John Ryland

The Character of the Rev. James Hervey

Late Rector of Weston-Favel in Northamptonshire

John Ryland

The Character of the Rev. James Hervey
Late Rector of Weston-Favel in Northamptonshire

ISBN/EAN: 9783337236328

Printed in Europe, USA, Canada, Australia, Japan

Cover: Foto ©Raphael Reischuk / pixelio.de

More available books at **www.hansebooks.com**

Rev. JAMES HERVEY, M. A.

LATE

Rector of Weston Favel, in Northamptonshire,

CONSIDERED,

A S A

MAN OF GENIUS AND A PREACHER—As A PHILOSOPHER AND
CHRISTIAN UNITED—As A REGENERATE MAN—As A MAN
ENDOWED WITH THE DIGNI I Y AND PREROGATIVES OF A CHRIS-
TIAN—As A MAN OF BEAUTIFUL VIRTUE AND HOLINESS.

By JOHN RYLAND, M. A.

LONDON:

, PRINTED BY W. JUSTINS, BLACKFRIARS, FOR R. THOMPSON,
No. 326, OXFORD STREET.

AND SOLD BY H. D. SYMONDS, PATERNOSTER-ROW, AND MUR-
GATROYD, CHISWELL-STREET.

M,DCC,XC.

LIFE of HERVEY.

To virtuous and ingenuous young Men.
To virtuous and amiable Women.
To young Students in Divinity.
To Tutors of Youth.

FIRST.

TO VIRTUOUS AND INGENUOUS YOUNG MEN,

MY DEAR FRIENDS,

I Have had, from my earlieſt youth, a ſincere love for ſuch perſons as you; and now
I feel a ſtronger affection than ever I had before:
I conſider you as the great ſupports of civil ſo-
ciety; as the ornaments of human nature; as
the hopes of the riſing generation; from you,
as the proper fountains, muſt flow wiſdom,
virtue, and happineſs; whilſt, from the wicked
and ungodly, there will continually iſſue
ſtreams of folly, vice, and miſery.

In the compofition of the following work, I have had your welfare very much at heart. My whole aim has been to write the truth, and nothing but the truth. I have fet down all that I knew concerning him with great fimplicity and integrity of heart; and I dare appeal to the tribunal of heaven: the omnifcient Judge of my foul knows that my grand defign was to difplay the illuftrious grace of CHRIST in the falvation and happinefs of this man.

If any perfon fhall cenfure me, as having faid too high or too kind things of his character, let them candidly confider that I was obliged to write the truth ; and what opinion would they have formed of me, if to avoid the appearance of flattery, I had concealed the truth ; a mind and life of fuch fuperior excellence could not have been written without the appearance of flattery ; but, however, I fhall difregard fevere cenfure, whilft I know that my grand aim was not to fet off the man, but to demonftrate the fovereign grace of GOD in CHRIST.

If GOD, from all eternity, decreed to illuf-trate his perfections in the uncommon natural genius, the peculiar and fhining excellencies, with the moft fublime fpirit of religion, in this fingular perfon, who, and what was I, that I fhould withftand GOD ? If I attempted to defcribe a rare and an uncommon work of the Almighty, I muſt defcribe it as being what it was, and not conceal any of 'its perfections: my bufinefs and duty was to trace out the wiſdom, power, and goodnefs of the LORD JESUS CHRIST in the formation of this excellent creature. It was my wifdom to relate what I faw, and my happinefs to have fuch a piece of exquifite workmanſhip fet before mine eyes. Here I could view, with rapture and aftoniſhment, the being and attributes of GOD, in the production of fuch a work. Here I could view the wonderful efficacy of redeeming blood, in recovering from darknefs, guilt, and corruption, a human foul that had been involved in all the ruins of the apoftacy. Here I faw a mind that was envenomed with pride and prejudice againft the dominion of GOD, in the gracious provifion of a free and abfolute falvation of a finner by CHRIST's righteoufnefs: I faw this mind enlightened, renewed, humbled in the duft, made fincere in its enquiries after truth, and happily brought into the enjoyment of that truth. I faw this mind under the conduct of the HOLY SPIRIT, gradually rifing from folly to wifdom, from unbelief to faith, from enmity to love, from pride to humility, from prejudice to unbiaffed integrity, from luke-

warmnefs

warmneſs to zeal, from inſenſibility and black ingratitude, to the higheſt thankfulneſs that ever dwelt in a mortal breaſt. Amidſt ſuch wonders of redeeming and ſanctifying mercy, what could I do but ſtand ſtill and admire, and ſilently adore; or elſe burſt forth in the praiſes of the moſt wiſe, the moſt gracious, the moſt holy, and the moſt juſt GOD! As I had the advantages above any other man now living to contemplate this mirror of the divine perfections, and this miracle of redeeming mercy, who can blame me for ſtanding ſtill to feaſt mine eyes with ſuch a charming ſpectacle, and to admire the grace of CHRIST, till my ſoul was loſt in holy adoration and ſecret praiſe?

If I had written upon this ſubject in a dull dreaming manner, without taſte, life, or ſpirit: if I had treated this illuſtrious creature of GOD with a cold indifference, or a contemptible lukewarmneſs of ſoul, what true Chriſtian is there to be found who would not have blamed and deſpiſed me? They would have ſaid, and that juſtly, that I had no true reliſh for the ſingular invincible and victorious grace of GOD in the redemption and holineſs of a loſt ſinner. If I had given to the world ſuch a dull unmeaning and inſipid performance, who would have read it? Not the corrupt part of mankind; they muſt

have

have works of genius, tafte, and fire : every new romance; every new.piece for the play-houfe, muft be animated with falt and'fpirit, in order to keep the town in a continual attention and burft of applaufe.

If I had given a cold narrative of Hervey's life and virtues, would fordid hypocrites have read my book ? No : they have fomething elfe to do : their grand bufinefs is to patch up and keep in repair their falfe profeffion of Chriftianity.

Would proud felf-righteous Pharifees have read my book ? No : they would not have borne to have heard one word againft their favourite idol, their own righteoufnefs, even if I had ex-preffed it in a cold unmeaning manner, and without one part of that ardent zeal which dwelt in the breaft of our admirable author.

Will proud felf-righteous Pharifees read my book? No : they will not; they have too high an opinion of their own virtue to read and relifh the character and temper of a man fo entirely oppofite to their own : they can never delight in a man of his principles, whofe grand defign was to humble the finner, to exalt the Saviour, and to promote vital holinefs to the very utter-moft.

To

To you, therefore, worthy young men, I turn myself: I expect you will read my work with attention, candour, and eagernefs. I truft you will here meet with fomething to inform your underftandings, to pleafe your tafte, to animate your virtues, to allure your fouls to excel in every good thought, word, and work. I leave the book in your hands, and commit that and yourfelves to the keeping and direction of the HOLY SPIRIT of GOD.

TO VIRTUOUS AND AMIABLE WOMEN.

It muft be allowed without flattery, that you are the chief ornaments of civil fociety; and if your underftandings are clearly enlightened; if your judgments are folidly fixed; if your tafte is delicate and correct; if your beft paffions are fet upon the fupreme good, and your whole lives devoted to the love and purfuit of truth, you will certainly become the greateft bleffings to the Britifh empire: you will be dutiful daughters, loving fifters, amiable friends, and wife and virtuous mothers, at the head of well-formed families.

Let me advife you to cultivate a generous ambition, to excel in every thing that is lovely and of good report. Do not give way to abject thoughts of yourfelves—dignity and honour

is

is a very different thing from pride : there may be pride without dignity, and dignity without pride. *Pride* is the high opinion that a poor little narrow foul entertains of itfelf, attended with a mean felfifhnefs, which prompts us to feek nothing but our own humour and our own honour. *Dignity* is a generous fenfe of our connection with CHRIST; a high conception of our immortal duration, with a vaft defire to live for the glory of GOD, and the happinefs of mankind. Cherifh this dignity with your whole heart: feek out for the beft motives to promote it : put yourfelves in the way of thofe motives : ftrive to underftand the force of thofe motives: comply with the grand defign of thofe motives, and beg of the SPIRIT of GOD to give an edge and force to thofe motives.

This book I dedicate to you: I had the good of your precious fouls at heart, whilft I was compofing it; and I publifh it with an high hope that I fhall have fome of the beft women in the Britifh empire to be my readers.

I know that all the vicious and wicked part of your fex will defpife this work. From them I expect no favour: the vain and trifling part of your fex, who can relifh nothing but plays, romances, and novels, with all the reft of the trafh of the age, thefe people will give me no attention;

attention; and from them I turn with a mixture of pity, indignation, and filent contempt.

Go on, my worthy friends, beg of God the
Holy Spirit to adorn you with all the perfonal graces of humility, meeknefs, patience, felf-
denial, contentment, prudence, chaftity, fortitude, and felf-poffeffion.

Beg of God the Holy Spirit to adorn you
with all the Chriftian graces of lively faith in
Christ : ardent love to his perfon : imitation
of his beautiful example, learning every leffon of
truth at his feet : obedience to him as your divine Mafter, and dependance upon him as your
powerful Interceffor.

Beg of the Holy Spirit to work into your
hearts all the divine graces, *i. e.* a clear knowledge of God in his natural and moral attributes; a holy fear of his divine majefty; a
lively love to his beautiful chara&ter; a deep
fubmiffion to his holy will, however made
known; a powerful truft in his divine providence and grace; and a lively communion with
him in the works of creation and providence,
in the words of falvation and grace.

Beg of the Holy Spirit to adorn your foul
with all the focial graces of love to your fellow
creatures; a fpirit of beneficence, or a delight
in doing good: the exercife of mercy to fouls
and

and bodies in mifery; in a forgivenefs of injuries; in a fpirit of juftice, truth, and faithfulnefs; and may the golden threads of fincerity,
zeal, tendernefs, and perfeverance, run through
the whole tenour of your life and converfation.

TO YOUNG STUDENTS OF DIVINITY.

My dear young friends, it concerns you above
all things to have the approbation of CHRIST
in your ftudies: it is impoffible for you to have
that approbation, unlefs your hearts are renewed, and fet right in the fight of GOD. You
muft be made uprightly to aim at his glory in
all things, and regard his intereft as the great
ufe of your eternal exiftence. It concerns you
very much to be employed in fevere felf-exami-
nation. Am I exercifing myfelf in the very
beft ftudies, and do I purfue the richeft objects
of knowledge in the beft manner? Does GOD
the SON ftand by me every moment? Does he
infpect my heart, my principles, and all my
views? Is the perfon of CHRIST the higheft
object of my efteem? And is it my great aim in
the ftudy of the original Scriptures, to find out
the glorious perfections and offices of the LORD
JESUS CHRIST? Do I fee the fitnefs of his
offices? Do I enjoy the fulnefs of his offices?
Do I feel the power of his offices? Do I dif-

b   cern

cern the beauty of his offices, to endear himfelf eternally to my foul? Are all my acquifi-
tions of fcience laid at his feet, made fubfer-
vient to his intereft, and confecrated to the
good of his church in the world? How do I
fpend my mornings? Are they loft in fleep and
idlenefs? Do I lay my plan of ftudy wifely for
every day? How do I conclude my evenings?
Are they loft in chattering and impertinence?
Have I a generous ambition to excel for the
edifying of the church, or is it my main ftudy
and defign to advance felf, to preach felf, to
feek the glory of being ftiled a man of parts, a
man of politenefs, and a man of elegance? If
thefe are my low and fordid views of the Chriftian miniftry, how can I ever look GOD in the
face, and with what a dreadful vengeance will
GOD look me in the face. And after I have
read this Life of Hervey, if my ftudies fhould
be conducted in a wrong manner, I muft ftand
fpeechlefs and fhivering before the tribunal of
GOD.

On the other hand, if my heart fhould be inclined by the grace of GOD the HOLY SPIRIT
to imitate this beautiful example, to imbibe his
amiable temper, and purfue the fame glorious
work, 1 fhall have the fmiles and approbation
of the Judge of the univerfe: I fhall hear him

fay,

fay, " *Well done good and faithful fervant, enter*
" *into the joy of thy Lord.*" Then I fhall be
affociated with all thefe great and excellent men,
and fhall mingle fouls, and fentiments, and joys
with them before the throne of GOD.

TO PIOUS TUTORS OF DIVINITY AND SCIENCE.

My dear and honoured friends, you are fome
of the moft important creatures of GOD, and
it becomes you to think fo : if you rightly
conduct the ftudies of valuable young men,
you will become the greateft bleffings to the
rifing generation, and the inftruments of honour
and happinefs to the Britifh empire. If you
conduct the ftudies of our Britifh youth in a
wrong manner, they will have reafon to curfe
you to all eternity, and to wifh they had never
fallen into fuch foolifh and unfaithful hands.

But if you are wife and worthy men; if you
direct your ftudents to the very beft objects of
knowledge; and if you invite and allure them to
reduce all their knowledge to the purpofes of
practical godlinefs, what an harveft of honour
and happinefs will you reap in this life, and
what glorious profpects will open to your eyes
from the invifible world through the blood and
righteoufnefs of the LORD JESUS CHRIST.

I have

I have a thoufand things to fay to you upon this occafion, but Dr. Watts's Improvement of the Mind, both parts; and Rollin's Method of Study, 4 vols. in duodecimo, will abundantly fupply all my deficiencies, and fet you right in the purfuit of every branch of knowledge.

I now deliver up this work into the hands of the eternal Son of God, for the fervice and good of the churches of Christ, and the rifing generation. Evangelical holinefs, and focial virtue, in all its branches, I admire and love. I pray God, from the depth of my foul, that I may admire and love them more every day. Every part of this book was written with a defign to promote fcience and true religion. I blefs God that I have a large number of true Chriftian friends who will read this book with candour and delight: they will fee its faults: they will difcern its fcope and tendency: they will read the life and temper of this great and good man with an ardent defire to imitate his example: they will pray moft paffionately that the fame good Spirit of God, which dwelt fo eminently in him, may dwell more powerfully and fweetly in them: they will make ufe of this book as a mirror, to difcern the beauties and blemifhes of their own fouls: they will here find many cautions

to avoid the blemishes of the Christian temper,
and many counsels to direct and stimulate them
to higher degrees of growth in grace and holinefs; to be the dignity and ornament of the
Christian church, and the reputation and glory
of their native country. Here let ambition
rife; let Godly ambition know no bounds or
limits: you cannot be too humble; but mean
and abject thoughts of yourselves is not humility, but the curse, and plague, and poison of
the foul: for a man to have mean and abject
thoughts of himself, is the way never to think
a great thought; never to speak a good word;
never to perform one generous action. Christian profeffors are too low in their views: too
contracted in their conceptions: too narrow in
their purpofes: too lukewarm in their purfuits; and what is the confequence? The glory
of God is obscured: the honour of CHRIST's
Godhead and righteousnefs is eclipsed: the
bleffed SPIRIT of God is grieved and affronted:
the holinefs of God in his law is undervalued:
the riches of the grace of the Gospel are not
displayed: awakened and enquiring souls are
difcouraged: lukewarm profeffors are confirmed
in their shabby profeffion, and unbelievers are
hardened in their infidelity. Thefe are fome of
the awful confequences of neglecting to imitate
　　　　　　　　　　　　　　　　　　fuch

such a character as that which is contained in this book.

I shall rejoice in the agonies of death, and in my departure into the invisible world, if I shall be well informed that this book has been of real and permanent service to the immortal souls of true Christians; and when GOD comes to declare my character, and fix my state in the invisible world, I shall appeal to his impartial and inflexible tribunal for the truth of what I have written. I know that GOD's eye can discern more errors and blemishes in my work, than can be discerned by all the men upon earth, and angels in heaven; but this blessed GOD is a most merciful Being, and I know that in his mercy I shall have a sure refuge, when I come to converse with the immortal spirit of Hervey in glory, and to give him an account of what I have been doing to compose and publish his life and character, when I shall assure him that I did this not to set off the man, but to display the sovereign and invincible grace of CHRIST in his salvation. He will give me full credit for my assertion, because he that was all candour and sweetness upon earth, cannot possibly be all sourness and severity in heaven. We shall therefore agree together to leave the

book

book to make its way upon earth, as the providence of God fhall direct, whilft we fhall
adore together, before the throne of God and
the Lamb for ever and ever.

Feb. 11, 1791.   John Ryland.

CONTENTS

OF

Mr. HERVEY's LIFE.

CHAPTER I.

*His Character as a Man of excellent Genius, and as a moft Evan-
gelical Preacher.*

His

C H A P. II.

The character of Hervey as a Christian and Philosopher
united.   -   -   -   -

C H A P. III.

The Character of Hervey as a regenerate Man.

CHAP.

CHAP. IV.

Views of Hervey as a Man endowed with the Dignity and Prerogatives of a Chriſtian.

XXVI. His

He

CHAP. V.

The Character of Hervey as a Man of Science and Virtue.

CHAP. VI.

The Character of Hervey as a Divine.

The.

The

The

PRELIMINARY DEFINITIONS.

XXVI. The

Of

He

RE-

REMARKS on Mr. HERVEY's LIFE and CHARACTER.

Rev. Mr. James Hervey, A. M.

JAMES HERVEY's Character arose from his will and understanding: his will was endued by the Spirit of GOD, with a permanent principle of holiness, freely determining his whole soul to act after such a particular manner as to increase the sum of happiness in the universe, and not, on the contrary part, for one moment, to increase the sum of misery in the great moral empire of GOD.

His Character likewise arose from his understanding, or an aptitude to excel in clear spiritual knowledge, which enabled him to instruct the people of GOD, and increase the happiness of the Church of CHRIST, and not on the contrary to increase ignorance, sin, and misery.

His Character also arose from his imagination and taste; or his clear sense of the most sublime, beautiful, and affecting objects in heaven and earth, and his

A 2   power

power to paint thofe objects in the moſt ſtriking language, to allure and captivate the hearts and paſſions
of mankind.

His Character likewiſe aroſe from the moral qualities of his ſoul, or the divine glories of his mind and
paſſions, which were all on fire for GOD his Saviour.

Conſequently his character aroſe from the regeneration of his whole ſoul, as having paſſed under a
mighty change in his moral powers and principles
of action; being endowed with the moſt excellent
kind of life, and made the ſubject of the nobleſt divine habits, his heart being inſcribed with the whole
divine law in a clear ſtrong ſenſe of its meaning, a cordial approbation of its purity, an ardent inclination to
obey it, and a real ability of will for that obedience.

His Character likewiſe aroſe from the image of
GOD impreſſed upon his whole eſſence, inclinations,
powers, and paſſions: the moral perfections of GOD
were ſtruck in ſtrong characters on his whole ſoul.

WISDOM ſhone in the ſerene brightneſs of his underſtanding.

GOODNESS, or an inclination to increaſe happineſs,
glowed like celeſtial fire.

HOLINESS, or the purity of GOD, ſhone in his ſoul
as a reſemblance, an imitation, and expreſſion of the
immaculate holineſs of the divine nature.

JUSTICE, or an ardent regard for the rights of his
GOD and SAVIOUR in his *righteouſneſs, redemption,* and
grace, poſſeſſed his will with a determinate purpoſe.
to preſerve thoſe rights inviolate againſt all kinds of
oppoſition.

TRUTH was a permanent principle in the nature
and eſſence of his ſoul. Truth ſhone in the conceptions of his underſtanding. Truth dwelt in the radical intentions of his will. Truth appeared in all the
words of his lips, as the tranſparent expreſſions of his
ſincere and upright heart. Truth ſparkled in all the
actions

actions of his life.   Truth appeared in his affections.
His admiration was fixed upon the great and wonderful REDEEMER.°   The object of his love was the fitnefs, fulnefs, and beauty of CHRIST: the objects of
his hatred were fin and error.   He hated fin more
than hell: he loved holinefs in a manner that refembled the love of GOD to holinefs.   Error was the
object of his contempt and fcorn: he had an holy
caution and fear of miftaking truth, and falling into
error.   His gratitude to CHRIST rofe as high as heaven; was as wide as unbounded fpace, and lafting as
eternity.   But the grand feature of holinefs in the
great foul of this man, was a permanent principle of
delight and joy in the *righteoufnefs* of CHRIST, imputed to him, or put down to his account and credit
by the act of GOD himfelf.   This he regarded as
the entire ground and matter of his juftification for
eternity.   Here his efteem, his defire, and benevolence, all rofe fublimely to forcible fire, and expreffed
itfelf in the moft magnificent eloquence.

Here he differed *toto cœlo* from many thoufands of
the Britifh clergy, and from all the Socinians in the
whole univerfe.

Let us now return and view him as a man of genius and tafte.   By genius, I mean an aptitude in the
imagination to excel in painting all the beauties of
nature and Scripture.   By tafte, I mean a clear fenfe,
and a lively relifh, for all the noble and beautiful objects in creation and revelation.   The attributes and
actions of GOD the REDEEMER were the objects of
his peculiar delight.   He had great elevation and penetration of thought: and he fpared no pains to edu-
cate his foul to grandeur, by impregnating his mind
with enlarged and generous ideas.

HERVEY's foul was near to CHRIST, and intenfely one fpirit with him.   He had the richeft privileges and bleffings from CHRIST, as we fhall fhew
                                                              in

in a separate essay, on his personal religion and happiness, in above sixty views of him.

His ultimate view and end was to make CHRIST's fulness and beauty conspicuous to the churches, and to all mankind, in the richest eloquence, and in the most illustrious manner; and to this end prayer was the life and joy of his soul. He had a glorious and daring freedom of thought on CHRIST's eternal divinity: he had such an amplitude of mind, and such a boldness of conceptions and passions respecting the grand works of creation and redemption, as distinguished him from other writers and preachers. He had lively images of all visible and invisible objects; and the warm and strong commotions, of his soul arose from the keen perception of beauty and deformity in the visible and invisible worlds.

HERVEY had the most pleasing and useful new things in his preaching, writings, and conversation.

First. His matter and subjects of discourse were new: his rich and fruitful invention was never exhausted. In the course of six years that I visited him twice a year, what astonishing charms of eloquence have I heard from him at family worship, as well as in the pulpit. Never did I hear from any other man such new turns and elevated range of thought and passion as I have heard from him times more than I can recollect, in the parlour, at family devotion. In a word, they were some of the best divinity lectures that ever were given to young students.

Second. His method was often new: he never moved on with the heavy pace of a pack-horse, but flew like an eagle, and ranged all over the skies.

Third. His proofs and demonstrations were often new: he knew such a variety of proofs from the fund of the Scriptures, that he was never at a loss for arguments. This appears with surprising beauty against Martin Tomkins, in his Letters, No. 24—27, in
which

which letters he nobly defends the perfonality and divinity of the Holy Spirit.

His ability for proving the great truths of the Gofpel brightly appear in his Dialogues and Letters of Theron and Afpafio: none can doubt of his fkill in reafoning, who have read, with attention, thofe works.

Fourth. His images and figures were new. He knew as well as any man the beft figures which contained a beauty, or expreffed a painful or pleafing commotion of the foul, and he feized with ardour the moft glowing images of all things.

He relifhed the moft daring and ftriking ideas, and painted them in fo lively a manner, as though you faw them before your eyes.

Fifth. His movements of heart and paffions, or the ftrong commotions of his delicate, pure, and holy foul, were new. He felt all objects to the bottom of his being, and found new fentiments rifing continually within the depth of his foul.

Sixth. His words and expreffions were often new. His ftyle was the copy of the conceptions of his ideas, and the feeling commotions of his heart.

He did not in a faftidious manner difdain plain words, and common forms of fpeech; nor did he, with a falfe and corrupt tafte, hunt perpetually for new forms of expreffion, and fuch words as were not of the ufual manner; but he had fuch powers to vary his language, fo as ever to appear pleafing, and not difguftful to his auditory, or to his friends in common converfation.

Seventh. His applications of his fermons were often new: his manner of addreffing the underftanding and confcience, the imagination, memory, and paffions of his different kinds of hearers, were unboundedly new; and he could afford to blot out, and throw away riches, fuperior to other authors.

He

He had a rich GENIUS for ELOQUENCE. Genius is an aptitude to excel in eloquence, or in any particular art or science.

If there ever was any man who had a talent or aptitude from the GOD of nature for excelling in any one thing whatever, then Hervey had an aptitude for eloquence.

If eloquence confifts in an ability or power of expreffing the nature of an object with exact propriety and decency of language, Hervey was one of the moft eloquent of all mankind.

If eloquence confifts in declaring, in the moft clear and forcible manner, the illuftrious power, beauty, fulnefs, and fitnefs of CHRIST, and the tendernefs and fweetnefs of his grace, to perifhing finners, then Hervey was a moft eloquent man.

If eloquence be a power of fuiting words and expreffions exactly to the perfon of CHRIST with admirable propriety and decency, then Hervey was the moft eloquent man that hath exifted in the whole world for feventeen hundred years paft.

In a word, he had fuch an unbounded fund of thought, imagination, and paffion; and fuch a variety of modes of expreffion, that he appeared to be never exhaufted, or at a lofs to difcover the conceptions of his underftanding. I will exprefs again what I before obferved, that he could afford to throw away riches enough to ftock the minds, writings, and fermons, of many other men.

He painted the hearts, the manners and characters of men, with wonderful clearnefs, evidence, and precifion.

He had an admirable talent for anatomifing the underftanding, the confcience, the memory, the will, and the paffions, as well as the thoughts and imaginations of the heart; as may be clearly feen in his awful difcoveries of the total degeneracy and univerfal depravity

pravity of all mankind in his THERON and AS-PASIO, Dialogue XI and XIII. And no man underftood better that amazing defcription of the depravity of man, vividly painted by Dr. Witfius, in his incomparable Economy of the Covenants, Book I. chap. v. fect. 8, and Book III. chap. vi. fect. 6. No fpirit in hell can be uglier, or more loathfome and horrible than the heart of man; and Hervey knew it more clearly than almoft any man in the world.

He was an excellent mafter of found logic, and true divinity, in a very high degree. See his manly reafoning againft the fly and malignant enemy to the divinity and perfonality of the Holy Spirit, mentioned before, page 6.

Hervey was a great mafter, of found divinity; and this was owing to the gracious influences of the divine Spirit. GOD the Holy Spirit infufed into his foul *habitual grace:* he had a new and gracious fpiritual life, or divine principle, created in his mind, by which he was changed in all his faculties and affections, and enabled to make noble exertions of love to every divine·object that was fet before him, with clear evidence of its coming from the GOD of truth; and this habitual grace is abfolutely effential to a true Gofpel minifter.

He was likewife bleffed with *actual grace*, which appears by his Letters, in a fmall degree, from 1733, in the 19th year of his age, as arifing from the principle of habitual grace infufed into his foul; and by very flow degrees, it grew in the ufe of the Scriptures, by ardent prayer, and the reading of fome good books, from 1734 to 1741. This appears by a letter in my poffeffion, directed to Mr. George Whitfield, dated from Biddeford, in the 27th year of his age. This letter, which will be·printed at the end of his Life, clearly and beautifully fhews that

B   CHRIST,

CHRIST, the pure original truth, was dawning upon his foul.

Actual grace in this great man's heart, was an influence of GOD the Spirit upon his powers and affections; it was the divine agency and affiftance working by his foul, any good fpiritual action, or duty whatfoever, without any pre-exiftence to that act, or continuance after it: GOD *working in him both to will and to do of his own good pleafure.*

This habitual and actual grace in Hervey's faculties and paffions, formed him, by flow degrees; and, in the diligent ufe of proper means, into a very judicious and excellent *divine.* It is a moft delightful employment, to mark the gradual progrefs of fcience and religion, in the good man's heart, from the 19th to his 45th year; that is, a courfe of 26 years. I could dwell upon it for an hundred pages together, and never grow weary of fuch a charming fubject of pleafing admiration.

It was this habitual and actual grace in his great foul that fpiritualized and beautified the whole creation, and turned all nature into a fchool of inftruction to his holy imagination. This grace taught him to read the two great books of Nature and Scripture with new eyes, and new commotions of the paffions.

This grace taught him to fee CHRIST and his precious righteoufnefs in every part of Scripture: he viewed the perfections of GOD the Son in every object in the univerfe. All his letters, except a few of the firft; all his Contemplations and Dialogues; all his Letters to Theron, to Lady Frances Shirley, to myfelf, and his other friends, appear to be tinctured and beautified with the grace and glory of CHRIST.

By the moft keen and inceffant attention to nature and Scripture, he rofe to fuch a pitch of facred knowledge and devotion, as few good men ever attained. It would be invidious to compare him with the eloquent Dr. Bates; the favoury and judicious Dr. Owen;

Owen; the accurate and copious Charnock; the great John Smith, of Cambridge; and the much greater man, Edward Polhill, Efq. the mafculine John Howe; the correct and nervous Hurrion; the fagacious prefident Edwards; the florid Dr. Watts, the fprightly and benevolent Dr. Doddridge, and the fervent zealous Whitfield, with the great and judicious Dr. Waterland. But this I may fafely fay, that Hervey had thofe peculiar excellencies which diftinguifh him from all thofe great men; and even that prince of all divines, Dr. Witfius, did not excel him in great conceptions, rich imagination, devotional criticifm, deep humility, and feraphic fire. Suffer me to make this remark, that through the defective and faulty methods of education, almoft all the above divines neglected the beauties of creation, and the charms of natural philofophy. Through this defect, their compofitions want that ftriking brilliance with which Hervey's writings abound.

This great and good preacher difdained to ufe any coarfe words, and low vulgar expreffions; fuch as debafe the true dignity of the pulpit, render the preacher mean and contemptible, give juft offence to good fenfe, and raife difguft in a refined and holy tafte.

Hervey had the keeneft perceptions, amidft all his deep condefcenfion to vulgar capacities. No man of true tafte could defpife him as mean and vulgar, even in the loweft addreffes to the meaneft of his flock.

Nor did he ever content himfelf with mere general difcourfes that affect no body, and are fo vague and unmeaning as to intereft neither the head nor the heart—that have no tendency to alarm the finner, nor animate and comfort the faint.

What a pungent manner does he ufe in his fermons on the Time of Danger, the Means of Safety, and the Way of Holinefs! How does he fearch Theron's confcience, in his Letter on Self-Examination; and

what

what a pointed addrefs to the foul, is that letter to the condemned malefactors in Northampton jail—it is a pattern for all preachers to the end of the world. See his Collection of Letters, No. 141.

He loved fimplicity in his *manner* of preaching: and with refpect to his ideas, they were very clear, and never obfcure and confufed. He had no complicated and perplexed conceptions; no crowd of thoughts to overwhelm his own underftanding, or the conceptions of his hearers and readers. He had a fimplicity of method in his preaching particularly. In all his fermons you might difcern a clear and eafy arrangement; nothing tedious; no long-winded periods; no perplexing parenthefes; no tirefome circumlocutions, but every thing adapted to the weakeft memory of his auditors.

He loved a fervency of *ftyle*, or the language and mode in which he expreffed the conceptions of his underftanding, and the pleafing or dreadful commotions of his heart.

He loved the SUBLIME to a moft ardent degree; the beautiful and the pathetic were the objects of his pureft delight. No man I ever knew loved the truly fublime and beautiful fo fervently as JAMES HERVEY. Longinus himfelf never had a higher conception of its nature and beauty. Not even our three Britifh Longinufes, Dr. Lowth, the late Bifhop of London; Dr. Smith, the Dean of Chefter; and Dr. Blair, the prefent Profeffor of Eloquence at Edinburgh, never poffeffed a higher tafte for the fublime and the beautiful, than the amiable and excellent *Hervey*. He had a fublimity of conceptions. His underftanding was capable of receiving great ideas, without pain or difficulty; of receiving new and uncommon ideas, without furprife or averfion; and he loved to furvey large trains of aftonifhing thoughts of the God and Saviour he adored.

He

He had great fublimity in his *paffions* : he felt and expreffed the higheft admiration and efteem for the LORD JESUS CHRIST. He had the moft ardent defire after his vital prefence; and he difcovered the ftrongeft exertions of benevolence and gratitude to CHRIST for his precious redemption. His hatred to fin was infinite; and his defire of difunion from it rofe as high as heaven, and lafting as eternity.

He had a fublimity of ftyle and language. It was quite natural to him to exprefs himfelf in the manner you fee. He never fought after uncommon modes of expreffion, or high-founding terms of art. His words are fimple, yet fublime. He certainly had a great luxuriance of imagination, and could afford to throw away a great ftock of riches; but amidft all his redundancy, you muft acknowledge, that in a thoufand places, his expreffions are very concife: his words are forcible, and full of fire.

He was an experimental and practical preacher: he entered deeply into all the parts of vital experience: he urged to particular duties, and oppofed particular fins upon Gofpel principles.

He always kept up a clear diftinction between the regenerate and the unregenerate, and marked their diftinct and oppofite characters in the moft decided manner. This is a great defect in many of our Calviniftic preachers: they do not dwell long enough, nor fpeak keen enough, on the diftinct nature of true and falfe conviction; the faith of an hypocrite, and the faith of a fincere believer; the true nature of regeneration, that iffues in happinefs, and the mere refemblance of it, that iffues in eternal ruin. They do not continually bring the great object of faith to the mental eye, nor reprefent the neceffity of the perpetual affiftances of GOD the Spirit, to keep up inceffant views of CHRIST's righteoufnefs.

He knew how to ftate the great doctrines of the Gofpel in a ftriking and judicious manner; and he

defended

defended and improved them in the moſt pungent and
ſpirited diction.   Hervey had ſuch wiſdom and ſkill,
to repreſent the truths of Chriſtianity in a pleaſing and
beautiful light, that was peculiar to himſelf.   He uſed
frequently to obſerve, that he did not wiſh to invent
any new doctrine, but he deſired to dreſs the good
old truths of the reformation in ſuch beautiful dra
pery of language, as to allure people of all conditions; but eſpecially thoſe in the higher ranks of life;
to contemplate thoſe truths from which we, as a nation, have ungratefully departed.   In this deſign, he
ſucceeded as well, and better, than any other man in
England.

We have had very able divines, who have ſtated
the great doctrines of the Goſpel, and improve them
in a very maſterly manner.   Witneſs Dr. Waterland,
Dr. Abraham Taylor, Dr. Calamy, and Mr. Sloſs,
on the Trinity.   Dr. Owen and Mr. Hurrion on particular Redemption.   Mr. Richard Rawlin on Juſtification, by Christ's righteouſneſs.   Dr. Doddridge's
ten Sermons on Regeneration.   Edward Polhill, Eſq.
on Christ, as the mirror of the divine perfections,
and vital union with Christ.   The Rev. Thomas
Hall, on Final Perſeverance.   Dr. Gill on the Reſur-
rection of the Dead.   With many other great and
good authors; but in point of eloquence and beauty, Hervey exceeds them all.

He deſpiſed and avoided all boiſterous noiſe; all
rude and violent vociferation in the pulpit: every
thing that was vulgar and coarſe; every thing that
was groſsly ſhocking and offenſive; every thing that
gave diſguſt to perſons of ſound ſenſe; every thing
that had the leaſt tincture of uglineſs or deformity;
every thing that was a diſgrace to the pulpit in temper, expreſſion, and action, he avoided with the utmoſt
prudence and caution.

On the other hand, his modeſty, in manners and
expreſſion, were moſt amiable and alluring.   Never
did

did I fee deportment more modeft and inviting to imitation, than in that of the moft amiable Hervey.

He had a moft tender love to immortal fouls. No man knew better than himfelf the infinite dignity or immenfe worth of an immortal foul. He ftudied the aftonifhing nature and powers of the foul. He knew the grandeur of the paffions; and he viewed the eternal duration of a foul in the light of CHRIST's blood upon the crofs; and in all he thought, fpoke, or wrote, he ftill had the worth of a foul in view. He did not defpife Sir Richard Blackmore's Demonftration of the Immortality of the Soul. He had the higheft efteem for Dr. Young's Demonftration of Immortality, Night Six and Seven. And if he had ever read Dr. Leng's Boylean Lectures on the Immortality of the Soul, he muft have given them his cordial approbation. Had Dr. Gill's moft excellent Difcourfe on Immortality been then known, and the great Andrew Baxter, whofe work upon the foul was publifhed by Dr. Duncan in octavo, 1779; and, to name no more, if Dr. Porteus, the prefent Bifhop of London, had then publifhed his three excellent Sermons upon Immortality, Hervey would have read them all with the higheft relifh and admiration.

He finely obferved all the decencies of the pulpit, in his whole conduct of preaching. There was a decency in the matter of his fermons; his fubjects were always very ferious and fublime: they might be well ranged under three heads, Ruin, Righteoufnefs, and Regeneration. There was a decency in his proofs and evidences; he always fteered a middle courfe, between a haughty pofitivity, and a fceptical hefitation. He made it an invariable rule to be thoroughly convinced of the truth and importance of his fubject, before he proceeded to ftate and defend it; but when he was once in poffeffion of a truth, he held it with the greateft fortitude and tenacioufnefs.

I never

I never obferved any thing of the fceptic in him, in the whole of our converfation and correfpondence.

He obferved the greateft decency in point of time, place, and the perfons to whom he addreffed himfelf. I believe no man ever faw the leaft violation in the fitnefs and decorum of behaviour, in the whole of his deportment. He obferved fuch a decency in all his actions, that it was impoffible for any man to take juft offence. He obferved the greateft decency with refpect to his age. You faw in him nothing of levity; nothing ludicrous; no marks of the light and frothy ftudent; no haughty or dignified referve; nothing that favoured of the four and peevifh old man. In a word, he had dignity without pride; modefty without meannefs; affability without groveling; and courtefy without flattery. There was great faithfulnefs in his friendfhip. He obferved the greateft decency in his expreffions, and would never fail to give you the moft pointed reproof for a fault. He could fting like the bee, who always affords a drop of honey to affwage the fmart.

He confidered very minutely the ftate and frame of all the hearts of his hearers. He knew as well as any man, the difference between a regenerate and unregenerate ftate: he did not preach to a promifcuous auditory, as though they were all converted to CHRIST; nor did he treat true believers as though they were in an unregenerate ftate: he diftinguifhed well between thofe who are in darknefs, and thofe who are in light; the blind and the feeing; the deaf, and thofe who have ears to hear; the dead and the living; the profligate and the pharifee; the hypocrite and the fincere: he diftinguifhed between the weak and the ftrong, the backflider and the man that advances in holinefs of heart. And he had a word proper and pungent to all thefe different characters in his auditory.

He

He had an ardor of love to the word of God, above millions of true Christians. Never did I see in a mortal breast, such love to the inspired Scriptures of God; such supreme esteem rising into the utmost veneration; such ardent commotion of desire that could never be satisfied; and you could not have pleased him better, than by bringing him any elucidation of a text of Scripture: even the very fragments of an exposition were always welcome to his heart: he had such supreme benevolence, or good will to the precious Bible, that far transcended the pleasures of a geometrician in Euclid; or the joys of an orator, in hearing the eloquence of Demosthenes. There was in him an unbounded delight, or a sweet agreement with the book of God, in love and joy, which discovered a superlative affection to the Bible; and hence arose his sublime criticisms on the force and beauty of the original phrases of the Hebrew Bible, and the Greek Testament; and every body must acknowledge, that his criticisms were all light and devout fire, mingled with elegance.

He had a high regard to his own dignity of character, and the grandeur and importance of his office. A Christian preacher's employment is of the highest dignity and usefulness in the eyes of devils and damned spirits; in the eyes of angels and glorified souls: in the eyes of God the Father, and his eternal Son and Spirit.

JAMES HERVEY, in this life, for *twenty-six* years, stood nearer to God's heart than millions of angels: he was more intensely united to Christ, joined or glued to the Lord, and made one spirit with him. He had the deepest interest in the eternal Council of Peace; that covenant, which was contrived with the highest wisdom, entered into with the most serious regard to man, in which there was the most perfect association of the three persons in God. He was bought with a price that was above the worth

C   of

of the ftarry worlds, and all the angelic legions. He felt the attractions of CHRIST's love, and difcerned more diftinctly and forcibly thofe attractions of love, than the angels of heaven. He knew that all the damned in hell were entirely defigned to difplay the glory of CHRIST: that all the faved fouls in heaven, in their ultimate deftination, were intended to difplay the greatnefs of CHRIST's Godhead; the fitnefs of his righteoufnefs to juftify; the fulnefs of his grace to make holy: the power of his arm to deliver, and the ravifhing beauty of his perfon to endear himfelf to the fouls of men.

He was governed in his whole temper and conduct by the fupreme ends of his miniftry, which were the utmoft glory of CHRIST, and the union of immortal fouls to him. All his thoughts and ftudies were tinctured with this defign. All his writings and fermons were animated by this principle. CHRIST was, in the higheft fenfe, his whole life: he lived *from* CHRIST as the fountain of his life: he lived *like* CHRIST, as the pattern of his life; and he lived *to* his glory, as the end of his life. His great aim and paffionate defire, was to bring fouls to *know* CHRIST; to make them *wife* men; to bring fouls to *love* CHRIST; to make them *good* men, and to bring fouls to *poffefs* CHRIST, to make them *happy* men. Whatever books or converfation had this tendency, it always met with his approbation. Whatever fermons or writings had a tendency to neglect, or pervert this end, they were fure to meet with his fublime contempt, and filent difdain. You could not pleafe him better, than by dropping a hint how CHRIST's perfonal and relative glory might be promoted; nor could you difpleafe him more, than by manifefting a neglect of the Godhead and righteoufnefs of CHRIST, or leffening his manifeftative glory in the world.

He

He felt powerfully, and he obeyed with alacrity the very best *motives* to rouse him to a most powerful zeal for the glory of CHRIST.   No man was more honest to put himself in the way of motives.   No man was more sincere in searching out for the best motives. No man had a keener sensibility, to feel the force of those motives ; and no man was more diligent and active to pursue the design of those motives.   All the peculiar discoveries of divine revelation, were the darling themes of his meditation.   He considered CHRIST as the grand mirror of all the divine perfections; and he considered all revealed truth as flowing out of, and to be resolved into the person and attributes, the righteousness and blood of GOD his SAVIOUR.   He felt every motive, addressed to *fear*, arising from the consideration of evil.   He felt every motive addressed to *hope*, or the consideration of good to be enjoyed. He felt all the motives addressed to the generous passion of *gratitude*, which indeed is not any one particular passion, but a combination of all the finest feelings of the human mind.   He felt all the motives addressed to the noblest *ambition*, and the highest glory. He considered glory as the fame of the most excellent virtue, attended with praise.   He was not insensible of the superior excellency of his own writings, and of their amazing reception in the world; and with a most amiable simplicity, has confessed to me, " I am " apt to have too good an opinion of my own works." But the grace of CHRIST, in a very superior degree, raised him above a passionate zeal for his own honour, and gave him a most ardent and commanding sense of the transcendent glory of CHRIST.   He accounted it the most solid glory, and real greatness of a Christian preacher, to throw himself into the shade.

The

The CHARACTER of HERVEY as a PHILOSO-PHER and a CHRISTIAN united.

PHILOSOPHY is the clear knowledge of the beauties of creation; the properties of matter; the laws of nature; the powers and immortality of man; the good and bad qualities of the human heart; and the ultimate intention of GOD in the production and preservation of the univerfe.

HERVEY was born a Philofopher; he carried in his mind that ftandard of good fenfe, which gave him a delicate and correct perception of the beauty of the world, before he had read any books, or received any inftructions in Philofophy. His genius, or aptitude to excel, led him to contemplate, with rapture, the grandeur of the univerfe. He had the unhappinefs to have the worft tutors that ever exifted. He was under one mafter for ten years, for claffical education. He told me with his own mouth, that his mafter never made but one remark in reading the Greek Teftament, and that was a very foolifh one. I wifh I could recollect it, for the fake of all fuch mafters, with which this country abounds. He was five years more under his tutor at Lincoln college, Oxford; that tutor behaved towards him with a falfe dignity and haughty referve.

You will then fay, how could this youth commence a natural philofopher? I anfwer, he had no tutor but the Providential agency of JESUS CHRIST, directing his own genius and tafte. The two firft years of his being at college, were fpent in fauntering and idlenefs; not fo much through natural indolence, as for want of a wife and faithful friend to direct him to proper ftudies: he was ordered, in a very carelefs manner, to read fuch and fuch books, which were altogether unfuitable to his tafte, and in an high degree afforded matter of difguft and difcouragement. If I were

were to name thofe authors, I fhould do it with an
indignant fcorn and contempt.   At laft, by the peculiar agency of Providence, he was led to read the
Abbe le Pluche's Nature Difplayed, well known by
the title of Spectacle de la Nature.   The intrinfic
beauty of the piece, allured his imagination and paffions; and when he had made an entrance into the
work, he read with inceffant greedinefs, improvement,
and pleafure.   This work cherifhed and fomented his
natural paffion for knowledge: he added Dr. Derham's Aftro-Theology.   This book, which is fuperior to every other of the kind, affifted him in his firft
learned ideas of the Starry Heavens, and led him into
views of the whole Newtonian Syftem of Philofophy.
His conceptions were farther aided by Ray's Wifdom
of God in Creation, and Dr. Derham's Demonftration of the Being and Attributes of God in his Phy-
fico-Theology.   To thefe books he added, Keil's
Anatomy, which he ftudied with fuch inceffant attention, and perpetual reviews, as to make himfelf the
greateft mafter of the knowledge and elegance of the
ftructure of the human body, above any man I ever
knew.   He went on to read Mr. Spence's Five Dialogues on Pope's Tranflation of Homer, which he
often affured me gave him a greater infight into the
nature and beauty of compofition, than any author
he ever read.   By the moft accurate digeftion of thefe
authors, in his underftanding, and a continual contemplation of the Book of Nature, he adorned his
mind, and polifhed his genius in the line of fcience.

   Philofophy roufed and refined his tafte, purged his
underftanding from Atheifm, and all corrupt ideas
of God: expelled a low fuperftition, or falfe ideas of
the character and attributes of God, and cleared off
all erroneous conceptions of the nature of religion.
Philofophy gave him noble conceptions of the moral
perfections of the Deity: expanded his underftanding,
to take in great and wonderful thoughts of the wif-
                                                    dom,

dom, power, and goodneſs of Goᴅ in creation. Philoſophy purified his reaſon from prejudices, and enlarged all his intellectual powers to a very great degree. Philoſophy exhilerated his grand imagination,
ſweetened his beſt paſſions, and gladdened his heart.
Philoſophy meliorated his will, or rational appetite
for goodneſs and beauty; inſpired dignity into his
temper, manners, and deportment: enlivened and
ennobled his converſation, and raiſed him above all
low groveling diſcourſe. Philoſophy invigorated his
public ſpirit, and rouſed him unto a generous love of
his country, and to all mankind. Philoſophy, connected with religion, made him the credit of his birth-
place, the honour of Great Britain, and the glory of
Europe. All theſe rich improvements of his mind,
he was free and zealous to declare, that they were not
owing to his own induſtry, or exquiſite powers of genius, but they were ſolely owing to the gracious influence of an omnipotent Goᴅ and Sᴀᴠɪᴏᴜʀ. He
was grateful to confeſs, that the Grace of Goᴅ the
Hᴏʟʏ Sᴘɪʀɪᴛ, freed him from ten thouſand narrow
conceptions of men and things : purged away all falſe
judgments and puerile prejudices, concerning the univerſe. He was nobly grateful to declare, that it was
the continual Grace of Cʜʀɪꜱᴛ upon his heart, that
fired up his meditations and devotional exerciſes; in
thought engaged, and attention fixed ; in thought inflamed, and attention centered in the perſon, glory,
and righteouſneſs of Cʜʀɪꜱᴛ. Under the influence
of Goᴅ the Spirit, he was formed to as great a degree
of philoſophy and religion, as any man in the Britiſh
empire ever poſſeſſed. Philoſophy, animated by vital religion, carried him directly into an heart-union
with Cʜʀɪꜱᴛ, enlarged the capacities of his underſtanding, reſtored him to ſelf-dominion and ſelf-en-
joyment : raiſed him to the higheſt end of his exiſtence, and enabled him to live up to the height of his
being and immortal powers. Philoſophy and devotion

produced

produced and cherished the greatest purity and serenity of soul, and inspired in him the deepest peace of conscience or friendship with GOD his SAVIOUR: infused into him a sense of liberty in GOD. He had a liberty of Grace, and a prospect of the liberty of glory. He could come with boldness to the throne of GOD, wrestle with his Almighty SAVIOUR, and say with Jacob, *I will not let thee go, except thou bless me.* His writings were always carried on by a daily converse with CHRIST; and his manuscripts for the press, (all which passed through my hands) were frequently beautified with continual aspirations to CHRIST, which, though often concealed by the erasement of his pen, yet I could peep under the covering, and read with great pleasure and improvement.

By found Philosophy and true Religion united, he spiritualized the whole system of the universe in all its parts, as illustrated by the amiable Le Pluche; the sagacious and devout Dr. Derham; the pious and elegant Archbishop of Cambray; the masculine Andrew Baxter, and demonstrated by Sir Isaac Newton. Enlightened and directed by these great authors, he flew like an eagle all round the globe, and ranged like an angel all over the skies.

Philosophy and Religion taught him to observe the motions of Providence; to adore the wisdom of Providence; and comply with the designs of Providence in every minute affair of his life. He realized the hand of CHRIST on every event, every day, every hour, every morning and evening, of his happy life. He saw much of GOD his SAVIOUR in every creature, and he considered every creature to be nothing without GOD. In all he thought, spoke, and acted, he was governed by this grand principle, " that every creature is that to us, and no more, than " what CHRIST makes it to be."

Philosophy, united to vital Religion, carried his soul, by an happy progressive motion, into GOD his SAVIOUR. Every time I visited him, in the course of

twelve

twelve half years, I obferved, with filent aftonifhment, what frefh progrefs he had made in a life of holinefs; his temper towards CHRIST, more animated
by faith and love; his attention to the perfon of
CHRIST, and his difpofition to fit at his feet, more
tender and fixed: his habits of imitation of CHRIST's
temper and dependance upon his interceffion, more
fenfible and evident. His perception of the natural
and moral attributes of GOD, more diftinct and forcible; his obedience to the divine will, more free;
his truft in divine Providence advanced to an higher
degree; his delight in the grandeur and beauty of
GOD, and his communion with him, in every moment
of his rational exiftence, and in all the vital emotions
of his paffions, more feeling and fenfible to himfelf,
and more convincing to his obfervant friends.

The cperations of vital holinefs in his heart, appeared more bright and amiable to others, than it did
to himfelf. His humility was carried to an excefs, if
it is poffible for any excefs to be in humility. He
had fuch a low opinion of himfelf, that he was almoft
ready, fometimes, to refign his underftanding to the
dictates of other men. I do not fay that he ever actually did it; but this I will affirm, that the greateft
foible I ever obferved in him, was too low an opinion
of one of the nobleft works he ever wrote: I mean
his Eleven Letters upon Juftification, by CHRIST's
imputed Righteoufnefs. Thefe letters were written
with his dying hand. And what is faid of a much inferior author, concerning a Poem upon the Lord's
Prayer, and the fear of GOD, may be more juftly applied to him, when compofing thefe letters.

    " *Wreftling with Death he did thofe lines indite,*'
    " *No other theme could give his foul delight.*"

                     WALLER.

If you confider the Character of Hervey as a Philofopher and Chriftian united, you fee in him the
                               fweeteft

sweetest meekness in the government of his anger. Never did I see him in a frame of mind that was not fit for immediate death. If the pride and petulance of one of the most false-hearted men that ever lived, could have moved him to undue anger, I should have seen it either in the features of his countenance; or the language of his lips; or in his letters to me; or in his superior letters to his enemy; but not a trace of improper commotion can be found. It was wonderful to consider how he could preserve such a beautiful temper of meekness in a consistency with his ardent zeal for the doctrine of justification, by the imputed righteousness of CHRIST, or CHRIST's active and passive obedience put down to our account and credit, by an act of GOD, as a Father and a Judge.

His contentment with the allotments of Providence was so great, that I never saw the least mark of dissatisfaction or fretfulness in him. His fortitude in bearing afflictions was wonderful; but his fortitude in defending truth was more so: he had no dread of any consequences: he had no slavish fear of any man upon earth; and if he had been called to preach before the King, Lords, and Commons, he would not have shunned to declare the whole counsel of GOD.

With respect to his temperance and chastity, I believe no man in Great Britain, or in the whole world, was ever a more perfect pattern; and all his graces and conduct were under the direction of the most consummate prudence. I never saw one instance of imprudence in his behaviour and conduct in the whole six years of my conversation with him.

His *social graces* towards mankind were most beautiful and exemplary: his benevolence had no other limits than the empire of GOD: every thing, except the sin and madness of men and devils, was the object of his love. If the definition of virtue given us by President Edwards, " that it is universal benevolence to being;" I say, if this be a right definition, and

nobody

nobody can prove that it is wrong, then Hervey was
one of the moſt virtuous men that ever lived. He
had the tendereſt regard for immortal ſouls : he had
the ſtrongeſt mercy to men, conſidered as ſinners and
miſerable : he had the tendereſt compaſſion for poor
men drawn into error, and could make the moſt candid allowance for the different impreſſions of truth
and religion, upon the human underſtanding and
conſcience : he kindly conſidered, that perſons who
had no education, and perſons who had received a
corrupt and bad education, had very different conceptions of God and truth, from thoſe perſons, who
in their earlieſt years were trained up in right ideas,
of all the parts of faith, worſhip, and morals. He had
yet greater candour, if it was poſſible, towards all
true Chriſtians, who differed in their apprehenſions
of ſome part of truth : he clearly ſaw that God did
not give equal impreſſions of the powers of the world
to come ; that is to ſay, inviſible perſons and inviſible tranſactions : he fully knew, that all believers
had not conceptions equally diſtinct, and equally forcible : he judiciouſly thought, that true believers had
different natural capacities, and that they had different age and ſtature in the Chriſtian life : he wiſely
diſtinguiſhed between new-born babes and little children : he did not confound theſe with ſtrong men and
fathers in Christ : he made all proper and juſt al-
lowances for perſons who laboured under great diſ-
advantages, by reading improper books, or ſitting
under a puerile and injudicious miniſtry : he clearly
diſcerned, that God, our Saviour, was an abſolute
ſovereign over his own grace ; and that he gave one,
or five, or ten talents, juſt as it pleaſed him ; and
that he calls ſome perſons to higher and more arduous ſervices ; and that by a greater force of underſtanding, and by having the advantage of a very correct and judicious education, by the effects of long
and hard ſtudy ; by a more free and ample converſe
with

with the Chriftian world; and above all, by the brighter illuminations of God the Holy Spirit, fome Chriftians would rife almoft to the ftature and beauty of angels; whilft other Chriftians refembled little dwarfs; that fome Chriftians had the elevation of the cedars of Lebanon, while others refembled the fragrant myrtle tree; others, like the green olive; and others, like the humble box-tree; yet all were fitted to beautify the garden of God.

His love and compaffion for the poor, rofe to fuch an aftonifhing degree, as I never difcerned in any other human being: he appeared to be nothing but bowels of mercy: he had a powerful difpofition to feed them, to clothe them, and inftruct them in the true method of falvation, by our Lord, Jesus Christ: he did but juft allow himfelf the neceffaries of life, in order that he might have the more to beftow on the people of God, and minifters of Christ. He kept no money by him, any longer than till he could difpofe of it to fome good ufe; yet he made no account of the money that he gave away; he tried to forget every thing he did, and could not bear to have any body mention any charitable action he had done.

His fpirit of forgivenefs of injuries was almoft unparalleled. If any body fpoke ill of him; if any perfon wrote him an abufive letter, his only pain was, to think that they were diftempered or bad people; and in proportion as they were malignant, they were miferable: it was always the joy of his heart to do good for evil; and he did that good with the greateft eafe and complacency.

His heart was the feat of moral juftice and truth; his will was endued with a permanent principle of juftice, which determined him to do all thofe things which his underftanding perceived fit and right to be done. He had the higheft regard to the rights of God, and the rights of man; and he defired to

give

give to God the rights of his law, and the rights of his Gospel: he was equally willing to give to all men their rights in the full extent, respecting their good name and reputation, their bodies, souls, and estates. Truth shone in the conceptions of his understanding, the intentions of the heart, the expressions of his pen and tongue, and in all the actions of his life.

Hervey was remarkably just and true in his friend-ships; if once he took a person into his heart, all the powers of earth and hell could never get him out; nothing but your own bad conduct, could make him alter his friendship for you; and that friendship, so long as you did not forfeit it, was not only steady and sincere, but remarkably tender and generous: if he thought you a wise and worthy person, his heart was all your own; his head contrived for your wel-fare; his tongue gave you the wisest counsel, and the most faithful reproof; his pen was employed to ani-mate your devotion, and cheer your heart. In the compass of above fifty years, I never found so wise and faithful a friend.

His sincerity was pure and transparent to the very bottom of his being: he never disguised his senti-ments of men, and books, and things; you saw at once, into the whole intention of his heart: he had not one sentiment of religion or science, that he wished to conceal: he had no disguises or doublings in his whole temper or deportment towards God or man: he had a passionate desire to please God in every thing: he desired to know the will of God in the most minute affairs of life; and he obeyed that will to the uttermost of his power: his thoughts, words, and actions, had a singular correspondence with each other: he was uniformly the same at home and abroad, in solitude and in company, and in all the conditions and circumstances of human life.

The

The CHARACTER of HERVEY as a REGENE-RATE MAN.

He had certainly paffed under a fenfible and mighty change, wrought in his foul by the efficacious grace of God the Holy Spirit. He had experienced the infufion of a vital principle, or a new mental habit, or difpofition to live to God. The law of God, and a divine nature, were put into and formed in the foul, enabling this man to act in a holy and pleafing manner towards God, and to grow up in the beauty of holinefs to eternal glory in the heavens.

Confider *Hervey* as a regenerate man, as having paffed under a change.—It was a real change, and not imaginary: it was a peculiar change, yet common to all true Chriftians: it was a change, quite contrary to his former temper of mind: it was every way as oppofite to his natural ftate, as light is to darknefs; as fummer is to winter; as day is to night; as heat is to cold; as fertility is to barrennefs; as fpirit is to flefh; as fweet is to bitter; as beauty is to uglinefs; as life is to death; as purity is to fin; as an angel is to a devil; as heaven is to hell.

This good and great man had paffed under a univerfal change, in his whole perfon of foul and body. This new creation bears a ftrong refemblance to the firft creation, and to human generation. It is throughout a new creation; intirely a new generation; a new birth in all its parts: it bears proportion to corruption in all the parts of it: tends to expel, by degrees, the whole frame and genius of original fin in every part of body and foul: it fpreads its influence through all the powers and paffions of the human mind.

The proper feat of grace is the fubftance or effence of the foul, and therefore it influences every faculty and affection; every fenfe and fentiment.

There

There is a gracious harmony of parts in the whole new man, in all the light of the understanding; the choice of the will; the tenderness of the conscience; the retention of the memory; the purity and grandeur of the imagination; the love and joy of the passions; the richness and fertility of the invention; the correctness and delicacy of the taste, for all that is holy and beautiful in heaven and earth.

This amiable man had passed under an inward change in principle, intentions, thoughts, and comforts: he had experienced a change of principle, or spring of action in the soul. Faith was the grand spring of all his holy actions, working by ardent love to GOD and man: no person better understood the nature of faith : no man more clearly knew the foundation of faith, and no believer produced richer effects and fruits of faith.

He had experienced a change of intention and end. His whole aim was the honour of GOD, and the glory of CHRIST's moral perfections.

Self, self is the sole end of the old man, the corrupt nature : GOD is the sole end of the new man. CHRIST's glory is the sole end and intention of the new and divine nature. The intention of GOD our SAVIOUR, in the new creation, is for himself to represent his wisdom and goodness; his holiness, justice, and truth.

The new creation is an evangelical impression upon the soul, and therefore corresponds in its intention, and holy inclination, with the grand design of the Gospel.

This new creation, is the bringing forth of the soul into a likeness to GOD, the REDEEMER, as the pattern and end of divine grace.

The end of the new creation, is to advance the soul above the power of sin, into the beauty of holiness; above the power of satan, into union with CHRIST; above the spirit of the world, into the bosom of GOD.   It

It is impoffible for a foul to have this new creation, without a change of intention and defign. This change of end or defign, doth alone fit the foul for its proper actions, fervices, and true felicity in CHRIST, our redeeming GOD.

View this excellent man in the change of his thoughts: thoughts are reflected perceptions of the mind: thoughts are the actions of the human underftanding on the objects of material nature, or on the invifible objects of the fpiritual world, difcovered by divine revelation. There was a fingular and remarkable change in the thoughts of Hervey, concerning all things in heaven, earth, and hell; all things vifible and invifible; all things good or bad; all things paft, prefent, or future.

He had a peculiar change, with refpect to his comfort and joys: he had no more joy in fin, or the perifhing things of time and fenfe; he had no more joy in the vain applaufes, the perifhing riches, or the vanifhing pleafures of a polluted world; but his joy centered in CHRIST; and his comfort flowed from GOD, the HOLY SPIRIT. Joy, is an agreeable fenfation, or pleafure, excited by the prefence of beauty and goodnefs, with the profpect of a full fruition of the fupreme good, by the perception of its real nature; by a vital union with its moft amiable beauty; a full reft of the foul in its effence, without interruption or feparation; a rich delight, without difguft or difappointment; a free ufe, without denial or diminution; and a full enjoyment of pleafure in the moft rapturous degree of inward fenfation and reflection on GOD, the REDEEMER.

Hervey experienced and exhibited an outward change, in all its beautiful effects; and with refpect to all external objects, he difcovered this outward change in all his natural actions. If there was ever any man, who eat and drank to the glory of GOD, Hervey was the man. In all his civil and moral actions, punctuality

ality was the maxim; CHRIST's glory was the end. In all his common converfation with good men, or bad, every thing was tinctured with religion; and if he had not CHRIST every minute on his tongue, he had him always in his heart. Need it then be told, that in all his religious actions, CHRIST was the principle, the pattern, and the end?

View Hervey, as poffeffed of a vital principle, or fpring of fpiritual action, in GOD, and from GOD: he knew what it was to pafs from fpiritual death to fpiritual life: he was quickened and enlivened, who had been dead in trefpaffes and fins; he was endowed with a living, powerful, felf-active, or divine motion, animating his foul and body for GOD.

The formal nature or effence of life, of every kind and degree, is very fublime, myfterious, and incomprehenfible: life is animated exiftence, and we cannot give a clearer definition of life. Yet, although we know, that life is felf-motion; its effence, and many of its properties, are quite above our underftanding. We have this comfort and fatisfaction, that no botanift can better tell us, what is vegetative life, than we can tell what is fpiritual life: no anatomift can more clearly declare, what is animal life, than we know what is divine life: I fay again, not the greateft metaphyficians in the world, even Locke, and Bifhop Berkely, can more clearly define what is rational life, than we can tell what is fpiritual life. Not the greateft metaphyficians in the world, can more clearly define what is rational life, than we can declare what are the properties of the religious life. We know for a certainty, that the religious life is a ftate of holy, active exiftence, or felf-motion, under the influence of GOD, the HOLY SPIRIT.

That great phyfician, Dr. Mead, defines life in this manner: life is a circulation of the blood from the heart, by the arteries, and its return back to the heart, by the fame canals inverted.

In

In this manner, we define spiritual life, it is an emanation from GOD the SON, who is the efficient life of every believer, and this stream of vital holy animation, circulates through all the powers and passions of the believer's soul, and returns back again to GOD, the efficient life, in streams of love, gratitude, and obedience.

First. Is natural life self-active existence under the agency of GOD the SPIRIT? So is spiritual life.

Second. Is natural life a power or ability for action? Thus spiritual life is a power or ability for holy action.

Third. Is natural life the result of union between soul and body? So spiritual life is owing to a vital union of the soul with CHRIST.

Fourth. Is natural life diffused through all the parts of the body? So spiritual life is diffused through all the powers of the soul.

Fifth. Does natural life stand in need of GOD's incessant agency? And do we live and move, and have our existence in GOD? So does spiritual life every moment depend upon the agency of the Spirit of GOD.

Sixth. Does natural life need every day fresh food, fresh air, supplies of meat and drink, warm clothing, and seasonable physic? Thus does spiritual life need the fresh air of the Holy Spirit, the flesh of CHRIST, which is meat indeed; the blood of CHRIST, which is drink indeed; the clothing of CHRIST's Righteousness, and the seasonable physic of fatherly afflictions.

Seventh. Does natural life operate by the five senses, seeing, hearing, feeling, tasting, and smelling? So does spiritual life: it sees the beauty of CHRIST: it hears his gracious and powerful voice: it feels the constraining force of his eternal love: it tastes that the LORD is gracious, and the sweetness of his promises: it smells the fragrance of his good ointments, or the graces of his Spirit.

E

Eighth.

Eighth. Does natural life exert itfelf in ten thoufand different operations, by walking, working, converfation, weeping, rejoicing, loving, and hating ; by hunger and thirft ; by pain and pleafure, and all the infinite variety of the primitive and derivative paffions, in their fimple and compound operations ? So does fpiritual life. Thus we have exemplified our affertion, that the religious and divine life, is every way as well known in its effence and properties, as animated exiftence in the vegetative, the animal, and the rational kingdoms of nature : and in all thefe various operations, Hervey difplayed himfelf a truly fpiritual and religious man.

View HERVEY as a Man endowed with a divine mental Habit, infufed into his Soul, by GOD the HOLY SPIRIT.

A divine mental habit is an inward frame of heart, or radical difpofition of the will, enabling a man to act with eafe and readinefs for the glory of CHRIST, and conformable to the divine holinefs.

First. This was a *real* habit, and not imaginary : it is poffeffed by every true Chriftian in heaven and on earth : it is a ftrong inclination or fixed bent of the will to GOD : it is a divine aptitude to excel in holinefs towards GOD the Redeemer, and all the objects of our free agency : it difcovers itfelf in ten thoufand modes of action ; and this holy bent of the will is neceffary for all gracious actions towards GOD the Father, Son and Holy Spirit, and towards all mankind. This habit is but one, as the foul of man is but one fimple principle of rational operation ; fo grace is but one fimple principle of holy operation.

This habit receives various denominations, or names, from the feat or fubject of it, that is, the foul in which it refides : in the underftanding, it is the knowledge of GOD our SAVIOUR : in the will, it is

the

the choice of God: in the affections, it is a motion towards God.

This habit receives different names from the objects by which it is diversified: as it closes with Christ crucified and dying, it is faith: as it rejoices in a delightful union with Christ living, it is love: as it lies at Christ's feet, it is humility: as it observes the will of Christ, it is obedience: as it submits to Christ's rod, it is patience and resignation: as it is satisfied with the appointments of Providence, it is contentment: as it burns for Christ's glory, it is zeal: as it teaches us to reflect upon sin with sorrow and indignation, it is repentance: as it feels an high degree of pleasure in Christ's person and perfections, it is joy.

Here we will take a view of the nature of regeneration in Hervey's soul, as it is a vital principle and a holy habit, united both together in one operation; it is therefore a motion to God, and a motion for God, as the result of a motion from God the Holy Spirit; and it must be, and really is, ready in disposition, and ready in activity of motion. First, it is ready in disposition for motion; it is disposed to every good word and work, when God calls and smiles, at any time, in any place, and upon any occasion whatsoever.

This readiness to God, and for God, is radically, in every regenerate soul in the whole world; yet it doth not always actually appear every day or every hour. This readiness to every good work, doth not actually appear in persons newly regenerated; the lowest degree of this habit, is a purpose of heart to cleave to the Lord Jesus, Acts xi. 23.

This spiritual principle and holy habit united, was the cause in Hervey's soul, which made him ready in active motion: it made him naturally active in motion towards Christ: all vital actions are from nature itself; and it is the nature and essence of the

divine

divine life to be felf-active, and always in motion towards God the Redeemer.

He was *voluntarily* active : he had a free choice not
forced by God or man : free grace always produces
free will to good : holy men are the only free-men of
God upon earth.

He was *fervently* active : his foul burned with ardour to do fomething noble for God every day of his
life : he was zealous, like godlike Phinehas againft
fin ; like David againft Goliath ; like Christ fcourg-
ing the buyers and fellers out of the temple ; like
Paul preaching at Athens, when his fpirit was ftirred
in him to fee the idolatry of the city.

Hervey was *unboundedly* active for Christ : he
knew no limits : he difdained all reftraints in his ardour for God, and againft fin : he was unbounded in
his affection for God : his foul burned with defire to
reft every moment in the bofom of Christ : he ardently wifhed even to a raging thirft for clearer perceptions of the divine attributes, a more intenfe union
with the foul and Godhead of Jesus Christ ; to feel
in him a reft undifturbed, and to have from him a
rich fruition, without denial or limitation. He had
an ardent delight in Christ without bounds ; and he
wifhed to increafe every moment, to eternity, in perceptions of his perfon ; of union of heart with heart ;
a reft in his love, and to have ftill deeper and deeper
delights in the ufe of all God's perfections.

His foul was unbounded in difaffection to fin : he
ardently defired to have an eternal difunion from fin :
he hated it with a mortal averfion ; that is, a defire
to kill it ; and at the fame time he had an immortal
hatred to fin, as long as God's holinefs fhould endure : he burned with rage againft fin : he was fully
refolved upon its death and utter ruin ; that is, a total deftruction of its being in the foul.

He was *powerfully* active for God. This fpiritual
life and holy habit united, gives aftonifhing ftrength,
vigour

vigour, refolution, and fortitude to the foul. Grace always adds ftrength to the mind, and fixes the determinations of the will for GOD : we have glorious examples of this kind in Scripture: it was 'this powerfully
active principle, that enabled Jacob to wreftle with
JESUS and prevail : it was this that gave a ftrength
of chaftity to Jofeph: this infpired fortitude into
Jofhua, and made Mofes not fear the wrath of the
king: this infufed courage into Caleb, to outbrave
three millions of Ifraelites : this gave a poor widow
ftrength of foul to refolve, never to part with her
mother-in-law in poverty: this infpired ftrength of
mind, into the ftripling David, to meet that monfter
of a man, Goliath: this principle enabled three heroes
to dare the flames for GOD; and enabled Daniel to
meet a den of lions, rather than ceafe to pray. This
gave to Mordecai, that ftout fpirit againft proud Haman: this infpired Paul with a godlike fortitude, to
fay none of thefe things move me; and what mean ye
to weep and break mine heart? I am willing not only
to be bound, but ready to die for the name of the
LORD JESUS: it was this victorious principle that
gave ftrength of mind to all the martyrs, to kifs the
ftake, and fing in the flames. And I know that
Mr. Hervey had the fame intrepid refolution, rather
to die, for the fake of the LORD JESUS, than to give
up one truth. He was a dreadnought, in defending
the glorious doctrine of juftification by CHRIST's imputed Righteoufnefs.

This fpiritual principle and holy habit united, made
him *eafily* active for CHRIST.

The motions of the foul are always eafy, when it
moves upon wheels nicely made, and oiled by the
freeft love of GOD. Every thing that Hervey faid
and did in religion, was done with wonderful eafe.
There was a freedom in his converfation, in his writings, in his fermons, that was almoft inimitable. Never did I fee dignity and freedom fo happily united.
This

This leads me to obferve, that he was *pleafantly* active for CHRIST; all his actions flowing from life and an holy habit, were agreeable and pleafant. His foul rejoiced to act for CHRIST, and to exercife himfelf for his glory, in great, new, and beautiful exertions of grace. He was pleafed in obedience, or in fuffering; in fevere ftudies and lofty contemplations, and in all kinds of devout exercifes of the heart, like the amiable Mrs. Rowe, or the accurate Dr. Witfius. His foul rebounded with joy, as much at an opportunity for pleafing and glorifying CHRIST, as John the Baptift rejoiced at the approach of the mother of our LORD.

He had a permanent activity for CHRIST all the days of his life. If ever any man obferved the fenfe and fpirit of an old good rule, " count that day loft on which the fetting fun fees from thine hand no noble action done," it was James Hervey. It is aftonifhing to think, that a man of fuch a feeble conftitution could go through fuch a conftant feries of elevated thoughts and contemplation: fuch inceffant writing for the public: fuch an extenfive correfpondence by letters, and fuch unwearied beneficence to the poor: Every day, and every week; every month, and every year, to the laft moment of his life, was filled up with love to CHRIST; love to his people, and to his country. With juft propriety he might affume Mr. Bradbury's motto, *Pro Chrifto pro patria*; I live for CHRIST and my country.

Grace is a ftate of active exiftence from GOD the HOLY SPIRIT: it is a perpetual motion of the foul in the life and perfections of the LORD JESUS CHRIST: he lived from CHRIST, as his principle: he lived like CHRIST, as his pattern; and he lived to CHRIST as his laft end. He might juftly fay with the apoftle Paul, for me to live is CHRIST; and he had a thoufand reafons for living to CHRIST, becaufe he had a new principle of grace out of the fulnefs of CHRIST:

he.

he had a precious vital union with Christ: he had daily rich supplies from Christ: he had a full conviction, that with respect to all outward mercies, it was too low and mean for him to live upon them. He had a most endearing love to Christ's person; and whenever he felt any withdrawings of Christ's presence, he found it very painful and distressing. He saw it was a dreadful thing to be without Christ, and that ten thousand worlds without him were but cyphers and bubbles. He valued Christ as the pearl of great price; and he had a feeling experience, that Christ's loving kindness was better than life in a thousand points of view. Christ had done and suffered great things *for* him, and he had received great things *from* him; wisdom, righteousness, sanctification, and redemption. He had received strong consolations for his conscience; that is to say, rich cordials, which are victorious over all opposition, and durable without ruin and decay. He expected greater things from Christ; better and better through life, and to eternity. He clearly saw that there was no object in the universe so glorious as the Lord Jesus Christ; and that the whole creation is empty trash without him. He knew as well as any man, that Christ had paid all his debts: that he had suffered for all his sins: that he had wrought out an everlasting righteousness for his justification: that he had begun a glorious work of sanctification in his soul: that he had secured the highest end of his existence, and that his security was greater than his interest: his interest was that of a created finite soul, but his security was that of an infinite uncreated God.

There was a beautiful order in all the activity and motions of Hervey's soul for the glory of Christ. Grace loves beautiful order and method in all its operations. The soul does all for God, in number, weight, and measure; in time, place, and manner. That which our moral philosophers speak of virtue,

is

is only true in the higheſt ſenſe of divine grace: they
ſpeak very much of the το πρεπον, the fitneſs of virtue; the το χαλον, the beauty of virtue; the το αγαθον,
the goodneſs of virtue. All this fitneſs, beauty, and
goodneſs, appeared in the temper and actions of this
great man.

Upon a review of the reſult of this divine change,
this ſpiritual principle, this gracious bent and habit of
holineſs, which was infuſed into Hervey's ſoul by the
Spirit of GOD; from a continued activity for GOD,
and towards GOD, we may obſerve, that there followed two grand effects; a predominance of grace
and antipathy to ſin. Theſe ſhone in the ſoul of
Hervey. Firſt, there was a predominance of grace in
his new nature. Grace will ſtrive reſolutely for the
maſtery over luſt and corruption: it will ſpeak the
laſt word for the King of kings. Grace is nobly ambitious to be abſolute monarch under GOD the RE-
DEEMER.—Secondly, there was in his ſoul, a difficulty
to ſin: no creature can act pleaſantly againſt a rooted
habit: it muſt be difficult to ſin againſt purpoſe of
heart, Acts xi. 23.

When a regenerate man commits a wilful ſin, he
has a thouſand barriers againſt the commiſſion of it;
he muſt ſin againſt a new heart; a new creature; a
divine nature; the root of the matter; the fear of
GOD put into the heart; a bent of will and taſte for
holineſs; a clear ſenſe of the beauty and dignity of
holineſs. Theſe are ſome of the difficulties that lie in
the way of ſin.

It is hard for a man to ſin who hath cordially cho-
ſen GOD for his portion. Pſalm cxix. 57. *Thou art
my portion, O* LORD. Lam. iii. 24. *The* LORD *is my
portion, ſaith my ſoul, therefore will I hope in him.*

N. B. This was the text of ſcripture, that ſet a
very good man in full fixed liberty for life.*

---

* The excellent Mr. Joſeph Williams, of Kidderminſter.

It

It is difficult for a true believer to contradict that new habit, with which he is so highly pleased, and which is a beautiful resemblance of God.

It must be difficult to act that sin, which by virtue of this holy habit, he is daily striving to eradicate and destroy.

It is difficult for the habit of sin, in a regenerate man, to do the same actions, after it hath received a deadly wound: as it is for a man deeply wounded, to do what he could when he was sound, wind and limb.

This new nature cannot be in a man without a universal enmity to sin every day of his life; although a Christian has not a universal victory, yet he can but half sin at most, when regenerate.

Some persons may object the cases of David and Peter. Mr. Henry wisely remarks, that even David did not repeat his lewdness; and with respect to Peter, who swore twice, and cursed himself once, and did as it were bind his soul down to damnation, yet a single look from CHRIST made him go out and weep bitterly. With respect to this holy man whose character we are writing, the power of sin was so far broken, and the principle and venom of sin so far wasted, that it was not only very difficult for him to commit sin, but it was exceeding difficult for him to avoid a delight and joy in God. This leads us to another prospect of regeneration.

View it as a law put into the heart, and written upon the everlasting tables of the soul, by the finger of God the SPIRIT.

Every creature animate and inanimate is under a law to God. The law of gravitation runs through universal nature, from a grain of sand to seventy-five millions of suns, each of them seven hundred thousand miles diameter.

The laws of vegetation run through all the plants, trees, and flowers, from the hyssop, that groweth on the wal l to the lofty cedar of Lebanon.

F

The

The laws of inftinct in the animal world, run through all the birds, beafts, fifhes, reptiles, and infects; and which laws they always obey. There are the laws of motion, belonging to all bodies on the face of the globe. There is the law of nature in man, and from which he cannot be releafed to all eternity.

There is the law of the new creature: the new and divine nature in a regenerate man, cannot exift without a law or rule of action. The new creature furely hath a law. GOD promifes, as a mighty blefling, *I will put my law in their inward parts, and write it in their hearts,* Jerem. xxxi. 33. xxxii. 40. Heb. viii. 10. It is ftiled by the apoftle Paul, the law of the mind, Rom. vii. 23.

Let us confider what is meant by the law put into the heart. This is a plain fign that it was blotted out in a fad degree before.

This law of the mind, or law written in the heart, is not only the fame with the great original law of nature; it not only includes that, but much more; it is a deeper impreffion of GOD's nature and will upon the foul of a regenerate man: it is a more beautiful impreffion; a more durable and lafting impreffion, never to be loft, but it fhall grow deeper and brighter for ever and ever. In the heaven of heavens, it is more than a law of reafon; it is a law of mighty grace, or a fenfe of a good will in GOD to us, and a good work of GOD in us.

It is a reftoration of that law which was the grand original law of nature; but it is more than a mere reftoration; this law is written in the heart wholly, and not in a piece-meal manner; every part of the law is written upon every part of the heart.

This law written in the heart, does not make the outward law needlefs and ufelefs; for that is ftill a rule: this inward law, written in the heart, is a conformity to the outward rule, and therefore is not a

rule

rule itſelf: it is the thing ruled, and not the rule itſelf. Some raw and injudicious Chriſtians, for want
of ſifting and comparing ideas, have talked and written like Antinomians, though we have reaſon to hope
they are good men; they have not been ſo wiſe as
they ſhould be, nor ſo wiſe as they might have been,
if they had taken more pains to ſearch after a clear
conception of the true nature of things.

Let us conſider, wherein conſiſts the writing of the
law in the heart, and putting it in the inward parts.
It appears in the following views of it; a knowledge
of the ſenſe and meaning of the law; an inward conformity of heart to the law; a ſtrong propenſity to
obey the law; an ardent affection for it; an intenſe
delight in it, with an actual ability to obey its commands.

Firſt. An inward knowledge of the law; a ſenſe of
its meaning and vaſt extent in the underſtanding; a
diſcernment of the exceeding great ſpirituality of the
law; a perception of the reaſonableneſs of its demands; the purity of its precepts; the perpetual obligation of it upon the ſoul, as enduring for ever. The
ſoul ſees, that in a conformity to this law, the dignity and beauty of the ſoul conſiſts; and the regenerate man adores GOD for its binding force to eternity;
which leads us to obſerve, that there is an inward
conformity of heart to the law; the ſoul is deeply
impreſſed with it; and the heart and the law fit exactly to each other, juſt as the ſeal and wax, where
every lineament anſwers to the impreſſion of that ſeal;
and the powers of the ſoul, are like the wards of a
lock, which are nicely adapted to its proper key.

There is a ſtrong propenſity to obey the law;
there is a bent of the will, or a powerful impulſe of
the new nature towards the law. The grace of GOD
produces an invincible inclination, an unconquerable
inſtinct or aptitude in the mind, will, and taſte, to

obey

obey the whole law of God, difcovered in every manner and degree.

Mr. Hervey had an ardent love to the law, and
an intenfe delight in the whole extent of its precepts :
his foul as really loved to obey the law, as he loved
the Gofpel. That man that loves not the law in the
whole extent of its commands, as it is a rule of duty,
and a ftandard of beauty, never loved the Gofpel for
one moment in his life.

He had an actual ability for obedience to the
law : an inward ftrength in his underftanding and
will; in his confcience and paffions, to obey the law
of God. God the Spirit, infufed an active ftrength
into the foul of this good man ; he created a practical power in his foul, to yield a free and perpetual
obedience. Thus you fee a complete and comprehenfive idea of what is meant by writing the law on
the heart; that there is included in it a fpiritual perception of the fenfe and meaning of the law; an approbation of the holinefs of the law, as it is a copy
of the rectitude and beauty of God, and a ftandard of
the rectitude and beauty of man. It includes likewife, a conformity of our natures, unto the purity of
its demands, and a ftrict avoidance of all that it for-
bids. There is likewife a propenfion of heart to
obedience, and a love and delight in that obedience :
a man is lovely to himfelf, when he feels the leaft degree of conformity to the divine law; and he is deformed
and deteftable in his own eyes, when he feels himfelf fall fhort of conformity to the law; but when
God gives the foul an actual ability to obey, he feels
more joy than in all the riches of the univerfe.

View regeneration, as it is the image of God, or
the likenefs of his moral perfections, impreffed upon
the foul. We are faid to be born of God, 1 John iii. 9.
and it is peculiarly remarkable, that we are faid to be
born of Christ, 1 John ii. 29. he may well therefore be called the everlafting Father. We are faid
likewife to be born of the fpirit, John iii. 5. We are
renewed

renewed in the image of him that created us, Colof. ii. 10. We are made partakers of the divine nature, 2 Pet. i. 4. Every true Chriſtian is the image and glory of GOD, 1 Cor. xi. 7. Let us take ſeveral views of this ſubject, and apply them to the amiable Hervey, as we proceed.

There is in the ſoul of man a natural likeneſs to the eſſence of GOD. GOD is a ſpirit incorporeal and inviſible, poſſeſſed of life and action, underſtanding, will, and affections. The ſoul of man is a ſpirit incorporeal and inviſible, endowed with life and action, underſtanding, will, and affections. This natural reſemblance of the ſoul of man to GOD, is common to bad men as well as good, and will continue amongſt devils and loſt ſouls for ever, as well as with ſaints and angels in glory: indeed, the eſſence of GOD is infinite and incomprehenſible; and, in that reſpect, there can be no participation with the eternal eſſence and being of GOD.

But in regeneration, there is a real participation of a divine nature; it is not a mere picture, but a nature divine in its origin, or fountain: divine in its reſemblance or likeneſs to GOD: divine in its bent and tendency, as it proceeds to a fruition of GOD.—GOD's moral perfections are in the new creature, by way of quality, which are in GOD by way of eſſence.

It is a real likeneſs to GOD, as the creature is capable of; and this likeneſs is laid in the firſt lineaments of it, in regeneration, and completed in the higheſt meaſures of it, by ſanctification in glory.

The whole image of GOD is drawn in the new creature; the man is renewed in knowledge, after the image of GOD that created him, Coloſſ. iii. 10. It is the image of GOD, not a part of his image; not a fragment of GOD's reſemblance, as a perfect child has every part of his body quite anſwerable to the father, ſo all the moral perfections of GOD are delineated on the human ſoul; there is an image of

his

his wifdom, or an ability to fuit the beft means to the attainment of the nobleft ends; there is an image of his goodnefs, or a bent of will to make other fouls happy, which is ftamped upon the foul by the Spirit of God.

As there is an impreffion of the wifdom of God on the underftanding, fo there is an equal impreffion of the goodnefs and holinefs of God on the will and affections.

It is more peculiarly a ftriking likenefs to Christ, wherein we partake of his nature: a new nature is a delineation of Christ; it is fuch a vivid likenefs to Christ's temper and conduct, that it feems to be as it were another Christ put into the foul. As the image of the fun in a veffel of water exactly refembles the fun in the heavens, fo the image of Christ in the foul of a believer exactly refembles the Sun of Righteoufnefs: we are predeftinated to be conformed unto the image of God's Son, Rom. viii.

Christ is formed in us, Galat. iv. 19. There is the fame mind in us which was in Christ Jesus, and believers are exhorted to arm themfelves with the fame mind, 1 Pet.

It is a likenefs to the Holy Spirit of God, who is the immediate caufe of it; hence the new creature is called Spirit, John iii. 8. all the graces are the fruits of the Spirit, Galat. v. 22—25. Believers are faid to mind the things of the Spirit; they have a tafte for fpiritual things; they have a clear fenfe of the beauty of fpiritual objects; they have a relifh for fpiritual bleffings; they have a bent and inclination for fpiritual exercifes; they have a delight in fpiritual perfons in heaven and earth.

Let us confider wherein this true likenefs to God confifts: as we are made partakers of the divine nature, we fhall find that it confifts in a likenefs to God, of affections, of actions, of holinefs. .

Firft. In a likenefs of affections, God, and his fervant, Hervey, had a love to the fame objects: God
delighted

delighted in him, and he delighted in God: God's love, and the love of this holy man centered in each other: they loved and they hated all the same objects; Sin was the object of God's hatred, and sin was the object of the most intense hatred of this holy man.

There was a likeness of actions and operations in God, and in this excellent man: all bad men naturally work like Satan; they operate like the impure spirits of hell; they are of their father the devil, and the works of their father they will do, John viii. 44. Now consider what is the opposite to the temper and actions of bad men. God works for his own glory, or with a view to the fame of his excellent perfections. This good man said, Amen; I will work for that too.

God loves the Church, and works for its good every moment: Amen, said Hervey; I love the Church, and will work for its good every day of my life. God aims to exalt Christ in all his thoughts, words, and actions: Amen, said this good man; I will exalt Christ and his righteousness for ever to the utmost of my power. God, in all his influences on the soul of this good man, aimed at its purity, beauty, and elevation to Christ: Amen, said this good man, that is what I ardently aim at, and chiefly long for.

In a likeness to the holiness of God, holiness is the shining purity of the divine nature in its powers, affections and operations. Hervey was made a partaker of God's holiness, Heb. xii. 10. He was born of Christ, that is, he was made partaker of the divine nature of Christ, 1 John ii. 29. This was the chief thing in which his excellent soul resembled God.

Let us view regeneration as it is a new birth, or being born again; there is a striking likeness between our first and second birth; our natural birth from

our

our parents, and our fpiritual birth from CHRIST;
our old birth from Adam, and our new birth from the
SON of GOD: our firft birth rifes from very fmall
beginnings, and our fecond birth is compared to a
grain of muftard feed, and to a little leaven, which
leaveneth the whole lump. If you read the firft
letters of this amiable man, you will fee divine grace
in its firft and fmalleft principle; who could ever
have thought, that fuch a feeble principle could ever
have taken deep root downward, and brought forth
fruit upward, in fuch an aftonifhing variety and
beauty.

In our firft birth we are wholly paffive: no man
has a hand in his own formation; no man has the
leaft degree of power to determine the features of his
face, the ftrength of his conftitution, or the powers
of his foul. Hervey was free and zealous to declare,
that regeneration was the motion of GOD in the creature, and that converfion was the motion of the creature to GOD; that in regeneration he received life,
and in converfion exerted that life; that regeneration
was an holy habit infufed, in which the ftructure of
the new man is infinitely fuperior in beauty and harmony to the ftructure of the human body: not the
tongue of an orator, nor the pencil of an angel, can
fully paint the beauty and harmonious affemblage of
the Chriftian and divine graces, the perfonal and focial virtues of a true believer. The amiable features of holinefs that appeared in Hervey's heart and
life, may teach men to imitate, and angels to admire.

In our firft birth we have new relations; there are
joyful and happy connections appear, which were unknown before; there is a fweet agreement between
the parent and the child; Jerufalem above, which is
the mother of us all, rejoices to fee a new-born child,
and all our brethren in CHRIST fhout for joy.

In

In our firft birth, there is a family likenefs; and as the child grows up, the features of the parent are marked in ftrong chara&ters upon the countenance of the child. Thus it is in the world of grace; you may know the parent by the child, and you may know the child by looking at the features of the father; in the wicked world there is a ftrong likenefs between Satan and his children, fo that you may eafily know who are of their father, the devil: you may fee the features of Satan upon the child, and you may know the child by looking at the features of the father. Certainly there muft be as ftrong a refemblance between God and his children, as there can be between the children of the devil and their father in hell, John viii. 44.

Our firft birth is incomprehenfible to all the underftandings of men and angels. That incomparable anatomift, Dr. William Harvey, who difcovered and demonftrated the circulation of the blood, was never able to explain the nature and manner of human generation; and our modern Harveys, who muft be allowed to be the moft acute anatomifts in the world; I mean Dr. John Hunter, and his late brother, with the prefent Mr. Cruikfhanks, are quite incompetent to the tafk: and we may venture to challenge all the fons of fcience unto the end of the world, ever to explain the beginning, rife, progrefs, and perfe&tion of the human body. Do we acknowledge fa&ts to be incomprehenfible myfteries in the world of nature, and fhall we be fo abfurd as to deny them in the world of grace.

Thus we have viewed Hervey as a regenerate man; we have confidered him as having paffed under a change in his underftanding, will, affe&tions, and tafte; in his principles, thought, intentions and end of life; we have viewed him as the feat and fubje&t of a divine and immortal life; we have confidered him as poffeffed of a divine habit; and we have

G   viewed

viewed the beautiful union and vigorous operations of this life and habit, as united together; we have viewed his foul as infcribed with the divine law, and have confidered what is meant by God's writing the law upon the heart: we have proceeded to defcribe the moral perfections of God, and the beautiful temper of Christ, as inftamped upon his foul. Laftly, we have viewed him as the feat and fubject of the new birth; and fhall we not difcern, adore, and admire the wife, the powerful, and good hand of God in this whole ftructure. Even this feeble delineation of his internal character, if viewed in the light of faith, and under the influence of divine grace, is fufficient to attract all hearts, and charm all eyes.

But if any reader has a ftrong paffion to fee the grandeur and beauty of regeneration in all its amplitude and extent defcribed in the very beft language, let him read the firft writer in the world upon this fubject; I mean the immortal Stephen Charnock, Vol. II. in folio.

View HERVEY as a Man endowed with the Dignity and Prerogatives of a CHRISTIAN.

THE dignity of a Chriftian is the refult of vital union with Christ: it confifts of being poffeffed of a radical and effential refemblance to God. The ftrongeft cordials of the Gofpel have the happieft tendency to promote and cherifh this dignity; a fpiritual privilege confifts in exemption from the worft evils, and in being endowed with a right to the very beft goods: a cordial is a vital and moft interefting truth that has a tendency to comfort and cheer the heart: a fpiritual prerogative is a right of diftinction and pre-eminence belonging to a Chriftian above all other men, and exclufive of the whole unregenerate world.

Before

Before we amplify the character of Hervey in his dignity, comfort, and prerogatives, let us take a short prospect of them in a miniature picture; in order to excite our esteem, inflame our desires to'be possessed of the same dignity, and encourage our hopes of enjoying the same strong consolation.

We shall enter upon this part of Hervey's Life and Character with two preliminaries:

PRELIMINARY I.

Let not the weakest true Christian upon earth, feel any disgust or discouragement at the superior degrees of holiness with which he was endowed, or the embellishments of genius and science with which he was adorned. Every true believer is possessed with the grand essentials of salvation and happiness, in as real a manner as this great and good man: he had no exclusive privileges of salvation; his dignity is common to all regenerate souls; the cordials of the Gospel are the right of every Christian; and the weakest servant of God, has a share in all the great prerogatives of a Christian, and an interest in those eternal distinctions and honours which God bestowed upon him.

PRELIMINARY II.

In the Covenant of Grace, which begins with this grand article, " I will be to you a God," every perfection in the divine nature is engaged to be exerted to the very uttermost, for the salvation of every believer: the infinite perfections of God the Son, or his boundless capacities for virtue and happiness, are all pledged to the true Christian. Christ will exert his three offices to the very uttermost, to remove the three plagues of a blind understanding, a guilty conscience, and a stubborn will: he will employ his three offices to the very uttermost, to answer three scruples of a doubting Christian: is he

G 2   able,

able, is he willing, is he commiffioned and fworn into his office by God? Christ will exert his three
offices of prophet, prieft, and king, to level three
mountains in the way to heaven: the juftice of God
declares you are guilty and deferve hell; the holinefs of God fwears you are filthy, and unfit to come
to heaven. The decrees of God are a profound depth,
which no underftanding can fathom or know. Christ
fatisfies divine juftice by his blood; he glorifies divine holinefs by his obedience; and he opens up the
thoughts of God, as containing nothing but thoughts
of peace, and not thoughts of evil towards his people. Christ, by his three offices, unravels the devil's
plots, that we cannot difcover: he anfwers the devil's charges, which we cannot deny; and he con-
quers the devil's forces, which we cannot refift. The
Spirit of God, in all his infinite perfections and operations, is engaged by his word and oath, to bring
home the redemption of Christ to the heart, and to
give us an holinefs and happinefs, vaft as our capacities,
and lafting as our immortal exiftence. With thefe two
preliminaries, we proceed to confider the dignity and
prerogatives of a Chriftian; firft of all in miniature,
and then with a greater amplitude and extent.

SECTION I.

This great and good man was born of God—
his birth-day was celebrated by all the millions of
holy angels.—He was the fon of a noble one, Jerem.
xxx. 21. He fprang from a nobleman, Luke xix.
12.—He was the reftored image of the living God
—His foul was inlaid with all manner of beauties and
ornaments—He was dignified with noble names and
titles of honour—He was married to the Prince of
Peace and Lord of lords, the incarnate God over
the whole earth—He was ennobled and enriched by
all kinds of union with Christ, his vital head—He
was a temple of God, the eternal Spirit—His foul
was

was brighter than the vifible fun in the expanfe of
heaven.

SECTION II.

His foul was of more worth and dignity than feventy-five millions of the fixed ftars—His immortal
foul was the end of the whole creation, vifible and invifible, mortal and immortal, rational and material
—His foul poffeffed greater riches than all the mines
of gold and diamonds in the Weft and Eaft-Indies—
He was an heir of the whole world ; a monarch of
the univerfe, Rom. iv. 13.—He had a liberal and
noble education, under the tuition of the omnipotent
and incarnate GOD—He had a foul formed to love
and delight in the natural and moral perfections of
the divine nature—All things muft needs work for
his temporal, fpiritual, and eternal good—The holinefs of GOD was the moft agreeable object in the
world to Hervey's pure illuminated exalted foul—He
lived by faith in the invifible ever prefent agency of
GOD the Redeemer, who was the author, object, and
life of that faith—He fhewed to the three worlds of
heaven, earth, and hell, the true dignity and pre-
eminence of man.

SECTION III.

Hervey could never die, his divine life was immortal; "his life was hid with CHRIST in GOD."—
His foul was moft agreeable to the correct tafte of
our LORD JESUS CHRIST—His foul was a bright
fun in a dark world.—CHRIST had an infinite delight
in this man, as he was cleanfed from guilt by his
blood ; as clothed with his divine and infinite righteoufnefs ; as adorned by the graces of the Holy Spirit ; and as a rightful heir to eternal glory. His excellent and holy foul was fuperior to all the unregenerate kings and monarchs in the world, wicked
princes, profligate lords, proud philofophers, artful
ftatefmen,

ſtateſmen, florid orators, and mighty warriors, with all other ſhining characters in the univerſe deſtitute of divine grace, were far beneath this great man. Glory is the fame of excellent virtue, attended with praiſe; and Hervey had more ſolid glory and real greatneſs of ſoul, than all the unconverted men upon the face of the whole earth. CHRIST, as a Chriſtian's life, deſcribed by that excellent man, Mr. John Gammon, was never better exemplified, than in the life and character of James Hervey. He felt an ardour of joy in GOD the REDEEMER, flowing from above ſixty funds or fountains of joy. His ſoul was the beauty of his birth-place; it was the ornament to the village, and gave dignity to the county in which he was born: he was the honour of Great Britain, the beauty and ornament of Europe, the glory of human nature, and a credit to the whole univerſe of GOD—GOD's life, and all his infinite attributes dwelt every moment in his precious ſoul—He felt the happineſs of heaven above him, around him, within him, flowing every moment as an emanation from GOD.

SECTION IV.

He was a ſpiritually learned man in the ſight of GOD—He was a truly wiſe man—He was a man endowed with wonderful prudence—He was really a happy man; happier than all the millions of the wicked world—He was a man of great benevolence and generoſity of ſoul—He was a man of eminent holineſs—He was a very juſt man; he loved eternal and immutable juſtice—He was a man of great truth, ſincerity, and faithfulneſs—He was a man endowed with aſtoniſhing fortitude—He had a chaſte ſoul in a chaſte body.

SECTION

SECTION V.

He was a man of wife zeal and diligence—He was
a very humble man—He was a man of great meeknefs and felf-denial—He was a man of the moft calm
contentment—He conquered all things by patience—
He was indefatigable in his labours for the glory of
CHRIST—He was fupported by a fure hope in GOD
his Saviour—He lived without a pagan folicitude
and heathenifh care concerning food and raiment—He
loved frugality for the fake of liberality, but he
hated a foolifh prodigality—The vifible and invifible
worlds were created for his fake, and all creatures
were at his fervice, and for his ufe and pleafure—His
foul was the moft beautiful bride of CHRIST, the
eternal and immutable JEHOVAH, the GOD of the
whole earth.

SECTION VI.

He lived and walked; he fought and conquered
by faith—His foul was enriched by the daily unction
of actual grace—He was an heir of GOD, and a joint
heir of CHRIST—He had an ardent and immortal delight in GOD—He was a man poffeffed of infinite
happinefs; he was happy in his fweet life, happy in
his pleafant death, happy in his glorious immortality.
The whole world of material nature, with all its productions, laws, operations and beauties, were infinitely inferior to his immortal foul—He was a noble
freeman in the city and kingdom of GOD—He was a
friend of GOD, and to him GOD was a cordial friend.
Friendfhip is a fweet attraction of the heart between
two perfons, forcibly inclining them to promote each
other's happinefs—He was endowed with all manner
of rights, and every kind of pre-eminence as a citi-
zen of heaven—His gratitude, praifes, and thankf-
givings were exceedingly pleafing to GOD—His foul
was a victorious conqueror over fin, Satan, felf, the
world,

world, and death—He was a divine Marlborough in
the armies of GOD—He was the rightful heir of
eternal life, a life of holinefs, and a life of happinefs;
he faw wicked men and devils beneath his feet: he
faw good men and angels all around him—Heaven
blazed upon his mental eye; the patriarchs, prophets, apoftles, and martyrs attracted his love; he
felt GOD his Saviour within his foul, and he was fure
of the fruition of this GOD for ever and ever.

Having viewed the miniature picture of Hervey's
dignity, and prerogatives as a Chriftian, let us now
take a more ample furvey of this beautiful and attractive object: let us confider every thing with refpect to ourfelves: let us always remember that Hervey had no monopoly of the bleffings of grace: he
pretended to no exclufive right to the cordials and
prerogatives of a true Chriftian; but he rejoiced to
fee the whole believing world as happy as his own
foul, as you may clearly difcern in his Rhapfody on
the Bleffings of the Gofpel, Dialogue xvii.

SECTION I.

I. He was a MAN born of GOD.

Our birth of natural parents implies, that we receive from them our exiftence, life, and likenefs; but
they are only inftruments under the agency of GOD:
they can give nothing by their own power; they can
neither determine our being, life, features, fex, conftitution, or beauty; but GOD can do all thefe. As
in nature, fo in grace; and to be fpiritually born of
GOD, implies that GOD gives us our entire being,
life, and likenefs, ftrength, ftature, conftitution, and
beauty!

'What an infinite honour; what a prerogative,
marked with an eternal diftinction, for Hervey, to be
born of GOD! and how glorious was the likenefs between the fon and the Father.

II. His

II. His Birth-Day was celebrated by all the Princes in the Court of Heaven.

There is joy in the presence of the angels over every repenting sinner, Luke xv. When we consider the nature, the number, the powers, and bright perfections of angels, we have reason to be astonished at their benevolence to man! They are mentioned in the Scripture no less than 170 times; and in every place there is a discovery of their good will and tender care of man.

These generous beings, in millions, and hundreds of millions, fly all round the globe: they watched over Hervey when he was a child: they attended him in his youth: they guarded his life at Oxford, Dummer, Stoke-abbey, Biddeford and Weston Favell: they attended all his night-studies, contemplations, writings, and sermons; and on Dec. 25, 1758, at four o'clock in the afternoon, they flew with his precious soul to the third heavens, and presented him with exceeding joy to our God and Saviour on his throne.

III. He was born of a Noble One, Jerem. xxx. 21.

אדירו Adiro, a noble one, not nobles, as our translation has wrongly rendered the text.

Christ is stiled a noble man, Luke xix. 12. Aν Θρωπος ευγενης, and the Bereans are said to be more noble than others, or better born, Acts xxii. 11. Hervey was born of this noble one, 1 John ii. 29. and his temper, passions, and actions, all favoured of nobility. No man ever exemplified the sublime discourse on the nobleness and excellence of true religion, by the great John Smith, of Cambridge, better than this exalted and godlike servant of Jesus Christ.

IV. He was the *restored image of* God.

The image of God is the shining purity of the divine nature, perfections, and decrees, according to

H   which,

which, and with infinite reafon, GOD operates in creation, providence, redemption, and glory.

Hervey made the fhining purity of GOD, the pattern of all his tempers, words, fermons, writings, and actions.

Every thing that favoured of the world, the devil, and the flefh, was the object of his hatred, indignation, and contempt. Every thing that favoured of holinefs, beauty, and the dignity of GOD, was the object of his efteem, rifing into veneration, and that rifing into a profound and eternal adoration of the character of GOD.

V. His SOUL was inlaid with all manner of lovely *ornaments* and *beauties*. Every thing that could adorn a man of fcience; every grace that could adorn a Chriftian; every perfection that could beautify an angel, and the lineaments of every feature of the incarnate GOD, were to be found in this holy man.

His firft beauty was vital faith, working by love. This was the fpring of all his beautiful writings, words, and actions: this was the general receiver of all GOD's bleffings: this led up the chorus of all the Chriftian and divine graces, of all the perfonal and focial virtues of his foul.

VI. Hervey was dignified with noble names and titles of honour. Thefe are the excellent names of true Chriftians in Scripture:—jewels—fheep—fervants of CHRIST—a friend of GOD—adopted fons of GOD—an old difciple—a bride—a ftar—a burning and fhining light—lights of the world—a city fet on an hill—a foldier—an heir of GOD—the falt of the earth—a merchant feeking goodly pearls—a palm-tree—a cedar of Lebanon—a pine-tree—a willow—a fragrant myrtle-tree—a hardy box-tree—a dove—a lion—a veffel of mercy—wheat to be gathered into the garner—a lively ftone—a fteward—the Lamb's wife—a prophet, prieft, and king—an heir of CHRIST—the honourable of the earth—an eternal excellency, and the joy of many generations, Ifai. lx. 15.

On

On the other hand, let us reprefent, by way of contraft, the wicked, who are marked with every epithet of opprobium and difgrace. Drofs—wolves —flaves—haters of God—children of the devil—rebels—an harlot—blacknefs of darknefs—outer darknefs—dogs and fwine—captives in a dungeon—fluggards—children of wrath and heirs of hell—falt that has loft its favour—a fool—thorns, Jofhua xxiii. 13. Numb. xxxiii. 55.—thiftles—briars—nettles—wild affes colts—veffels of wrath—chaff and tares to be burned—having hearts of adamant—thieves and robbers—fornicators—without underftanding—in condemnation and bondage—children of hell—a generation of vipers—the troubled fea—foxes for craft—goats for luft—leopards for fiercenefs.

N. B. Thefe contrafts ftrike the mind and illuftrate each other.

VII. He was married to the Prince of Heaven, the King of kings, and Lord of lords, the incarnate God of the whole earth.

This glorious Prince efteemed the perfon of Hervey; he defired to have his heart, Prov. xxiii. 26. he bore an ardent good will to his foul, and delighted in the thoughts of a vital union of fpirits.

On the other hand, Hervey efteemed the Prince of Peace; he defired his vital prefence; he bore a ftrong good will to his perfon and kingdom, and he found a fweet delight in his love.

Thus a conjugal union began, which will never end to eternity; incomprehenfible dignity; the richeft privileges of a Chriftian, the rights of a Son of God, are the glorious effects and confequences of this marriage, which leads us to obferve,

VIII. That he was ennobled and enriched by all *kinds* of *union* with the eternal Son of God. There are *natural unions* of root and branches of the vine and its twigs, graft and ftock, head and members, foul and body.—*Moral unions*, friend with friend, hufband and wife.—*Civil unions*, king and fubjects,

captain

captain and foldiers, counfellor and clients, advocate
and criminals, furety and debtor, captives and redeemer, prieft and offenders, phyfician and patients
with broken bones, fhepherd and fheep, tutor and
fcholars*.—*Spiritual and divine union*, of foul with foul.
This union refembles that of the divinity and humanity in the one perfon of GOD the SON: this likewife
refembles the union of the three glorious intelligent
agents in the undivided being of GOD, John xvii.

Note. Our underftandings can go no higher into
this glorious myftery.

IX. He was a *Temple* of GOD the eternal SPIRIT.
A temple is a peculiar dwelling-place of GOD, exclufive of all other perfons and things; it is a ftructure
built entirely for GOD, and confecrated wholly to the
adoration of his perfections, and the celebration of his
praifes: know ye not, that your bodies are the
temples of the Holy Spirit? What an idea of the
infinite dignity of a Chriftian, and what refined and
beautiful morals fhould we have, if we lived like
Hervey, under the lively fenfe of this privilege? GOD
the Spirit lived in his whole foul and body; he actuated his underftanding and will, his confcience and
paffions; he kept him as the apple of his eye, and
hid him under the fhadow of his wings.

X. His SOUL was brighter than the *vifible fun* in
the expanfe of *heaven*. The vifible fun is dead matter; he was a living fpirit; that fun is void of
thought; he was a thinking being to eternity—that
fun has no underftanding; he had a power of mind,
to difcern all the perfections of GOD—That fun has
no felf-motion; his foul has eternal felf-activity in
GOD.—That fun has no choice of will; no power to
do a thing, or let it alone; his foul, under grace,
had a felf-determining power freely to choofe CHRIST

---

* *Artificial union:* as foundation and building: corner ftone,
and the whole ftructure. *Incorporated union:* as bread of life:
meat and drink indeed.   John vi. 43.

and

and vital holinefs.   Thus you fee, Hervey's foul was brighter and better than the fun in the heavens.

SECTION II. .

XI. His soul had greater *dignity* than all the fixed *ftars* in the *univerfe.*

That excellent writer, the Aftronomer and Optician, in Fleet-ftreet, Mr. George Adams, in his late Treatife, obferves, that it is now agreed, we have above 75 millions of fixed ftars, which are all funs equal in magnitude to the fun, in our fyftem.

And the greateft of all practical Aftronomers, Mr. Herfchell, when I vifited him on Monday, May 9, 1785, affured me he had difcovered one hundred and fixteen thoufand ftars in fifteen minutes, with his incomparable telefcope.

Now they muft have an immenfe magnitude, and a pure innate light and fire, in order to be feen at all: but if we put all thefe into one fcale, one foul of the immortal Hervey will outweigh them all! See Dr. Bentley's Sermons at Boyle's Lecture, No. viii.

XII. The *immortal foul* of this good man, was the *end* of the whole *creation,* vifible and invifible, mortal and immortal, rational and material.

All things are for your fakes, 2 Cor. iv. 15.

All things are your's, 1 Cor. iii. 21.

All angels, ftars, funs, planets, empires, monarchs, beggars, good men, bad men, devils, all the damned millions of atheifts, infidels, profligates, madmen, fools, heretics, tyrants, perfecutors, pains, difeafes, and death itfelf, are all put into the believer's inventory, and are parts of his Bank ftock.   Confequently,

XIII. Hervey's soul poffeffed greater *riches* than all the banks of money in Europe, with the rich treafures of all the jewellers in the whole world, joined to all the filver mines of Mexico and Peru, with all the gold and diamonds of the Weft and Eaft Indies.

Thefe

Thefe riches are nothing but dead matter, deftitute of thought, life, intelligence, and reafon. Much more without grace and holinefs, the image of GOD, the Redeemer, in all its moral perfections and glory.

The grand and fublime ideas of the divine underftanding, were hid in GOD from eternal ages, the archetypes of all creations, and efpecially of elect fouls, which were hid in the underftanding of GOD, the Redeemer, were in part revealed to the foul of this great man.

XIV. He was the *heir* of the *world*, Rom. iv. 13. the *monarch* of the *univerfe*. See Dr. Witfius's fublime ideas on this fubject, Oecon. Book III. chap. x. fect. 30, 31.

Our great father Abraham was the heir of the world, and all believers are joint heirs with him. What a noble idea of the dignity of a true Chriftian does this thought fupply ! An heir of the whole creation : the wonders of fpace : the revolutions of nature : the fucceffions of the feafons : the alternate changes of day and night: the graces of the patriarchs, the great conceptions of the prophets : the magnanimity of the apoftles: the fortitude of the martyrs: the fcience of the reformed divines, with all the glorious gifts, fermons, expofitions, writings, and eloquence of the beft and brighteft preachers of the laft and prefent age, are all for the fervice and good of true believers.

XV. He had a *liberal* and *noble education* from the *omniprefent* and incarnate GOD.

Hervey's tutors in human learning, were fome of the worft in the world; his divine tutor was the very beft in the univerfe.

Education confifts in giving clear ideas of GOD— in cherifhing right inclinations of the will and choice —in animating the paffions, and regulating and directing them to proper objects, producing the fitnefs

and

and decorum of the whole deportment towards GOD and all mankind.

That great man, Milton, in his Treatife on this fubject, confiders a right noble and generous education as that which enables a man with wifdom and juftice, with goodnefs and greatnefs of foul, to perform all the duties which we owe to GOD, to ourfelves, and to our country, in fuch a manner, under the aids of divine grace, as fhall make us dear to GOD, and famous to all ages. Such an education Hervey received from CHRIST, his divine Mafter; it was conducted by CHRIST, with the utmoft delicacy, with the fweeteft and moft elegant decency, and which raifed him to the utmoft correctnefs of tafte: his faculties and paffions were wrought up to moft exquifite perfection, and he had the cleareft fenfe of the grandeur and beauty of creation and revelation, above any other man I ever knew. How happy would it be to fee thoufands of the preachers of Chriftianity in England and France, educated in the fame manner!

XVI. He had a SOUL formed to love and delight in the *natural* and *moral perfections* of GOD.

He had a clear fenfe of the omniprefence and eternity of the Deity, and he rejoiced in all the difcoveries of his life and power; the almighty ftrength and active exiftence of GOD, was a noble and affecting object to entertain the fublime tafte of his large and capacious foul: he could take in great ideas of the divine nature; he received new and uncommon difcoveries of GOD with rapture and pleafure.

The moral perfections of GOD are the fame in kind with moral perfections in men and angels, though infinitely different with refpect to degrees: the genuine idea of the word perfection is this, it is a capacity for virtue and happinefs.

The moral perfections of GOD confift in the rectitude of his will, and the clearnefs and purity of his underftanding; his will is invariably inclined to do
what

what his pure mind fees right and beft to be done ; confequently we may conceive this clear idea of the moral perfections of the LORD JESUS CHRIST, that they confift in a permanent and immutable principle which determines him to act in one particular holy manner, and not in the leaft contrary to what his clear and boundlefs underftanding perceives to be proper and right to be done.   Hervey agreed with the great Polhill, in confidering CHRIST as the mirror of all the divine perfections : without CHRIST we cannot have one glimpfe of the Godhead for our comfort and joy to eternity.

XVII. *All things* in *heaven, earth,* and *hell,* worked together for his temporal and eternal *good.*

All good things under the direction of Providence, did actually work for his benefit ; good men and good books, efpecially the Book of GOD, worked for his fpiritual welfare ; bad perfons and things were over-ruled by the wifdom and power of GOD the SON, to make fin more odious, CHRIST more precious, the devil more deteftable, and the ways of GOD more pleafant to his foul. This part of divinity is difplayed with all the charms of eloquence, and brightnefs of imagination by Dr. Watts, in his difcourfes on the Apoftle's words, " All things are your's."   But if any judicious and inquifitive Chriftian wifhes to fee this truth in all the force and glory of demonftration, let him read the incomparable Charnock, in his Dif-courfe upon Divine Providence, 8vo, 1680.

XIX. The *holinefs* of GOD was the moft agreeable *object* to *Hervey's* pure and illuminated *foul.*

The holinefs of GOD is the moft fhining purity of his nature and perfections, according to which, and with the moft perfect reafon he invariably operates in nature, providence, and redemption. GOD never thinks but with holinefs ; he never fpeaks in his pro-mifes and threatenings, but with holinefs ; he never acts towards good men or bad, towards devils or

angels

angels, but in a manner agreeable to the shining purity of his perfections.

Hervey loved the Scriptures for their spotless purity and holiness; he had a clear perception of the purity of GOD revealed in Scripture; he had a vital union with that purity; he had a rest in the holiness of GOD with his will, and he delighted in it with all his best passions of love and joy; he loved every particle of pure light in the Scriptures. Thy word, O GOD, is very pure; therefore thy servant Hervey loved it: witness his excellent Letter on the Book of Job, written in Latin to the Rev. Mr. Thayer, near Northampton.

XX. He lived by *faith* in the invisible and ever present GOD the REDEEMER, the friend and life of his *soul.*

He had a strong persuasion of the power and grace of CHRIST to save: he received CHRIST's whole person into his soul, and he committed his all to CHRIST for time and eternity. Faith, true vital faith, was in him a settled confidence in the truth of CHRIST. Faith took CHRIST at his word, and trusted resolutely and chearfully, in his free transparent promise. Faith treated CHRIST as an upright undissembling GOD.

Unbelief treats GOD as a liar, as a false-hearted being, who makes a voluntary disagreement between his mind and speech, and speaks contrary to light shining in his understanding, with an intent to deceive.

Faith, on the contrary, treats GOD as true—true in his existence—true in his conceptions without error—true in his intentions without hypocrisy—true in all his expressions without lying—true in his actions without unfaithfulness; and in this manner Hervey treated GOD, from the first moment of his establishment in grace, till the last hour and moment of his life.

I   SECTION

SECTION III.

XXI. He was a *glorious instance* and *example* of the true *dignity* and *pre-eminence* of *man*.

All dignity of soul arises from vital holiness; all holiness arises from a living union with the person of God the Son: and there can be no dignity without holiness, nor holiness without union. Man is equally fallen from God with the devils, only with this difference; we live in a world surrounded with goodness; they live in a world surrounded with darkness and despair.

Conceptions of the dignity of man are carried to a vast height and extent in the Night Thoughts and the Centaur, not fabulous, of Dr. Young; and amidst a constellation of bright and beautiful thoughts, there are some extravagant and erroneous notions concerning the freedom of the human will, and the power of man to attain virtue. Hervey exhibited all this dignity without one spark of that pride and arrogance which eclipses and diminishes the glory of sovereign and invincible grace.

N. B. The dignity of man is displayed in the brightest and most beautiful light, by that excellent and incomparable scholar and divine, Edward Polhill, Esq. in his Treatise on Union with Christ, 12mo. and his Palmarian Book, entitled *Speculum Theologiæ in Christo, i. e.* The Mirror of Divinity in the Person of Christ; which is equal, if not superior to Dr. Owen's glorious book on the Person of Christ, 4to, 1679.

XXII. *Hervey* could never DIE; it was impossible for *him* to *die*; his divine LIFE was *immortal*, for his LIFE was hid with Christ in God.

The clear and distinct idea of life is this: that it is self-motion, or animated existence, but still dependant upon God. When we speak of life as self-active existence, we do not mean that this life exists with-

out

out God; we live and move in God, according to the order of nature; and more so, if possible, according to the order of grace.

God alone is original and essential life: he only is the immutable and perfect life: he alone has eternal life in himself: and he only is the efficient life of all creatures. Natural life flows from him, as the God of nature: rational life flows from him as the God of reason: a gracious life flows from him as the God of grace: and a glorious life flows from him as the God of glory. Hervey knew that his life of nature, reason, grace, and glory, all flowed from Christ, the true God, and eternal life.

XXIII. His soul was most agreeable to the *taste* and *conceptions* of the Lord Jesus Christ.

Christ had a clear sense of the noble and beautiful qualities, which adorned the soul of this great man; and well he might, for he was the author of them all: he loved his soul, and took pleasure in its prosperity; he loved to look at him, and as Dr. Witsius expresses it, to stand still and feast his eyes with the beauties of a holy, humble, generous mind.

Christ could see more beauty in Hervey, than in the sun and moon, the planets, and all the millions of the fixed stars.

He could see more beauty in this one holy soul, than in all the wicked monarchs, the profligate lords, the proud philosophers, the artful statesmen, and haughty conquerors of the whole earth.

There were a thousand objects of Christ's taste and delight in the soul of this one man; the sincerity of his heart; the sweetness and candour of his temper; the benevolence and beauty of his passions; the chearfulness of his mind; his ardent zeal for the divine glory; the new graces and affections that were rising up continually; his habitual joy in God; his lively gratitude for divine mercies; his generosity to all

I 2   mankind;

mankind; his liberty of foul in prayer; his liberality
of fentiments towards all true Chriftians; his grand
and holy imagination; his pure friendfhip with
CHRIST and all his people; his wonderful thoughts
and images reflected from the greatnefs of his foul;
and all thefe perfections and good qualities under the
conduct of a delicate and correct tafte, afcending to
GOD in a flame of divine fire, were the objects of
CHRIST's delight.

XXIV. His SOUL was a SUN in a dark *world*.

Who can meafure the immenfe magnitude of the
fun? Who can declare the boundlefs extent of the
capacities of a foul?

What language can defcribe the light of the fun
in the finenefs of its particles, the velocity of the motions of its beams, the expanfion of its rays, through
unknown millions of miles, and in all directions every
way, and every way equally through the boundlefs
expanfe: the beauty of its colours, which are the
grand caufe of all the beauty in the univerfe?

The fun difcovers wonders; the foul of man difcovers greater wonders: light reveals new, and great,
and beautiful objects, to excite our love; light reveals
ugly, terrible, and abominable objects, to excite our
hatred: the light of grace in the foul, difovers the
beauties of heaven, to roufe our efteem and defire.
This light alfo reveals the horrible deformity of fin,
to the end, that we may hate it more than the damnation of hell. The purity of the beams of the fun
is very peculiar and remarkable: who ever knew that
the foul fteams of a dunghill, or the filth of a puddle,
could defile the light of the fun? And what moral impurity can defile the new nature in a holy foul? The
fun is moft excellently ufeful in its chearing and enlivening rays, to make every thing pleafant and joyful in the creation of GOD; but the emanations of
grace, from Hervey's rich and glorious foul, has
fpread a greater chearfulnefs through the rational
creation,

creation of GOD, and will continue to do so through millions yet unborn, quite down to the burning of the world. The sun promotes universal fruitfulness in the spring and summer seasons of the year: it is, under GOD, the great parent of universal fertility; but who can tell the amazing fruitfulness in holiness and good works, which Hervey's writings, under GOD, have produced and cherished in the believing world. The sun has been unboundedly good and beneficial to all mankind every hour, for almost six thousand years; the productions of Hervey's eloquent and divine pen have done *more* spiritual good to immortal souls, from the first hour of the publication of the Meditations amongst the Tombs, to this moment, and will continue to spread their happy influence, till the day, when a nation shall be born at once, popery destroyed, the Jews converted, and the spiritual reign of CHRIST commence in its utmost glory.

XXV. This great MAN was happy to think of CHRIST's rejoicing in the habitable parts of the *earth*, and that his delights were with the *sons* of *men*.

He knew that CHRIST could take two views of his people; he could view them in their apostate head, as guilty, and under obligation to punishment; as naked and exposed to everlasting vengeance; as full of the ugliness and deformity of hell, and justly obnoxious to the vengeance of eternal fire. His soul was infinitely pleased to think that CHRIST could delight in his people, as viewing them cleansed from guilt by his blood, and all obligation to punishment for ever dissolved—as clothed with his divine and infinite righteousness, and made perfectly spotless in point of justification before the divine tribunal—as adorned and sweetened by the graces of the Holy Spirit, and made exceeding beautiful in point of sanctification and gospel holiness: he saw that CHRIST could delight in his people, as rightfully entitled to

eternal

eternal glory in the heavens, and that this right was indefeasible and for ever the same.

XXVI. His excellent and holy soul, was superior in real *dignity* and solid *glory*, to all the unconverted men upon *earth,* and angels in *heaven.* *Glory* is the fame of excellent virtue, attended with praise.—*Honour* is a state of dignity beyond the reach of just suspicion, superior to the influence of unrighteous censure, and in defiance of all the calumny in the world. *Honour* is the emanation of virtue, the renown of real holiness ; it is a superior degree of resemblance to Christ, surrounded with praise.— Solid *glory* is the well-established fame of the nobleness and excellence of true religion, advanced to a very high degree, and surrounded with the esteem and approbation of God, and the rational applause of angels in heaven, and all good men upon the face of the earth.

XXVII. Christ was the sole *spring* and *source* of his divine *life.*

The nature and properties of his life flowed from Christ : he enlarged the extent of it : he preserved the calmness and serenity of it : he emboldened and strengthened it : He was the great increaser and feeder of his life : He spiritualized his genius, and increased the bent and taste of his life : He gave him a strong and invincible bent to pursue all the beauties of creation and Providence : He led him into the superior beauties of Scripture, and taught him the simplicity, energy, and spirit of the sacred originals. This rendered him superior to most scholars and divines, in explaining and illustrating the inspired Scriptures of God.

XXVIII. He felt an unbounded ardor of joy in God, the Redeemer, as issuing from different *funds,* and flowing from distinct *fountains* into his happy soul.

All

All the funds of joy; all the fountains of fweet and folid pleafure; all the mighty fprings of triumph and tranfport, are to be fought and found in the perfon and offices, in the righteoufnefs and , blood of GOD the SON.   Joy is pleafure;   pleafure is an agreeable fenfation of the foul, arifing from the prefence and fruition of the fupreme good, with the profpect of enjoying that good, without any lofs to eternity.

It is the will of GOD, that every true believer fhould have ftrong confolation.

Confolation is the relief of the mind under any trouble, arifing from the prefence of a good, out-balancing the evil which we feel or fear.

Confolation, may be faid to be ftrong, when it has a firm foundation, and is made victorious over all oppofition, and felt to be durable without ruin or decay.

GOD's people have the firmeft ground for ever-lafting joy in the exiftence and perfections of the living and true GOD.

Believers rejoice to think of the certainty of the divine exiftence, and every perfection of Godhead is the ground-work of their joy : they rejoice in all the relations of GOD to them, as he is the *Creator* of their exiftence, and the *Owner* of their exiftence, with all their powers and good qualities; they rejoice to think that GOD is the *Governor* of their exiftence : they feel with unfpeakable pleafure, that he is the *Benefactor* of their being; and that all the ftreams of light, life, liberty, and purity, flow from GOD, through the perfon of CHRIST, into their happy fouls : they rejoice to feel that GOD is the eternal *Judge* of their exiftence, and that their immortal being and happinefs will be determined by the immutable volitions of his will. They rejoice in the divine infpiration and authority of the Scriptures; they believe the doctrines re-vealed; they obey the precepts prefcribed, and live upon the bleffings promifed. They rejoice in the

perfon

perfon of CHRIST, as GOD-MAN: his eternal divinity, is the object of their faith, love, and adoration: they rejoice in the conftitution of CHRIST's perfon, as the moft glorious manifeftation of the wifdom, love, and power of the Godhead: they rejoice in the *fitnefs* of his perfon, to do them good; in the *fulnefs* of his perfon, to give them all poffible good; in the *greatnefs* of his perfon, to excite in them the higheft ardor of aftonifhment and delight: they rejoice in the power of his arm, to fave to the very uttermoft; that is, to the uttermoft of their dangers, of their defires, and immortal duration: they rejoice in the gracious willingnefs of his heart to fave, and that he feels all the infinite delights of a GOD, in the falvation of all his people, without the leaft lofs or difappointment: they rejoice in the *beauty* of his perfon, to endear himfelf to their fouls, and to make himfelf eternally precious in their efteem.

They rejoice in his three offices of prophet, prieft, and king: his offices confift in the different modes of the manifeftation of the divine perfections: his wifdom removes the plague of darknefs from their underftanding: his obedience and fatisfaction removes the plague of guilt from their confciences: his Almighty Power, blended with Grace, removes the plague of ftubbornnefs from their will and affections: he demonftrates to the mental eye of their faith, that he is able and willing, and commiffioned, and fworn into his offices, by GOD the FATHER. He has perfectly fatisfied GOD's juftice by his death: he has perfectly pleafed the divine holinefs by his obedience; and he has opened up the profoundeft depths of GOD's heart, as containing none but thoughts of peace, and no thoughts of evil.

They rejoice to fee that CHRIST, as a wife prophet, has unravelled all the devil's plots which they could not difcover; that CHRIST, as a meritorious prieft, has anfwered all the devil's charges, which
they

they could not deny: that CHRIST as an omnipotent GOD and King, has broke and conquered all the devil's forces, which they could not refist.

Another fund or fountain of joy to true believers, is the interest and kingdom of CHRIST in the world. CHRIST's interest does not confist in external forms and ceremonies; in worldly glare and grandeur; but in vital holinefs implanted in the fouls of men; in a divine nature created, and every moment fupported by GOD the Spirit. This conftitutes the true glory and folid greatnefs of the Church of CHRIST upon earth: it wants no fupport from the arm of mighty kings; the arts of deep politicians; the wifdom of proud philofophers; the harangues of eloquent orators; the riches of wealthy bankers; or the glittering trappings of gold and jewels. Thefe are all extraneous and foreign to the true interest of CHRIST; and though he condefcends fometimes to make ufe of them, yet he can do without them to all eternity.

True believers rejoice in the profpect of the fpiritual reign of CHRIST, in the latter day glory.

They confider, in the light of prophecy, and with an eye of faith, that there will be a vaft increafe of fpiritual knowledge all round the world: that *Holinefs to the* LORD *fhall be written upon the bells of the horfes;* that is, that all the common employments of life fhall be confecrated by holy fouls to the glory of CHRIST; and that love to each other, will be every way proportionable to their holinefs towards GOD: they view with rapture and pleafure, the vaft extent of this knowledge, holinefs, and brotherly love: it will fpread all round the globe, from pole to pole; and every empire, kingdom, and ftate, with all the iflands of the fea: in fhort, every habitable fpot that rolls at the foot of CHRIST's throne, fhall be wafhed in his blood, clothed with his righteoufnefs, and adorned by the graces of his Spirit. All the enemies of the church will be utterly deftroyed, and all the

K   Pagans,

Pagans, Mahometans, Papifts, Jews, and the whole world of Proteftant infidels, that will not bow to the fcepter of Christ's grace, fhall break under the iron rod of his juftice. They view with joy the fubmiffion of all the kings and queens, the nobles, and mighty men of the earth, to the church of Christ. God declares that they fhall bow down to the foles of her feet. They confider, with joy, that this fpiritual profperity will be of longer continuance than any period of happinefs fince the creation of the world: they view with joy the converfion of all the twelve tribes of the Jews, their acceffion to the church of Christ; their full and univerfal return to their own land, and their being placed in holinefs and honour at the head of all the nations upon earth. In the light of faith they view the Lord Jesus Christ, after a fhort period of the drowfy Laodicean ftate, defcending from heaven with a fhout, with the voice of the archangel, and the trump of God; and the dead in Christ fhall rife firft. They fee in the morning of the thoufand years, the whole world of God's elect ftanding upon their feet: in one moment they fee the living changed, and the whole affembled world of holy fouls in their new-raifed bodies afcend as fwift as light to meet the Lord Jesus in the air: they fee them ftand at the right hand of Christ. In a moment, in the twinkling of an eye, the conflagration will begin; the earth, with all her works, fhall be burned up; the loftieft mountains, which are twenty thoufand feet high, fhall be diffolved like a pile of fnow; the folemn temples, the gorgeous palaces, the moft populous cities, with the pooreft villages, and the vileft cottages, fhall be blended in one promifcuous ruin: the wicked, which are then living, fhall have their bodies diffolved into afhes by fire, and thofe afhes fhall be thrown under our feet: they fee the creation of the new heavens and the new earth: they fee the New Jerufalem formed, the walls erected,

the

the gates made of folid pearl fet up, the ftreets paved
with pure gold like tranfparent glafs; the river of life
running through the city; the tree of life arifes and
fpreads its branches, with their twelve manner of
fruits, over the whole breadth of the river: they defcend with their glorified LORD, and here they reign
as kings a thoufand years. In the light of faith, they
fee the grand employment of the inhabitants of the
new earth: they fee them all fparkling with holinefs,
and every Chriftian as a mirror to reflect the fun
beams of his REDEEMER's countenance: all our labours, fervices, fufferings, will then be reviewed,
and GOD our SAVIOUR will reward his own grace.
In the evening of this day, and at the conclufion of
a thoufand years, they fee their glorious LORD afcend
into the expanfe of heaven, with all the millions of
his faints with him: they fhall ftand at his right hand:
they will fee the wicked dead all arife: in a moment
they fhall ftand upon their feet; their characters will
be all declared; the qualities of their wicked hearts
all difplayed: their fprings and motives of action
laid naked and open to the whole affembled world of
faints, angels, and devils: their final ftate of mifery
will be fixed: they muft hear the fentence, *Depart ye
curfed into everlafting fire, prepared for the devil and his
angels.* It is the language of infinite hatred; it implies the everlafting averfion of GOD's nature to the
wicked: they are words that contain indignant fcorn
and contempt: they imply an unalterable refolution
in GOD's nature and will, never to relent: the wicked
fhall be driven off firft; CHRIST and his people fhall
keep the field of victory and triumph. In the light
of faith, they fee the tranfports and horrors of the
two eternal worlds; the one to demonftrate pure juftice without any mercy, the other to difplay infinite
grace in all its brightnefs, to all eternity.

Thefe are fome of the funds or fountains of the
Chriftian's joy; and from thefe fountains Hervey's

foul was richly replenifhed, all through the laft
twenty-fix years of his happy life.

XXIX. He was a truly LEARNED MAN in the
SIGHT of GOD.

Learning confifts in a clear knowledge of books
and facts, in a juft acquaintance with the characters
of men, times and ages, antient and modern; in an
accurate and fagacious fearch into the fprings and
caufes of things, in order to explain the laws and operations of nature, the rational and immortal powers of
man, his connections with GOD, his dependance upon
him, and obligations to love and adore him; his connections with mankind, and with the whole univerfe,
that we may point out and purfue the great ends of
our eternal exiftence; the beft ufe of our rational capacities; the higheft tafte for our virtuous enjoyments; the wifeft application of our nobleft faculties
to polifh and dignify our nature, and advance the glory
of CHRIST as the true caufe of our exiftence, and
the fource of our holinefs and happinefs.

In all thefe views Hervey was a truly learned man.

Knowledge is the conception of ideas of truth; and
comparing them with each other, and difcerning their
agreement with each other, or their difference from
each other, and from the nature of things.

A learned man is one who has a large ftock of
clear ideas upon all the fciences or branches of knowledge, and who is able beautifully to difcourfe upon
any fyftem of fpeculative or practical truth, fo as to
inftruct and pleafe mankind.

There were few of the liberal fciences with which
Hervey had not a familiar acquaintance, but he
had the wifdom to purfue thofe moft which were beft
adapted to his genius and tafte. With his ufual fimplicity and fweetnefs of temper, he has faid to me,
" My friend, I have not a ftrong mind; I have not
" powers fitted for arduous refearches, but I think I
" have a power of writing in fomewhat of a ftriking
                                        " manner,

" manner, fo far as to pleafe mankind, and to re-
" commend my dear REDEEMER." Happy if all our
learned men were to make the fame ufe of their genius and talents.

XXX. He was truly a WISE MAN in the fight of
GOD.

Wifdom confifts in the ftrength of the underftanding,
to confider the relation of things under the notion of
means and ends, and their fitnefs or unfitnefs, to pro-
mcte our holinefs and happinefs.

This is true wifdom to know the grand end of our
exiftence, and the very beft means of purfuing and
attaining that end : the devils knew that Hervey was
a wife man; good men and angels knew that he was
a wife man; the LORD JESUS CHRIST loved him as a
wife man; the divine FATHER and HOLY SPIRIT delighted in him as a wife man ; that blefſed Author of
all wifdom and goodnefs had taught him to be wife;
he enabled him to propofe the very beft end of his
exiftence ; he taught him to ufe the beft means to attain that end ; he affifted him as to the circumftances
of action, to do every thing in the fitteft time, and
moft beautiful manner: he taught him to fecure himfelf from all bitter repentance, and forrow for doing
wrong: he fecured him from wifhing that he had taken
better meafures, and ufed better means to attain his
end. In a word, he taught him to know CHRIST's
righteoufnefs, which made him a wife man: he taught
him to love CHRIST's perfon, which made him a good
man: he brought him into a vital union with CHRIST's
heart, and a fweet fruition of his eternal love, which
made him an happy man.

Hervey was truly prudent in the fight of GOD : as
wifdom is practical knowledge, fo prudence is practical wifdom.

Guarding againft repentance, chagrin and difappointment, is the hardeft part of prudence, and where
almoft all men fall and fail.

Hervey

Hervey did not fall or fail in this point, with refpect to the final iffue of things; but before he attained his ftrength of mind and underftanding, to enjoy his God and Saviour in a free and full union of
foul with foul, he hurt his health by night ftudies, and
broke his delicate conftitution beyond the power of
recovery.   Here it was that the great Toplady
miftook his way, and ruined his health; the great
John Milton loft his eyes by the fame miftaken
ftep.   Thefe three men were truly wife, and are now
eternally happy: but let us never make them patterns for our imitation in that, which was the greateft
blunder of their lives.

S E C T I O N IV.

XXXI. Hervey was a happier man than all the
millions of the wicked on the face of the earth.   See
this difplayed in his fublime and beautiful triumph and
gratitude to Christ in his noble rhapfody on the bleffings of the Gofpel, Dialogue XVII.   In order to
your poffeffion of this noble rhapfody, you muft feel
that rich affurance of faith, Dialogue XVI.   It is of
infinite confequence for a Chriftian to ufe the moft
ftrenuous exertions in prayer to Christ, for this great
affurance of faith, and boundlefs joy in the bleffings
of the Gofpel.

God's people live below their dignity and privileges in Christ: they fail exceedingly in their practical regards to Christ: they do not live up to the
height of their being in union with God the Redeemer, who is the light, life, and glory, of every true
Chriftian.

Here Hervey excelled, and was a pattern to all
believers to the end of the world.

If you compare Hervey with all the great men of
Greece and Rome, you will fee him fuperior in happinefs and holinefs, in wifdom and dignity, above all
the heroes of antiquity.   You will fee in him fuch

pre-

pre-eminence in fublime tempers and delicate tafte,
that you will not bear with patience the comparifon:
you will think it an infult upon his memory to mention the greateft men of Greece: fuch' were Socrates
and Plato, Ariftotle and Ariftides, Homer, Demoft-
henes, and Epictetus.   If you inftitute a comparifon
between him and the greateft men among the Romans,
there is not one man that will bear to be mentioned
with him.   You will turn away your face with difdain
upon the mention of Scipio and Cato, Virgil and
Horace, Cicero and Quintilian: and even Seneca's
temper and conduct will not bear one moment's comparifon.   In a word, if you go through all Plutarch's
lives, and compare them with the divine and Chriftian
graces, the fweet and focial affections which fhone in
Hervey's temper and life, you will find that Hervey
fhines like the fun in the expanfe, which extinguifhes
and drowns all the light of the ftars by his fuperior
brightnefs.

If you compare Hervey with all the moft celebrated geniufes of modern times, he will appear to great
advantage on the comparifon.   Call up to view
Shakefpeare, Pope, Bolingbroke, Hume, Hobbes, and
Lord Herbert.   Go over to France, compare Hervey with Voltaire, and all the herds of infidels : what
do you think of him now, when fet in contraft with
fuch faints as thefe.   O Hervey! the palm is thine!
for ever thine.

Compare Hervey with Fauftus Socinus, whofe famous words are thefe,

" *Præcepta veteris Fœderis maxima ex parte ejufmodi*
" *fint, ut difficile fit creditu, illa* DEO *manare, adeo vel*
" *levia, vel vana, vel fuperftitiofa, vel etiam ftulta ac ri-*
" *dicula, et in fumma, parum* DEO *digna videri queant.*"

In Englifh thus:

" The precepts of the Old Teftament are, for the
" moft part fuch, that it is hard to believe that they
" proceed from GOD: they are either fo light, or vain,

" or superstitious, or even foolish, or ridiculous ; and
" upon the whole, they seemed not to be worthy of
" God," Here is one specimen out of a thousand of
Socinus's great piety!

See this paragraph in his first volume folio, page
499, of the Amsterdam Edition, 1656.

One more proof of Socinus's great piety in his capital work *De Christo Servatore*, Part III. Cap. vi.
page 204. Vol. II. of his Works speaking of the
Satisfaction of Christ, has these words:

" *Ego quidem non semel sed sæpe id in sacris monimentis*
" *scriptum extaret ; non idcirco tamen ita rem prorsus se*
" *habere crederem, ut vos opinamini.*"

The English of which passage is this :

" As for my part, indeed, though such a thing
" (i. e. the satisfaction of Christ) should be found
" not once, but frequently in the sacred records ; I
" would not, on that account, believe it to be so."

Surely the remark of Dr. Witsius is just : " *Quan-*
" *do de reipsa liquet, semper pro Deo contra stultæ rationis*
" *nostræ cæspitationes statuendum est. Monstrum hor-*
" *rendum infandæ hæresios et profanæ arrogantiæ parturit*
" *qui quod Socinus facit non erubescit scribere.*" De Oecon.
Lib. II. Cap. v. Sect. viii.

" When the fact is plain, we are always to vindicate
" God against the sophistry of our foolish reason-
" ings.—That man is certainly the author of a
" monstrous, horrible, and detestable error, who, like
" Socinus, is not ashamed to write the above words."

Let us now seriously compare the temper and piety
of Faustus Socinus with James Hervey. Let us
view our author in his temper towards God the Father : his clear perception of the divine perfections :
his ardent love to the beautiful nature of God : his
high veneration for the divine Majesty : his trust in
God's faithful promises : his obedience to the orders
of the divine law, and most affectionate communion
with God, in providence and grace.

View

View him in his temper and difpofition towards God the Son: he had a clear underftanding of Christ's eternal divinity; a lively faith in his righteoufnefs and blood; a moft delightful union in heart, with his perfonal beauty; a moft accurate imitation of his perfect example; an humble fubmiffion to his infallible dictates; with an inceffant dependance on his powerful interceffion, founded on his fatisfaction.

View him in his temper and conduct towards God the Holy Spirit. He regarded Him as the fpirit of wifdom and revelation, Eph. i. 17. He loved him as the fpirit of truth, John xiv. 17. He confided in him as the fpirit of comfort and ftrength, John xiv. 26. Colof. i. 11. He applied to him as the fpirit of holinefs, Rom. i. 4. and he rejoiced in him as a fpirit of love and goodnefs, Pfalm cxliii. 10.

View Hervey in his temper towards himfelf, as the refult of union with Christ. He was humble in the opinion of his own underftanding and goodnefs: he was meek and patient, and contented in his ftation: he was chafte, fober, and temperate in his appetites: he had the fortitude of the lion, the wifdom of the ferpent, and the harmleffnefs of the dove.

Confider Hervey in his temper and conduct towards all mankind: the Spirit of Christ influenced his heart, and gave him an aptitude to excel in benevolence and beneficence: he had a tender mercy to the fouls and bodies of men: he had a fpirit of generous forgivenefs to all offenders. Union with Christ, produced in his foul a temper of juftice, truth, and candour. Faithfulnefs fhone in his univerfal conduct. Sincerity and tendernefs, punctuality and perfeverance, in good works, under the direction of prudence, adorned all his actions, and rendered him a lovely object to men, to angels, and even to God himfelf.

Now compare this perfon with Fauftus Socinus, and fee which is the greateft Chriftian. See the Life

L   of

of Fauſtus Socinus at large, by Mr. Toulmin, 8vo.
6s. With reſpect to morality, theſe are his genuine
ſentiments, which you may ſee in his Expoſition of
the 5th chapter of Matthew, and many other parts of
his works. " He believed that officious lies are
" lawful : that the motions of concupiſcence are not
" vicious : that idle or obſcene words, gluttony,
" drunkenneſs, riot, luxury, and all impure deſires
" and luſts, were not forbidden till CHRIST's time,
" and conſequently were no ſins."

XXXII. Mr. Hervey was remarkable for a ſpiritual underſtanding of the revelation of the Goſpel,
concerning the divine perſon of the eternal SON of
GOD.

He clearly ſaw in the light of vital faith, that GOD
the SON, was the glorious mirror of all the divine
perfections, and the repoſitory of all evangelical truth.
He viewed him as that adorable object, in which
alone the wiſdom of GOD was diſplayed in the moſt
tranſcendent light and beauty : having a ſweet aſſociation and union of the divine and human nature in
one perſon ; and in whom was to be ſeen the richeſt
conjunction of juſtice and mercy in GOD. In the
ſufferings of this adorable perſon, he ſaw a moſt wonderful conjunction of puniſhment and obedience, and
a rich aſſociation of full ſatisfaction and infinite merit, even the merit of all poſſible grace ; and afford-
ing a rich example of the beauty of grace, to excite
our imitation.

Hervey clearly ſaw, that CHRIST in the characters
of Saviour and Redeemer, exceeded that of Creator
and Preſerver, in the moſt amazing and tranſcendent
degree.

XXXIII. Theſe ſublime views of the wiſdom of
CHRIST in our redemption, were attended with proſ-
pects of equal brightneſs and beauty, with reſpect to
the goodneſs of CHRIST. How great is his goodneſs !
How great is his beauty ! Zech. ix. 17. CHRIST,

in

in giving himfelf *to* us and *for* us, has given us a
greater gift than all the legions of angels and millions
of worlds—and the manner in which he gave himfelf
was fo fweet, fo condefcending, and 'generous, as
tranfcends all expreffion and conception of his people
to eternity!—If we confider to whom CHRIST gave
himfelf! to us, that were creatures lefs than nothing,
and worfe than nothing—and if we recollect the infinite evils, moral as fin; and natural evil, which is
punifhment; which are the two greateft plagues in the
world!—If we view all the goods CHRIST has procured, temporal, fpiritual, and eternal. Temporal
for the body; fpiritual for the foul; and eternal goods
for foul and body in heaven. If you confider the
eafy and free manner and grounds on which we enjoy
this fupreme good, and that GOD the SON, comes
nearer to us in a double union, than he did to Adam
in Paradife: by a perfonal union of his divine with
his human nature, and a vital holy union with our
fouls, what objects which were hid in GOD from eternity, are here laid open; and what ravifhing entertainments did they yield to the holy and contempla-
tive foul of this great and good man!

XXXIV. From a view of the wifdom and
prudence in harmony with the juftice and mercy
of GOD—of the harmonious conjunction of punifhment and obedience: of the beautiful union of fatisfaction and merit in the actions of CHRIST: and the
wonderful conjunction of the merit of all grace, and
of example, by its divine beauty, to allure imitation:
from all thefe views, Hervey's foul was mightily excited and roufed to feek and practife the moft exquifite holy prudence and difcretion.

Religious prudence is an ability of judging what
is the very BEST in the choice of ends and means.
Prudence is the leading grace in vital godlinefs; for
without prudence to guide and guard all the virtues
and graces, every virtue would be tarnifhed, and

L 2   every

every grace would be diftorted or put out of place;
every virtue would degenerate into a folly or a vice;
religion would degenerate into atheifm or fuperftition;
zeal into bigotry and perfecution; temperance into
aufterity; courage into rafhnefs; humility into ab-
jectnefs and meannefs of foul; meeknefs into an infipid temper, or rife into anger, fury, and malice;
diligence into anxiety or flothfulnefs; love into a
foolifh fondnefs or violent hatred; chaftity into luft
and impurity; friendfhip into a doating idolatry, or
into averfion, loathing, and difguft.

Thus we might go through all the virtues and
graces, and fhew that every virtue would be fpoiled,
every grace would be tarnifhed, without prudence to
guide, and guard them in their exercife.

His Prudence judged of the beft end, and the beft
means adapted to the very beft end.

Prudence gave him a knowledge of PERSONS, and
a knowledge of ACTIONS.

1. A KNOWLEDGE of himfelf: his natural powers,
genius, or aptitude to excel in divinity, philofophy,
and eloquence; his tafte and bias of temper; his
real abilities, knowledge, and confequence to the
world.

2. His KNOWLEDGE of other MEN: their capacities,
paffions, quality in life, bias of mind.—Humours,
fancies, foibles.—Favourite taftes, education, and real
characters in the eye of GOD.

His PRUDENCE included a knowledge of ACTIONS:
the intrinfic nature of actions—the eftimate of actions
in the eyes of all the world—the circumftances of
actions.—the effects of actions. or the genuine confequences that flow from good and bad actions, according to their nature and genuine tendency.

1. He had a keen perception of the intrinfic nature of actions, as full of goodnefs and dignity, or
malignity and bafenefs, as adorned with beauty, or
tarnifhed

tarnifhed with deformity! as enlivened with pleafure, or attended with pain and mifery. He thoroughly underftood all actions, whether good, evil, or indifferent.

2. He had a ftrict regard to the eftimate of actions in the eye of the world, whether they were of good report, or evil report, amongft mankind. His exquifite prudence always enquired, " Will the action " give a handle for cenfure? Will the action be of- " fenfive to friends, or fcandalous to be reported by " enemies? Is the action of evil report, or good re- " port, in the eyes of bad men or good men?"

3. He gave a keen attention to the *circumfances* of actions, with refpect to the *time when*, the *place where*, and the *manner how*, they were done.

4. His confummate prudence obferved the confequences of actions: it was this profpective faculty that was the chief characteriftic of his true manly prudence. He could forefee events at a diftance, and he provided accordingly. It was from this that his prudence came to be of fo great importance and advantage in the conduct of life.

In order to his forming this judgment of future confequences, his prudence kept in view the time paft. He always reviewed the actions and deportment of his life, and by comparing fimilar caufes and events, he proceeded with a greater confidence and bravery of mind, becaufe he knew that the fame things come round again in human life.

Prudence is the art of conjecturing. The objects of fcience are things effentially true and neceffary. The objects of prudence are things contingent, which may fall out one way or another. He knew that it was well worth our while to come as near to certainty as poffible, and to regulate our conduct accordingly. Now, in this uncertainty of events, what did this wife man do? He obferved, as for his life, thefe maxims of prudence.

Maxim

Maxim I. He attempted nothing from which there was a prospect of more evil arising than good.

Maxim II. He did what appeared most adviseable, and committed the event to Providence.

Maxim III. He considered the uncertainty of things, and made allowance for it in the schemes which he formed, and the hopes and expectations which he entertained. Upon the whole, these two things he considered as essentially necessary to the idea of prudence.

1. Due consultation concerning such things as demand it, in a right manner, and for a competent time, that the resolution taken up may be neither too hasty and precipitant, nor too slow.

2. A faculty of discerning proper means, when they occur.

To the perfection of his prudence, he had three things that were very remarkable.

1. A *natural sagacity*; prudence to appear with any lustre and beauty must, in part, be a gift of the God of nature, though in the grand affair of all, the salvation of our souls, it is our happiness that every convinced sinner is welcome to be prudent in giving up his soul to God the REDEEMER; to be saved by his precious blood, and imputed righteousness.

2. A firm *presence of mind*, and such a ready turn of thought, as helped him to expedients on a sudden push, when he had no time to make many reflections. The Duke of Marlborough was remarkable for this presence of mind in the day of battle; but no Marlborough had more fortitude than James Hervey.

3. *Experience*, or knowledge, gained by observation, made on men and things. This was of great use to improve his natural sagacity. The Book of Proverbs is the result of observation and experience, aided by the inspiration of the HOLY SPIRIT, and no man was ever more attentive to that book.

XXXV. Hervey

XXXV. Hervey had a very deep and powerful fenfe of the holinefs of God conftantly abiding on his foul and confcience, and exciting him to the moft intenfe hatred of fin; or a defire to have an eternal difunion from it.

He confidered holinefs as the beauty and glory of the divine nature, and as the fhining purity of the nature, powers, and affections of man. Yea, he confidered it as a thoufand times more divine than the foul itfelf. He fet this glorious attribute before his MENTAL EYE; and confidered what manner of perfon he ought to be in all holy converfation and godlinefs, GOD ACTS LIKE HIMSELF. He acted like God. He judged that his decorum of temper confifted in an holy affimilation to the moral qualities of God our SAVIOUR, and to refemble his imitable perfections: to be full of love, mercy, holinefs, and patience, as CHRIST is. This is to be, and act like a Chriftian. One fhining virtue or another of God was continually breaking out from Hervey's heart, to tell the world that he was a true Chriftian: his love and mercy to his fellow creatures declared his fenfe of the infinite love and mercy of God to himfelf: his patience under injuries bore a refemblance to thofe riches of forbearance, which God the SAVIOUR exercifed towards his own foul.

All his holy graces appeared as fo many rays of God, who is the great fountain and pattern of holinefs. He walked worthy of God, and in imitation of CHRIST: and this was to walk condecently to himfelf; and in an high correfpondence to the DIGNITY of a CHRISTIAN. God does all things for himfelf, for his own glory; and Hervey's aim was to do all things for God; an higher and nobler end than God cannot poffibly be; and no thing fhort of this would ever content the foul of this great and generous man of God.

Read the immortal work of Polhill on the Holinefs of God, page 26—41. *Speculum Theologiæ in Chrifto,* 4to.

4to. 1678. The richeſt book ever written in the Engliſh language; a book unknown, and conſequently diſregarded.

XXXVI. This great and wiſe man had the higheſt veneration for the eſſential and immutable juſtice of GOD.

That attribute, which all wilful ſinners abhor: that glorious divine perfection which Socinians would be glad to have deſtroyed; or for ever cloſed up in GOD without one ſingle exertion againſt ſin or ſinners.

This attribute, in all its glory and terror, Hervey loved and adored: this was the grand reaſon why he fied to CHRIST's righteouſneſs, and rejoiced in the bleſſed plan of ſalvation; a plan in which we ſee wonders upon wonders: miracles of power uniting with miracles of mercy, and all the TERRORS of JUS-TICE mingling with the triumphs of everlaſting grace. Salvation would not, it could not take place, without a full proviſion for the utmoſt rights and demands of eternal juſtice: nor would Hervey have taken plea-ſure in his own ſalvation, if it could have been effected at the expence, eclipſe, and ruin of GOD's natural and eſſential juſtice.

The ſum total of religion is, to imitate the GOD we adore.

Hervey had a divine permanent principle in his will, determining his ſoul to actions of juſtice; and not the contrary. He was juſt in his diſpoſitions to-wards GOD, in giving him the full glory of his grace in the juſtification of a ſinner. Juſt in his temper to GOD the Son, in giving him the whole glory of his precious imputed RIGHTEOUSNESS. Juſt in his temper towards GOD the HOLY SPIRIT, in giving him the full glory of regeneration and conſolation. Juſt to the Church of CHRIST, and to all mankind; and juſt to his own ſoul, by ſeeking his eternal happineſs and ſalvation.

Let

Let us now proceed to confider Hervey in that point of light in which confifts the folid glory and real greatnefs of a believer, and a preacher of the Gofpel.

XXXVII. He had the higheft efteem and admiration for CHRIST as GOD the Truth, Deut. xxxii. 4. Ifai. lxv. 16. The amen or truth, Rev. iii. 14. The truth and the life, John xiv. 6.

When man departed from GOD, he intirely fell out of the truth into the effence and fpirit of the father of lies.

The greateft lovers of truth I ever read were, Dr. Witfius, Edward Polhill, Efq. Dr. Owen, Stephen Charnock, Dr. Gill, and John Brine: and Hervey was equal to them all in ardent love of eternal divine truth in the perfon of GOD the Son, CHRIST JESUS our LORD.

Hervey had the higheft ftrongeft faith in CHRIST's exiftence as the TRUE GOD, and not an unexifting fiction. All mankind treat CHRIST as a cypher and a lie, till omnipotent grace changes the qualities of the foul. Then, and not till then, they confider GOD the REDEEMER, as the greateft reality of exiftence and nature, above all created perfons and things.

The truth of CHRIST's exiftence is fo real and great, that nothing in the univerfe is fo fure and certain.

All things are fictions and fhadows, when compared with Him. And fo Hervey treated all creation: he confidered the earth and ftarry heavens as fhadows without CHRIST. All trees, and plants, and flowers; all gold and filver, and precious ftones; all birds, and beafts, and fifhes, as fictions and cyphers, feparate from CHRIST.

When he compared the real and glorious exiftence of GOD the Son with kings, ftatefmen, and philofophers, he confidered them all as bubbles and fictions of a moment. All the nine hundred millions of

M

mankind

mankind on the face of the earth, he confidered as
fhadows, as a lie, a dream; as fictions and painted
nothings before GOD! GOD incarnate! GOD every
where prefent! GOD all in all!

He confidered and revered the truth of CHRIST's
conceptions, in oppofition to error and miftake. This
confifts in CHRIST's infinite underftanding, having a
true perception of the nature of all things, in oppofition to a miftaken apprehenfion of the nature of
things in heaven, earth, and hell; and in the nature,
powers, and moral qualities, of actions in men, devils, and angels.

He had the higheft efteem for the truth of CHRIST's
intentions, in oppofition to hypocrify. Hypocrify is
diffimulation in the moral difpofition and character:
it is not acting up to a permanent principle of fincerity and truth. The effence of hypocrify confifts in
appearing different from the reality of internal fentiments. Hervey knew that GOD our SAVIOUR is not
an infincere being, of a double diffembling heart.
His intentions are all pure, and tranfparent to the very
bottom of his being. He hates hypocrify in men
and devils with his whole foul; and will he ever practife it himfelf?

He loved the truth of GOD the Son in his expreffions, in oppofition to lying and falfehood. GOD the
REDEEMER fpeaks out his heart in doctrines and facts;
in predictions of future events; in laws and precepts;
in threatenings and promifes. He never fpeaks contrary to truth fhining in his underftanding. There
is no voluntary difagreement between his mind and
fpeech in all that he fays to good men and bad. This
great and good man had the higheft confidence in the
promifes of GOD; and he compofed little collections
of thofe promifes, and gave them away in thoufands,
to be pafted within the covers of the bible.

Hervey had the higheft efteem and veneration for
the truth of GOD in his actions, in oppofition to
                                            ficklenefs

fickleneſs and unfaithfulneſs. He rejoiced with full confidence in the thought that there can be no diſagreement between his declarations and actions. GOD's promiſes, laws, threatenings, doctrines, prophecies, all harmonize, coincide, and agree with his uniform conduct and actions in Providence. He formed a very clear idea of the truth of GOD, in his underſtanding, which removed from his conceptions all fictitious, fabulous, and imaginary exiſtence. Millions of mankind treat GOD as a fictitious being, a feigned GOD, an imaginary being. Men treat GOD as nothing, and a lie; and they treat this world in its ſenſual luſts, ſordid riches, and vain honours, as the only real and ſolid good in the univerſe. This they do every moment of their lives. Not ſo this wiſe and holy man. He viewed the truth of GOD as removing from his conceptions all ideas of error in GOD's underſtanding; all miſtakes in his perceptions and ideas. GOD has no miſapprehenſions of the nature of men or angels, or the quality of moral actions. GOD has no miſconceptions of himſelf, or of things paſt, preſent, or to come, in future ages.

Hervey had ſuch a high value for the truth of GOD, as removed from his mind all ideas of hypocriſy, or a deſign to deceive and cheat his creatures. He knew that GOD had no intention to amuſe or flatter mankind. His eſteem for the divine truth removed from his conceptions all ideas of lying or ſpeaking contrary to truth in his promiſes and threatenings. His conceptions of GOD's truth removed from his mind all ideas of unfaithfulneſs in the actions of the divine REDEEMER, or his acting contrary to his declared words and ſentiments. He knew that GOD never would act contrary to his profeſſions.

Hervey had the moſt profound veneration for the properties of divine truth. He conſidered GOD the Son as *eſſential* truth: it is eſſential to his very being: he cannot exiſt without truth: to conceive of CHRIST

without

without truth, is to conceive of him as a cypher, and no being at all.

You cannot conceive of a foul without thought or confcioufnefs. You cannot conceive of a body without folid ·extenfion and divifibility. So you cannot conceive of a GOD without truth, which is every way as effential to his being, as thought is to a foul, or folid extenfion to a body.

He viewed GOD the Son as *original* truth: all kinds of truth flow from GOD—The truth of creation—truth in fcience and learning—truth in revelation, laws, promifes, doctrines, and threatenings—all the truth of vital religion in the heart—the divine life—the holy habits of grace—the truth of the divine law—the truth of GOD's moral perfections—the divine change, and the new birth, all flow from the truth and goodnefs of our LORD JESUS CHRIST.

He confidered GOD the Son as the *primary* truth. As GOD is the firft being, fo he is the firft truth. There are millions of truths in the minds of men; but they are all fecondary truths: they are derived from GOD the original truth: there are millions of ideas of truth in the underftandings of angels, but they are revealed by GOD, who gives them an aptitude of mind to contemplate the works of creation, and to ftudy the nobler work of redemption.

He confidered GOD the Son as *pure and perfect* truth: pure without the leaft mixture of error, deceit, or unfaithfulnefs: perfect, without the leaft defect in his being, conceptions, or actions.

He confidered GOD the Son as *eternal* truth. Eternity is duration without beginning, fucceffion or end. It is perpetuity of exiftence, exifting all at once without fucceffion of moments. GOD the Son never began to be true, and will never end in his truth. As truth was in him from eternity; fo truth will fhine out from his nature in heaven and hell to eternity. Truth will give the greateft twinge of torment to

damned

damned finners, and afford the higheſt ſatisfaction and joy to redeemed ſouls. Truth and GOD's decree are the great gulph fixed between the two worlds, and all damned ſinners will find that the eternal and immutable truth of GOD's decree, is the impaſſable barrier between heaven and hell.

Hervey conſidered GOD the Son as *immutable* truth. Truth is not immutable in the minds of angels and men. Truth was not immutably ſeated in the minds of the angels, for they abode not in the truth, John viii. 44. and thus they became liars and devils.

Truth was not immutable in the minds of our firſt parents; they abode not in the truth, nor did the truth of GOD's omnipreſence abide in them; if it had, they would never have fled like atheiſts to hide from GOD, and then tell lies to his face to excuſe their crime. Here you ſee the horrors of departing from the truth, in the firſt infidels of the human race.

Wiſe and good men, in all ages, have had the truth in their minds, but the truth did not always ſhine immutably ſtrong even in the beſt underſtandings. The wiſeſt men, and the moſt holy lovers of truth, have been liable to weakneſs, inattention, and an eclipſe of the underſtanding, when GOD the Spirit of truth has ſuſpended his light and influence. Witneſs Noah and Abraham, Moſes and David, Solomon and Peter; but in GOD our SAVIOUR it is infinitely impoſſible for a ſuſpenſion of thought to betray him into error for one moment. Truth in his underſtanding, is the ſame from eternity to eternity, without any variableneſs or ſhadow of turning.

Hervey wiſely conſidered that GOD the Son, the Author of our being, has given us a ſtrong common ſenſe, or that power of the mind which perceives truth, and commands aſſent, by a ſudden impulſe, independent of our will; independent of all reaſoning and books; independent of all education, and acquired habits; operating on all mankind in every age and

and nation all around the globe, and therefore ſtiled common ſenſe.

Hervey conſidered the LORD JESUS CHRIST as the great Author of that divine common ſenſe which perceives ſpiritual truth in a moment, whenever the grand object is preſented. Propoſe this object whenever you will, in any point of Scripture light, and this holy common ſenſe will aſſent and approve, admire and adore; and this is common to all true Chriſtians in every age and nation.

This great and good man conſidered that GOD our SAVIOUR in his nature and choice, requires us to be true in our conceptions; ſincere in our intentions; upright in our expreſſions; exact and full of veracity in our words; faithful in our promiſes, actions, and conduct.

GOD the truth requires this by the law of nature in the whole world of mankind. He requires it in his revealed law from every man where that law is publiſhed. He ſeverely requires it above all in his own people, and can he allow the reverſe in his own mind, in his own words and actions? The holy GOD knows that it is impoſſible.

Hervey knew that if GOD the Son could ſpeak contrary to truth, always ſhining in his mind; or make a willing diſagreement between his thoughts and his words, with a deſign to deceive good men or bad, he could not hide it from himſelf; and it muſt fill his mind with a painful conſciouſneſs at himſelf, and all his perfections would reproach him, and bear witneſs againſt him for ſpeaking and acting utterly unworthy of a GOD. To conceive of GOD as eternally reproaching himſelf, is a moſt horrid idea; a ſelf-upbraiding GOD is a notion full of horror.

Hervey knew, that if ſuch a perſon as GOD the Son, who is beyond all poſſibility of receiving advantage from lying and unfaithfulneſs, 'was to be guilty of it, he would be ſo much the more inexcu
                                                        ſable

fable and deteftable, and be an object of abhorrence
to men and angels. Good men would hate him, becaufe they could not truft him. Angels would be
filled with horror, and expect their own ruin every
moment. Bad men and devils would be ftartled into
aftonifhment, and cry out to CHRIST, " What! art
" thou become like one of us?"

Hervey well knew that if GOD the SAVIOUR could
be deceitful and a liar, fo as to fpeak contrary to
truth for one moment, all love to him would be loft.
If GOD could be erroneous in his conceptions, hypo-
critical in his intentions, falfe in his expreffions, and
unfaithful in his actions, heaven might be turned into
hell. Abraham and Mofes might perifh—Ifaiah and
Paul might be damned to eternal wretchednefs—
Judas and Rabfhakeh might have an efcape out of
prifon—and Hervey and Witfius thrown into their
condition. Thus all gratitude to GOD, and confidence in his faithfulnefs, muft be loft out of heaven
and earth.

Hervey knew that GOD the Son had no need to
make a promife to increafe his own riches, multiply
his own pleafures, or augment his own honour and happinefs.

GOD has no need to fpeak any falfe words to increafe his own happinefs, becaufe he is infinitely happy now. He has no reafon to tell a lie to avoid any
evil, becaufe he is infinitely fuperior to all evil. He
has no need to fpeak a lie to increafe his own honour
or fame, becaufe his honour is boundlefs, and his fame
eternal; therefore if GOD the Son tell a lie, or fpeak a
falfehood, it muft be without any motive whatfoever.

The above thoughts on Mr. Hervey's knowledge
of the nature of truth and honefty in the fearch after
it, I know to be a fact; and I dare aver, in the prefence of GOD, and before the whole world, that I
firmly believe there has not exifted an human being,
fince the days of infpiration, who had a greater love

to

to the whole fyftem of evangelical truth than James Hervey. This! this is the folid glory of a learned man; and all learning is trafh, moon-fhine, and a lie, without the love of truth. A learned man is no better than an embellifhed devil, and all his pompous fcience will be only like a talent of gold fufpended on a man's neck in the fea, finking him fooner and deeper into the ocean of perdition.

As this is an age infamous for the hatred of truth in CHRIST, and of malice at his eternal perfon as GOD over all, I will endeavour to fearch out the original fprings and caufes of Hervey's love to the truth, which will be a ftriking contraft to the prefent gene-ration of infidels, and traitors to the Gofpel.

Know then, my dear reader, that the grand fprings and caufes of Hervey's love to truth, were a powerful and glorious REGENERATION of his foul by GOD the Eternal Spirit, and a clear forcible conception of the truth and veracity of GOD revealed in Scripture. The firft fpring of his love of truth I have already defcribed in the former pages. The fecond fpring I will now difplay from the grand volume of Infpi-ration.

Hervey had a clear, extenfive, and fpiritual under-ftanding of the fenfe and beauty of the following paffages in the book of GOD. Exod. xxxiv. 6. The LORD GOD abundant in goodnefs and truth. Deut. xxxii. 4. The GOD amen—GOD the truth. Genefis xxiv. 27. GOD hath not left my Mafter deftitute of his TRUTH. Gen. xxxii. 10. I am not worthy of all the truth of GOD. Numb. xxiii. 19. GOD is not a man that he fhould lie. 1 Sam. xv. 29. The ftrength or eternity of Ifrael will not lie. Deut. vii. 9. The faithfulnefs of GOD to a thoufand generations. Jofh. xxi. 45. There failed not ought of any good thing— all came to pafs. Jofh. xxiii. 14. Ye know in all your hearts—not one thing hath failed. Ver. 15. All good things are come upon you, which the LORD

your

your God promifed. 1 Kings viii. 15. which he fpake with his mouth, and hath with his hand fulfilled it. Ver. 20. The Lord hath performed the word that he fpake. Ver. 24. Thou fpakeft with thy mouth, and haft fulfilled it with thine hand. Ver. 56. There hath not failed one word of all his good promife which he promifed by the hand of Mofes his fervant. Gen. xxii. 16. By myfelf have I fworn, that in bleffing I will blefs thee. xxvi. 3. I will perform the oath which I fware. Deut. ix. 5. That he may perform the word which he fware unto thy fathers.

Note. An oath is God's folemn appeal to all his moral perfections, for the truth of any promife or affirmation : calling upon his attributes to bear witnefs againft him, if he proves worfe than his word.

The judgments, or wife determinations of the Lord are true, Pfal. xix. 9. Thou art a man of God : the word of the Lord in thy mouth is truth, 1 Kings xvii. 24. Thy God will not forget the covenant, Deut. iv. 31. All the paths of the Lord are truth, Pfal. xxv. 10. Thou haft redeemed me, O Lord God of truth, Pfal. xxxi. 5. God fhall fend out his truth, lvii. 3. Thy truth is great to the clouds, ver. 10.

. All his works are done in truth, Pfal. xxxiii. 4. Mercy and truth are met together, lxxxv. 10. Thou Lord art plenteous in truth, ver. 15. Truth fhall go before thy face, Pfal. lxxxix. 14. I will make known thy faithfulnefs to all generations, Pfal. lxxxix. 1. Once I have fworn by my holinefs, I will not lie unto David, nor fuffer my faithfulnefs to fail, Pfal. lxxxix. 35. His truth fhall be thy fhield and buckler, Pfal. xci. 4. He fhall judge the world in truth, Pfal. xcvi. 13. He hath remembered his truth, Pfal. xcviii. 3.

His truth endureth for ever, Pfal. c. 5. Give glory for thy truth, Pfal. cxv. 1. His works are verity

N   and

and truth, Pfal. cxi. 7. Thy faithfulnefs reacheth to
the clouds, Pfal. xxxvi. 5. Thy faithfulnefs round
about thee, Pfal. lxxxix. 8. Thy faithfulnefs as the
very heavens, ver. 2. My faithfulnefs fhall be with
him, ver. 24. A faithful witnefs in heaven, ver. 37.
Thy faithfulnefs in the congregation of the faints,
ver. 5. Thy commandments are very faithful, Pfal.
cxix. 86.

In faithfulnefs thou haft afflicted me, Pfal. cxix. 75.
Thy faithfulnefs to all generations, ver. 90. I will
praife thee for thy truth, Pfal. cxxxvii. 2. In thy
faithfulnefs anfwer me, Pfal. cxliii. 1. Thy law is
truth, Pfal. cxix. 142. Thy word is true from the
beginning, Pfal. cxix. 160. Thy teftimonies are very
faithful, ver. 138. My covenant I will not break,
nor alter the thing that is gone out of my mouth,
Pfal. lxxxix. 34. To fhew forth the faithfulnefs of
GOD every night, Pfal. xcii. 2. Shall thy faithfulnefs
be declared in deftruction? Pfal. lxxxviii. 11.

I have declared thy faithfulnefs, Pfal. cxl. 10. He
keepeth truth for ever, Pfal. cxlvi. 6. Faithfulnefs is
the girdle of his loins, Ifa. xi. 5. I will fweep Babylon with the befom of deftruction, Ifai. xiv. 23, 24.

Note. There are feventy-eight threatenings againft
Babylon in Ifaiah and Jeremiah.

I will haften my word to perform it, Jer. i. 12. I
will bring my words upon this city for evil, and not
for good, Jer. xxxix. 16. Every purpofe of the
LORD fhall be performed, Jer. li. 29. The LORD, a
true and faithful witnefs, Jer. xlii. 5. I will fay the
word: I will perform it, faith the LORD GOD, Ezek.
xii. 25. He fhall blefs himfelf in the GOD Amen,
(or truth): He fhall fwear by the GOD Amen, Ifai.
lxv. 16.

I will betroth thee to me in faithfulnefs, and thou
fhalt know the LORD, Hof. ii. 20.—Note. Betroth is
mentioned three times—All his works are truth, Dan.
iv. 37. I will perform the oath which I have fworn,

                                                    Jer.

WITH DIGNITY AND PREROGATIVES. 99

Jer. xiv. 5. Thou wilt perform the truth which thou haft fworn, Mic. vii. 20. I have fpoken it, and I will bring it to pafs, Ifa. xlvi. 10, 11.

A VIEW *of the* TRUTH *and* FAITHFULNESS *of* GOD *the* SON *in the* NEW TESTAMENT.

To perform the mercy he promifed, the oath which he fware, Luke i. 72, 73. He that fent me is true, John vii. 28. He that fent me is true, John viii. 26. The only true God, John xvii. 3. Sanctify them by thy truth, John xvii. 17. The Spirit of truth, John xiv. 17. The Spirit of truth, John xvi. 13. The Spirit is truth, 1 John v. 6. I am the truth, John xiv. 6. As GOD is true, 2 Cor. i. 18.

The promifes of GOD in Him are amen, 2 Cor. i. 20. GOD is faithful, 1. Cor. i. 9. GOD is faithful, 1 Cor. x. 13. Faithful is He who hath called you, 1 Thef. v. 24. The LORD is faithful, 2 Thef. iii. 3. He abideth faithful, 2 Tim. ii. 13. GOD is not unrighteous to forget your work and labour of love, Heb. vi. 10. GOD cannot lie, Titus i. 2. It is impoffible for GOD to lie, Heb. vi. 18. He is faithful that hath promifed, Heb. xi. 23.

She judged him faithful who had promifed, Heb. xi. 11. The faithful word, Titus i. 9. A faithful Creator, 1 Pet. iv. 19. He is faithful and juft, 1 John i. 9. We are in him that is true. He is the true GOD, 1 John v. 20. He that is holy and true, Rev. iii. 7. The amen, the faithful and true witnefs, ver. 14. How long holy and true, Rev. vi 10. He is the faithful witnefs, Rev. i. 5.

Let GOD be true, but every man a liar, Rom. iii. 4. He is faithful and true, Rev. xix. 11. Thefe words are true and faithful, Rev. xxi. 5. Thy counfels of old are faithfulnefs and truth, Ifai. xxv. 1. Thefe fayings are faithful and true, Rev. xxii. 6.

Thofe things which God before fhewed, he hath fulfilled, Acts iii. 18. My counfel fhall ftand, I will do all my pleafure, Ifai. xlvi. 10.

Thus we have given you the Scripture demon-ftrations of the truth and faithfulnefs of God the eternal Son, as the grand fpring and caufe of Her-vey's ardent and permanent love of truth: and in this view of him, he was a moft glorious contraft to all the infidels and Laodiceans of the prefent day.

XXXVIII. Let us now proceed to trace out that glorious diftinguifhing feature in Hervey's beau-tiful CHARACTER, his DISPOSITION and propenfity of heart towards the divine and precious RIGHTEOUS-NESS of the Lord Jesus Christ, as placed to his account for JUSTIFICATION before God.

This! this is the grand effential of a true Chrif-tian: it is this that marks the difference between the weakeft believer, and the moft refined hypocrite, or meer moralift in the whole world.

Hervey had a clear perception, and a folid under-ftanding of the nature and defign of Christ's righte-oufnefs.

He knew that God had this precious righteouf-nefs from all eternity in his eye and decree, as the fole matter of a finner's juftification before God.

God faw with infinite complacency the right habits, and the right actions of Christ's holy foul, as acting in the room and ftead of his people: and no man on earth had a better underftanding of the divine and in-finite dignity and excellence of this obedience, than the author of Theron and Afpafio. This was the real glory of his character: this raifed him above millions of mankind in the Chriftian world: this raifed him in folid greatnefs of foul above all the angels of heaven.

His capacious mind viewed this righteoufnefs as difcovered to our firft parents, difplayed to Abel, Enoch, and Noah: as fet in a brighter light before the mental eyes of Abraham, Mofes, and Job: as
                                        farther

farther revealed in its glorious brightnefs to David, all through the book of Pfalms: and more abundantly difcovered to the prophet Ifaiah, and his excellent fucceffors, Jeremiah, Ezekiel, and Daniel; and at laft exhibited in its cleareft glory in the perfon and actions of the incarnate God. Here you fee the ruler of all worlds, fubmit to his own law, and become obedient to death, even the death of the crofs: this righteoufnefs was difplayed by the Apoftles in its noon-tide glory, before heaven, earth, and hell.

He had a pungent fenfe and keen conviction of his want of this RIGHTEOUSNESS to juftify him before God. This lively and forcible conception arofe from a view of the eternal and immutable extent of the divine law: and the immaculate holinefs and inflexible juftice of God. Without this conviction every man will have more pride than devils, and will treat the righteoufnefs of Christ with contempt and difdain.

Human nature in all ages has always been proud of its own virtue; but Cicero and Seneca, with the other Pagan philofophers, were never equal in pride to our modern infidels, who treat our Redeemer with contempt, difguft, and abhorrence; and reject his fatisfaction and righteoufnefs as the ground of our acceptance with God.

Not fo our author and dear friend: no man in the whole world had a more piercing fenfe of the impurity of his nature and his guilt before God. This he has demonftrated in his eleven letters*, beyond any

---

* Thefe letters were juft upon the point of being fuppreffed, and loft to the Chriftian world for ever. If that had been the cafe, I fhould have reafon to regret the lofs to the day of my death. Soon after Mr. Hervey's death, thefe excellent letters were put into my hands for twelve or fourteen weeks. From a principle of foolifh and falfe delicacy, I did not take a copy of them, which I ought to have done. Happy for the church, the manufcript fell into the hands of three of my friends, who had more fincerity, zeal, and courage, than I had; and thus the manufcript was refcued from deftruction: and the original copy at laft brought to light. This is fuch an event as I fhall blefs God for to all eternity.

other

other man that has ever written on this glorious fub-ject.

HERVEY had a very ardent defire, a moft violent hunger, and vehement thirft, after this RIGHTEOUS-NESS. Hunger is a painful fenfation of a want of food, as thirft is a painful fenfe of the want of water, or fome liquid, to cool our parching tongues. Thefe are the Scripture images of the reftlefs and raging appetites of the foul, after the righteoufnefs of. CHRIST for juftification, before the burning tribunal of GOD.

GOD the HOLY SPIRIT formed the foul of this great and good man, into a difpofition for a cheerful acceptance of this righteoufnefs, as the free rich gift of GOD to a perifhing finner.—A clear and diftinct perception of the nature and defign of this righte-oufnefs—a pungent fenfe of our want of it—and a vehement thirft after it, always iffues in a joyful and pleafing acceptance of it. And however reluc-tant the proud heart of a finner may be to this pre-cious obedience; and however he may at firft be goaded by neceffity, and a fight of his damnable condition to fly to it, yet, like the man flying from the avenger of blood, when got within the walls of the city of REFUGE, he finds fuch rich provifions and fafety from dangers, as fhall excite him to blefs GOD for fuch a gracious appointment, and to live with cheerfulnefs amidft the beft of company, the moft fpacious palaces, and the joyful elegances of human life. Thus did Hervey enjoy himfelf in CHRIST.

An humble and intire dependance on this righte-oufnefs, was a very vifible and beautiful feature in the foul of this wife and great believer.

He had by nature a very proud opinion of his own virtue, and a contempt for the righteoufnefs of CHRIST. He has frequently faid to me, " I hated. " the righteoufnefs of CHRIST, and I wondered at a " good old man, a member of Dr. Doddridge's

         •   " church,

"" Church who, when I was applauding the excellency
" of felf-denial," replied, " Mr. Hervey, you have
" forgot the greateft act of that grace, which is to
" deny ourfelves of a proud confidence in our own
" obedience for juftification."—" I looked at the
" man with aftonifhment and difdain, and thought
" him an old fool. I have feen clearly fince who
" was the fool, not the wife old Chriftian, but the
" proud James Hervey."

No man had a more genuine, deep, and undiffem-
bled HUMILITY, or a deeper conviction of his inceffant and immediate dependance on the precious righteoufnefs and Spirit of the LORD JESUS
CHRIST for acceptance with GOD, and ability to live
in conformity to the rectitude and beauty of GOD.

He had the utmoft contempt and fcorn for his own
righteoufnefs, when fet in competition with the divine and infinite obedience of the LORD JESUS
CHRIST.

Hervey was no Antinomian. He loved and practifed every branch of moral virtue in the beft manner, and on the pureft and moft noble principles.
No man upon earth exceeded him in love to holinefs,
in heart, lip, and life.

He was no Arminian. He did not depend for one
moment on himfelf for wifdom, righteoufnefs, fanctification, and redemption. No man loved virtue *more*;
no man depended on it *lefs*, than himfelf.

He judged concerning his own righteoufnefs with
the Scriptures, that it was but filthy rags ; and counted it but dung, σκυβαλα, i. e. *offal*, or dog's meat, that
he might win CHRIST, and be found in him, not having on his own righteoufnefs. He had too fine a tafte
to live upon offal or dog's meat. He left fuch foul
feeding wholly to the Arminians, who have the moft
indelicate and incorrect tafte, with refpect to the food
of the foul, and the matter of our juftification.

Not

Not fo the correct genius and delicate tafte of our excellent friend, who had a clear fenfe of all the gradations of beauty in heaven and earth, and who knew that Christ's righteoufnefs was the chiefeft object among ten thoufand, and altogether lovely.

He had a vaft *admiration* and *efteem* for the righteoufnefs of Christ, as put down to his account and credit for his juftification.

He admired the boundlefs wifdom of God's underftanding, which devifed this method of a finner's acceptance.   He admired the wifdom and condefcenfion of Christ, in coming into our nature, and fubftituting his foul in our room and ftead.   He admired the wifdom of the Holy Spirit, in giving us fuch a clear revelation of this Righteoufnefs all through the Scriptures; fo clear, that none but men befotted, and prejudiced by the devil, and the pride of their own hearts, can defpife and deny it.

He had the higheft efteem for this righteoufnefs: he fet an infinite price upon it: he valued it above ten thoufand worlds of men and angels.   He compared all created objects with this righteoufnefs, and found them to be worthlefs trafh and vanity.

Whenever I vifited him in the courfe of fix years, I always found Christ, and his precious righteoufnefs, to be uppermoft in his thoughts and affections; and if he was for a few minutes diverted from his beloved object, by any impertinent and extraneous converfation, he would fit filent as midnight, and cold as death, till he had a fair opportunity to renew his delightful theme: and if any perfon ftarted a divine fubject, his imagination and paffions catched fire in a moment, and he was fure to be firft to encourage the wife and holy thought, and difplay it in the moft agreeable and pleafing manner.

He had an habitual DELIGHT in Christ's imputed righteoufnefs.   Delight is a mixture of love and joy, in an object confidered as good and beautiful, and

every

every way fit to make me eternally happy in the fruition of that good.

DELIGHT is ftyled the mafter bee in the hive of human paffions: they all hearken to its tone, and obey its voice: whatever object we delight in, is fure to be the object of our attention, our paffions, our converfation, and our purfuits.

This was the temper and habitual tafte of Hervey's mind and underftanding. Nothing gave him fo much fatisfaction and joy: and in this he eternally diffented from all devils and infidels: there is no object that they hate with fo much malice and malignity. Nothing gives a Socinian fuch pain, fuch indignation, and bitternefs, as the eternal Godhead and imputed Righteoufnefs of CHRIST. It would fill him with tortures and unfpeakable mifery, to be for a thoufand years obliged to hear of nothing to fee, nothing but this object. That which is the higheft heaven to the believer, would be to him the moft tormenting hell: and you could not more fting up to all the tortures and madnefs of the damned, than to oblige a Socinian to all eternity to fee nothing, to hear of nothing, but the divinity and righteoufnefs of our GOD and SAVIOUR.

That object which conftitutes the higheft beauty and pleafure of heaven to us, is to them the moft difguftful uglinefs and plague of hell. Thus it has been, and thus it will be, as long as GOD and immortal fouls fhall live in the vaft eternity of the invifible world.

Hervey felt the deepeft GRATITUDE, and expreffed the fweeteft THANKFULNESS to GOD for the gift of this righteoufnefs.

Gratitude is a compound paffion: it is a compofition of all the fineft feelings of the human foul. Gratitude hath feven ingredients, which go into its whole idea and nature: it includes a fenfe of the bleffing: a fight of the generous benefactor: an ardent bent

O   of

of mind to make the beft returns: a defire to have better ability and power to be more grateful: a determinate purpofe never to lay gratitude afide: a difpleafure and pain when we feel an ungrateful heart: and an high approbation of ourfelves, when we feel gratitude grow into all its power, life, and beauty.

Such was the tafte and temper of Hervey's great and generous foul. This was the bent and tendency of his mind, through the courfe of twenty-fix years of his holy happy life.

I declare moft ferioufly, before God, that in the courfe of fixty years, in which I have been capable of making fome obfervation on men and things, I never have feen a man equal to James Hervey, in gratitude and thankfulnefs for the righteoufnefs of CHRIST.

All the fprings and fountains of the great deep of his foul were thrown open on this object; and thefe fountains rofe as high as heaven; fpread as wide as the univerfe; and flowed into the eternity of God's duration and happinefs. All his thoughts, words, and actions, were fwallowed up, and loft in this infinite ocean of the pureft and richeft grace.

Now, my dear Reader, I wifh you the fame happy tafte; the fame holy tendency; the fame fpiritual perceptions; the fame divine ideas; the fame vaft underftanding; the fame Godlike mind.

XXXIX. Let us now rife up to the very higheft glory of Hervey's Character, which confifted in the moft ardent and fupreme love to the eternal perfon, divinity, and offices of the LORD JESUS CHRIST.

Here let us confider the nature of his love to CHRIST: the grounds and reafons of his affection: the actions and exercife of this love: the excellent properties of his love: with all the pungent and mighty motives, to roufe and enflame this love: with the fincerity of Hervey's heart, to put himfelf in the way of the beft motives to increafe this glorious affection of love to the REDEEMER, and God of his falvation.

His

His love, in the nature of it, confifted of four ingredients, or was made up of four conftituent parts,
efteem and defire, benevolence and delight.   Efteem
is a refpectful thought of CHRIST in the underftanding, confidered as good and worthy in himfelf.   Defire is a warm emotion of the heart towards him, as
fit to do us good, and make us happy.   Benevolence
is a pleafing emotion or good will to CHRIST, confidered as fit to receive good from us ; and delight is
a mixture, or compofition of love and joy in Him, as
an object of complete goodnefs, truth, beauty, and
perfection.

The grounds and reafons of his love to the perfon of
CHRIST, were the names and titles He bears ; the perfections He poffeffes ; the love that He exercifes towards us ; the unions and relations in which He ftands
to us ; the aftonifhing fufferings and death He has endured for us ; and the bleffings and rich comforts He
beftows upon us.

He felt, in a moft powerful manner, all the glorious actions and exercifes of love to CHRIST.

His thoughts and conceptions were raifed to an noble elevation and penetration, on the eternal perfon of
the Son of GOD : his mind difdained every object
that was put in competition with him : he had a moft
fublime contempt and fcorn of all his former idols,
trafh, and vanity.   The world! the world to him was
all mere title page, and no contents or folid good to
fatisfy his vaft and boundlefs mind : yea, fuch was
his value for CHRIST, that he undervalued his own
fine genius, and natural parts, and capacities for learning, fcience, and virtue, when compared with CHRIST.
I declare what I know to be true, that he could not endure to fpeak one word in praife of himfelf ; and he
could not, without pain and difguft, hear one word
fpoken of his perfon, virtues, and writings : while
Socinians are admiring themfelves, and applauding
each other, as men of vaft powers of genius, wonder-

O 2   ful!

ful penetration and learning, aftonifhing fcience and virtue. Hervey had all thefe objects in contempt, when compared with the tranfcendent glories of GOD his SAVIOUR.

He defired CHRIST's prefence for his own foul to make him happy. He defired CHRIST's grace to enable him to ferve his caufe and intereft in the world: but above all, he defired CHRIST, on the account of his eternal dignity and excellence, as the fupreme and only good: the ocean of all perfection: the fum of all that is bright and beautiful in heaven and earth.

His joys in CHRIST were unbounded and eternal; on his own account, as he found himfelf infinitely happy, in an ocean of perfections and grace: and his joys on the account of CHRIST's undiminifhed glory and happinefs, rofe higher than the heavens, and endured to eternity.

His LOVE to CHRIST appeared in a moft bright and lovely manner, in his ardent love to the WORD and SPIRIT of CHRIST.

He had the firmeft faith in the infpiration of the Scriptures. He believed that all the hiftorical parts of the bible were written by the infpiration of direction; and no fact was omitted through forgetfulnefs; no fact was mifreprefented through prejudice; no fact added by human invention; but that all was the plain fimple narrative of GOD himfelf.

He believed that all the rapturous and devotional hymns and pfalms of the Scripture, were written by the infpiration of elevation. That the HOLY SPIRIT fet fire to the contemplations and paffions of the facred writers, and every devout fong was the language of ardent imagination and enlivened paffion, but under the conduct of the pureft reafon, and the cleareft wifdom and prudence.

He firmly believed that all the doctrines of the Gofpel; all the predictions of future events; all the promifes of rich grace, came wholly from GOD. He

learly

clearly knew that all the doctrines, prophecies, promifes, and threatenings of Scripture, were hid in
GOD from eternal ages: i. e. eternal duration. And
that all the men upon earth, and all the angels in heaven, could not have ftarted one thought concerning
thefe grand, new, and wonderful objects; but they were
all the pure revelations of GOD the HOLY SPIRIT.

This led him to a very high conception of the dignity and glory of the HOLY SPIRIT; and to the utmoft love and veneration for his divine perfon and
character.

I never knew but one man who equalled him in a
tender love and veneration for the perfon and operations of GOD the HOLY SPIRIT; and that was the
moft holy and judicious John Brine, the greateft mafter of the Socinian controverfy, above and beyond
every other man in the whole world.

Hervey fhewed his love to CHRIST, by the entire
refignation of his foul and body, to the difpofing
will of CHRIST's Providence—to the commanding
will of His law—and to the fanctifying will of His
Spirit. Never did I fee in any mortal breaft, fuch
a confidence in the peculiar Providence, and fuch a
moft profound and abfolute refignation to the will of
GOD, however made known in the oeconomy of nature, and the order of grace. He appeared to have
no will of his own feparate from the will of GOD.
He lived as much as a man in this imperfect ftate
could well live to the will of GOD his SAVIOUR, and
his will feemed fwallowed up and loft in the will and
pleafure of his divine REDEEMER.

He was always pleafed with his own exiftence and
powers, when he felt a grateful difpofition; and he
was grieved and difpleafed with his own foul, when
he found any workings of an ungrateful frame of
heart. He was not lovely to himfelf, when he felt an
ungrateful heart: on the other hand, he was pleafed
with his own eternal exiftence and immortal powers,

when

when he felt a foul glowing with gratitude, under the influence of celeftial fire.

Let us now take a furvey of all the excellent and glorious properties of his love to CHRIST: and in the firft place we view it as a RATIONAL LOVE: what is reafon, but a power to fee the truth of certain principles which GOD has eftablifhed, and to draw fure conclufions from clear principles: and was ever any principle revealed by GOD fo noble and divine as this, that CHRIST is the moft lovely object in all worlds: and what furer conclufion can holy reafon draw than this; therefore I ought to love him with a fupreme and eternal affection and delight.

There are a fet of men in our nation, who ftile themfelves, and compliment one another with the dignified title of RATIONAL CHRISTIANS. I wifh to know wherein their rationality appears to be fuperior to that of James Hervey. Does it confift in an outrage on the eternal and immutable truth of GOD: in a moft impudent infult of his natural and moral perfections: in a proud contempt of the peculiar doctrines of the Gofpel: in a malicious rancour at the GODHEAD of JESUS CHRIST: in a contempt of his divine and infinite fatisfaction and righteoufnefs: in a determined fpite at regeneration by GOD the HOLY SPIRIT? If it does, they may take all their RATIONALITY to themfelves: we defire to have nothing to do with it, to eternity.

RATIONAL CHRISTIANS! who are they? the men who defpife CHRIST's perfon and divinity, or the men that efteem him above ten thoufand worlds! If it be fuperior wifdom to love the higheft beauty, and to feek for the richeft fruition of the fupreme good, in the exercife of vital faith; then Hervey was in the nobleft fenfe a RATIONAL CHRISTIAN.

If it be the utmoft folly and madnefs, for a man to try with all his might to damn his own foul, and the fouls of all mankind, then Socinians are in the worft
fenfe

sense of the terms IRRATIONAL CHRISTIANS, i. e. no Chriftians, but infidels and enemies to GOD and the whole moral world.

His love to CHRIST was sincere and fervent. He loved CHRIST with a pure heart fervently, 1. Pet. i. 22. He loved our LORD JESUS in sincerity, i. e. with incorruptness εν αφθαρσια, Eph. vi. 24.

Hervey was no hypocrite in his love to CHRIST: an hypocrite is a person professing Christianity, without a divine principle in his heart: he has no desire to please GOD in any thing: he is never honeft in his enquiries after truth: he never desires to know the whole will of GOD : he never applies himself to practise every duty and virtue: he never puts his neck under CHRIST's *whole* yoke : he hath always a loophole for some sin: he ever gives way to some darling luft. He is never uniform in his thoughts, words, and actions: there is a very great inconsistency between his profession, and his secret practice.

Not so this great and good man: he was the very reverse of an hypocrite in all his thoughts, words, and actions. No man could ftand the test of Mr. Crook's famous book, describing the hypocrite, in a folio volume, better than James Hervey.

He was honest to put himself in the way of the *very best* motives to excite his foul to love CHRIST. He was sincere to search into those *best* motives: he was upright in ftriving to underftand the *best* motives: he was honest in being heartily willing to feel the utmost force of the *best* motives : and he was equally honest in freely complying with the design and end of those motives, to bring us into an eternal resemblance and fruition of CHRIST.

He put himself in the way of all the motives addressed to fear, hope, gratitude, interest, pleasure, honour, ambition, glory, and shame; and he felt the keenest and utmost force of those motives, commanding all the powers and affections of his foul.

He

He had a keen fenfe, and a mighty conviction, that all invifible objects were very near to his foul. This roufed his FEAR of caution, and kept the defenfive paffions in their full tone and exercife. He had a clear fight of the faithfulnefs of CHRIST in his promifes. This raifed his HOPES to full truft and confident expectation: he had a feeling fenfe of redeeming love; and this roufed his GRATITUDE to immortal force and fire: he had a ftriking view of the brave men in all ages, who had gone before him to heaven; and this fired up his AMBITION to excel. He had a clear fenfe of the bafenefs and ingratitude of not loving CHRIST, and this awakened the paffion of SHAME; i. e. forrow and felf-contempt; and his paffion for folid GLORY, and real greatnefs, was raifed by a confcioufnefs of the dignity and intrinfic excellence of loving the REDEEMER with a fupreme and unrivalled affection.

He could look GOD our SAVIOUR in the face, and fay, "LORD JESUS thou knoweft all things, thou knoweft that I love thee", John xxi. 17.

When he confidered the ftate of England with refpect to religion, and the artful and malicious oppofition to the divinity and righteoufnefs of CHRIST, it raifed in his foul the moft powerful emotions of compaffion for miferable finners, and the moft ardent ZEAL, i. e. a mixture of love and anger: of love for the whole fyftem of truth, and anger at the oppofition to it, by the deceit and malice of all its enemies.

He deeply confidered that every infidel and enemy to CHRIST's perfon and righteoufnefs, was branded with this black mark; that he was a confederate with devils and damned fpirits in a felf-deftroying war, againft all poffible and infinite power and goodnefs.

XL. Having viewed Hervey in his regard to truth and faithfulnefs of GOD; in his glorious difpofitions and tafte for CHRIST's RIGHTEOUSNESS, and his ardent love to his eternal perfon and divinity.

Let

Let us now view him in the SOLID GLORY and real GREATNESS of his CHARACTER as a DIVINE, who clearly underſtood, and highly valued, that grand canon

The ANALOGY of FAITH.

This is the univerſal rule for underſtanding the true ſenſe of Scripture: every doctrine you would found on the Scripture, muſt be agreeable to the analogy of faith; for thoſe doctrines cannot be grounded on Scripture, which are contrary to the analogy of faith. For the underſtanding of what we mean by this glorious canon, let it be obſerved, that no young ſtudent in divinity, or preacher of religion, is for one moment fit to teach, or qualified to inſtruct the church of CHRIST, who is himſelf chargeable with ſcepticiſm; or at a loſs to determine what is the mind and will of CHRIST in the Goſpel, as though he knew not where to ſet his foot, or heſitated concerning thoſe great, important, and glorious diſcoveries of the truths which were hid in GOD from eternal ages, which are not mentioned ſlightly, or by the bye, or in a meer occaſional manner, but are clearly and ſtrikingly revealed, and are to be found in every part of the Goſpel; ſo that we muſt go back from the known ſenſe of words, if we deny them; and we muſt renounce the general ſenſe and experience of all true Chriſtians, if we deny theſe common principles.

Theſe doctrines, a worthy young ſtudent in divinity, is always ſuppoſed to believe and love; and therefore, whatever ſenſe of Scripture is not agreeable to theſe firſt grand principles, hath a tendency to ſap and ruin the foundations of our faith, which we muſt either lay aſide and renounce, or elſe we muſt explain every other doctrine we embrace, in a full conſiſtency with thoſe clear principles.

An EXEMPLIFICATION *of what we mean by the Analogy of Faith.*

Thus, if we can prove by undeniable arguments

that

that man is guilty before GOD; and that this guilt
cannot be removed, but by an atonement, or satisfaction made for it; and that this atonement, or divine
satisfaction, was really made by the obedience and
death of CHRIST, and that our justification and right
to eternal life, is founded upon this righteousness and
death; then whatever doctrine or notion of the Socinian tends to subvert this truth, it must be quite
contrary to the analogy of faith.

The Socinians and Arminians may reply, that
which is agreeable to my faith as a Calvinist, is not a
standard for the faith of other men, who differ from
me.

I do not deny this.—But then that which is agreeable to my faith, is a rule by which I proceed in judging of the truth of doctrines, and in giving the sense
of those Scriptures that are supposed to maintain those
doctrines; so that persons must either wholly lay aside
and reject these essential doctrines, or explain all others
consistent with them.

Now, my dear Reader, you shall have the analogy
of faith farther explained, as a grand theorem in divinity, which is of more use to a Christian, or a minister of the Gospel, than the mariner's compass and
polar star, is to a sailor; or the aphorisms of Hypo-
crates to a physician; the axioms in geometry to a
mathematician; the adjudged cases in law, to a counsellor, or pleader at the bar; or the maxims of war
to a Marlborough.

The analogy of faith is the proportion that the
doctrines of the Gospel bear to each other; or the
close connection between all the truths of revealed
religion.

It is the universal harmony that subsists between all
the principles of Christianity; so that if you destroy
one, you destroy them all; and if you hold one, you
are obliged to hold them all, otherwise you must incur
the

the charge of being an abfurd reafoner, and an inconfiftent preacher or writer.

This glorious analogy of faith, is the uniform defign of God, in the whole fcheme of falvation, by the
righteoufnefs and blood of Christ.   It is the fweet
confent of all the parts of truth with each other ; the
harmonious connection of the great doctrines of
grace, or the wife adjuftment and concurrence of all
revealed truths, to advance the glory of God's grand
defigns in the falvation of men, in which the end and
means are fo clofely connected together, that one of the
truths of the Gofpel cannot be denied, but all the reft
muft follow its fate, and be likewife denied ; nor one
of thefe capital truths be held faft, but you muft hold
the other truths faft in like manner.

This may be explained and exemplified through
all the great truths of the Gofpel : they glorify God's
free grace to the uttermoft : they humble the pride of
man into duft and afhes : they afford ftrong confolation to diftreffed confciences : they cherifh and promote holinefs in heart and life : they are all confiftent
with each other, and exempt from all abfurdity and
contradiction of ideas in the human underftanding.

God the Eternal Spirit had fo deeply impreffed on
his underftanding, confcience, and memory, the fenfe
and excellent ufe of the ANALOGY of FAITH, that
neither men, with all their artifice ; nor devils, with all
their feductions and force, could wreft it from him.
He knew the excellence and glory of this grand THE-
OREM in divinity too well to part with it ; and it
would be happy for all our tutors and ftudents, if
they had as keen a fenfe of its dignity and ufefulnefs:
if they had, we fhould have no Calvinifts go over to
the infidel fcheme of the Socinians, as they have lately done to the deftruction of their own ufefulnefs, and
the grief of all their beft friends in the churches of
Christ.   O ! how do I wifh, from the depth of my
foul, that we had once again a Dr. Owen, at Oxford ;

an

an Arrowfmith, at Cambridge; a Brine and Gill, in London; a Witfius, in Holland; a Rollin, in France; an Halyburton, in Scotland; an Ufher, in Ireland; and Prefident Edwards, in America: Men that under'ftood the analogy of faith as well, or better, than any divines in the whole world; efpecially if we add that prodigy of genius in true divinity, Polhill, the author of Speculum Theologiæ in Chrifto, which bears the fame rank in theology as Sir Ifaac Newton's Principia holds in Natural Philofophy.

And if GOD our SAVIOUR fhall pleafe to blefs our ftudents with the fame humble mind, and divine aptitude to learn, like our Hervey, we fhall then fee men in our pulpits who fhall be more ufeful and important than the angels in glory.

We fhall now exhibit the grand object of Hervey's faith and love, in what I would call CHRIST's beauty and glory in his perfonal and relative characters of GOD and man: the Prophet and Teacher: the Prieft and Righteoufnefs: the King and Governor, of his church, in heaven and earth.

A VIEW of GOD the SON as JEHOVAH.

Hervey's faith confidered him as that JEHOVAH who fware an oath to Abraham at Mount Moriah. The angel or meffenger, JEHOVAH, faid, *By myfelf I have fworn*, Gen. xxii. 16. Heb. vi. 13—18. Could this be a meer creature of GOD? If fo, he was the greateft blafphemer in the world.

I AM *that* I AM, Exod. iii. 14. is expreffive of the name JEHOVAH, the felf-exiftent and immortal GOD—JEHOVAH GOD of your fathers. This is applied to CHRIST, Acts vii. 30. JEHOVAH fent fiery ferpents, Numb. xxi. 6. The people fpake againft GOD, ver. 5. They tempted CHRIST, 1 Cor. x. 9. therefore CHRIST is JEHOVAH.

Jofhua worfhipped CHRIST as the Captain of the LORD's hoft. Jofhua faid, What faith JEHOVAH to

to

to his fervant? Jofh. v. 14. CHRIST is the Captain of our falvation, Heb. ii. 10. therefore CHRIST is JEHOVAH. JEHOVAH afcended on high, a'nd led captivity captive, Pf. lxviii. 18. This is applied to CHRIST, Eph. iv. 8. therefore CHRIST is JEHOVAH.

In JEHOVAH we have righteoufnefs, Ifa. xlv. 24. CHRIST is made unto us righteoufnefs, 1 Cor. i. 30. therefore CHRIST is JEHOVAH.

CHRIST the Branch is JEHOVAH our righteoufnefs, Jer. xxiii. 6. Of GOD he is made unto us righteoufnefs, 2 Cor. v. 21. therefore JESUS is JEHOVAH.

I will fave them by JEHOVAH their GOD, Hof. i. 7. He fhall fave his people from their fins, Matt. i. 21. therefore CHRIST is the true JEHOVAH.

Thefe are all plain clear Scripture declarations and folid conclufions. It requires only common fenfe: it requires nothing but an honeft love of truth to feel their evidence; and I leave them in the hands of every upright Chriftian in the whole world. A man muft outrage GOD and truth, and common fenfe, if he fhall attempt to deny them, or evade their evidence.

This vital faith in Hervey's foul, viewed CHRIST as GOD, with a rich variety of additional titles, as the mighty GOD, Ifai. ix. 5. GOD and none elfe, Ifai. xlv. 22. The GOD of the whole earth, liv. 5. The LORD their GOD, Hof. i. 7. God over all, bleffed for evermore, Rom. ix. 5. The great GOD, even our SAVIOUR JESUS CHRIST, Tit. ii. 13. He is the true GOD and eternal life, 1 John v. 20. The only wife GOD our SAVIOUR, Jude ver. 25. The GOD of glory appeared unto our father Abraham, Acts vii. 2. The LORD of glory, 1 Cor. ii. 8. του κυριε ημων Ιησου Χριστε της δοξης; Our LORD JESUS CHRIST of glory, James ii. 1. He is LORD of all, Acts x. 36. LORD of lords, Rev. xix. 16. The firft and the laft, Ifai. xli. 4. The Alpha and Omega; the firft and the laft, Rev. i. 8. The GOD of Abraham, Exod. iii. 6, compare with Acts vii. 32. The image of the
invifible

invisible God, the first-born of every creature, or
rather the first Producer of every creature, Col. i. 15.
πρωτοτοκος πασης κτισεως. Lord of the dead and the living, Rom. xiv. 9. Prince of life, Acts iii. 15. Thy
throne, O God, is for ever and ever, Pf. xlv. 6. Heb.
i. 8. The God Amen, (אמן) Ifa. lxv. 16. compared
with Rev. iii. 14. (the Amen) Εγω ειμι η οδος, και η
αληθεια, και η ζωη. I am the way, the truth, and the
life. John xiv. 6. Thy God, thy glory, Ifai. lx. 19.
My Lord and my God, John xx. 28.

He confidered CHRIST *as* MAN.

The feed of the woman, Gen. iii. 15. compared
with Gal. iv. 4. The feed of Abraham, Gal. iii. 16.
The feed of Ifaac, Gen. xxvi. 4. The feed of Jacob, Gen. xxviii. 14. The fecond man, 1 Cor. xv.
47. The laft Adam, 1 Cor. xv. 42. The man
Christ Jesus, 1 Tim. ii. 5. The Son of man,
Matt. xvi. 13. One man, Jesus Christ, Rom. v. 15.
The heavenly man, 1 Cor. xv. 49. Fairer than the
children of men, Pfal. xl. 2. A tender plant, and a
root out of a dry ground, Ifai. liii. 2. A rod out of
the ftem of Jeffe, Ifa. xi. 1. The fruit of the body
of David, Pfal. cxxxii. 11. The fon of David, Matt.
xxii. 42. A righteous Branch unto David, Jer. xxiii.
5. The Branch of righteoufnefs, Jer. xxiii. 15. The
firft-born fon of Mary, Luke ii. 7. The bleffed
fruit of Mary's womb, Luke i. 42. The holy thing
which was born of Mary, Luke i. 35. A child born,
and a fon given, Ifa. ix. 5. A ftar out of Jacob,
Numb. xxiv. 17. The lion of the tribe of Judah,
Rev. v. 5. A child, whofe name is Immanuel, Ifa. vii.
24. The holy child Jesus, Acts iv. 27. A woman, fhall (תסובב) compafs, or furround, a man,
Jer. xxxi. 22. A man with a writer's ink-horn by
his fide, Ezek. ix. 2. The man clothed with linen,
ver. 3. The man who had the ink-horn, ver. 11.
The appearance of a man above the firmament, or

expanfe,

expanse, Ezek. i. 26.   He fpake to the man clothed
in linen, Ezek. x. 2.—Note.   This is three times repeated.—A man like the appearance of brafs, with a
line of flax, and a meafuring reed of fix cubits long,
i. e. nine feet, Ezek. xl. 3, 5.   And the man ftood by
me, and faid unto me, the place of my throne, and the
place of the foles of my feet, Ezek. xliii. 6, 7.

A certain man clothed in linen, Dan. x. 5.   A man
among the myrtle trees, Zech. i. 10.   A man whofe
name is the Branch, Zech. vi. 12.   The man that is
my fellow, or equal, Zech. xii. 7.   Jesus, a man approved of God, Acts ii. 22.   That man whom he
ordained, Acts xvii. 31.   Go to my brethren, John
xx. 17.   He is not afhamed to call them brethren,
Heb. ii. 11.   I will declare thy name to my brethren,
Heb. ii. 12. made like unto his brethren, ver. 17.

The firft-born among many brethren, Rom. viii. 9.
Jesus of Nazareth, Mark i. 24.   Jesus thou fon of
David, Mark x. 47.   The Holy One of God, Mark
i. 24.   Thou waft with Jesus of Nazareth, Mark
xiv. 67.   Ye feek Jesus of Nazareth, Mark xvi. 6.
He fhall be called a Nazarene, Matt. ii. 23.   The
word was made flefh, John i. 14.   God's righteous
fervant, Ifai. liii. 11.   Behold my fervant, Ifai. xlii. 1.

My fervant fhall deal prudently, Ifai. lii. 13.   The
apple tree, Cant. ii. 3.   A green fir tree, Hof. xiv. 8.
The true vine, John xv. 1.   The good olive tree,
Rom. xi. 17.   A goodly cedar, Ezek. xviii. 23.   A
plant of renown, Ezek. xxxiv. 29.

Hervey loved and admired the Lord Jesus Christ
as a

PROPHET.

This glorious character and office requires infinite
underftanding to know the whole fyftem of truth in
God, and infinite faithfulnefs and infallibility in the
difcovery of truth, to the underftanding and confcience.   It fuppofes almighty power and grace to
enlighten

enlighten and ftrengthen the mind to receive truth, and to give us a ftrong ardent tafte for the truth, goodnefs, and beauty, of the Holy Scriptures. Thus CHRIST appears in all his fitnefs, fulnefs, power, and will, to fave us from the plague of a dark underftand-ing, and to unravel all the plots of hell and earth, which are formed for our deftruction.

This renders CHRIST a moft amiable object to every convinced finner who knows the weaknefs of his mind, to difcern, to receive, and retain, the truths of divine revelation.

CHRIST was to be a prophet like unto Mofes, Deut. xv. 18. This is moft beautifully exemplified in near thirty inftances by the late Dr. Newton, in his Differtations on Prophecy, Vol. I. 8vo. Mofes was perfecuted as foon as born: fo was CHRIST. Mofes was educated in all the wifdom and learning of Egypt: CHRIST hath all the treafures of wifdom and knowledge. Mofes fled into the wildernefs of Ara-bia: CHRIST was led into the wildernefs to be tempted of the devil. Mofes led the children of Ifrael out of Egypt: CHRIST leads all his people out of a ftate of nature. Mofes fed the people with manna: CHRIST feeds his people with his own flefh and blood. Mofes received the two tables of the law, written by the finger of GOD: CHRIST received the whole law, written on his heart. Mofes had to treat with a moft perverfe peo-ple all his days: CHRIST preached to a moft perverfe and faithlefs generation. The wicked Ifraelites fpake of ftoning Mofes: the Jews took up ftones to kill CHRIST. The face of Mofes fhone when he came down from the mount: the face of CHRIST fhone when he was on the mount, Matt. xvii. 2. Mofes ftruck the rock to give the people to drink water: CHRIST was himfelf ftruck with the rod of divine juftice, to bring forth the waters of life. Mofes went up to die on Mount Nebo: CHRIST went up to die on Mount Calvary. Mofes left Jofhua to fucceed

him

him in leading the people into Canaan, CHRIST fent the HOLY SPIRIT to lead all his people to heaven.

Thefe, with a great variety of other beauties, appear, on a comparifon of Mofes with CHRIST; and Hervey's foul catched fire at every view of the fuperior glories of the LORD JESUS.

A Prophet fhall the LORD your GOD raife up, Acts iii. 22. A great Prophet, Luke vii. 16. The Prophet—This is of a truth that Prophet, John vi. 14. Wifdom, Prov. viii. 1. Matt. xi. 19. Light, John iii. 19. The true Light, John i. 9. Light of the world, John viii. 12. The Light of men, John i. 4. A great Light, Ifai. ix. 2. A Light to lighten the Gentiles, Ifa. xlix. 6. The Day Star, 2 Pet. i. 19. Thy Light, Ifai. lx. 1. The LORD is my light, Pfal. xxvii. 1. A Sun, Pfal. lxxxiv. 11. An everlafting Light, Ifai. lx. 19. Thy GOD, thy Glory, ver. 19. Sun of Righteoufnefs, Mal. iv. 2. Thy fun fhall no more go down, Ifa. lx. 20. The Lamb is the Light of the New Jerufalem, Rev. xxi. 23. The Way, the Truth, John xiv. 6. The Amen, or Truth, Rev. iii. 14. The GOD Amen, or Truth, Ifai. lxv. 16. The Counfellor, Ifai. ix. 6. A Teacher come from GOD, John iii. 2. The Author, Object, Feeder, and Finifher of Faith, Heb. xii. 2. He that hath the key of David, who openeth, and no man fhutteth, i. e. he opens the meaning of the Scriptures, and the human underftanding, Rev. iii. 7. Faithful and true, Rev. xix. 11. The faithful Witnefs, Rev. i. 5. A Shepherd that feeketh out his flock, Ezek. xxxiv. 12. One Shepherd, ver. 13. The chief Shepherd, 1 Pet. v. 4. The good Shepherd, John x. 11. The LORD is my Shepherd, Pfal. xxiii. 1.

Thefe are fome of the bright and beautiful difco-veries of CHRIST, as the fupreme and infallible

Q   Teacher

Teacher of fouls ; and thefe views were perpetually kept up in the mind of our excellent friend.

Hervey had a moft endeared love and veneration for the character of CHRIST as a

PRIEST.

CHRIST affuming this character, and executing this glorious office, has difcovered one of the greateft and moft wonderful modes in which the divine nature is exerted, in the falvation and final happinefs of the people of GOD. By this office, a facrifice is offered up : a redemption is effected : a fatisfaction to the RECTORAL JUSTICE is made : an obedience or righteoufnefs of divine and infinite worth is wrought out, and brought in before the tribunal of GOD for our juftification.

The interceffion of CHRIST is grounded on this fatisfaction and righteoufnefs ; and our LORD, as a Prieft, can and will beftow all poffible bleffings on his people. Thefe were the three great parts of the high prieft's office under the Mofaic difpenfation, to offer a facrifice : to intercede for the people : and blefs the congregation : and thus the type was a lively reprefentation of the prieftly office of CHRIST. Hervey loved this glorious character, as the great central glory of the whole Gofpel.

We will now give the difplay of it from divine revelation.

The Mediator of a better Covenant, Heb. viii. 6. The one Mediator between GOD and man, 1 Tim. ii. 5. The Mediator of the New Teftament or Covenant, Heb. ix. 5. An High Prieft for ever, Pfalm cx. 4. Heb. vi. 20. The High Prieft of our profeffion, Heb. iii. 1. A Surety of a better Covenant, Heb. vii. 22. JESUS, the Mediator of the New Covenant, Heb. xii. 24. Such an High Prieft became us, i. e. was fuitable to us, who was holy, harmlefs, undefiled, feparate from finners, higher than the heavens, Heb. vii.

vii. 26.   A Covenant of the People, a Light of the
Gentiles, Ifa, xlii. 6. A merciful and faithful High
Prieft, Heb. ii. 17.

My Redeemer, Job xix. 25.   Thy Redeemer, Ifa.
liv. 5.—*Note.* De Gols obferves, that the word Redeemer is ufed fix hundred times.—The Lamb of
GOD, John i. 29.   The Lamb without Spot, 1 Pet.
i. 19. The Lamb flain, Rev. v. 12.—N. B. CHRIST
is called a Lamb twenty-nine times in the book of the
Revelations.—CHRIST our paffover is facrificed for
us, 1 Cor. v. 7. Made fin for us, 2 Cor. v. 21. Made
a CURSE for us, Gal. iii. 13.—Dr. Gill obferved to me,
that this is a phrafe never ufed, even of the devils or
damned fpirits.— Our Peace, Eph. ii. 14.   Our Life,
Col. iii. 4.

The Bread of Life, John vi. 48.   The Bread of
GOD, ver. 33. The Tree of Life, Rev. ii.,7. xxii. 14.
The Refurrection and the Life, John xi. 25.   The
plague and deftruction of death, Hofea xiii. 14.
The Saviour of the body, the church, Eph. v. 23.
The Saviour of the world, 1 John iv. 14. A Saviour and a Great One, Ifa. xix. 20.   O GOD of Ifrael the Saviour, Ifa. xlv. 15.   A juft GOD and a Saviour, ver. 21.

To you is born this day a Saviour, Luke ii. 11.
A Prince and a Saviour, Acts v. 31.   We look for
the Saviour, Phil. iii. 20. My Spirit rejoiceth in GOD
my Saviour, Luke i. 47. The commandment of GOD
our Saviour, 1 Tim. i. 1.   In the fight of GOD our
Saviour, 1 Tim. ii. 3.   The living GOD is the Saviour, 1 Tim. iv. 10. The appearing of GOD our
Saviour, 2 Tim. i. 10.   The kindnefs and love of
GOD our Saviour, Titus iii. 4.   The commandment
of GOD our Saviour, Titus i. 3.   The LORD JESUS
CHRIST our Saviour, ver. 4

The

The glorious appearance of the great GOD our Saviour, Titus ii. 13.   The righteoufnefs of GOD our Saviour, 2 Pet. i. 1.   The knowledge of the LORD and Saviour, 2 Pet. ii. 20.   Grow in grace and in the knowledge of our Saviour, 2 Pet. iii. 18.   The Father fent the Son to be the Saviour, 1 John iv. 14.   To the only wife GOD our Saviour, Jude 25.   They forgat GOD their Saviour, Pfal. cvi. 21.   The Holy One of Ifrael thy Saviour, Ifa. xliii. 3.   Befides me there is no Saviour, ver. 11.   I JEHOVAH am thy Saviour, Ifa. xlix. 26.   So he was their Saviour, Ifa. lxiii. 8.   I will be to them a little fanctuary, i. e. a Saviour, Ezek. xi. 16.   The Rock of our falvation, 2 Sam. xxii. 47. Pfal. xviii. 2.   The Well of falvation, Ifa. xii. 3. The Horn of falvation, Luke i. 69.   The Captain of our falvation, Heb. ii. 10.   I have waited for thy falvation, Gen. xlix. 18.   The Rock of our falvation, Pfal. xcv. 1.   JEHOVAH is my falvation, Exod. xv. 2.   I rejoice in thy falvation 1 Sam. ii. 1.

He fhall be my falvation, Job xiii. 16.   JEHOVAH is my light, and my falvation, Pfal. xxvii. 1.   Such as love thy falvation, Pfal. xl. 16.   The falvation of GOD, Ifa. l. 23.   O GOD of our falvation, Pfal. lxv. 5.   Thy faving health, or healing falvation, Pfal. lxvii. 2.   Let fuch as love thy falvation be glad, Pfal. lxx. 4.   My mouth fhall fhew forth thy falvation all the day, Pfal. lxxi. 15. Shew forth his falvation from day to day, Pfal. xcvi. 2.   The LORD hath made known his falvation, Pfal. xcviii. 2.

All the ends of the earth have feen the falvation of GOD, Pfal. xcviii. 3.   All the ends of the earth fhall fee the falvation of GOD, Ifa. lii. 10.   JEHOVAH is my ftrength and fong, and is become my falvation, Pfal. cxviii. 14. My foul fainteth for thy falvation, Pfal. cxix. 81.   Mine eyes fail for thy falvation, ver. 123.   I have hoped for thy falvation, ver. 166.   I have longed
for

for thy falvation, ver. 174. God is my falvation, Ifa.
xii. 2.   Let them bring forth falvation, Ifa. xlv. 8.
Salvation in Zion for Ifrael my glory,' Ifa. xlvi. 13.

My falvation fhall not tarry, Ifa. xlvi. 13. The gar-
ments of falvation; the robe of righteoufnefs, Ifa. lxi.
10.   Salvation as a lamp that burneth, Ifa. lxii. 1.
Behold thy falvation cometh, ver. 11.   All flefh fhall
fee the falvation of God, Luke iii. 6.   I will joy in
the God of my falvation, Hab. iii. 18.   Thou fhalt
call his name Jesus, for he fhall fave his people from
their fins, Matt. i. 21.—*Note.* The whole Gofpel is
comprehended in this one word—Jesus.

Hervey regarded Christ as a
K I N G.

This is another mode of God's difcovering himfelf
to the church, in order to difplay the divine glory in
our happinefs.

We have not only the plague of a weak blind underftanding, and the torment of a wicked guilty confcience; but we have alfo the plague of a ftubborn
and rebellious will, which is always at war with every
attribute, and every perfon in the Godhead.   This
moft defperate enmity muft be fubdued, or the foul
be loft for ever.

Nothing but Omnipotence, at the command of infinite love, and under the guidance of infinite wifdom, can apply the great redemption of Christ to
millions of immortal fouls, in every period of time.

A King on my holy hill, Pfal. ii. 6.   David, a
king and a prince, Ezek. xxxiv. 23, 24.   David my
fervant fhall be king over them, Ezek. xxxvii. 24.
Captain of the Lord's hoft, Jofh. v. 14. ftiled
Jehovah, vi. 2.   Lord of the living and the dead,
Rom. xiv. 9. A Leader and Commander to the peo-
ple, Ifa. lv. 4.   Messiah the Prince, Dan. ix. 25.
A Gover-

A Governor that shall rule my people Israel, Mic. v. 2. Matt. ii. 6. A Great King over all the earth, Psal. xlvii. 2. Sing ye praises with understanding, five times repeated, ver. 6, 7. The Prince of Life, Acts iii. 15.

The King of the daughter of Zion, Zech. ix. 9. A Great King, above all gods, Psal. xcv. 3. The King that is fairer than the children of men, Psal. xlv. 2. The LORD reigneth, Psal. xciii. 1. David their King, Hosea iii. 5. Their GOD, and David their King, Jer. xxx. 9. He is born King of the Jews, Matt. ii. 2. The Horn of David, Psal. cxxxii. 17. He reigns over Jacob for ever, Luke i. 33. The King of Israel, John i. 49.

The King of Righteousness, Heb. ii. 7. The King of Peace, ibid. Higher than the kings of the earth, Psal. lxxxix. 27. The King of kings, Rev. xvii. 14. The LORD of lords, Rev. xix. 16. The Prince of the kings of the earth, Rev. i. 5. The King's Son, Psal. lxxii. 1. The King of Glory, Psal. xxiv. 8. —*Note.* This is five times repeated.—The LORD of glory, 1 Cor. ii. 8. James ii. 1.

MISCELLANEOUS NAMES expressive of the GLORIES of CHRIST.

The Apostle and High Priest of our profession, Heb. iii. 1. A Deacon, (ο, διακονος) or a Minister, Rom. xv. 8. A Minister of Holy Things, των αγιων λειτουργος, Heb. viii. 2. The Angel, or Messenger of the Covenant, Mal. iii. 1. The Servant of GOD, Isai. xlix. 6. The Desire of all nations, Hag. ii. 7. The Elect of GOD, Isai. xlii. 1. A Worm and no man, Psa. xxii. 6. The LORD and Son of David, Psal. cx. 1. Matt. xxii. 43. The Day Spring from on high, Luke i. 78. Rabbi, or my Great Master, John i. 49. Rabboni, or my Master, John xx. 16.

A Stone

A Stone laid in Zion—a tried Stone—a precious Corner Stone—a fure Foundation; or as it is in the Hebrew, מוסד מוסד a foundation—a foundation, Ifai. xxviii. 16.

Other Foundation can no man lay than that is laid, JESUS CHRIST, 1 Cor. iii. 11. A Stone, the Head of the Corner, Pfal. cxviii. 22. A Stone of Stumbling, and Rock of Offence, 1 Pet. ii. 8. The Forerunner, Heb. vi. 8. An Advocate with the Father, 1 John ii. 2. The true Redeemer and near Kinfman, Lev. xxv. 25. Ruth iv. 4.—*Note.* The word Goel, גואל, or Redeemer, is mentioned fix hundred times. See De Gols on the Divinity of CHRIST.—A Sower, Matt. xiii. 3. Solomon, Cant. iii. 7. King Solomon, iii. 11. The Rofe of Sharon, ibid. ii. 1.

Thou whom my foul loveth, Sol. Song iii. 1, 2, 3. My Brother, ibid. viii. 1. The Lamb in the midft of the throne, Rev. v. 6. The Lamb is the Temple of the New Jerufalem, Rev. xxi. 22. The Lamb is the light of the New Jerufalem, ver. 23.—*Note.* CHRIST is ftiled a Lamb twenty-nine times in the Revelations.— A Bundle of Myrrh, Sol. Song i. 13. A Clufter of Camphire, ibid 14. Fair and Pleafant, ibid. i. 16. My fervant the Branch, Zech. iii. 8. The man whofe name is the Branch, Zech. vi. 12.

He feedeth among the lilies, Sol. Song ii. 16. vi. 3. He feedeth in the gardens, Sol. Song vi. 2. A Stone cut out without hands, Dan. ii. 34. The Stone became a great mountain, and filled the whole earth, Dan. ii. 35. His countenance is as Lebanon, excellent as the cedars, Sol. Song v. 15. A man of war, Exod. xv. 3. Mighty to fave, Ifai. lxiii. 1. Moft mighty, Pfal. xlv. 3. He treadeth the wineprefs alone, Ifai. lxiii. 2, 3. Shiloh—a quiet peaceable Prince, Gen. xlix. 10.

A no-

A noble man, Luke xix. 12. A noble one, אדירין
Jer. xxx. 21. A ftronger man, Luke xi. 22. My
ftrength, my fong, my falvation, Ifai. xii. 2. A
ftrength to the poor, Ifai. xxv. 4. A ftrength to the
needy in diftrefs, ib. ver. 5. A refuge from the ftorm,
ibid. A fhadow from the heat, ibid.—*Note*. All thefe
four glories of CHRIST are in one verfe.—An hiding
place from the wind: a covert from the tempeft:
rivers of waters in a dry place: the fhadow of a great
rock in a weary land, Ifai. xxxii. 2.—*Note*. All thefe
four glories are in one verfe.—My GOD fhall be my
ftrength, Ifai. xlix. 5.

He that liveth and was dead, and is alive for evermore, Amen. He hath the keys of hell and of death,
Rev. i. 18. Our hope, 1 Tim. i. 1. CHRIST in us
the hope of glory, Col. i. 27. Zerubbabel, Zech. iv.
6. Hag. ii. 3. O JEHOVAH my ftrength, and my
fortrefs, and my refuge in the day of affliction, Jer.
xvi. 19. Thy hufband, Ifa. liv. 5. Pfal. xlv. 10.
The portion of Jacob, Jer. x. 16. A light to lighten
the Gentiles, and the glory of thy people Ifrael, Luke
ii. 32. Ifa. lx. 19. The hope of his people, and the
ftrength of the children of Ifrael, Joel iii. 16. Having falvation, Zech. ix. 9.

The Keeper of Ifrael, Pfal. cxxi. 4. The Angel
which redeemed me from all evil, Gen. xlviii. 16. I
will fend an angel before thee to drive out the Cana-
anite, Exod. xxxiii. 2. The arm of the LORD, Ifa.
liii. 1. li. 9. The Bridegroom, Matt. xxv. 1. Ifa. lxii.
4, 5. The Heir of all things, Heb. i. 2. The Head
over all things to the church, Eph. i. 22. A Sceptre
fhall rife out of Ifrael, and a Star out of Jacob,
Numb. xxiv. 17. The Bleffed One who comes in
the name of the LORD, Pfal. cviii. 20.

Bleffed be the LORD GOD, doing wondrous things,
Pfa. lxxii. 18. The LORD ftrong and mighty in battle,

tle, Pfal. xxiv. 8. God ftandeth in the congregation; he judgeth among the Gods, Pfal. lxxxii. 1.
The Judge of the living and the dead, Acts x. 42.
The Judge of all the earth, Gen. xviii. 25. God
is Judge himfelf, Pfal. l. 6. The chiefett among
ten thoufand and altogether lovely, Sol. Song, v.
10. White and ruddy, ibid. My Friend, ibid. 16.
Chrift is all in all, Col. iii. 11.

Let us now view the paffion of Love, which is
expreffed towards this glorious and divine perfon,
by all chafte virgin Chriftians, in all ages to the
end of the world.—*Note.* Christ is ftiled David.
דוד i. e. Beloved no lefs than thirty-two times in
the Song of Songs; which fhall be thus exemplified:
The Beloved, Sol. Song. i. 13. My Beloved,
ver. 14. My Beloved, ii. 3. My Beloved, ver 8.
My Beloved, ver. 9. My Beloved, ver. 10. My
Beloved, ver. 16. My Beloved ver. 17. Thy Beloved, iv. 16. My Beloved, v. 2.

My Beloved, Sol. Song, v. 4. My Beloved, ver.
5. My Beloved, my Beloved, ver. 6. My Beloved,
ver. 8. Thy Beloved, thy beloved, ver. 9. My Beloved, ver. 10. My Beloved, ver. 16. Thy Beloved, thy Beloved, vi. 1. My Beloved, ver. 2. My
Beloved, my Beloved, ver. 3.

My Beloved, Sol. Song. vii. 9. My Beloved,
ver. 10. My Beloved, ver. 11. My beloved, ver.
13. My Love, viii. 4. Her Beloved, ver. 5. My
Beloved, ver. 14. Thy Love, ii. 1. My Well Beloved, Ifa. v. 1. Thou whom my foul loveth is
repeated four times, Sol. Song. i. 7.—iii. 1, 2, 3.
Note. Christ is ftiled the Beloved, with aftonifhing repetitions in the Song of Solomon. In this
manner the Scriptures reprefent the genuine paffion
of love to Christ; and in this manner the excellent

R   Hervey

Hervey expreſſed his paſſion in all his holy thoughts,* words, and writings.

Note. All ungenerate perſons, wherever the Goſpel comes, as they do not love Chriſt, they are adulterous lovers of ſin and the world, and they are lovers of damnation in the cauſes of it, i. e. infidelity, and enmity to CHRIST.

Let us cloſe all our views with a ſong of ſevenfold praiſe, due to the LORD JESUS CHRIST, Rev. v. 12. Worthy is the Lamb that was ſlain, to receive, 1. power, 2. riches; 3. wiſdom; 4. ſtrength; 5. honour; 6. glory; 7. bleſſing; and every creature which is in heaven, and on the earth, heard I, ſaying, " Bleſ-" ſing and honour, glory and power, be unto the " Lamb, for ever and ever," and the four living creatures ſaid, Amen.

Hervey's faith was the confident expeEtation of things hoped for. The clear demonſtration and convincing evidence of inviſible objeEts, i. e. inviſible perſons, inviſible attributes, inviſible tranſaEtions, and inviſible bleſſings. GOD the HOLY SPIRIT, by a phyſical, moral, and gracious influence, and real operation, wrought into his underſtanding, a perſuaſion of CHRIST's almighty power and grace to ſave: he opened his heart to receive CHRIST in all his offices, and to make a full and eternal ſurrender of his immortal ſoul into CHRIST's hands, to be ſaved intirely in his own method of grace and ſalvation.

It was this vital and peculiar faith of the operation of GOD, which marks the diſtinEt charaEter, and conſtitutes the real difference between a true believer, and all the unbelievers in the world. This faith enabled him to treat CHRIST according to the revealed idea of him; and from the names and charaEters of CHRIST in the preceding pages; and

* Read Dr. Lowth's LeEtures on the Song of Songs.

from

from the clear difcoveries of his divine attributes, and works of creation and redemption, and the divine worfhip paid to him by the patriarchs, prophets, apoftles, martyrs, and true Chriftians in all ages: this great and good man formed his conceptions of Chrift, and expreffed the beft affections for his perfon, intereft, and glory, in the world.

He confidered CHRIST in his eternal exiftence, or exifting all at once without fucceffion of moments, or change of time or place; and confequently, immutable, and every where prefent, with all fpace: the living GOD and·Friend of his precious foul. He kept up a continual converfe with him by faith and prayer: he lived in him: he lived with him in habitual joy and increafing delight. He faw future things as eternal, and eternity juft at hand: and by his vital union with the perfon of GOD the SON, he could call eternal bleffings and felicity all his own. This infpired his mind and paffions with a dignity and majefty of HOLINESS peculiar to his character: and by virtue of this holinefs, fhining in his underftanding, he contemplated the boundlefs power, the exquifite wifdom, and exuberant goodnefs of CHRIST, in all his works of creation, providence, and redemption; and every frefh profpect of the glories of CHRIST, transformed his foul into a brighter refemblance of the moral perfections of his GOD.

He clearly difcerned, that every natural and moral perfection of GOD the FATHER, was equally afcribed to GOD the SON; and he faw CHRIST in all the works of creation. He confidered that CHRIST gave being to our world and the ftarry heavens, which, without his agency, would have no exiftence: that he upholds the univerfe, which would, if left to itfelf, tumble into ruins: that he actuates every living creature, vegetable, animal, rational, and angelical, which would otherwife be intirely a lifelefs mafs: and he recovered our fyftem when it was

all

all doomed to deftruction, for the apoftacy and rebellion of man. He has beautifully difplayed thefe grand
truths in his contemplations on a flower garden: and
his defcant on creation, which are everlafting monu-
ments of his wonderful genius, and devotional tafte.

He imitated all the patriarchs, prophets, and apoftles, in the inceffant ardent worfhip he offered up
to our LORD JESUS, as God above all; and he purfued the glory of CHRIST, as the final caufe of his immortal exiftence.

We now come to confider the character of Hervey
as a man of SCIENCE and VIRTUE; and in this point
of light, propofe him for an example to the rifing
generation. His natural fenfibility was exceeding great:
his perceptions of beauty were exquifitely fine: he
had a clear fenfe of beauty in all its gradations: and
when this was connected with true piety, it worked
up his natural fenfibility to its utmoft perfection.

While he was a fchool-boy, and had not the leaft
advantage in the tuition of the fciences, the beauties
of the vegetable and animal creation, ftruck him very
ftrongly; and before he had the leaft learned acquaintance with the fcience of aftronomy, the glories of
the ftarry heavens poured themfelves into his foul.
He ufed to obferve, that when he took a walk into the
fields in the night feafon, he paufed, pondered, trem-
bled, and adored: he found an unknown fomething
within him, which fuggefted ftrongly, that there was
a moft wife, mighty, and good Being, at the head of
the univerfe, who governed and difpofed of all things.
When thefe natural fentiments and fublime feelings
of foul came to be cultivated by reading Dr. Derham's Aftro-theology, and Le Pulche's Dialogues on
the Starry Heavens, thefe enlarged the capacity of
his underftanding, to take in great and fublime ideas,
without pain or difficulty; to receive new and uncommon ideas, without an ignorant furprife and averfion. Thefe excellent books, with others written in
the

the fame ftrain and tafte, had a happy tendency to enable him to furvey vaft trains of great ideas without pain or difficulty.

The NATURAL HISTORY of air and water, in their diftinct properties and ufes, were open to his mind: the different claffes of minerals that lay within the bowels of the earth, were all familiar to his foul: the furniture of the furface of our earth, in graffes, plants, trees, and flowers, highly gratified his tafte, and gave pleafure to his imagination. The various claffes of birds, beafts, fifhes, and infects, paffed in review before his mental eye; and knowing himfelf to be a redeemed and recovered creature of GOD, and difcerning that CHRIST was the Creator and Redeemer of all thefe objects, he felt more divine pleafure than Adam could in Paradife.

Hervey was a great mafter of the fcience of LOGIC: he underftood the nature of ideas, and the objects of perception, as well as any man: he had a very clear and diftinct conception of all fubftances and qualities, material and immaterial, vifible and invifible, mortal and immortal, temporal and eternal.

He had a more clear and forcible conception of the nature of GOD and human fouls, as well as devils and angels, than moft men in the whole world, and a more comprehenfive idea of divine objects; and a more compleat perception of all their properties and parts, as difcovered by divine revelation, with a very extenfive apprehenfion of the various kinds and qualities of the glorious doctrines of the Gofpel.

He had an aftonifhing degree of elevation and penetration of thought, to reach into the future events which are coming upon the univerfe in the latter day: the ruin of Popery; the converfion and reftoration of the Jews; the fpread of the Gofpel through all the nations of the earth; and the difplay of the grandeur of GOD the SON.

He

He had a clear knowledge of the prejudices of the human underſtanding:—He himſelf had been the ſubject of the ſtrongeſt prejudices againſt the Goſpel. We have the utmoſt reaſon to believe, that he had never heard a ſingle ſermon on the perſon and righteouſneſs of CHRIST, for the firſt *ſeventeen* years of his life. When he went to Oxford, matters were not mended; the two firſt years were paſſed over in ignorance and indolence. He then fell into the hands of men that were ignorant of the method of acceptance with GOD. Theſe men became his ſpiritual phyſicians; and fooliſh phyſicians they were: their religion conſiſted in a ſet of outward obſervances, and a punctilious regard to rules of their own deviſing—riſing at ſtated hours—faſting ſeveral times in the week—giving the food they ſaved by faſting to the poor—ſaying prayers at certain hours—viſiting the priſoners in the jails—frequent attendance upon the ſacrament—binding themſelves by vows and covenants, to certain virtues and practices. This was the ſum total of their religion: they had no ſpiritual perception of the perſon of CHRIST; no underſtanding of his glorious righteouſneſs for our juſtification: no acquaintance with the ſpirituality and vaſt extent of GOD's law: no ſenſe of the immaculate purity of GOD: no conviction of the plague of their own hearts; no deep diſcernment of the power, deceit, and malignity of indwelling ſin: no ſight of the abſolute neceſſity of regeneration by GOD the HOLY SPIRIT: no knowledge of his divine perſon, and the infinite importance and neceſſity of his operations in the ſcheme of our ſalvation: no experience of the pleaſures of vital religion. In this dark, ſad, joyleſs ſtate, he lived for *eight* years; that is to ſay, from the *ninteenth* year of his age, till he was *twenty-ſeven.* All this time was ſpent in reading improper books, truſting to his own virtue and righteouſneſs for juſtification; and without the joys of GOD's ſalvation. He had no

friend

friend in all the world, to recommend to him the
beſt books : no friend to explain to him the true
ſenſe and meaning of the Holy Scriptures.   All his
external obſervances and his attempts to practiſe virtue, had a tendency to build up a ſtrong barrier between CHRIST and his ſoul.   He uſed to lament it as
one of the greateſt loſſes of his whole life, that the
œconomy of the covenants, by the *incomparable Witſius*, was never ſo much as mentioned to him ; and
whilſt he was at Stoke-Abbey, in Devonſhire, his
dear friend, *Paul Orchard*, Eſq. who was in the
ſame ſpirit of enquiry after happineſs with himſelf,
joined with him in reading a vaſt variety of treatiſes,
and a great deal of religious traſh they peruſed ; a
number of legal books they ſtudied, which had no
other tendency, than to eclipſe the glory of the LORD
JESUS, and leave their ſouls in froſt and darkneſs :
among the reſt, they ſtumbled upon one good
book, and that was *Eliſha Cole's*, on the Sovereignty
and Righteouſneſs of GOD ; on Election, Redemption, Effectual Calling, and final Perſeverance.   Their
minds were ſo incruſted with prejudice, and ſo envenomed with enmity againſt the dominion of GOD,
that they threw the book away, not only as worthleſs,
but pernicious ; and reſumed the reading of books
more adapted to their legal pride.   In this joyleſs
ſtate of religious obſervances, they continued ſome
years : at laſt, in the year 1741, the LORD JESUS
CHRIST began to dawn upon his ſoul ; then it was,
that he wrote the letter from Biddeford, marked
No. I. in the Appendix to this book.

Hervey had ten thouſand prejudices to ſurround
and poiſon his underſtanding : prejudices ariſing from
words : ariſing from the difficulty and obſcurity of
things : prejudices ariſing from bad or improper
books, and artful and malignant men who lie in wait
to deceive : but above all, prejudices ariſing from the
depravity and corruption of his own heart.

By

By flow degrees, God the Holy Spirit enabled him to furmount all the prejudices which had poifoned his underftanding, and framed him to a noble and firm determination to review and examine all his ideas and principles, as to their fitnefs or unfitnefs; goodnefs or moral evil; truth or falfehood; and he rejected with a fublime difdain, all that he found to be wrong or difagreeable to the revealed will of God.

As a found and mafculine mafter of logic, he well underftood the principles and rules in matters of fenfe; in matters of reafon and fpeculation; in affairs of human prudence; in matters of morality and religion; in the nature and evidences of infpiration, and knew thefe principles and rules, with a degree of intuitive readinefs and familiarity: and he could difcern, with great fagacity, the principles and rules of judging concerning things paft, prefent, and to come. How happy would it be for young ftudents of genius and piety, to imitate Hervey in the exercife of reafon, in their honeft enquiries after truth.

The greateft glory of the human underftanding, is to reafon well on all fubjects and all occafions whatfoever, but efpecially upon the moft divine and heavenly fubjects. The worft difgrace of the human underftanding, is to reafon ill, efpecially on divine fubjects. The next greateft glory of the human underftanding, is to unravel fophiftry, and detect error in all the parts of philofophy and divinity. Nothing can be a greater fhame to a man that ftiles himfelf a philofopher, than to reafon in a corrupt and erroneous manner.

It was the greateft glory of Hervey's underftanding, to receive and difcern the moft fpiritual and heavenly objects; and he purfued thofe objects with an unbiaffed integrity: no fophifms of men or devils could warp his underftanding. He kept truth for ever in his eye, and purfued it with unfainting perfeverance. In all his reafonings, he never loft fight of
the

point in debate. He took the utmoft care to lay
down found premifes, and to draw folid conclufions
from thofe premifes. He was deeply concerned not
to reafon inconclufively. He was honeftly willing
and zealous to follow wherever truth led the way.
I would, with the utmoft candour, compare his methods of reafoning with fome of the moft mafterly lo-
gicians in the world; I mean Chillingworth, Bifhop
Bull, Dr. Waterland, Dr. Owen, Dr. Witfius, and
Mr. Brine. Thefe great men underftood the force
of direct demonftration: they were exceeding careful to lay down none but clear and fure principles;
and they drew the moft genuine and legitimate inferences from thofe principles. On the other hand,
men of weak or corrupt underftandings, are not
careful to lay down found principles; and if their
principles are falfe, their conclufions muft be bad:
or otherwife, they draw corrupt inferences from true
principles; and thefe are the things that conftitute all
fophifms whatever.

Hervey was as careful, as of his life and foul, not
to be impofed upon by fophiftry: all the powers of
earth and hell could never drive or feduce him from
the love of truth: the authority of the greateft bad
men had no influence: the love of fame never fwayed
his underftanding: the riches of the world, except to
do good with them, had no charms for his imagination. Senfual pleafure could never feduce his underftanding into an error: he faw the infamy and
madnefs of unlawful pleafure, and was crucified and
dead to all criminal gratifications.

Hervey had a vaft ftock of ideas upon all forts of
divine fubjects: he had the keeneft readinefs at all
kinds of fcriptural arguments: no man better underftood the force of the apoftle Paul's reafoning, on the
great doctrine of juftification by CHRIST's imputed
righteoufnefs: it never entered into his mind, that
the apoftle reafoned inconclufively; and no man, ex-

S   cept

cept the great Mr. Brine, had studied this subject with
more fixed attention.

The highest excellency of this good man, consisted
in the spirituality of his understanding, and his love
of truth. There were many other men that excelled
him in several branches of learning; but no man went
beyond him in a discernment of divine things. Newton and Dr. Barrow, were superior to him in geometry; and yet, without his knowing it, he pursued the
very best method of geometrical reasoning. Judge
Hales, and the great Judge Blackstone, were infinitely superior to him, in the knowledge of laws and
government; but he understood the meaning of the
divine law better than both of them. The great
Locke, was superior to him in metaphysics; but he
understood the dignity of CHRIST, and the worth of
his own immortal soul, better than all the Lockes in
the world. The great Sir Isaac could anatomize the
rays of light, and penetrate the nature and properties
of colours, beyond any man upon the earth; but
Hervey had more spiritual light, than ever Newton
himself possessed. Demosthenes and Cicero, excelled
him in natural and political eloquence; but they have
no share with him, in a bright display of CHRIST's
person and righteousness.

This great and wise man accustomed himself to
clear and distinct ideas: to evident propositions; to
strong and convincing arguments on all the subjects
of divinity. Aspasio's Dialogues with Theron, and
Hervey's eleven letters on justification, by CHRIST's
imputed righteousness, are glorious evidences of the
excellency of his understanding.

He enlarged his general acquaintance with things
daily, in order to attain a rich furniture of ideas, by
which those propositions, which occur, may be either
proved or disproved: but he did especially meditate
and enquire, with great diligence and exactness, into
the nature, properties, circumstances and relations of
the

the particular fubject, about which he reafoned or
judged : he furveyed a queftion round about, and on
all fides; and extended his views, as far as poffible,
to every thing that had a connection with it.

In fearching the knowledge of divine things, he
always kept the precife point of the prefent queftion
in his eye: he took earneft heed, that he added nothing to it while he was reafoning, nor omitted any part
of it. By keeping the fingle point of enquiry in his
conftant view, he was fecured from fudden rafh, and
impertinent determinations; which fome have obtrud-
ed, inftead of folutions and folid anfwers, before they
perfectly knew the queftion. When he had exactly
confidered the precife point of enquiry, or what was
unknown in the queftion, he then confidered what and
how much he knew already of the queftion, or of the
ideas of which it is compofed. In choofing his arguments to prove any queftion, he always took fuch
heads of truth, which are fureft and leaft fallible, and
which carry the greateft evidence and ftrength with
them. He was not fo folicitous about the number,
as the weight of his arguments ; efpecially in proving
any propofition which admitted of divine certainty
and complete demonftration. A growing acquaintance with fcience and divinity, and a daily improvement of his underftanding in divine fubjects, did beft
teach him to judge and diftinguifh, in what cafes the
number of arguments adds to their weight and force.
He proved his conclufion, as far as poffible, by fome
propofitions, that were in themfelves more plain,
evident, and certain, than the conclufion; or at leaft,
fuch as are more known, and more intelligible to the
perfon whom he would convince. If we neglect this
rule, we fhall endeavour to enlighten that which is
obfcure, by fomething equally or more obfcure ; and
to confirm that which is doubtful, by fomething
equally or more uncertain. He laboured in all reafonings, to enlighten the underftanding, as well as to

S 2   conquer

conquer and captivate the judgment: he argued in
such a manner, as might give a natural, distinct, and
solid knowledge of divine objects to his readers; as
well as to force their assent, by a mere proof of the
question.   Now to attain this end, the chief medium
of his demonstration was fetched, as much as possible,
from the nature of the thing to be proved, or from
those things which are most naturally connected with
it.   He distinguished well between an explanation
and an argument; and neither imposed on himself, nor
suffered himself to be imposed upon by others, by
mistaking a mere illustration for a convincing reason.
Axioms, or self-evident propositions, may want an
explanation or illustration, though they are not to be
proved by reasoning.   Similitudes and allusions, have
oftentimes a very happy influence to explain some difficult truths, and to render the idea of it familiar and
easy.   In his whole course of reasoning, he kept
his mind sincerely intent on the pursuit of truth, and
followed solid arguments wheresoever it led him.—
No party spirit, no love of fame, no vile avarice or
love of money, no polluted passions, nor the jaun-
dice of any prejudice whatsoever, stopped or averted
the current of his reasoning, in the pursuit of true
knowledge of his GOD and SAVIOUR.

When we set this great and good man in his honest and admirable methods of reasoning, in contrast
with the proud enemies of the Gospel, we shall see
in him every thing to raise our admiration and
esteem; and every thing in them, to rouse our indignation and contempt.   He loved solid facts and divine reasonings: they love scepticism and sophistry:
they are frequently guilty of a mistake of the question,
that is, when something else is proved, which has neither any necessary connexion or consistency with the
thing enquired; and consequently gives no determination to the enquiry, though it may seem at first sight
to determine the question.   They are guilty of begging
the

the thing in queſtion, or a ſuppoſition of what is not granted; that is, when any propoſition is proved by the ſame propoſition in other words, or by ſome-thing that is equally uncertain and diſputed. They are guilty of another ſort of fallacy, which is called a circle. This is very near kin to the ſophiſm, which is called a begging the queſtion; as when one of the premiſes in a ſyllogiſm is queſtioned and op-poſed; and we intend to prove it by the concluſion.

The Papiſts are famous at this ſort of fallacy, when they prove the Scripture to be the word of God, by the authority or infallible teſtimony of their church: and when they are called to ſhew the infallible au-thority of their church, they pretend to prove it by the Scripture. The next kind of ſophiſm is called, the aſſignation of a falſe cauſe. There is ſcarce any thing more common in human life, than this ſort of deceitful argument: if any two accidental events hap-pen to concur, one is preſently made the cauſe of the other.

This ſophiſm was found in the early days of the world: for when holy Job was ſurrounded with un-common miſery, his own friends inferred, that he was a moſt wicked man; and charged him with aggravat-ed guilt, as the cauſe of his calamities; though God himſelf, by a voice from heaven, ſolved this uncharit-able ſophiſm, and cleared his ſervant Job of that charge. The way to relieve ourſelves from thoſe ſophiſms, and to ſecure ourſelves from the danger of falling into them, is an honeſt love of truth, and an ardent enquiry into the real nature and cauſes of things; with a conſtant attention and fixed watchful-neſs againſt all thoſe prejudices, that might warp the judgment aſide from truth in that enquiry. How ex-ceedingly abſurd and contemptible is the ſophiſtry of the Socinians, which they exerciſe againſt the grand doctrines of revelation. They are continually guilty of a miſtake of the queſtion, between Socinians and

Calviniſts :

Calvinifts : in a thoufand inftances, they form a bold and impudent fuppofition of what is not granted; and are guilty of a mean begging the thing in queftion, without any fort of proof. They are continually guilty of the affignation of a falfe caufe of man's falvation. In the prefent day, feveral Calvinifts of good natural parts, of amiable manners, and whofe gifts promifed ufefulnefs in the churches, have gone over from Calvinifm to Socinianifm. Heaven forbid, that I fhould indulge a fpirit of perfecution againft thefe men. Perfecution confifts in hurting a man in his natural or civil rights, merely on account of the faith he profeffes, and the worfhip he practices, without his being guilty of any civil forfeiture or crime. We renounce perfecution as being full of abfurdity and iniquity, in all its kinds and degrees.

Thus we have viewed Hervey as a man fkilled in found logic, being well acquainted with the nature of ideas, the objects of perception, as matter and fpirit, with their different qualities : having viewed the different kinds of perception, as fenfible, fpiritual, and intellectual; as clear and diftinct; or obfcure and confufed; as comprehenfive in all their properties ; complete in all their parts ; extenfive in all their kinds; and orderly in due method.

The clearnefs of our conceptions may be illuftrated by a microfcope, which views things clearly in their own nature. The comprehenfivenefs of our conceptions of the properties of all divine objects, may be illuftrated by a terreftrial globe turning upon its own axis, and exhibiting, in a few moments of time, the different empires, kingdoms, republicks, and cities ; the iflands, rivers, fprings, and lakes, on the face of the whole earth. We would then confider every divine object as complete in all its parts. This may be illuftrated by an anatomical knife, which divides the human body into all its component parts ; as bones and cartilages, mufcles and tendons, which
are

are the terminations of thofe mufcles: as divided into arteries and veins, which are the fame canals inverted : as divided into the brain, fpinal marrow, and nerves; which nerves, are only the brain and fpinal marrow, carried into different ramifications, and fpread all over the body, to the ends of our fingers and toes.　He confidered divine objects in all their different kinds ; and this may be illuftrated, by a glafs prifm, which refolves and analyfis light into its feven original colours; as violet, indigo, blue, green, yellow, orange, red; and the compofition of all thefe colours makes a complete white, or no colour at all.　Hervey went on to confider the nature of judgment, and the different kinds of propofitions: he confidered the different fources of human knowledge, as fenfe, intelligence, confcioufnefs, reafon, infpiration, and human teftimony.

He traced, in a very accurate manner, all the different prejudices or falfe judgments of mankind.　He entered deeply into himfelf; confidered the falfe judgments which he had formed, arifing from improper words; arifing from bad books and bad men; but efpecially, from his own bad heart; of which he had the deepeft confcioufnefs of any man, except the great Brine, which I ever knew.　This wife and good man, entered into the nature of clear and found fyllogifms: he underftood the major and the minor propofitions, as well as any man; and knew how to draw the conclufions with the utmoft diftinctnefs and force. He purfued his reafonings with the greateft honefty and attention, and never loft fight of his grand object, pure and immutable truth.　Truth was the fovereign of his foul, the miftrefs of his affections, and the darling of his heart; and to this, he facrificed all vain honours, fordid riches, and fenfual pleafures ; and if the whole world had been offered him, to be bought at the price of truth and virtue, he would have

fcorned

ſcorned to have opened his mouth and ſaid, I will buy it.

Having given a ſhort ſketch of Hervey's character as a ſound and good logician, let us in the next place view him with reſpect to his knowledge of
NATURAL PHILOSOPHY,
or a clear perception of the greatneſs, variety, beauty, and ends of the whole CREATION.

We have taken a ſhort proſpect of him in this point of light already: let us here view him in the higheſt exertions of his vaſt underſtanding, in the grand principle and foundation of all philoſophy; and that is the great law of UNIVERSAL GRAVITATION. He darted, with the whole fire and force of his underſtanding, into GOD and gravitation, beyond the conceptions of millions of mankind; and ſaw deeper and farther into this grand object, than moſt philoſophers in the whole world. He ſaw, with intuitive rapidity of perception, that GRAVITATION is only another name for the action of GOD our SAVIOUR, upon all matter in the univerſe: and the fundamental laws of nature are nothing elſe but the wiſdom, power, goodneſs, and omnipreſence, of GOD the Son, acting every where in his own world; and every moment ſuſtaining and actuating the whole creation.

Moſt men who ſtile themſelves philoſophers, ſuffer their minds and underſtandings to be *debauched* with mere dead matter; or poiſoned with ſuch deteſtable infidelity, that they ſee nothing; they believe nothing: they love nothing that relates to the perſon, the attributes, the actions, and glories of the LORD JESUS CHRIST.

Not ſo the great and ſublime Hervey: he ſaw GOD in every creature: he was attentive to the agency of GOD the REDEEMER every day and every hour of his life: it became habitual to him for many years before he died to live in CHRIST, and to be ONE SPIRIT with
· him.

him. This gave fuch an immortal dignity to his
mind, and fuch a grandeur to his conceptions, volitions, and paffions: and fuch a majefty in his actions,
and in all his deportment, as I never faw in any other
man in my whole life. .Whenever I came afrefh
into his prefence, I was ftruck with veneration and
delight: he feemed to me above the rank of other
men: a being that defcended from the celeftial world,
and breathing in the air of Paradife: his temper and
underftanding had a certain Godlike manner, as I
know not how to exprefs. It was impoffible to think
of him with contempt, unlefs you were a brute, or a
fool, void of all common fenfe, and deftitute of all
learning and virtue. If you were a man of any genius, tafte, and piety, you muft, in proportion as you
rofe in dignity of mind, efteem and venerate his fuperior character.

I have converfed with learned men and philofophers almoft fifty years: and I have found the greateft
number of them no better than PRACTICAL ATHEISTS,
deftitute of all right knowledge of GOD, fecret or
open enemies to divine revelation, with a temper as
determined in hatred of CHRIST, as the devils or the
damned fpirits; and all their fcience and philofophy
only ferved them to do more mifchief to mankind,
and to render them fo much the more deteftable in
the eyes of all wife and good men. Hervey valued
no man for his learning alone, unlefs joined with ardent devotion to the perfon of his GOD and SAVIOUR.

Hervey's fkill in the HEBREW LANGUAGE.

He began the ftudy of the Hebrew about the nine-
teenth year of his age, by the inftigation of an acquaintance, who gave him no manner of affiftance.
The only book he took up was, the Weftminfter
Hebrew Grammar. That book feems to be contrived by the devil to prevent the pleafing learning of
the Hebrew language: it is dark and obfcure, with-

out any light: it is harſh and unpleaſant, without any
taſte: it is ugly and diſguſtful, without any beauty:
and it is dull and lifeleſs, without any ſpirit. One
would think that all the powers of darkneſs had ſat
in council for a thouſand years paſt, to prevent the
rational and pleaſant ſtudy of the Hebrew language.
We have reaſon to believe that ninety-nine Gram-
mars out of an hundred, were invented by hell, to
ſpoil the moſt uſeful and beautiful language in the
world. Hervey took up this Grammar by the inſti-
gation of an Egyptian taſk-maſter, who urged him
to work and make bricks without ſtraw: he never
gave him the leaſt aſſiſtance in the language, which
Mr. Hervey found ſo harſh and difficult, that he
threw it by in deſpair. Some time after, he was urged
by the ſame taſk-maſter to learn the Hebrew language. He attempted the matter again, by the ſame
abſurd Grammar. He ſtuck a long time at the heemantic nouns, and was not able for his life and ſoul to
go on. Theſe heemantic nouns, at the beginning of a
Grammar, is another invention of the devil, to ſpoil
the learning of one of the moſt important languages
in the world.

After a long time, and much perplexity, great diſ-
couragements, chopped hay, prickly furze-buſhes,
and tormenting ſtinging nettles, by a happy Providence, there was another fellow of Lincoln college,
far different from the former tyrant. Seeing Mr.
Hervey in his painful embarraſſment, he pitied him,
and took him into his boſom: he conducted him to
the firſt chapter of Geneſis, and analized every word:
he taught him to reduce every noun to its proper pattern: he inſtructed him to trace every verb to its proper root, and to work every verb through the active
and paſſive conjugations of *kal* and *niphal*; of *pihel*
and *puhal*; *hiphil* and *hophal*, with the reciprocal
form of the verb *hithpael*. If the devil could have
had his way, we had loſt one of the fineſt Hebrew
ſcholars in the world.   After

After Mr. Hervey had learned to analize the firſt chapter of Geneſis, he went on like a race horſe, or a giant: he entered into the ſimplicity, the energy, the imagery, and the majeſty of the firſt language ſpoken upon earth; and to my certain knowledge, he was one of the firſt ſcholars in Europe for a familiar knowledge in the Hebrew Bible; and whilſt the greateſt part of the miniſters of religion hardly know the beginning from the end, or the top from the bottom of the ſacred Scriptures of GOD, in their original language, this excellent man converſed with the Hebrew Scriptures with the critical knowledge of a Jewiſh Rabbi, and the devotional ſpirit of a lively Chriſtian.

Hervey's ſkill in the GREEK LANGUAGE.

He was ſent to the Grammar Free School in Northampton, at ſeven years of age. His father was miniſter at Hardingſtone, one mile from Northampton, where Hervey was born. He went as a day-ſcholar for ten years. Here he learnt nothing but Latin and Greek. He ſoon got before many of the boys who had been ſome time in the ſchool; but his ungenerous and ſordid maſter checked his progreſs, leſt he ſhould go beyond his own ſon. Thus one of the fineſt geniuſes in the world was hindered in his improvement, to gratify the meanneſs of a bad maſter, and perhaps to cover the ſhame of a dull boy. His maſter had no ſort of taſte for the beauties of literature: never made any remarks on the excellent paſſages in the claſſics, nor did he ever lay before him a map, to aſſiſt him to underſtand the deſcriptions in the hiſtorians and poets. In the courſe of ten years, he muſt unavoidably have acquired a vaſt ſtock of Latin and Greek words; and when his underſtanding and imagination began to bud and bloſſom, he would, from his own reflections, begin to ſee their beauties, and taſte their ſweetneſs. He was grown ſo

exceed-

exceedingly tall at feventeen years of age, that he was
afhamed to go as a fchool-boy any longer: he then
petitioned his father that he might go to Oxford: accordingly a little exhibition of twenty pounds a year
was procured for him at Lincoln college.   Here he
was left to himfelf, by a proud indolent tutor; and
if a gracious God had not took care of him, he
would have been plunged in vice, and loft for ever.
After two years fpent in idlenefs, and non-improve-
ment, owing chiefly to the improper books that
were laid before him; books quite unfuitable to
his tafte and capacity, and only fitted to fill him
with difguft and defpair: he was roufed from his
drowfinefs by the fecret and flow ftimulations of
divine grace: he then began to recollect the claffical
knowledge he had acquired, in a dry and dull manner,
at the grammar fchool: he reviewed his Greek: he
read the Greek Teftament with diligence: he reviewed Homer and Xenophon, and began to difcern
the aftonifhing beauties in thofe works of genius
and eloquence; and at laft arofe to as mafterly
an acquaintance with Homer's Iliad and Odyffey, as
moft fcholars in the whole world.   Perhaps no man
had a greater fenfibility to the beauties of that daring
genius, Homer: no man entered with greater elevation, and penetration of thought, into the characters,
the fpeeches, the actions, the ardent imaginations, the
powerful paffions, and the daring actions of valour in
Achilles, Hector, and the other heroes in the Greek
and Trojan armies: it fet his foul all on fire.

   In a courfe of eight years Hervey had perufed,
with great attention, the felect beauties of the Greek
and Roman claffics; but in the year 1741, divine
grace drew him from the feet of Homer and Demoft-
henes, to the feet of the LORD JESUS CHRIST, his
heavenly tutor; and there he abode for eighteen
years. Now the Greek Teftament was the darling object of his foul; and in conjunction with the Hebrew
                                                    Bible,

Bible, were the great medium of his acquaintance
with CHRIST. He roved through the flowery fields
of the four Evangelifts with unutterable furprize, admiration, and efteem. He found the LORD JESUS
the object of the higheft benevolence and gratitude.

Hervey's fkill in the LATIN LANGUAGE.

He underftood the beauties of the Latin tongue
as well as any man ; and perhaps better than moft
claffical fcholars in the world. He did not content
himfelf with a mere dry plodding over letters and
fyllables, merely to underftand the grammatical fenfe
of words, but he entered with genius and fpirit into
the meaning of the authors he read, and the beauties
of fentiment and compofition. A dull fecond-rate
claffic had no charms for him, and therefore he laid
them by with coldnefs and indifference. An author
who wrote with ardent imagination, and enlivened
paffion ; who painted the characters of great men ;
entered into the fprings of their actions ; defcribed the
battles of heroes ; reprefented the grand effects of peace
or war ; the erection or ruin of kingdoms ; the awful
convulfions of nature ; the amiable charms of corn-
fields ; the pictures of rural nature ; the cultivation of
land ; the policy ; the good government and order of
bees ; their exquifite productions of combs and honey ;
with a thoufand beautiful dialogues of fhepherds—

Thefe, with innumerable other beauties, fet fire to
Hervey's imagination ; raifed his paffions to the higheft
tone and energy, and took poffeffion of his whole foul.
All thefe beauties Hervey found in one author ; but
for the laft years of his life, his tafte for holinefs, and
his devotion to CHRIST, had almoft expelled the love
of Virgil out of his heart. To fhew my love and
refpect for him, as foon as ever Bafkerville's beautiful edition of Virgil in quarto was publifhed, I carried it to him as a prefent. He received me with his
ufual fweetnefs, and expreffed the tendereft gratitude

for

for my regard to him. Said he, " My dear friend, if
" I intended to keep this book, I would accept it; but
" as I ſhall never read it, you muſt allow me to pay
" for it, for I ſhall ſurely give it away."

Let me obſerve, that amongſt many of the claſſic
authors, as he had one favourite among the poets, ſo
he had one that he valued above all the proſe writers,
and looked upon as a maſter-piece of eloquent deſcription, and that was the ſecond part of Tully's
book *De Natura Deorum*. If Tully had done as well
on the firſt and third part of that book, he would have
deſerved the approbation and praiſes of the whole
world.

Hervey had a clear ſenſe of the grandeur and beauty of ſentiments and language in the orations of De-
moſthenes and Cicero; and if he had poſſeſſed health
and ſpirits equal to his genius and taſte, he could have
transfuſed them into the Engliſh language with energy
and beauty peculiar to himſelf, diſplaying of the
lively beauties of the Engliſh language, of which he
was ſo great a maſter.

His knowledge of
GEOGRAPHY and ASTRONOMY.

His claſſical tutor, who taught him the languages of
Latin and Greek for ten years, was one of the moſt
negligent and unfaithful men in the whole world. He
never made but one remark upon the Greek Teſtament, and that was a remark fit only for a fool to
make. When he led him in his abſurd method through
the claſſics, he never laid before him ſo much as a
ſingle map of any of thoſe countries which are deſcribed by the Greek and Latin hiſtorians and poets.
His tutor at Lincoln college, in Oxford, was the ſame
lazy and worthleſs character: he took no ſort of care
and pains in his education; of which, out of a thouſand proofs, this is one; that after Mr. Hervey had
entered into orders, he happened to be in company
with

with fome gentlemen, who were fpeaking of Jerufalem: he was fo ignorant, as not to know where Jerufalem ftood : he knew nothing of the ·latitude of the
place, nor the quarter of the world where it was built.
He was fo ftung with fhame at his own ignorance,
and roufed to indignation at his tutors, that he went
immediately and bought a book of maps, and ftudied
Geography in all its parts, with fuch diligence and attention, that he became one of the firft Geographers
in the whole world.

He was equally ignorant of Aftronomy, or the fcience of the Sun, Moon, Planets, and Starry Heavens.
He ftudied Dr. Derham's Aftro-theology, with fuch
inceffant diligence, and unbounded delight, that he
made himfelf mafter of the Newtonian Syftem of the
Heavens. This enlarged the capacity of his underftanding to a moft extraordinary degree, and enabled
him to take in great and fublime ideas of GOD, in his
being, attributes, and perfections, and to receive new
and uncommon ideas of the Godhead and glory of
CHRIST, without a childifh furprize, or abfurd averfion. This enabled him to furvey ten thoufand grand
ideas in a beautiful arrangement, and a regular fucceffion.

Hervey's admirable fkill in ANATOMY.

He thoroughly underftood the ftructure and œconomy of the human body. He was well acquainted
with the fyftem of the bones, and cartilages by which
thofe bones were connected. He was well acquainted
with the doctrine of the mufcles, and the tendons in
which thefe mufcles terminate. He was clearly acquainted with the whole fyftem of the arteries, by
which the blood is conveyed from the heart, to all
parts of the body and the veins, which are the fame
canals inverted, by which the blood is brought back
to the heart again. He had an exquifite knowledge
of the nature of digeftion, nutrition, and circulation:
he

he traced the chyle from all its veffels, to its grand receptacle at the left kidney : he followed it up through
its glorious tube, the thoracic duct, 'till it poured
its vital treafure into the right auricle of the heart :
he purfued it into the right ventricle, and from thence
by the pulmonary arteries, to both the lobes of the
lungs : he purfued it by the fame canals inverted,
called the *pulmonary veins*, to the left auricle of the
heart : from the left auricle, he faw it into the left ventricle ; and from thence he purfued its vital tour by
the grand artery, down by the back bone, to the end
of the toes ; and by another beautiful artery to the
top of the head, and to the ends of the fingers.   And
thus, at the rate of fixty ounces in a minute, and at
the length of feventeen yards in the fame time, the
blood has played itfelf off ever fince we were born.

Let us now view Hervey, who, on the principles of
the glorious Gofpel, had a moft exquifite knowledge of
MORAL PHILOSOPHY.
This beautiful and glorious fcience confifts of two
parts, HAPPINESS and VIRTUE.

Happinefs confifts in the fruition of the fupreme
good.   The fupreme good is an object defirable for
its own fake.   It is that which removes all poffible
evil from the body and foul of man.   It muft, by its
own virtue, remove all natural evil, which is pain,
difeafes, poverty, and death.   It muft remove all moral evil, or an habitual violation of GOD's eternal and
immutable law, with all charge of offence, which is
guilt, or an obligation to punifhment.   It muft remove all eternal evil, confifting in the pain of lofs, or
an eternal difunion from the fupreme good ; and
from the pain of fenfe, which is an eternal feeling of
the holy juftice of GOD, giving us a lively confcioufnefs of GOD's hatred and wrath againft our perfons
and crimes.

The

The fupreme good muft have another property; it muft be immutably and univerfally the fame, without any difcontinuance and lofs; that is, to fay, it muft be as frefh and lively after the fruition of ten thoufand ages, as it is now; being known it muft make a wife man; being intenfely loved, muft make a good man; and being richly enjoyed, muft make a happy man.

Enjoyment, or fruition, confifts in five things; perception, union, reft, ufe, and delight. It is impoffible for any man to be happy without a fpiritual perception of CHRIST: no man can be happy without a vital union with CHRIST: no man can be happy without a total reft in the perfon and blood of CHRIST: no man can be happy without a free and full ufe of the righteoufnefs of CHRIST: no man can be happy without a delight in CHRIST; that is to fay, an habitual love and joy in his perfections and beauty. No man can be happy without an ardent zeal for his glory, as the ultimate end and intention of his eternal exiftence.

Hervey knew CHRIST as the fupreme good, as well as any man in the world; and he knew that vital virtue, flowing out of the fulnefs of CHRIST, was the only means of bringing him to the fruition of this fupreme good.

All the Pagan philofophers were blind and miferable men; they profeffed themfelves to be wife, but became fools. The epicureans placed happinefs in fenfual good; the difciples of Ariftotle and Zeno; the one placed happinefs in the habits of virtue; the other placed happinefs in the actions of virtue. Plato, and his followers, afferted, that happinefs confifted in a perception of the divine goodnefs and beauty; but he never knew, for one moment, the right method of attaining an union with, and enjoyment of the fupreme beauty and good. The Platonic world, by wifdom, knew not GOD.

U   How

How ought we to love and adore the infinite goodnefs and mercy of GOD, in giving us a revelation of the fupreme good. We were totally ignorant of the LORD JESUS CHRIST, who is an object infinitely defirable for his own fake, and not for the fake of any thing elfe; for then that object would be before him, and above him, and confequently he would not be the fupreme good; our LORD JESUS CHRIST has another property of the fupreme good, and that is, He is able wholly to remove from us all natural, moral, and eternal evils; and he is equally able and willing to beftow upon us, all natural, moral, and eternal good. He can give us a happinefs as large as our wifhes, and lafting as our fouls; a happinefs which an immortal foul fhall never outlive, and an eternal GOD fhall never ceafe to communicate.

Our GOD and SAVIOUR is an unperifhing good, and the fruition of him will be as lively and frefh after millions of ages are rolled away, as he was at the beginning of our enjoyment of his prefence. Hervey knew as well as any man, by happy experience, the nature of the fruition of the fupreme good: he had a clear perception, a forcible underftanding of the nature of this good: he felt an intenfe union with it, an entire reft of heart in it, a free and full ufe of CHRIST's perfon and righteoufnefs; an habitual delight in him, as the ftrength of his heart, and his portion for ever.

Let us now take a view of the fecond part of moral philofophy, which is VIRTUE.

Virtue is a free and intentional conformity of our nature and actions to the nature and will of GOD.

Here let us confider the feat and fubject of virtue —*The underftanding, will, and affections.* The underftanding may be confidered as fpeculative or practical. The underftanding as fpeculative, is that power of the foul which fimply views the exiftence

and

and nature of all objects, without any regard to our happiness, or the consequences of actions. A man's understanding may be said to be sound, when he has a clear perception of the nature of all things in heaven, earth, and hell; when he has a complete conception of an object in all its parts, and a comprehensive conception of all its properties; when he has an extensive conception of any being in all its kinds; and when he has an orderly conception or understanding of a subject in due method.

The practical understanding, considers the nature of actions in their moral qualities; and the consequences of actions, with respect to time and eternity. In this view, the understanding may be said to be in a sound state, when it clearly conceives of the eternity and immutability of the divine law, and our infinite obligations to obey its commands, with the fitness and reasonableness of that obedience: when we have a strong sense of the immaculate purity of God, and a very keen conception of the infinite evil of sin, as it strikes at all possible and infinite good, and fixes a stain in the soul to an infinite duration; as it makes the soul subject to suffer the loss of an infinite good, and to feel that infinite loss to all eternity.

The moral understanding may be considered in a sound state, when it has a forcible apprehension of the fitness, goodness, and beauty of Gospel holiness, and feels that perception attended with the highest admiration and esteem, with the utmost veneration and benevolence.

The WILL of MAN

Is that rational appetite of the soul, which pursues every object that appears good, and avoids every object that appears evil. The will may be said to be in a sound state, when all its volitions and determinations are conformable to the will of God: it is this that constitutes the essence of virtue. On the other hand, the will is in an unsound and corrupt state, when its

volitions

volitions and determinations are continually oppofite to the revealed will of God.

The effence and life of fin, confifts in the habitual inclination of the will to difobey the will of God; and the fum total of the madnefs and rebellion of mankind, confifts in a perpetual attempt to fubject the will, glory, and majefty of God, to the corrupt determinations, humours, and lufts of men. Hence fpring all the miferies that have plagued, and will plague and ruin the human race to eternity. On the other hand, if we view our lovely author, I muft declare once more, in the divine prefence, that I never faw a human will fo totally abforbed in the will of God: not a fimple motion in Providence, but he ftrictly attended to it: not a hint of the good pleafure of God, but he freely obeyed it. He clearly faw, that in a moft chearful and lively conformity of his whole foul, to the pleafure and commands of God his Saviour, the whole dignity, glory, and felicity of man, entirely confifts.

The acquifition of the dominion of our fyftem, and the poffeffion of all the riches and glory of the univerfe, had no charms for him, when compared with a little farther conformity to the holinefs of God in his law.

Let us now confider the nature of virtue, as it is feated in the AFFECTIONS.

The affections are fenfible motions of the foul, arifing from an unufual object fuited to excite that motion. The paffions of the foul are to be confidered as primitive or derivative; as fimple or compound.

The primitive paffions are admiration, love, and hatred; efteem and contempt; benevolence and malevolence; complacency and difplicency.

The derivative paffions are defire and averfion; hope and fear; joy and forrow; gratitude and anger. All thefe paffions in Hervey's heart were confecrated
entirely

entirely to the pleafure and glory of GoD his RE-
DEEMER.   His admiration was fixed upon an object
the moft grand, new, and beautiful in the univerfe
—he difcerned a perfon, whofe name is

פֶּלֶא יוֹעֵץ אֵל גִּבּוֹר ׀
אֲבִי עַד שַׂר שָׁלוֹם ׀

WONDERFUL: COUNSELLOR: The STRONG or
MIGHTY GOD: The FATHER of ETERNITY: The
PRINCE OF PEACE.

L O V E.

Love is the moft powerful paffion of the human
foul: it is a delightful union of the heart, with an
object confidered as good.   Hervey knew where to
find the true good, the greateft good: he knew that
this good was fuited to the higheft and nobleft powers of the human foul: that it was adapted to the
nature of man in every period of time, and in every
nation all round the globe.   He knew that this good
would fupport a fteady ferenity amidft all the vexations and troubles of human life: that it would en-
liven and fweeten all other lawful enjoyments: that
the fruition of this good would ftand the teft of the
moft fevere reflection: that it would improve upon
longer experience; and upon the moft frequent repetition, yield ftill higher fruitions: that it might be
enjoyed without blufhes and fhame, or the leaft painful remorfe of confcience: that it was fuperior to our
greateft capacities for happinefs, and lafting as our
eternal exiftence.

If we fet the fupreme good in a vigorous contraft
with the honours, riches, and pleafures of this world,
it will appear greatly heightened by the comparifon.

Temporal good is not fuited to our higheft faculties: it is not adapted to the nature of man: it will
not fupport a fteady ferenity under all the vexations
of life: an excefs in worldly gratifications imbitters
and poifons the common comforts of life: worldly
enjoy-

enjoyments will not ftand the teft of cool and deliberate reafon: worldly lufts grow more bitter and
tormenting, upon longer experience: the more flat,
infipid, and naufeous, are all worldly pleafures, on frequent repetition: worldly lufts can never be enjoyed
without blufhes and fhame; that is, forrow and felf-
contempt; for a man knows himfelf to be a fool, whilft
he is gratifying luft; and he can never enjoy the approbation of his own heart. Worldly pleafures are all
inferior to our capacities of happinefs; and we feel
them too little for the mighty grafp of an immortal
foul. Worldly lufts die away: they are vanifhing as
a fhadow; empty as a bubble, and lighter than a fea-
ther: the power of gratification is foon loft: the objects of fruition fly away as fwift as lightening, and
leave nothing behind but ftench and darknefs, and the
tortures of the damned.

Hervey's great underftanding faw the truth of all
thefe things in the cleareft and ftrongeft point of
light: he flew with the force and quicknefs of celeftial fire, from all ungodlinefs and worldly lufts;
and his will and paffions darted with their full force
and fire into the infinite beauty of GOD his SAVIOUR.

The PASSION of HATRED

Is a defire of difunion from an object, confidered as
intrinfically evil, ugly, and deteftable; pernicious and
deftructive of our peace and happinefs. The firft
object of hatred in the univerfe, is fin, or moral evil,
which is a departure from the beautiful order of GOD;
a violation of his revealed will, and a defperate enmity to infinite goodnefs.

No creature ought to be the object of our hatred,
confidered fimply as the production of GOD, devils,
and bad men: viewed as clothed with evil qualities,
may be hated, and ought to be hated as the enemies
of GOD. No man had a more intenfe hatred of fin
than our excellent friend; and as holinefs grew more
rooted

rooted in the habits, and rofe higher in the exertion of the actions, his hatred of fin continually increafed.

We have already viewed him in his efteem for CHRIST, confidered as an object good in himfelf: in his benevolence to CHRIST, confidering him as worthy to receive good: in his defires after CHRIST, confidered as fit to do us good, and fuited to make us happy: he had a complacency in CHRIST, confidered as an object of perfect beauty and delight.

His contempt, averfion, malevolence, and bitter difguft, were all pointed at the deteftable uglinefs of moral evil.

His hope in the righteoufnefs and fatisfaction of CHRIST, rofe as high as the third heavens: his fear filled him with awe of the great GOD: made him dread to offend him, and eager to pleafe him. His joys all terminated in CHRIST, as an ocean of infinite perfection: his forrows arofe from a confcioufnefs of his paft unkindnefs to his dear REDEEMER, and a keen fenfe of prefent depravity of heart: his gratitude had no other bounds than the infinitude of GOD's exiftence and duration. He had the moft delicate fenfe of the excellency and worth of bleffings received. " I know, " (faid he, when dying,) what my dear REDEEMER " has done for me." He had the moft lively perception of the fpirit and fpring of his REDEEMER's actions and fufferings, and that was felf-moving love. He had an ardent defire to make all poffible returns: he wifhed for better ability to be more grateful, and he determined never to lay gratitude afide, but with the extinction of his being, and his total lofs of all confcioufnefs. He was always difpleafed with himfelf, when he felt the leaft failure in gratitude; and he delighted in his own exiftence, when he found a grateful heart.

We have already obferved, that the paffions are either fimple or compound. We muft not pretend to go through all the vaft variety of the paffions of the heart:

heart: their number, nature, caufes, appearances, pains, pleafures, ends, and ufes, if confidered as they de-ferve, would make a large treatife by itfelf. Let us only confider the combination of the fimple paffions in a very few inftances.

Honour is a generous fenfe of right and wrong, and is always attended with the compound paffion, ftiled ambition. Ambition is compofed of vivid wonder and vaft defire: it admires an object, confi-dered as great: it defires that object, confidered as good. A holy ambition was created by God, in the firft formation of the human foul: its grand defign and ufe was to attach man to God for ever and ever. This paffion man wickedly tore from his breaft. In regeneration, Christ re-infufes it into the foul, on purpofe that man might live in an eternal union with himfelf, as the fountain of all honour. Hervey was one of the moft ambitious men in the whole world: he had a moft intenfe defire of the eternal approbation of his great Mafter: no-thing fhort of the delight of Christ in the hap-pinefs of his foul, could fatisfy his immortal mind.

Glory is another compound paffion: it is made up of immenfe joy in an object, and boundlefs felf-love, animated by a fenfe of our intereft in that object. Notwithftanding the feeblenefs of Mr. Hervey's con-ftitution of body, and the precarioufnefs of his health, with the langour of his fpirits, and the preffures of his animal ftructure upon the powers of his mind, he had within him the feeds of immortal glory: thefe feeds of divine fire flafhed out into meridian brightnefs on a thoufand occafions: witnefs that paffage in his Me-ditations among The Tombs—" Wonder! O man! be loft in admiration at the events which are com-ing on the univerfe!"—Witnefs his expofition of that paffage in the firft Book of Kings, chap. viii. *Will* God *in very deed dwell with man upon the earth!* Witnefs his moft fublime reflections on that paffage in Rev. x.

Time

Time shall be no longer. Witnefs his rhapfody on the bleffings of the Gofpel; Dialogue XVII. Witnefs the aftonifhing grandeur of his thoughts on the heavens and earth flying away from the prefence of the Son of God, Rev. xx. Witnefs his Palmarian eloquence, which tranfcends every thing, his Meditations on the 40th Chapter of Ifaiah, page 60, in his Eleven Letters on Christ's Imputed Righteoufnefs. But who can number all his beauties. I muft only add his unparalleled Expofition of thofe words: " The " loftinefs of man fhall be bowed down, and the " haughtinefs of men fhall be made low, and the " Lord Jesus alone fhall be exalted in that day," Ifai. ii. 10, 22.—See the Eleven Letters, page 79—82.

The RULE of VIRTUE

Is the will of Christ grounded in the conftitution and powers of man, and made known by the light of reafon and divine revelation. God our Saviour has given common fenfe to the whole world; and in this view he is the light to every man that comes into exiftence.

Common fenfe is a power of perceiving truth by a fudden impulfe, independent of our will, prior to all reafoning, and to all kinds of education: it is effential to the human mind, to fee that all things are not alike true, nor alike falfe, nor alike fit, nor alike unfit, nor alike good, nor alike evil, nor alike beautiful, nor alike deformed, nor alike happy, nor alike miferable.

Thefe perceptions of common fenfe take place in a moment, whenever their objects are prefented; and thefe decifions of common fenfe, are like a fudden impulfe, much quicker than any reafonings whatfoever, and prior to all inftructions from mankind.

Moral good and evil are wifely marked out by the different natural effects which they produce: moral good always produces natural good, that is, pleafure

X   and

and happineſs: moral evil always produces natural
evil, that is, pain and miſery: moral good always
iſſues in honour: moral evil always iſſues in diſgrace and ſhame: moral good is always attended
with gain and advantage: moral evil is always attended with loſs and damage. Theſe invariable effects, which take place in all mankind all round the
globe, in every period of time, are the wiſe inter-
pretations of the will of CHRIST, and the eternal and
immutable ſanctions of his law.

All theſe explanations and demonſtrations of the
law of nature, are illuminated, enlarged, improved,
and enforced, by the ſuperior light of divine revelation.

Hervey ſaw, as clearly as any man, the inſuffici-
ency of the light of reaſon in its preſent ſtate, to
lead us to happineſs and virtue. This gave him a
moſt endeared and tranſcendent eſteem for the Holy
Scriptures. He loved every particle of truth in the
Hebrew Bible and the Greek Teſtament: he ſcorned
to read the Bible with other mens eyes: he diſdained
the fault of being on a level with the boy that wiped
his horſes heels. This is ſuch an indignity to the
character of a preacher, which no man of genius,
ſpirit, and good ſenſe, will ever endure; a generous
preacher will be aſhamed to aſcend the pulpit ignorant
of the ſacred originals, and the contents of his great
Maſter's commiſſion and inſtructions: and he will,
by inceſſant attention and prayer, form a familiar acquaintance with the inſpired Scriptures of GOD.

The NATURE of VIRTUE.

. Virtue is a free and intentional conformity of our
whole nature and choice to the rectitude, purity, and
determinations of the will of our LORD JESUS
CHRIST, manifeſted by common ſenſe, reaſon, and
revelation.

Vice

Vice is the difconformity of our nature, will, actions, and paffions, to the will of GOD.

Virtue is the production of the greateft happinefs to mankind: it is the conformity of our actions to the public good—vice is the production of pain to mankind: it is the increafe of mifery in the univerfe.

Virtue is the knowledge of GOD's moral attributes —vice is an ignorance of the nature and perfections of the DEITY. Virtue is an ardent union of the will with GOD—vice is a determined enmity of the will to GOD. Virtue is a high veneration for the divine character—vice is an infinite contempt of the being and dignity of GOD. Virtue is a fixed regard to the divine will, and a free fubmiffion to the divine dominion—vice is a wicked refiftance of the will of GOD, and a vile attempt to fubject GOD's pleafure to our humours and lufts. Virtue is a noble truft in the care of divine Providence—vice is a diftruft of the honour and faithfulnefs of GOD. Virtue loves to converfe with the DEITY in all his works of creation and providence—vice is blind to GOD in the ftructure and operations of the univerfe. Virtue loves to fee GOD in every thing—vice difcerns GOD in none of the works of his hands. Virtue loves to converfe with GOD in the Sacred Scriptures—vice hates the Scriptures with the venomous malice of the devil.

Virtue clearly perceives the fitnefs, fulnefs, power, beauty, and grace, of the LORD JESUS CHRIST— vice fees no fitnefs in him, defpifes his fulnefs, defies his power, hates his beauty, and fcorns his grace. Virtue loves to imitate the example of our LORD JESUS CHRIST—vice loves to copy the example of the devil and all bad men. Virtue loves to fit at CHRIST's feet to learn of him every thing great, good, venerable, and wonderful—vice loves to fit at the feet of the devil, and to be led captive by him at his will. Virtue loves a full confidence in CHRIST's in-

terceffion

terceffion—vice fcorns that interceffion, and re-
nounces it for ever.

Virtue loves the divinity, perfonality, and operations of God the Holy Spirit—vice hates the divine
perfon of the Spirit of God, and fcorns all his gracious influences. Virtue loves the fpirit of truth—
vice loves the fpirit of error. Virtue loves the teaching and guidance of the Spirit—vice loves the inftructions and guidance of the devil. Virtue loves to
be fealed with the image of Christ—vice loves to be
inftamped with the refemblance of fatan. Virtue loves
the fpirit of wifdom and revelation—vice loves the
fpirit of folly and darknefs.

Virtue loves the whole world of mankind with
ardent and intenfe affection—vice hates all the human race, and ardently loves their utter deftruction.
Virtue delights in the whole houfhold of faith—vice
would perfecute all Chriftians to the death. Virtue
loves the beauty of univerfal juftice—vice delights
in all kinds of unrighteoufnefs. Virtue delights in
fincerity of heart—vice loves hypocrify and deceit.
Virtue teaches our lips the utmoft veracity—vice
infpires our tongues with the fpirit of lying. Virtue loves faithfulnefs in all our actions—vice
makes us falfe and fickle in all the relations of life.
Virtue infpires us with a fpirit of candour, in judging the perfons and actions of mankind—vice is intenfely cenforious and unkind to the whole human
race. Virtue has ftrong compaffion for poor men as
miferable—vice is cruel as the grave, and barbarous as hell. Virtue is exceedingly merciful to mens
fouls—vice aims to murder them all. Virtue has a
fpirit of generous forgivenefs of all offences—vice
fays, " I will never forgive or forget, but purfue
" every offence with a fweet revenge." Virtue is a
fpirit of deep humility—vice is a fpirit of haughtinefs and pride. Virtue is a fpirit of meeknefs and
quietnefs—vice is a fpirit of rafh anger and boifterous
rage.

rage. Virtue is a fpirit of patience and contentment—vice is a fpirit of fretfulnefs and murmuring at divine Providence. Virtue is a fpirit of felf-denial in all things, but efpecially a denial of our own righteoufnefs for juftification—vice is a violent and corrupt felfifhnefs, and a vain confidence in our own works to juftify us before GOD. Virtue commands our appetites into fobriety and temperance—vice inflames our appetites for rioting and drunkennefs. Virtue teaches us chaftity in body, foul, paffions, and imagination—vice inflames the blood, enrages the paffions for impurity, pollutes the imagination, and renders foul and body a flave to luft.

Through all thefe virtues which fhone in Hervey's temper and character, there appeared fome fignal qualities which animated and adorned all the reft; fuch were fincerity, tendernefs, zeal, prudence, and perfeverance.

SINCERITY was the life blood of all his graces: it was the golden thread that ran through the whole web of his Chriftian life. Sincerity animated him to an ardent intention to pleafe GOD in every thing through his whole courfe. Sincerity prompted him to enquire into the whole will of GOD, and actuated him to ftrive after a total compliance with that will, as far as he knew it. Sincerity was the caufe of an exact correfpondence between his thoughts, words, and actions: he had no wifh or intention to deceive GOD or man: he was the fame uniform great character through life.

TENDERNESS is an exquifite and lively fenfibility of the prefence of GOD with the human mind: it includes in it pungent remorfe of confcience, whenever we violate the eternal rule of right and wrong; a tender regard for the honour and glory of CHRIST, as the true GOD, and eternal life; a tender refentment of the leaft injury done to his divine character and righteoufnefs; a tender regard for his holy law and
Gofpel:

Gofpel; and a tender concern for the intereft and happinefs of his people, and the advancement of his kingdom in the world.

ZEAL is a compound paffion, made up of love and anger: love to an object, confidered as beautiful and good; and anger at every perfon and thing which have a tendency to injure that object. The original Hebrew word, which we tranflate zeal, fignifies refentment for the deareft thing. Hervey had a moft powerful and ardent love to CHRIST: had the utmoft regard for his precious righteoufnefs; confequently his anger muft rife againft every thing which eclipfed the glory of that perfon, or depreciated the worth of that righteoufnefs. His zeal appears through all his works, but it fhines in its meridian glory in many pages in his Eleven Letters on Juftification.

Whenever Pagan or Chriftian fyftems of moral philofophy were fet up in competition with CHRIST, to eclipfe his righteoufnefs, or to rival the excellency of evangelical holinefs, he treated them with infinite fcorn and indignation.

All fyftems of moral philofophy, without CHRIST, were with him upon an equal footing with Ariftotle's Ethics, and Tully's offices.—" Give me," faid he to me, " any of their fyftems of morals, I will take all " their heathen virtues, and turn them into Chriftian " graces: I will reprefent them as flowing from vital " union with CHRIST; as animated by the Spirit of " CHRIST, and enforced by motives drawn from the " Gofpel of CHRIST."

This excellent zeal in Hervey's bofom was a permanent principle of habitual love to, and concern for, the glory of CHRIST's perfon and grace; and ten thoufand creations offered him as a price to deny or diminifh one tittle of CHRIST's honour, would have met with infinite indignation and abhorrence.

PRUDENCE confifts in propofing the nobleft end of all our actions; in ufing the beft means to attain that end;

end; in obferving the fitteft circumftances of time, and manner of action; in preventing all reafons for bitter repentance, and guarding againft every thing that may defeat the higheft end and intention we have in view.   If we try Hervey's character by this defcription of prudence, we fhall have reafon to efteem and venerate him in the higheft degree.   The end that he propofed, was the difplay of the boundlefs glory of CHRIST.   The means that he made ufe of, were faith and love, and the gracious promifes of the Gofpel.   In all his converfation, ftudies, preaching and writings, he obferved the fitteft circumftances of time and manner; and by the affiftance of GOD the Holy Spirit, he fecured himfelf from bitter repentance, and guarded againft all defeat of his fupreme end.

PERSEVERANCE implies a continuance in all gracious habits of the heart, and holy actions in the life. It fcorns to ferve our LORD JESUS CHRIST by fits and ftarts, being fometimes as hot as fire, and at other times as cold as ice; fometimes ferving GOD, and other times ferving the devil; fometimes purfuing the pleafures of fin, and at other times the pleafures of religion; fometimes running with their faces towards hell, in company with the people of this world; and at other times running our race with true Chriftians, after the prize of celeftial glory.

Hervey defpifed this inconfiftent conduct, this deteftable duplicity of character.   He was not always in one equal frame of lively devotion and joy, but he was habitually ready to receive any frefh notices of celeftial truth ; and he had an habitual difpofition to catch fire whenever the great object was propofed ; that object of his faith which was the chiefeft among ten thoufand, and altogether lovely.

MOTIVES TO VIRTUE.

A motive is the confideration of good or evil, which determines the choice, and excites to action:

it

it is an impulfe to move by the fenfe of good, to be
enjoyed, or evil to be avoided. To propofe a motive, is to give an impulfe to the mind and paffions
by propofing fuch objects to the underftanding, will,
and paffions, which have the fitteft tendency to roufe
the fprings of action to purfue all that is good, and
avoid all that is evil.

Thefe motives, drawn from reafon and fcripture,
are addreffed to fear, hope, gratitude, intereft, gain,
lofs, honour, difgrace, pain, pleafure, ambition, fhame,
and glory.

Thefe motives pour in upon us from all quarters,
like light from all the parts of the ftarry heavens;
and ftreams from all the fprings, fountains, and rivers, of the known world; heaven, earth, hell, time
paft, prefent, and future; men, devils, angels, the
alluring beauties of creation, the events that are
coming upon the univerfe, the defcending God, the
burning world, the concluding fcenes of creation, the
tranfports of the faved, the terrors of the damned,
and the opening fcenes of a vaft eternity, all furnifh
motives to fting and ftorm the foul into the higheft
advancements in virtue.

Out of an immenfe mafs of motives to virtue,
which offer themfelves to our confideration, let us
felect a few of the moft pungent and alluring nature.

God ardently loves virtue wherever he fees it;
the virtue of the patriarchs, prophets, and apoftles,
were the objects of his moft intenfe delight. All the
primitive Chriftian fathers, the throng of glorious
confeffors, and the noble army of martyrs, with all
the divines and Chriftians in every period; to the
prefent time, have been the objects of his higheft
approbation and efteem. God is now carrying on one
grand fcheme of wifdom, virtue and happinefs, which
he will never ceafe to execute, till the laft foul fhall
be born of God.

GOD

GOD loves virtue fo intenfely, that if he could fee one good thought in any unregenerate man upon earth; yea, if he faw one good thought or holy voli- tion in a devil, or a damned fpirit, it would be his approbation and delight.

On the other hand, if he could fee an evil thought in an angel or faint in glory, he would abhor it; and although he loves his people upon earth with a moft intenfe affection, yet he never loved their fins, nor ever will: they were always hated; they are now hated, and will be totally expelled from the foul. The dominion of fin, in believers, is gone for ever: its reign is abfolutely irrecoverable: it reigns not, nor fhall reign in the faints.

CHRIST has bought all virtue with his blood, to put into our hearts; and he has bought our hearts with his blood, to be the feat and fubject of eternal virtue.

GOD the HOLY SPIRIT, inclined the will of this great and good man, to put himfelf in the way of motives: he affifted him to underftand the nature of motives: to feel the force and energy of motives: to comply with the defign and intention of motives: and practically to obey with joy the great end of the beft motives in the world.

No man in a ftate of nature loves to put himfelf in the way of the beft motives: no man underftands the nature of the beft motives: no man feels the force of the beft motives: no man difcerns the defign of the beft motives: no man chearfully obeys the influ- ence of the beft motives.

This is the great and effential difference between a true Chriftian and every other man. This is the *differentia conftitutiva* which marks the internal cha- racter of a regenerate man, and diftinguifhes him from all other perfons in the world: fuch a man was Hervey.

Y   I never

I never knew any man more free from corrupt
fprings and impure motives, in his whole temper,
language and conduct: pure love to GOD his SAVI-
OUR; boundlefs benevolence to the whole univerfe,
and peculiar delight in the image of CHRIST, found
in all true Chriftians, were the grand fprings of his
action. He faw and felt that the objects in the eternal and invifible world were every moment near to
his foul. He confidered millions of good beings in
heaven, as very near him every moment, and millions of bad beings in torment, as not very diftant
from the prefent ftate of things in the vifible world.
His foul catched fire at the fight of all great characters for virtue which have appeared in the Jewifh
and the Chriftian world. He wifely confidered that
a great and good foul could not employ itfelf in a
worthy manner, except in vital virtue towards GOD
and man.

He ftrongly felt, and clearly difcerned, how much
great and good work true virtue would accomplifh in
the world, and in the churches of CHRIST: He confidered virtue as the greateft glory of the human character; for what is glory but the fame of the moft
excellent virtue, attended with praife. It is by this
that the greateft and beft of men in all ages have
obtained a good report, and that good report will be
made afrefh at the burning bar of CHRIST, amid fur-
rounding worlds of devils, men, and angels. He
knew that virtue would eternally live in the brightnefs of the underftanding; in the rectitude of the will;
in the ftrength of the memory; in the delicacy and
correctnefs of confcience; in the grandeur of the imagination; in the fire of the great paffions, it fpreads
health, ftrength, and beauty through the whole foul.

GOD the Holy Spirit fet before his mental eyes,
the pleafure, the riches, and the honours of virtue.
Pleafure is a confcioufnefs of agreeable fenfations,
arifing from the prefence of beauty and good. Virtue

tue always produces the pleasures of contemplation, the pleasures of action, the pleasures of fruition, and the pleasures of hope and beautiful prospects, which terminate in nothing short of the everlasting duration of God. Riches are a competent supply of our real wants, and a satisfaction of mind, with that competence. Honour is the fame of virtue; attended with eternal praise. Praise and renown have always been the rewards of real virtue, and fire up a generous ambition to excel; to consider what patterns of virtue are gone to heaven before us; what prudence, justice, temperance, and fortitude, shone in the tempers and characters of the great and good men of the Old and New Testament. The great Basils, Chrysostoms, the Bradwardines; the great Bacons, the Boyles, the Miltons, the Polhills the Owens, the Witsiuses, the Charnocks, the Bateses, the Howes, the Hurrions, the Wattses, the Doddridges, the Brines, the Gills, the Edwards, the Hallyburtons, the Fenelons, the Rollins; with millions of heroes more, all flashed their brightest virtues upon Hervey's understanding, imagination, and passions; and roused him to an unbounded ardor to excel in every virtue, and rise and shine in every Christian grace.

Nor did he ever forget his great and wonderful poet, Dr. Young, whose Night Thoughts, and the great Longinus* of the present age, whose Lectures on the Hebrew prophets, in their original composition, and their present elegant translation, by Dr. Gregory, which must be considered as the standard of taste to the learned world, and exceed all commendation and praise.

His hatred and indignation against vice, were roused to the highest degree, by a view of the worst characters in all ages and nations: the monsters of vice before the deluge; the polluted sinners of Sodom; the tyrant Pharaoh, and his outrageous and cruel army; the rebellious Israelites in the wilder-

---

* Dr. Lowth late Bishop of London.

nefs;

nefs; the fhocking impudence of Zimri and Cofbi; the gigantic heights in blafphemy and vice appearing in Korah, Dathan, and Abiram; the black atheifm and deteftable ingratitude in the Canaanites: the vice of avarice in Achan: of lewdnefs and folly in Sampfon; the horrid profligacy of the Benjamites, Judg. xix. 25. xx. 15.   The moft daring atheifm and blafphemy of Hophni and Phinehas; the vile hypocrify and rebellion of king Saul; the defperate unchaftity, adultery, and murder in David; the horrid inceft of Amnon; the murder of that wretched man by his own brother; the tranfcendent rebellion of Abfalom; and the undefcriptive and undefcribable lewdnefs of that horrid parricide.   The dreadful apoftacy of Solomon: the unparalleled and inexpreffible infolence of Rabfhakeh; the horrible madnefs and atheifm of the wicked bible burners, Jehoiakim, Antiochus, and Dioclefian: the daring impiety of Belfhazzar; the infinite crime of Judas Ifcariot; the murder of the LORD of life; the murder of Stephen; the cruel madnefs and rage of Saul the perfecutor; the unbounded wickednefs of Nero; and his moft barbarous murder of the apoftle Paul.   With all the immenfe crimes againft GOD and man, which have rifen up to public view in every age, and in every nation under heaven.

All thefe crimes, which ftrike at an infinite GOD, and fix a guilt in the foul through an infinite duration; and all this guilt and infinite malignity, which expofe every foul to the lofs of an infinite GOOD, through an infinite duration, unlefs cleared off by the fatisfaction and righteoufnefs of GOD the Son: I fay, all thefe crimes and infinite deformities of vice, rofe up before the mind and underftanding of this great and good man; and filled him with eternal hatred and horrors unfpeakable.

God has decreed to infufe virtue and holinefs into our hearts; and his promifes are the copies of his decree.   The

The promises muſt be viewed as abſolute, or evidential. The abſolute promiſes put grace into the heart: the evidential and deſcriptive promiſes draw grace into exerciſe.

A promiſe is a declaration that we will do ſomething for the ſervice and good of another perſon. A condition is that on which a promiſe is ſuſpended, and made to reſt; and which being performed, gives a right to the good promiſed. There are properly no conditional promiſes in the book of God; for thoſe promiſes that are made to graces and duties, ſuppoſe that God has abſolutely put grace into the heart: and wherever there is the appearance of a condition, the ſagacity of faith will quickly find out an abſolute promiſe to enable us to perform that condition.

A View of GOD's ABSOLUTE PROMISES.

I will be to them a God, and they ſhall be to me a people: they ſhall all know me from the leaſt to the greateſt: I will be merciful to their unrighteouſneſs, and their ſins and iniquities I will remember no more, Heb. viii. 10, 12. I will give them a heart to know me, that I am the Lord, and they ſhall be my people, and I will be their God; for they ſhall return unto me with their whole heart, Jer. xxiv. 7. A new heart alſo will I give you, and a new ſpirit will I put within you; and I will take away the ſtony heart out of your fleſh, and I will give you a heart of fleſh, and I will put my ſpirit within you, Ezek. xxxvi. 26. xi. 19. I will not turn away from them to do them good: I will put my fear in their hearts, that they ſhall not depart from me: yea, I will rejoice over them to do them good, with my whole heart, and with my whole ſoul, Jer. xxxii. 38, 41. The Lord thy God will circumciſe thy heart, to love the Lord thy God with all thine heart, and with all thy ſoul, that thou mayeſt live, Deut. xxx. 6. I will bleſs thee, and thou ſhalt be a bleſſing. I will bleſs them that

bleſs

blefs thee, and curfe him that curfeth thee, Gen. xii.
2, 3.   I will not leave thee 'till I have done that
which I fpoke to thee of, Gen. xxviii. 15.   Thou
faidft I will do thee good, Gen. xxxii. 12.   I will do
you no hurt, Jer. xxv. 6.

Ye fhall be a peculiar treafure to me above all
people, Exod. xix 5.   Thy fhoes fhall be iron and
brafs, and as thy days, fo fhall thy ftrength be, Deut.
xxxiii. 25.   The eternal GOD is thy refuge, and un-
derneath are the everlafting arms, ver. 27. Let them
that love him be as the fun when he goeth forth in his
might, Judg. v. 31.   I will be with thee; I will not
fail thee, nor forfake thee.   Be ftrong and of a good
courage, Jofh. i. 5, 6.   I will never never leave thee: I
will not; I will not; I will not forfake thee, Ου μη σε ανω,
ουδ' ου μη σε εγκαταλιπω, Heb. xiii. 5.   The righteous
fhall hold on his way; and he that hath clean hands
fhall be ftronger and ftronger, Job xvii. 9.   He with-
draweth not his eyes from the righteous, Job xxxvi. 7.
Whatfoever he doth fhall profper, Pfal. i. 3.   Thou
wilt prepare their heart, and caufe thine ear to hear,
Pfal. x. 17.   I will inftruct thee, and teach thee in
the way which thou fhalt go; I will guide thee with
mine eye, Pfal. xxxii. 8.   No evil fhall befall thee,
neither fhall any plague come nigh thy dwelling,
Pfal. xci. 10.

EVIDENTIAL PROMISES.

Thefe evidential or defcriptive promifes are made
to diftinct graces and duties.   They are wifely contrived to mark out the character of true Chriftians;
to fhew the neceffity of the diligent ufe of the means
of grace; to bring us to a continual dependance upon
GOD the Holy Spirit: to roufe us to a vigorous exercife of all grace, and draw us to a generous performance of all duties to GOD and man; with dignity
and chearfulnefs.   Afk and it fhall be given you:
feek

feek and ye fhall find: knock and it fhall be opened unto you, Matt. vii. 7.   Seek firft the kingdom of God and his righteoufnefs, and all things fhall be added unto you, Matt. vi. 33.   How much more fhall your heavenly Father give the Holy Spirit to them that afk him, Luke xi. 13.   The Comforter, the Holy Ghoft, fhall teach you all things, and bring all things to your remembrance, John xiv. 26.   He that loveth me fhall be loved of my Father, and I will love him, and will manifeft myfelf to him, John xiv. 21.   If a man love me he will keep my words, and my Father will love him, and we will come unto him, and make our abode with him, ver. 23.   Becaufe he hath fet his love upon me, therefore will I deliver him: I will fet him on high, becaufe he hath known my name: he fhall call upon me and I will anfwer him.   I will be with him in trouble: I will deliver him, and honour him, Pfal. xci. 14, 15.   I drew them with cords of a man, with bands of love, Hof. xi. 4.   All that the Father giveth me, fhall come to me, and him that cometh to me, I will in no wife caft out, παν ο διδωσι μοι ο πατηρ, προς εμε ηξει και τον ερχομενον προς με ου μη εκβαλω εξω, John vi. 37.   No man can come to me except the Father draw him, ver. 44.   If any man lack wifdom, let him afk it of God that giveth to all men liberally and upbraideth not, and it fhall be given him, James i. 5.   I counfel thee to buy of me gold tried in the fire, Rev. iii. 18.

THREATENINGS and TERRORS of GOD againft all Kinds of VICE.

A Threatening is a denunciation of natural evil; i. e. pain, fhame, and death, on account of moral evil committed againft God.   Guilt is an offence againft the law, and an obligation to punifhment for that offence.   Punifhment is natural evil inflicted for moral evil acted againft God.

1. If

1. If any man worſhip the beaſt, and receive his mark, the ſame ſhall drink of the wine of the wrath of GOD, which is poured out without mixture into the·cup of his indignation, and he ſhall be tormented with fire and brimſtone, Rev. xiv. 10.

2. The wicked ſhall be turned into hell, and all the nations that forget GOD, Pſal. ix. 17.

3. Conſider this, ye that forget GOD, leſt I tear you in pieces, and there be none to deliver, Pſal. l. 22.

4. With GOD is terrible majeſty, Job xxxvii. 22.

5. Sinners in Zion are afraid. Who among us ſhall dwell with devouring fire? Who among us ſhall dwell with everlaſting burnings? Iſai. xxxiii. 14.

6. There is no peace, ſaith my GOD, to the wicked, Iſai. lvii. 21.

7. For in the hand of the LORD is a cup, and the wine is red: it is full of mixture, and he poureth out of the ſame; but the dregs thereof all the wicked of the earth ſhall wring them out, and drink them, Pſal. lxxv. 8.

8. Upon the wicked he ſhall rain ſnares, fire, and brimſtone; and an horrible tempeſt: this ſhall be the portion of their cup, Pſal. xi. 6.

9. Can thine heart endure, or can thy hands be ſtrong in the day that I ſhall deal with thee? I the LORD have ſpoken it, and will do it, Ezek. xxii. 14.

10. Thou ſhall not be purged from thy filthineſs any more, till I have cauſed my fury to reſt upon thee, Ezek. xxiv. 13.

11. How can ye eſcape the damnation of hell? Matt. xxiii. 33.

12. That they all may be damned who believe not the truth, 2 Theſſ. ii. 12.

Having viewed the *abſolute* promiſes of GOD, which infuſe grace into the heart by the agency of the Holy Spirit; and the *evidential* promiſes which draw grace and virtue into action; and having viewed the threatenings

enings and terrors of divine juftice againft all fin and vice, let us clofe our fketch of the fyftem of moral philofophy, with a profpect of the final mifery of vice, and the final happinefs of virtue; 'and then proceed to confider Hervey as a found and judicious divine.

VICE is HELL; or the final mifery of the vicious and wicked.

Vice is always attended with torment: it is always followed by tortures of mind and body: it is the fanction of GOD's natural law: that like caufes fhould produce like effects in the moral world. This is a noble idea, which is not enough attended to by the rifing generation of young preachers, and young people in general. " That moral evil, which is fin, fhall always produce natural evil, which is pain; and moral good, which is true virtue, fhall always produce natural good, which is pleafure, or eafe of mind, health of body, and a fine flow of fpirits and joy. This grand law of nature Hervey knew to the very bottom, and could difplay as well as any man upon earth.

Vice is torment of confcience, or painful feelings in the underftanding and memory, arifing from a fenfe of an offence againft the law of GOD in our nature.

Confcience is that knowledge which a man hath of his own actions with relation to a law; and from a violation of this law: a confcioufnefs of offence will immediately take place, and painful fenfations will arife in the mind. This will be attended with a fenfe of GOD's hatred, or his will to difunite himfelf from the criminal: his hatred or will to punifh, includes three ideas; an hatred of averfion; an hatred of oppofition; and hatred of profecution; all which exift in GOD the SON, the Judge of the world. From a fenfe of GOD's hatred of vice, there arifes in the foul, an hatred of GOD, fettled into malice, or a fixed

Z   habit.

habit and averſion; oppoſition, and perſecution. This is attended with eternal hardneſs of heart, or an inflexible reſolve never to relent or yield to the will of God to eternity.

Vice likewiſe iſſues in black deſpair, and wild impatience, at the loſs of all good; never to be regained; impoſſible to be reſtored.

Vice feels the torture of raging deſires for eaſe, never gratified; ardently wiſhing for a drop of pleaſure, but never for one moment indulged. Deſire and utter diſappointment, are the tormenting pains of vicious loſt ſpirits in the inviſible eternity.

Vice feels the moſt vexing envy at all happy ſouls in heaven and earth. Envy is pain at ſeeing other perſons happier than ourſelves: envy is pain felt at the ſight of excellence, at the ſame time that we know we are far below that excellence, and never can ariſe to it, but ſhall be ſinking lower and lower to eternity, although our eyes and our pride hate the conviction; and we feel the keeneſt hatred of another man for his happineſs or ſucceſs in virtue. This is a lively and true idea of the torments of the damned in hell, eſpecially if we add another thought.

Vice dreads every hour new tortures, and hath horrible fears of freſh puniſhments burſting in upon the ſoul from the holy juſtice and diſpleaſure of God.

Now place all theſe thoughts in one view, and you have a clear and extenſive idea of hell. Torture and remorſe of conſcience, a ſenſe of the hatred of God, and his dreadful anger; a bitter hatred of the perſon of Christ; ſettled into malice, the malice of averſion, the malice of oppoſition, the malice of perſecution, eternal hardneſs of heart, and inflexible obſtinacy in vice and wickedneſs—black deſpair of mercy; and wild impatience at the loſs of all good—raging deſires after eaſe, never gratified—vexing envy

at

at the welfare and happinefs of others, and hourly dread of new tortures from an angry GOD, never to be appeafed in his wrath: never to be altered in his will to punifh a defperate and impenitent finner againft GOD.

Thefe are the motives addreffed to the fears, and terrors, and horrors, of an immortal foul, to deter it from vice, and roufe, and fting, and ftorm the foul to virtue. Thefe operated powerfully on the mind of Hervey for eight years *, till more generous fprings and principles took place in his fublime and exalted foul, which leads us by an eafy tranfition to obferve.

VIRTUE IS HEAVEN; that is, the final happinefs of the righteous to all eternity.

VIRTUE infpires peace of confcience. Peace is a fenfe of pure friendfhip with GOD. Friendfhip is a fweet attraction of the heart between two perfons, inclining each perfon to promote mutually their in-tereft, honour, and happinefs. Such a friendfhip fubfifts between GOD the SON, and every believer in the world. Such a friendfhip fubfifted between the immortal Hervey and his divine and glorious RE-DEEMER, the LORD JEHOVAH JESUS CHRIST: in CHRIST his life was hid: CHRIST was his glory: his tongue fpoke his praife; his pen proclaimed his boundlefs perfections, and his whole life and deport-ment declared his Godlike temper and actions.

VIRTUE is attended with a fenfe of GOD's love; a perfuafion that GOD the SON ardently defires an union of his heart with us, and our heart with him: that GOD hath a love of good-will, and a love of delight: that his felf-fprung love rejoices over us to do us good with his whole heart, and his whole foul.

VIRTUE is a fettled delight in the perfon of GOD the SON. Delight is a compound paffion; made up

* From 1733, to 1741.

of

of love and joy. We have already obferved, that
Delight is the queen bee in the hive of human
paffions, whofe voice and tone governs all the reft.
Nothing doth fo attach the foul to the perfon of
CHRIST, as an intenfe, unbounded, and eternal
delight.

VIRTUE fweetens the temper, and foftens the paffions of the foul. As vice poifons and embitters all
the great paffions, and transforms us into the temper
of devils, fo virtue purifies, refines, and exalt all
the fineft feelings and emotions of the foul, and
transforms us into the likenefs of angels and of GOD ;
and never did I fee, in any creature, fo lively a
refemblance of CHRIST, as in this glorious and immortal man, fcholar, Chriftian, and divine.

VIRTUE iffues in unbounded joy. Joy is a great
quantity of pleafure. Pleafure is agreeable fenfation, arifing from the prefence of the pureft good.

VIRTUE is joy in the Being of a GOD: it is pleafure in the effence and attributes of GOD: it is delight in all our relations and connexions with GOD:
it is an high joy in all our obligations to our Creator,
Preferver, Governor, Benefactor, Judge, and Redeemer: it is pleafure of mind to feel the influence
of GOD the SPIRIT in his phyfical, moral, and gracious operations on the human underftanding, will,
and affections.

VIRTUE is pleafed at the happinefs of millions of
immortal fouls equally with ourfelves: and in this
Hervey was a glorious pattern of unbounded benevolence.

Socinian principles are cruel to the fouls of all
mankind: there is no benevolence in the whole
fyftem of Socinianifm: it makes no provifion for
the fure falvation of one foul, in all the world:
but we can prove that it doth infallibly ruin the
whole human race. That fcheme, which is ufually
ftiled CALVINISM, detached from the errors of

Calvin,

Calvin, and purged intirely from the fpirit of perfecution.   I fay this fyftem of religion is the only
fcheme in the world that has any mercy, good-will,
or generofity in it; and thefe two affertions I am
ready to demonftrate in the face of the whole world.
The proof is ready at any time, but it is too
copious to be inferted in this part of our Friend's
character, he himfelf was a living evidence of the
truth.

Virtue expects greater and better things from
God the Redeemer every day; and every hour of
life.

Frefh fountains of divine knowledge: new impreffions of grace and holinefs: fweet fprings of joy
burfting out of the heart of God, to enlighten,
beautify, and refrefh the happy fouls of all thofe who
are made perfect in virtue; and whofe underftandings are full of light to fee Christ in his higheft
glory: whofe wills and affections are fixed on
Christ, as the fupreme good and beauty for ever
and ever.

Thus you fee that moral Philosophy, viewed in
Christ, is not impietas in artis formam redac-
ta, which is the juft cenfure of Dr. Cotton Mather
on all our dry, fpiritlefs, deiftical fyftems of moral
philofophy.   (See my Edition of Dr. Cotton Mather's Student and Preacher, page 40) but morality,
as flowing from Christ: as arifing from. union with
Christ; as animated by the fpirit of Christ, and
directed by the precepts and example of Christ, is
a glorious fyftem, full of light, life, and beauty.

Let us place all thefe thoughts in one view, in
order to have a clear and extenfive conception of the
virtue and glory of heaven, or the final happinefs of
the virtuous.

Peace of confcience, and ferenity of underftanding:
a fenfe of God the Redeemer's love or will to make
me happy: a fettled delight in Christ's perfon and
offices:

offices : a fweetnefs of temper, and foftnefs of paffions : unbounded joy in the fitnefs and fulnefs, the
power and beauty of Christ : eafe in all the powers;
and pleafures in all the affections : joy to fee other
virtuous fouls as happy as ourfelves : and feeling high
fatisfaction in their eternal felicity.

Expecting new profpects of God every hour, and
new joys every moment of life through eternity.

The CHARACTER of HERVEY as a DIVINE.

I write what I know to be truth, and I will make
no apology for a moft free and faithful declaration of
the great principles of his faith.

No man loved truth with more ardor and honefty :
and no man was more cautious againft every error in
all the grand articles of his religion.

He believed the exiftence of one living and true
God, the firft caufe of all worlds : the Sovereign
Lord of the fouls of all mankind : the Supreme
Good to all real Chriftians, and the Laft End of the
whole univerfe.

A man has nothing to do but to open his eyes;
and on the firft glance of common fenfe, he muft
fee marks of defign in the world around him : and
in the ftructure of his own body and foul, he fees ten
thoufand evidences of the exiftence of a God.

The cleareft and beft method of demonftration of
the divine exiftence, is to confider the agreement of
all the objects in the vifible world with the idea of a
God; and for this grand purpofe Hervey had as keen
a tafte, and as good a genius, as any man upon earth.
He had an enthufiaftic fondnefs for the beauties of
creation ; and when he fat for his picture to Mr. John
Michael Williams, in the year 1751, he chofe this for
his motto, *Quælibet Herba Deum.* Every vegetable
fhews a God; and he found it the eafieft way of difplaying God to the rifing generation.

By

By that glorious power of common fenfe, he faw in a moment the Being of a God. He faw with eafe the amazing extent of the vifible univerfe, and that the wonders of SPACE agree with the idea of a God.

He faw that fpace had three apparent attributes of God. Eternity; for when did fpace begin to exift? Immutability; for who ever knew any change in fpace? Omniprefence; for can it be excluded or fhut out from any part of the univerfe?

And yet fpace is not God: and God is not fpace: nor will any man of common fenfe affert that fpace is God; but it agrees in its wonderful properties with our idea of a God: and the myfteries of fpace have puzzled all the powers of a Newton: and will puzzle all the keeneft Philofophers to the end of the world. I defy the moft piercing mind to explain all the wonders of fpace: the chief ufe of fpace, is to confound and mortify human pride.

He faw by the firft glance of common fenfe, the aftonifhing magnitude, and the amazing minutenefs of millions of creatures: and that all thefe agree with the idea of a God.

MOUNTAINS, and rocks, and globes, and worlds, down to a grain of fand; a particle of duft, even to the laft divifion of matter.

TREES, from the lofty cedar of Lebanon, of ninety feet in circumference, down to the hyffop that groweth on the wall.

BIRDS, from the tall oftrich of ten feet high, to the little humming bird, which weighs a few grains.

BEASTS, from the monftrous elephant, down to the mites which are but juft difcernible, as fpecks of animated exiftence.

FISHES, from the mountainous whale of an hundred feet in length, to the fmall minnow, the anchovy, and the diminutive fprat.

REPTILES, from the enormous rattle-fnake, to the fmall eels in vinegar and four pafte, which are not feen without a microfcope. In-

INSECTS, without number, and without end; which furpafs all numeration, and defy all defcription. All thefe agree with the idea of a GOD; and all poured their evidence of a divine exiftence into Hervey's admiring underftanding and enraptured foul.

The aftonifhing numbers, and amazing variety of creatures in unbounded fpace, agrees clearly with the idea of a GOD.

Are there not above one hundred and fifty kinds of quadrupeds, or four-footed beafts, wild and tame ?

Are there not above five hundred kinds of birds, all claffified by their beaks; and do not thefe agree with the idea of a GOD ?

Are there not unknown numbers of all kinds of fifhes ; and thefe claffified by their fins and perpendicular or horizontal tails; and do not they all agree with the idea of a GOD ?

The immenfe number and variety of fhell fifh, exceed all computation; and is not their exquifite beauty a ftriking demonftration of a GOD?

Are there not above fixteen thoufand kinds of plants, trees, and flowers, in twenty-four claffes, and about one hundred and twenty orders; and do not all thefe agree with the idea of a moft wife and powerful GOD?

Does not the great philofopher, RAY, reckon there are twenty thoufand different kinds of Infects ; and do they not, in their admirable beauty, agree with the idea of a GOD ?

Who can reckon up all the Reptiles and Serpents in their unbounded variety ! but do they not all agree with the idea of a wife, powerful, great and omniprefent GOD ?

Doth not that great promoter of fcience, and moft amiable genius, Mr. GEORGE ADAMS, of Fleet-ftreet, in his excellent Treatife on Aftronomy, obferve, that it is now agreed, by the greateft men in Europe, that

there

there are reckoned to be about feventy-five millions of fixed ftars in the whole univerfe, or concave of the heavens? that is to fay, funs, for they all fhine by their own light like our fun. Now only ftand ftill and confider the wondrous works of God! Job xxxvii. 14. Confider, ponder, paufe, wonder, tremble, and adore, on the furvey of fo many funs, and probably every one as big or bigger than our fun; and all agree that his magnitude is SEVEN HUNDRED thoufand miles in diameter. Now only think, till your under-ftanding is quite wearied out and overwhelmed, and drowned and loft: fay within yourfelf, what do I fee? what do I contemplate? Seventy-five times ten hundred thoufand funs, and each of them feven hundred thoufand miles in diameter; all fhining maffes of fire: letters and words written in characters of light, and all agreeing with the idea of a moft wife, omnipotent, bountiful, ever active, and ever prefent God.

Now, who can view with an eye of common fenfe, all thefe aftonifhing numbers of creatures, beafts, birds, fifhes, fhell fifhes, plants, trees, flowers, in-fects, reptiles, and ferpents; planets, moons, comets, and fixed ftars; or funs, in the vaft unbounded fpace! I fay, who? What man of common fenfe can fur-vey all thefe wonders, and not confefs that ALL thefe objects agree with the idea of a God! And who but a fworn atheift will not admire, adore, and praife this great, and good, and moft beautiful boun-tiful God!

Great and moft excellent JEHOVAH, thou Creator and Redeemer of loft mankind, thy fervant HERVEY faw thee in every object; admired thy works of beauty, and praifed thee as that dear and immortal Friend, on whom he every moment depended for the felicities of his genius, and immortal happinefs.

HERVEY darted the eye of his redeemed underftand-ing into God and gravitation, with invincible force and vivid fire!

A a

Gravi-

Gravitation is a force impreſſed on all bodies; by which they mutually attract, or tend towards each other, according to the quantity of matter they contain; and in proportion to their diſtances.

He underſtood this grand fundamental principle of all philoſophy better than moſt ſcholars in the learned world.

And as CHRIST had redeemed his genius, imagination and taſte, from depravity and pollution; he devoted them all to the glory of his divine Friend, Redeemer, and GOD.

He ſaw GOD with every glimpſe of his reaſon; and catched fire at every diſcovery of his Friend.

HERVEY ſaw, by the force of his underſtanding, that this grand ſimple principle of gravitation, accounts for the regular motion of the planets, ſo neceſſary to the beauty and order of the viſible world—that gravitation accounts for the preſſure of the air, ſo uſeful to the preſervation of all animal life—that gravitation accounts for the aſcent of vapours, and their deſcent, when collected and condenſed, in refreſhing rains—that gravitation accounts for the perpetual flux of rivers; for the ebbing and flowing of the ſea and oceans—that gravitation accounts for the ſtability of the earth, ſupporting innumerable living creatures, with all convenient furniture, for their accommodation—that gravitation is the foundation of all human mechanical arts, without which life would not be tolerable—that gravitation accounts for the growth of all vegetables and animals.

But this ſimple cauſe, productive of ſo many important appearances in nature, he always attributed to GOD the SON, as the firſt mover; as his work; for it is not to be explained, without having recourſe to the power and will of the great REDEEMER.

It is evidently an active force, and therefore cannot be aſcribed to matter, which is wholly and eſſentially inactive; and whatever appearance of action it
has,

has, can only be by the contact of its superficial parts;
whereas the force of gravity penetrates to the center
of all bodies, and affects them at the greatest distance:
therefore it must be the immediate operation of the
first cause himself; for what agent can act every where,
except God the Father, Son, and Holy Spirit?

Let us resume the views of Hervey's darting all the
force and fire of his vast understanding into the grand
laws, by which the immortal God governs the world:
that is to say, the law of universal gravitation, which
God has commanded all bodies to observe: the beautiful law of the planets, describing equal areas in equal
times; and the grand law first discovered by John
Kepler, "that the squares of the periodical times are
"in a wise proportion to the cubes of the distances
"of all the planets from the sun, which is the grand
"center of all their motions."

1. MERCURY.

His period is 88 days. His distance from the sun
is 36,000,000 of miles. His velocity 109,000 miles
per hour. His diameter is 3000 miles. The sun
is 26,000,000 times bigger than Mercury.

2. VENUS.

Her period around the sun is 224 days. Her distance from the sun is 68,000,000 miles. Her velocity is 80,000 miles an hour. Diameter near 8,000
miles.

3. OUR EARTH.

Her period is 365 days. Her distance 95,000,000
miles. Her velocity annual 1,000 miles per minute. Her diurnal velocity 1,000 miles an hour.
Her diameter 7,970 miles.

4. MARS.

His period round the sun is 686 days. His distance
from the sun is 140,000,000 miles. His diameter

is 4000 miles. His velocity round the fun 55,000 miles per hour.

5. JUPITER.

His period round the fun is 4,332 days, or near twelve years. His diſtance from the fun 494,000,000 miles. His velocity round the fun is 22,000 miles per hour. His diameter is 94,000 miles.

6. SATURN.

His period round the fun is 29 years and 167 days. Diſtance from the fun is 900,000,000 miles. His diameter 78,000 miles. His velocity round the fun is 22,000 miles per hour.

7. GEORGIUM SIDUS

Was diſcovered by Dr. Herſchell in the year 1781. His period is 83 years. His diſtance 1,800,000,000 miles.

N. B. This grand diſcovery of the Herſchell planet, was made March 13th, 1781, by the firſt aſtronomer in the world, Dr. Herſchell, at Windſor.

HERVEY ſaw, with unbounded admiration, and the moſt ſublime delight to his imagination and paſſions, the three grand laws by which GOD governs the whole beautiful ſtructure of the univerſe; and theſe are, the law of univerſal gravitation mentioned before; and the harmony between the times and diſtances, with reſpect to all the planets and their moons; and likewiſe the third beautiful law, that the planets deſcribe equal areas, in equal times, in all parts of their periods: and theſe THREE LAWS GOD has kept up, in their full force and glory, for near ſix thouſand years.

Theſe three laws are the great foundations on which Sir Iſaac Newton's Natural Philoſophy is built, and they will endure till GOD ſhall burn the univerſe, and deſtroy the viſible creation.

With

With refpect to that grand law, "that the fquares "of the periodical times of all the planets are as the "cubes of their diftances," let us a little farther give a clear explanation and illuftration of it, for the entertainment of my young readers, who have an inquifitive mind, and love to have their underftandings conducted into the knowledge of the nobleft truths in NATURAL PHILOSOPHY.

VENUS revolves round the fun in 224 days. The earth revolves round the fun in 365 days. The diftance of the earth from the fun is ninety-five millions of miles. Hence, according to Kepler, as the fquare of 365 is to the fquare of 224, fo is the cube of ninety-five millions of miles to a fourth number, which is the cube of Venus's diftance from the fun: and if the cube root of this number be found, it will give about fixty-eight millions of miles for her real diftance; fo that by this rule, if the times of the periodical revolutions of the planets be known, and the diftance of any one of them from the fun, the diftances of all the reft may be determined by a fimple proportion, or the golden rule of three direct*; and this rule is not only applicable to the planets, but it is alfo equally true with refpect to their fatellites, or attendants. The moons of Jupiter and Saturn are found to follow the fame law in revolving round their primaries, as is obferved by thofe primaries in revolving round the fun. Thefe are the difcoveries by which Kepler enriched the fcience, and obtained an immortality of renown to all ages in the world. This great philofopher was born at Wiel, in the Dutchy of Wirtemberg, in Germany, on the 27th of December, 1571. He

---

* Every ingenious young perfon who can readily work the golden rule, or rule of three direct, may foon learn to extract the fquare and cube root in the common method; but the roots are extracted with much more eafe and elegance by the ufe of Logarithms.

Read that moft excellent Treatife of Arithmetic, recommended by that confummate mathematician, HumphryDitton---the author, John Hill, page 214---236. By Logarithms, page 213---321.

died

died on the 15th of November, 1631, in the 59th year of his age.

Let us ftand ftill and review the underftanding and the pleafures of this great man Hervey: he had a foul feelingly alive to every fine impulfe of beauty in the whole creation of GOD.

If we confider the amazing extent of the whole creation, it gives us a notion of power incomprehenfible in the production and prefervation of the univerfe. The limits of creation are to us, and to every created mind, unfearchable: its extent is beyond all the power of fight which we have or can have from the affiftance of the beft telefcopes.

The diftance from the earth to the fun is prodigioufly greater than any man can conceive, who is unacquainted with aftronomy; and yet how vaft foever this diftance is, it is very inconfiderable, in comparifon of the diftance from the fixed ftars which are vifible to our naked eye: and yet more fo in comparifon of thofe which are fo remote, as not to be feen without the beft glaffes: and how many more there may be which by reafon of their vaftly greater diftance are invifible, we cannot guefs, though we have reafon to believe them to be an inconceivable number; and thefe being all funs to fo many fyftems of other planets attending them, muft require fuch an immenfe fpace for their feveral revolutions, without interfering with one another, as tranfcends all human conception to imagine*.

HERVEY had a clear fenfe of the prodigious number and variety of creatures contained in this unbounded fpace, and he had a power to feel pleafure from this

* When I vifited Dr. Herfchell, May 9th, 1785, at his houfe in Datchet, near Windfor, he affured me that he had feen, with his grand telefcope, 116,000 ftars in the fpace of fifteen minutes. He has likewife obferved, in his letter to the Royal Society, that the Georgium Sidus, or the new planet, which he difcovered, is eighteen hundred millions of miles diftant from the fun. This is but the femi-diameter of its orbit, confequently its whole diameter is thirty-fix hundred millions of miles.

clear

clear sense of their variety: he was feelingly alive to the wisdom and contrivance of that GOD, whose understanding was equal to that infinite power that produced them.

When he took a view only of this earth, with which he was best acquainted, as having the nearest means of knowing it, which is but a point in comparison of the universe, what an amazing variety did it afford him: under the earth, how many kinds of fossils, stones, gems, minerals, and metals: upon the surface, what an incredible number of vegetables, trees, plants, shrubs, grasses, with their several distinct seeds, leaves, flowers, and fruits: upon the earth, in the waters and in the air, how many thousand sorts or tribes of animals of different bulk and figure; beasts, birds, fishes, reptiles, and insects: and if the various kinds are so many, how many millions are the individuals of each kind! it may also be observed, that there is a wonderful variety among the individuals of the same species. Even in several nations of mankind, there is an incredible diversity as to colour, stature, and language; but we have a most striking instance of the wisdom of GOD in that inimitable variety in the faces of men, of which not one of so many thousands and millions is so like another, as not to be easily distinguished.

If we extend our thoughts and views farther, and consider that the number of fixed stars, especially since the improvement of telescopes, is not so much pretended to be guessed at, and that the planets about them may be replenished with creatures, both animate and inanimate, as different in kind as they are distant in place from those with which we are acquainted, is very probable; and there may be as many more kinds of them, and as many more individuals of each kind, as the places they are lodged in will contain. What an astonishing multiplication of their number and variety will this then amount to: it is here the excess of

power,

power, and wifdom, fo infinitely beyond our capacity, and not the want of it, which dazzles our underftanding, as the exceffive light of the fun blinds our eyes.

Hervey faw with intuitive rapidity of perception, or an underftanding feelingly alive: he difcerned with rapture and admiration the exquifite minutenefs of millions of creatures, and the feveral parts of which each diftinct creature, either animate or inanimate, is compofed: this heightened his admiration of the infinite fkill of God, who framed them. There are ten thoufand millions of entire and perfect animals endued with life and motion, fo very fmall, that they cannot eafily be difcerned by the naked eye; and yet, by the help of good microfcopes, are difcovered to have their feveral organical parts as curioufly framed, and fitted to their feveral motions and ufes, as thofe monftrous animals, an elephant fifteen feet high, or a whale an hundred feet long. And how furprifingly fmall muft thofe parts be, fingly taken, in a fmall creature, when a compounded body made up of fo great a number, is hardly big enough to be vifible. The like may be faid for the fine texture of the minute parts of larger animals, and even of plants, and all diftinct kinds of vegetables, of which the firft ftamina are fo fmall as to be imperceptible to our unaffifted fenfes. And even the moft fimple, and feemingly lefs compounded bodies, of how infinitely fmall particles do they confift ? Who can, by his fenfes, difcover the figure of the conftituent parts of fluids, which yet are not fo clofely united, but that there is much vacuity between them? Who can difcern the texture of the parts of water, which makes it fo difficult to be compreffed by any human force? Or whoever faw the particles of air and wind, which, though compreffible, yet how great is their force of refiftance? So that the *minima naturæ* are as much beyond our capacities to difcover, as the magnitude of the univerfe.

What

What an infinite wifdom then muſt it be, how intenſe, as well as extenſive, which at once ſo intimately reaches, and ſo accurately manages, both
theſe extremes.

HERVEY had a clear ſenſe of the beauty of creation, with a power to feel pleaſure from that beauty.
Beauty is that quality in objects which excites love.
A man cannot open his eyes and think like a man,
but he muſt perceive the beauty, order, and regularity, of every diſtinct ſpecies of things; and the
more a man exerciſes the power of common ſenſe,
the accuracy of the divine underſtanding will more
brightly appear. Though the number of GOD's
works be ſo incomprehenſibly great, and their kinds
ſo various, yet each of them ſingly is directed, fitted
up, and finiſhed, with as much ſkill and exactneſs,
as if it were the only thing attended to. Every one
of the creatures is wrought with more art and curio-
ſity, than the moſt ſkilful human artiſt can attain to
imitate, though he were to ſpend all his time and
pains upon a ſmall piece of work. What our bleſſed SAVIOUR ſays of the flowers of the field, *that
even Solomon, in all his glory, was not arrayed like one
of theſe*, is no hyperbolical expreſſion. The moſt
curious poliſhing, gilding, or painting of human art,
cannot vie with that of ſome ſmall inſects, ſeeds,
and flowers.—The moſt curious works of art, the
ſharpeſt fineſt needle, doth appear as a blunt rough
bar of iron, coming from the furnace or the forge:
the moſt accurate engravings or emboſſments, ſeem
ſuch rude bungling deformed works, as if they had
been done by a mattock or a trowel.

So vaſt a difference is there between the ſkill of
nature and the rudeneſs and imperfection of art. See
Biſhop Wilkins's Principles and Duties of Religion,
Book I. Chap. v.i. Nor is the order, regularity, and
proportion conſtantly obſerved in the ſeveral parts
of the viſible creation, leſs to be admired than the

beauty and elegance of each work, that fo many degrees of creatures, animate and inanimate, fhould be
always conftantly kept in their proper rank; fo that
they appear to be the fame in their inftincts, through
all generations, notwithftanding every thing appears
in perpetual motion, is utterly repugnant to the nature of chance, and muft evince a wife GOD, that
orders all things in number, weight, and meafure.

The harmonious correfpondence of each part of
nature to each other part, fhews a comprehenfive
wifdom that has one entire view of all things at
once; fuch a fkill as hath no occafion to mend or
new model one part of its work to make it fit for
another, but which makes both great and fmall parts
anfwer one another fo exactly, that notwithftanding
all the various motions and directions of motion in
the world, there is no diforder or difturbance created
by it in the whole, but every part and every motion
of that part is every way as well preferved, as if all
the reft had been particularly defigned for that only:
and though we can never be able to difcover all the
ufes and defigns for which every particular part of
the creation was made, or to which it ferves, yet
from what we can difcover, we may reafonably conclude, that every part has its ufe in the whole, and
that every thing is wifely fuited to fome excellent
purpofe or other, though we cannot find it out.

In every part of nature, of which we have any
tolerable acquaintance, even from the vaft heavenly bodies, as the fun, moon, and planets, down
to the fmalleft infect on earth, we may obferve one
thing fuited to another with a moft exact and beautiful fitnefs; fo that we are forced to fay, all nature is
but one mighty work of one almighty and all-wife
GOD. But then that there is a goodnefs as well as
wifdom and power fhewn in the formation of all
things, does more evidently appear from the animal
and rational part of the world, which being endued
with

with fenfation, are capable of pleafure and fatisfaction, as all creatures which have animal life are in different degrees, for they all rejoice in their powers of fenfation and perception, and are well pleafed with their own exiftence. No man had a more forcible conception of the wifdom, power, and goodnefs of God, in the creation of the animal and rational parts of the world, and in giving them the fenfations of pleafure in the fruition of good, than the author of the Meditation on the Flower Garden, and the Defcant upon Creation. This great and good man entered into the moft fublime contemplations on the curious ftructure of fo many different fpecies of animals; and he obferved how exactly they were fitted in their outward make and figure, as well as inward difpofitions and inftincts to their ftates and conditions of life, and what fuitable provifion is made for their fatisfaction, as well as for their prefervation, continuance, and propagation of their feveral kinds. He could not but admire the bounty as well as the wifdom of Providence. How aftonifhing is the diftinction of fexes in all animals, that being the means by which the fpecies is continued, and the due proportion of the numbers of each fex to the other fex, which has been conftantly kept up from the beginning. This quite deftroys all fuppofition of fpontaneous generation; even in leffer animals, and fhews the abfurdity of thinking that any real animal, and efpecially mankind, could ever be produced by CHANCE, or a cafual motion, and concourfe of atoms, of which they confift.

We may farther take notice of the exquifite formation and difpofition of the feveral organs of fenfe, as the eye, the ear, the tafte, the noftrils, the nerves, ramified through the whole body, for the purpofes of feeling; and with what wonderful contrivance and nicety they are adapted in every creature to their proper bufinefs and manner of life; and though they are fo curious, and

of

of so fine a structure, yet how well they are guarded
against any thing that may hurt or annoy them.
These things are displayed with all the charms of
eloquence, by Mr. Hervey himself, in his twelfth
Dialogue, on the wonderful structure of the human
body.

HERVEY saw, with a clear understanding, that
GOD is a Being infinitely good, the wise and powerful cause of the universe. He saw with a Godlike
mind, that the planets receive all their light and
heat from the body of the sun, and that this is a
glorious evidence of infinite wisdom, power, and
goodness; therefore consummate prudence, and not
wild chance, nor blind fate, made this constitution
of things.

He saw that a compound force is the cause of the
revolution of the planets around the sun, and that
this force, which is called the centrifugal and centri-
petal motion, is a most striking mark of intelligence
and design.

He saw that space is perfectly a void; that there is
nothing to resist or retard; nothing to guide or divert
the motion of the planetary worlds; and this is an
astonishing evidence of the wisdom and power of
GOD.   He clearly discerned that the situation of our
earth, and its distance from the sun, is infinitely better than if it were nearer or farther off.   If the sun
was nearer we should be burnt to ashes; and if it was
farther off, we should perish with cold, and the sea
would be frozen into ice to the very bottom.

His penetrating mind knew that the earth revolves
with a double motion; that is to say, a daily motion
on its own axis, at the rate of one thousand miles per
hour; and an annual motion around the sun at the rate
of above a thousand miles a minute; that is, sixty
times faster than the diurnal motion.

HERVEY wisely compared the admirable proportion of the daily and annual motions of the earth, as
                                                    distinct

diftinct from each other; and he clearly faw, that thefe very different degrees of velocity fupplied him with abundant reafon to admire and adore the exquifite wifdom and goodnefs of God.

He confidered, with the higheft aftonifhment and delight, the admirable mode of the daily and annual motion, by the axis of the earth making an angle with the plain of the ecliptic*, the quantity of which angle is twenty-three degrees and an half. Here he faw reafon for vivid wonder and delight; becaufe by this happy contrivance we have the four feafons of the year, Spring and Summer, Autumn and Winter, with the different lengths of the days and nights through the whole year.

Hervey faw, with ardent devotion, that the atmofphere, or body of air, and the frame and face of the globe, difplayed wonderful marks of wifdom and defign, with rich evidences of abundant goodnefs and almighty power.

He confidered that the ample provifion of waters, in the oceans, feas, rivers, and fprings, wonderfully difcovered wifdom without bounds, power without limits, goodnefs without end, to the glory of an eternal and omniprefent God.

Hervey contemplated with rapture and devotion, the lofty mountains of fifteen and twenty thoufand feet high, with all the beautiful fruitful vallies, as evincing, in the moft ftriking manner, the marks of the wifdom, power, and goodnefs of a moft glorious God.

---

* It appears plain enough in the parts and model of the world, that there is a contrivance and a refpect to certain reafons and ends, how the fun is placed near the middle of our fyftem for the more convenient difpenfing of his light and influence to the planets moving about him: how the plain of the earth's equator interfects that of her orbit, and makes a proper angle with it, in order to diverfify the year, and create a ufeful variety of feafons, and the regular gradations of day and night. Thefe things, though a thoufand times repeated, will always be pleafing meditations to good men and true fcholars.—See Religion of Nature, by William Wollafton, Efq. 4to. 1724.

In

In this beautiful manner HERVEY traced out the exiftence, the perfections, and the works of the moft glorious GOD; and in this manner all tutors* of divinity ought to train their pupils from the firft moment they come under their care.   This would lay a ftrong foundation on the principles of good common fenfe, on which to build the grand fuperftructure of revealed religion, and all the branches of moral virtue, which, under the influences of the bleffed SPIRIT, would not fail to make them RATIONAL Chriftians, in the richeft fenfe of the word.

We fhall now proceed to trace out Hervey's knowledge of the aftonifhing powers and affections of the human foul, with the ftriking proofs of its immortality.   We fhall view his clear conviction of the infufficiency of reafon, without revelation, to lead us to eternal happinefs.

His rich acquaintance with the nature of infpiration, and the evidences of it arifing from miracles,

---

* The learned and pious author of the Enquiry into the Nature of the Human Soul, on the Principles of Reafon and Philofophy; who is likewife the author of Matho, is a man of fuch uncommon excellence, that I have no words equal to my conceptions of his worth: and I cannot but feel an aftonifhment, mingled with contempt and indignation, at the ftupidity and ingratitude of the prefent age, which appears to know nothing of this great man, or his writings. I will not mention the name of this almoft unknown man, who deferves the efteem and veneration of the learned world, and the whole rifing generation.

There is another great man, who has been treated with the fame ingratitude and neglect: his Sixteen Sermons at Boyle's Lecture exceed almoft every thing of the kind, for clear thought, elevated conceptions, and mafculine language.   I have endeavoured to do juftice to this moft excellent author, by giving feveral pages from his Seventh Sermon of his Boylean Lectures, which muft charm every reader of true tafte, and allure him to read the whole volume, compofed by Dr. John Leng, late Bifhop of Norwich.

I am likewife indebted to another excellent author, for an eafy explanation of Kepler's Grand Law, concerning the beautiful harmony between the fquares of the times, and the cubes of the diftances of all the planets.   This is now made eafy to every ingenious youth in Great Britain, in the moft pleafing Letters on Aftronomy, by the fagacious Mr. Bonnycaftle, of the Military Academy, at Woolwich.

prophecy,

prophecy, the goodnefs of the doctrine, and the moral character of CHRIST, with his prophets and
apoftles. His views of the three Pérfons in one divine nature, arifing from the numerous plurals in the
Hebrew Bible; with the rich variety of views of the
agency of the facred Three in creation, providence,
and falvation. We fhall take a fhort furvey of his
ideas of the natural and moral perfections of GOD;
and the peculiar character of CHRIST in Scripture,
as the Son of GOD. We fhall then be able clearly to
underftand all the fubfequent articles of his faith,
from his own immortal writings.

We fhall clofe the work with a variety of pleafing
and inftructive remarks on his temper and conduct in
private life; and a concife review of his works, in
order to allure ingenuous and pious young perfons of
both fexes to an arduous and delightful imitation of
his example.

We are obliged to pafs by a thoufand other evidences of the being of a GOD, for want of room;
otherwife we fhould go through all the inftincts which
GOD hath infufed into the different claffes of birds,
beafts, and fifhes. We fhould have obferved, that
thefe inftincts have been ever the fame; the different
claffes of birds have the fame genius and manner of
life, as they had almoft fix thoufand years ago. The
beafts, both wild and tame, have the fame aptitude to
excel, in the purfuits of their food, the prefervation of
their lives from danger, and the continuation of their
fpecies: the fifhes have the fame impreffions, the
fame purfuits, and the fame methods of preferving
their lives in every part of the ocean and rivers, as
they had in the beginning of the creation.

The many thoufand kinds of reptiles and infects have the fame genius and fagacity to preferve
their lives, and continue their kind as they had at their
firft production.

The

The confideration of the famenefs of inftinct in all animals round the globe, from pole to pole, is to me, as it was to Mr. Hervey, a moft mighty demonftration of the being of a God.

Hervey had, by reading books on Natural Hiftory, and efpecially the Abbe le Pluche's Spectacle de la Nature, or Nature Difplayed, fo richly furnifhed his mind with views of animated nature, that he feemed to me to gràfp the whole creation in his underftanding. Every creature he faw, gave a frefh pleafure to his imagination, and raifed a devout and adoring thought of God his Saviour.

God had given this great and amiable man a foul above the common part of the human race: it is no extravagance or flattery to fay, that he poffeffed in his firft formation, and in all his after improvements, a vaft capacity of underftanding, to take in great and fublime ideas without pain or difficulty; a power of mind to receive new and uncommon ideas with delight, and an ability to furvey great trains of thought without confufion or diforder.

He was therefore one of the fitteft men in the world to defcribe the powers, affections, and operations of the immortal foul: and in every view of it he confidered the agreement of the idea of a foul with the idea of a God.

The objects and actions of the underftanding: the objects and actions of the will: the objects and actions of the imagination: the objects and actions of the paffions: the memory: the confcience: the genius and tafte of the foul, all clearly agree with the idea of a moft wife, powerful, and immortal God.

Hervey clearly faw that a fpiritual being, which has fuch a vaft underftanding, to take in an immenfe number of ideas of the nature, attributes, and actions of God, muft be truly immortal, and cannot be a perifhing effence. The idea of a fpirit of fuch knowledge, wonderfully agrees with the idea of a God.

God. He clearly faw that a fpiritual being, which has conceptions of eternity itfelf, and its amazing grandeur and terror, muft be immortal; and a foul which can think of eternity; that apprehends and conceives of eternity itfelf, agrees with the idea of a God.

Eternity is duration, exifting all at once without any fucceffion of moments, divided and diftinguifhed into paft, prefent, and future duration. Eternity is unfucceffive duration, incapable of being fhortened; incapable of addition, or being lengthened or growing older or younger for ever.—God's duration is effential, eternal, perfect, and immutable: he exifts all at once, and can neither grow older or younger through an infinite duration.—The idea of eternity ftruck Hervey's underftanding with the keeneft force. He thus fpeaks in his Meditations among the Tombs. O Eternity! *Eternity!* How are our boldeft, our ftrongeft thoughts loft and overwhelmed in thee! Who can fet land marks to limit thy dimenfions, or find plummets to fathom thy depths? *Arithmeticians* have figures to compute all the progreffions of time: *Aftronomers* have inftruments to calculate the diftances of the planets; but what numbers can ftate, what lines can gauge, the lengths and breadths of eternity? It is higher than heaven; what canft thou do? Deeper than hell; what canft thou know? The meafure thereof is longer than the earth, broader than the fea. Myfterious, mighty exiftence! A fum not to be leffened by the largeft *deductions!* An extent not to be contracted by all poffible *diminutions!* None can truly fay, after the moft prodigious wafte of ages, " So " much of eternity is gone." For when millions of centuries are elapfed, it is but juft commencing; and when millions more have run their ample round, it will be no nearer ending. Yea, when ages, numerous as the bloom of fpring, increafed by the leaves of autumn, and all multiplied by the drops of rain, which

C c

drown

drown the winter—when thefe, and ten thoufand times ten thoufand more—more than can be reprefented by any fimilitude, or imagined by any conception—when all thefe are revolved and finifhed, eternity, vaft boundlefs amazing eternity, will *only* be *beginning!*

HERVEY clearly faw that the idea of a foul, a rational intelligent being, which feels pain or uneafinefs at the fad defects of its own knowledge, agrees with the idea of a GOD; and a fpiritual being, which feels the tormenting defects of its own underftanding, muft be immortal.

Birds, beafts, and fifhes, foon arrive to their *ne plus ultra*, and can go no farther in the improvements of fenfe, in the fagacity of their faculties, or in their advancement in the arts of addrefs to eternity. This is the cafe with the moft fagacious creature upon earth, the elephant; all his art and fagacity is foon at an end; but man can improve in fcience, and the delicate arts and luxuries of life, through ten thoufand ages, and never come to the laft pitch of improvement. That fpiritual being, which feels that it hath not knowledge in proportion to the powers and capacities it poffeffes, muft be immortal.

And the idea of a foul, which has not knowledge of the liberal fciences, the languages, and divinity, in proportion to its vaft and aftonifhing faculties, muft agree with the idea of a GOD.

That fpirit which has a boundlefs defire after the knowledge of GOD, and which feels an inextinguifhable thirft for brighter conceptions of the divine attributes, muft be immortal.

The idea of a foul feeling an infuppreffible ardour after more knowledge every day and every hour, agrees with the idea of a GOD.

All thefe fentimental feelings were conftantly prefent with Mr. Hervey's foul every day of his life.

The

The objects and actions of the will brightly demonſtrate a God.

That being whoſe will hath for its object immenſe goodneſs, muſt be immortal; and the idea of a ſoul, whoſe object is eſſential and unbounded good, wonderfully agrees with the idea of a God.

That ſoul which is able to love and chooſe God as the ſupreme good, muſt be immortal.

The ſoul can unite itſelf to God in an eternal adheſion of the will, by the agency of the divine ſpirit: it can cleave to God in ardent inextinguiſhable love and forcible fire, therefore it muſt be immortal; it cannot but be an unperiſhing eſſence.

The idea of a ſoul that can love God with vaſt admiration and eſteem, that ardently delights in him with unbounded benevolence and gratitude, agrees with the idea of a God.

That being which hath unſatisfied deſires all through life.

Deſires of knowledge are not ſatisfied to the full; deſirës after virtue and holineſs are not fully ſatisfied; deſires after happineſs in the goodneſs of God are not fully ſatisfied.

The ſoul longs for more knowledge, for more virtue, for more holineſs, and Godlike dignity, and a more correct and delicate taſte for a happineſs in God, eternal as our exiſtence: ſuch a ſoul muſt be immortal, and the idea of ſuch a ſoul agrees with the idea of a God.

That being which acts with freedom and ſovereign dominion like a God in ten thouſand operations, muſt be unperiſhable and immortal.

The ſoul acts with amazing liberty, whether in hell or earth, or the heaven of heavens; whether as a ſinner or ſaint, as a devil or an angel, it is free in acts of ſin, madneſs, and rebellion. It is free in acts of holineſs and devotion to God: the idea of ſuch a ſoul agrees with the idea of a God.

That

That being whose will is never weakened by difeafe or age, but is moft active and vigorous in its operations, even when the body is dying in a confumption, or as weak as a child with difeafe in the agonies of death.

How clear is the underftanding to conceive of the eternity of GOD: how active and vigorous the will when on the verge of eternity, as appears by the ardour of its defires for the death of the body, and the fire of its paffions to go to GOD, when a man is holy and full of love: the idea of this wonderful being agrees with the idea of a GOD.

The OBJECTS and ACTIONS of the IMAGINATION demonftrate a GOD. This great and good man well underftood the nature and pleafures of the imagination; and no man in the European world better underftood the ufes of the imagination for the purpofes of contemplation and devotion.

Imagination is the power of receiving lively images of fenfible objects; of reprefenting, by recollection, fuch ftrong pictures of things, and giving fuch defcriptions as force the image of the object defcribed upon the mind. Thus a compleat idea of imagination confifts of three parts; a power of receiving images; a power of recollecting images; and a power of ftrongly painting images on the minds of other men.

Imagination is the fimple apprehenfion of material objects when prefent, and the power of painting the images of thofe objects to the underftanding when abfent.

Imagination is that faculty by which the mind not only reflects on its own operations, but affembles the various ideas conveyed to the underftanding by the fenfes, and treafured up in the repofitory of the memory, compounding or difjoining them at pleafure, and by its active power of inventing new affociations of ideas, and of combining them with infinite variety,

is

is enabled to prefent a bold creation of its own, and to exhibit new fcenes which never exifted in nature. As this was a favourite fubject with Mr. Hervey, let us take a farther view of the pleafures of imagination from Mr. Addifon's lively effays, in eleven papers in the Spectator, Vol. VI. No. 411—421. Mr. Addifon obferves, on the pleafures of imagination, that the perfection of our fight above our other fenfes, greatly affifts us in thefe pleafures. The pleafures of imagination arife firft of all from the eyes ; and thefe pleafures are divided under two heads, primary and fecondary ; and thefe pleafures of the imagination are in fome refpects equal, if not fuperior, to thofe of the underftanding. The extent, or vaft abundance of the pleafures of the imagination, demand our peculiar notice ; and likewife the rich and high advantages which a man of true genius and tafte receives from a relifh of thofe pleafures.

The beft ways of repeating and increafing thefe pleafures, is to ftudy all the grand images in the vifible univerfe, and to take an extenfive furvey of all the fcriptural images and hiftorical facts. Thefe views will enable us to difcern in what refpects the delicious pleafures of the imagination are preferable to the pleafures of the underftanding.

In No. 412, Mr. Addifon fhews that there are *three* fources of the pleafures of the imagination in our furvey of outward objects; that is to fay, the GREAT, the NEW, and the BEAUTIFUL. He fhews how what is great pleafes the imagination : how what is new pleafes the imagination : how what is beautiful pleafes the imagination. He treats of the beautiful in our own fpecies; the beauty of countenance, of body, of action, of voice, of addrefs, of converfation, of eloquence.

He fhews how what is beautiful of the creation in general pleafes the imagination. He fhews that other accidental caufes may contribute to the heightening of thefe exquifite pleafures. In

In No. 413, he fhews that the original efficient caufe of all the innocent pleafures of the imagination is God himfelf.

The neceffary caufe of our being pleafed with what is new, beautiful, and great, is unknown.

But the final caufes are more known and more ufeful for us to know.

The final caufe of our being, pleafed with what is great, is this: the infinite God has fo formed the foul of man, that nothing but himfelf can be its laft adequate and proper happinefs; becaufe, therefore, the whole of our happinefs muft arife from the contemplation of his being and perfection, that he might give our fouls a juft relifh of fuch a glorious contemplation, He has made them naturally delight in the apprehenfion of what is great and unlimited like God.

Our admiration, which is a very pleafing motion of the mind, immediately rifes at the confideration of any object that takes up a great deal of room in the imagination, and by confequence will improve into the higheft pitch of aftonifhment and devotion, when we contemplate God's nature and perfections, which are neither circumfcribed by time or place, nor to be comprehended by the largeft capacity of men or angels. The attributes of God are unbounded by time, therefore eternal: unbounded by fpace, therefore omniprefent: unbounded in power, therefore omnipotent.

The final caufe of our pleafures in whatever is new, rare and uncommon, is this: God has annexed a fecret pleafure to the idea of any thing that is new or uncommon, that he might encourage us in the eager and keen purfuit after knowledge, and inflame our beft paffions to fearch into the wonders of his creation, fcripture, and falvation; for every new idea brings fuch a pleafure along with it, as rewards any pains we have taken in the acquifition of it, and confequently ferves as a ftriking and pathetic motive to

put

put us on frefh difcoveries in God, and the revelation of his eternal Son and Spirit, with all the wonders of creation and providence.

The final caufe of our pleafure in beauty in our fellow creatures, is this: God has made every thing that is truly beautiful and pleafant in our own fpecies, that we might exercife generous love and benevolence to all mankind.

The beauty of countenance, of voice, of perfon, temper, and behaviour, all confpire with their fineft impulfes to ftrike our fenfes and imagination with delicate pleafure.

The final caufe of beauty in the creation, is to pleafe and regale the imagination.

God has made every thing that is beautiful in all other objects pleafing to our tafte.

He has created fo many objects to appear beautiful, that he might render the whole creation more cheering and delightful.

He has given almoft every thing about us, the power of raifing an agreeable idea in the imagination ; fo that it is impoffible for us to behold his works with coldnefs or indifference, and to furvey fo many beauties of creation and Scripture without a fecret fatisfaction and complacency.

The final caufe of beauty in revelation, is to pleafe the tafte, and charm the imagination. There is a beauty in miracles: there is a beauty in the prophecies: there is a beauty in the fingular providences and the noble actions recorded in Scripture.

The final caufe of beauty in Scripture images, and lively figures, is to ftrike the imagination with a delicate impulfe of pleafure, and charm the devout and virtuous tafte of a true Chriftian's heart and underftanding.

This may be exemplified in a great variety of Scriptural facts and characters in the Old Teftament, and

in

in the parables and actions of our LORD JESUS CHRIST in the New.

The final cause of beauty in the doctrines, laws, and promises of the Gospel, is to allure and fasten the attention of the whole soul of a real believer to his GOD and SAVIOUR.

The final cause of the beauty of the numerous names of CHRIST, with his perfections, offices, and lovely characters, in Psalm xlv. Proverbs viii. Song of Songs v. Heb. i. Col. i. Rev. i. with ten thousand other beauties of his person, is to allure and attract the souls of millions of men into the most forcible love and admiration.

The final cause of the beauties of virtue and holiness, is to excite love and imitation amongst mankind; and this great end has been wonderfully answered by the temper and writings of our excellent friend.

The final cause of greatness, novelty, and beauty, in the latter day glory: the conversion of millions of Jews and Gentiles: the utter ruin of Pagan, Mahometan, and Popish wickedness, is to strike our imagination. These are all designed to rouse our attention; to fix our studies; to fire up our eager searches, and to elevate us to the utmost pitch of sublimity of sentiment and passion; and thus to spread through the whole soul a rational and Godlike enthusiasm.

This is likewise the final cause of the discoveries of the ultimate glory of heaven in its certainty, nature, variety of pleasures, degrees of joy, changes of employment, perpetual additions of happiness, and eternity of duration.

OBJECTS in the NATURAL WORLD suited to the IMAGINATION.

The rising of the morning sun in its utmost glory.

The same object viewed in the midst of the Atlantic ocean.

The

The beauty of the fetting fun in a ferene fummer evening.

The fame object viewed by fea, when remote from land fome thoufands of miles.

The calmnefs of the vaft ocean hufhed to fleep like a child in the cradle.

The ferenenefs of the ftarry heavens by night.

The beauties of a fmiling meadow, and the fertile corn fields by day.

The grand chorus of all the birds warbling forth the praifes of their Maker.

OBJECTS of GRANDEUR and TERROR united.

Suppofe yourfelf fufpended in boundlefs fpace; that you have a vaft profpect of eternal duration; the world of waters under your feet; a fudden eclipfe of the moon increafes the darknefs of the night; you fee in a moment aftonifhing flafhes of lightening; you hear the prolonged roar of thunder; in a moment a dreadful ftorm at fea arifes, and toffes the waves twenty thoufand feet high, which is the height of the loftieft mountains: a terrible earthquake fhakes cities to pieces, and involves them in flames: at the fame moment volcanoes burfting out in ftreams of liquid fire twenty miles long, feven miles broad, and fixty feet deep: at the fame inftant you hear cataracts of water four hundred feet high, and the crafh of falling rocks, which difcover the foundations of nature: whilft all thefe objects combine together, fnatch your foul to the margin of eternity, make you feel yourfelf in the hands of omnipotence, and place you in the immediate profpects of the burning tribunal of GOD.

OBJECTS of GRANDEUR and TERROR in Scripture, fuited to the imagination, agreeing with the idea of a GOD, and evincing the immortality of the foul.

D d   The

The dreadful deluge: fire and brimſtone rained from heaven in an unexpected moment: the ten terrible plagues, and the ruin of the tyrant and his hoſt: the mount all on fire, and trembling to its baſis: Korah, Dathan, Abiram, with all their families, ſwallowed alive: a buſh all on fire, yet not conſumed: Jordan riſes up like mountains: the walls of Jericho fall flat in a moment: the ſun and moon ſtand ſtill a whole day, for the ruin of God's enemies: David's battle with a monſter: 185,000 rebels ſtruck dead by God's juſtice in twelve hours: three heroes defy the ſevenfold rage of fire: a viſible hand ſprings out of the wall, and writes the eternal doom of a tyrant: the lions devour whole families of the nobles in a moment: Haman hurled from the apex of honour, and hanged like a dog.

Jeruſalem twice devoured with tremendous famine, ſword, and fire.

OBJECTS of BEAUTY and NOVELTY ſuited to the imagination.

1. Judah's affecting addreſs to his brother Joſeph.

2. What an object of newneſs and beauty was the ſudden ſurpriſing diſcovery of Joſeph's perſon and love to his brethren! And what a lively type of an infinitely greater perſon, and his tranſcendent love! Joſeph's ſudden advancement from a priſon to a throne, is a new, ſurpriſing, and beautiful object.

3. Jonathan's ardent love and friendſhip for David.

4. The happy interpoſition of the wiſe and virtuous Abigail ſaved her huſband and family from inſtant deſtruction.

5. Solomon's dedication of the temple.

6. Queen of Sheba's interview with Solomon.

7. Ahaſuerus's grand feaſt.

8. Our SAVIOUR at the marriage of Cana.

9. CHRIST feeding 5,000.

10. CHRIST's transfiguration on the mount.

11. Reſur-

11. Refurrection of Lazarus.

12. Our Saviour's calming the tempeft.

13. Surrounded with the children.

14. His appearance to Mary Magdalen.

15. His converfe on going to Emmaus.

16. His appearance to the twelve and to five hun-dred brethren at once.

17. His afcenfion from Mount Olivet.

18. The glorious day of Pentecoft.

19. His appearance to John in the firft chapter of the Revelations.

20. His appearance at Paul's converfion.

The Objects and Actions of the Passions of the foul, agree with the idea of a God, and clearly prove its immortality.

Passions are unufual motions of the foul, arifing from new objects, fuited to produce that emotion.

A great, new, and agreeable object, produces that pleafing and unufual motion of the mind, which is ftiled admiration: how great is his goodnefs, and how great is his beauty! Zech. ix. 17. How mani-fold are thy works! in wifdom haft thou made them all! Pfal. civ. 24.

An object that appears good and fit to make us happy, produces that motion which iffues in a de-lightful union with the object, ftiled love.

An object appearing deformed, evil, and ugly, and fit to do us a terrible injury, excites that unufual motion in the will to fly from, and be difunited from the object: this is ftiled hatred.

Now admiration at new objects, love of good and beautiful objects, and hatred of all ugly objects, all agree with the idea of a God, and wonderfully prove our fure immortality of duration in a future and in-vifible world.

Efteem and contempt—defire and averfion—bene-volence and malevolence—complacency and delight

—diſplicency and difguſt, at the proper objects, all agree with the idea of a God, and demonſtrate our eternity of exiſtence.

Hope and fear—joy and ſorrow—gratitude and anger, all proclaim the ſoul immortal, and wonderfully agree with the being of a God.

All the pleaſing paſſions, and all the painful paſſions, clearly ſhew the immortality of the ſoul, and ſtrongly evince the being of a God.

The PLEASING PASSIONS all agree with the idea of a God; admiration, love, eſteem, benevolence, complacency, or delight ; deſire, hope, joy, gratitude, ambition, glory, fortitude, veneration, congratulation, cheerfulneſs, ſerenity, emulation, zeal, gladneſs, modeſty, adoration, candour, officioſity, hoſpitality, equanimity, public ſpirit: all theſe declare the ſoul to be immortal.

The PAINFUL PASSIONS agree with our ideas of a God, and equally ſhew the immortality of the ſoul, hatred, contempt, malevolence, diſplicence, averſion, fear, ſorrow, anger, ſhame, conſternation, fluctuation, loathing, envy, ſcorn, diſdain, indignation, deſperation, jealouſy, repentance, ſurpriſe, terror, horror, ſpite, rage, fury, rancour, malice, revenge, anguiſh, anxiety, melancholy, difguſt, cruelty, ſelfiſhneſs, impurity : all theſe paſſions agree with the idea of a juſt and angry God, and loudly proclaim the immortality of the ſoul.

The OBJECTS and ACTIONS of the memory clearly agree with the idea of a God, and convincingly prove the immortality of the ſoul.

Memory is the power of recollecting facts, or of reviving thoſe ideas which have lain out of ſight.

A good memory is ready to receive the various ideas of facts and words: it is large and copious to treaſure up facts and characters: it is ſtrong and durable to retain thoſe facts; faithful and active to ſuggeſt
and

and recollect, on every proper occasion, all those words, thoughts, and facts, which have been committed to its care, and treasured up in this store-house of the foul. The wonderful power of memory, clearly shews the amazing wisdom and goodness of God.

Without memory, the foul would be an universal blank: it is the grand repository of languages and science: it is the store-house of divinity drawn from the pure Scriptures of God.

Memory is of infinite service in history, by retaining facts, characters, and events, of the most striking and awful nature: to drive us from vice, and of the most striking and beautiful nature to allure and stimulate us to the practice of universal virtue. How brightly does the being of a God shine forth in the powers and uses of memory in the mind of man!

The OBJECTS and ACTIONS of CONSCIENCE, prove the immortality of the foul, and clearly agree with our idea of a God.

Conscience is a power of the rational foul, by which it knows its own actions with regard to a law, and judges of their fitness and unfitness, or the moral good or evil that is in them, according to that light which the mind possesses, and with reference to the judgment and will of God.

Conscience is God's vicegerent in the foul: it acts for him, and under his just government: it receives its authority and direction from God, and is accountable to him, and to no other power in heaven or earth.

Conscience observes all the thoughts, actions, and words of a man's whole life, from the very first dawn of reason, to the moment of death and to eternity.

Conscience writes down every act of sin and holiness, and records, as on tables of brass, or pillars of marble, all the moral and immoral actions of our foul and body.

Conscience

Confcience is a bold, refolute, and honeft witnefs of our actions; a moft accurate and dreadful regifter of our crimes; an impartial judge to condemn or juftify; a moft exquifite tormentor of vice and wick-ednefs, and a moft generous rewarder of goodnefs and virtue.

An evil confcience is blind and ignorant, dull and ftupid, partial and fcrupulous; as in the cafe of Saul, who was very fevere about a little honey, and yet could deliberately kill, at one and the fame hour, four-fcore priefts of God.

An evil confcience is liable to perpetual forrow and fadnefs, trouble and diftrefs, anguifh or pungent grief, which often rifes to horror and defpair. It makes a wicked man flee when no one purfueth, Prov. xxviii. 1. whilft the righteous are as bold as a lion.

A guilty confcience trembles at the thoughts of death, and dreads its approach: it looks forward with terror to the day of judgment, the appearance of the eternal Judge, and the burning tribunal of the invifible world.

The OBJECTS and ACTIONS of GENIUS and TASTE, agree with our ideas of a GOD, and evinces the im-mortality of the foul.

GENIUS is an aptitude to excel in the line of fcience and virtue.

Tafte is a clear fenfe of all that is great and good, true and beautiful, in heaven and earth; it is a power of receiving pleafure from the beauties of creation and revelation; the beauties of characters and virtu-ous actions; the excellencies of hiftory and eloquence, diffufed through the whole body of the Holy Scrip-tures.

Tafte is the exquifite fenfibility of the foul to every fine impulfe of beauty, truth and goodnefs. This tafte is wrought up to perfection and delicacy, by education, ftudy and devotion; by which means the
mind.

mind becomes able to difcern with an intuitive force
and readinefs, how much true beauty and pleafure
every object in heaven and earth can give us.

In the words of the judicious and eloquent Rollin,
we obferve that tafte is a clear, lively, and diftinct
perception of all the beauty, truth and juftnefs, of the
thoughts and expreffion which compofe a difcourfe or
treatife. It diftinguifhes what is conformable to eloquence and propriety, in every character, and fuitable
in different circumftances. And whilft with a delicate
cate and exquifite fagacity it notes the graces,
turns, manners, and expreffions moft likely to pleafe,
it perceives all the defects which produce the contrary effect; diftinguifhes precifely wherein thofe blemifhes confift, and how far they are removed from
the ftrict rules of eloquence, and the real beauties of
nature.

This happy faculty of tafte is a kind of natural
reafon, wrought up to perfection by a refined education, clofe attention, and thought; by a lively converfe with the great Friend and Teacher of man, the
only wife GOD our SAVIOUR.

This good tafte is not confined to literature; it
takes in alfo all fciences and branches of knowledge.

It confifts, therefore, in a certain juft and exact difcernment, which points out to us, in each of the
branches of knowledge, whatever is moft curious,
beautiful, and ufeful; whatever is moft effential, fuitable, and neceffary to thofe who apply to it; how far,
confequently, we fhould carry the ftudy of it, what
ought to be removed from it, and what deferves a
particular application and preference before the reft.

Read Rollin's Reflections on a good Tafte, in his
admirable method of ftudy, Vol. I. page 41—53.
Eng. Edit. 12mo.

Read Mr. Addifon on Imagination—Spectator,
Vol. VI. No. 411—421.

Thus

Thus we have confidered the objects and actions of the underftanding; of the will; the imagination, the paffions, the memory, the confcience, the genius, and tafte; and we fee in a moment that thefe are evidences of the immortality of the foul; and we fee the agreement of thefe ideas with the idea of a God; and if we proceed farther to confider the moral perfections of God, we fhall fee the clear agreement of the ideas of a foul with thofe moral perfections. The wifdom and goodnefs of God, evince its immortality: the holinefs and juftice of God, demonftrate its immortality: the truth, fincerity, veracity, and faithfulnefs of God, proclaim the foul immortal.

But after all, Hervey knew, as well as any man, the utter infufficiency of reafon, to lead us to true virtue and happinefs in the fruition of God.

Reafon is a power of judging of the nature, relation, and ufes of things; the fitnefs or unfitnefs; the good or evil qualities of actions, and the truth or falfehood of propofitions.

Reafon is a power of the underftanding, to difcern that all things are not alike true, nor alike good, nor alike fit, nor alike beautiful; and to fee that all actions, tempers and qualities, are not alike evil, nor alike unfit, nor alike wrong, nor alike ugly and deformed.

Reafon alone, without the aid of revelation, cannot give us eafy and plain notices of a God, fuch as are clear to the weakeft mind, affecting to the moft ftupid heart, and fuitable to the meaneft underftanding.

Reafon cannot give fpecial and diftinct ideas of God, to enable the foul, in a moment, to diftinguifh God from all other beings, and to give him that veneration which his dignity demands.

Reafon is infufficient to give us certain and convincing notices of a God, fo as to bind the underftanding to affent to the truth of God's exiftence; to

convince

convince it of the reality of the divine perfections, imprefs the confcience with a fenfe of divine juftice, and perfuade the will to fubmit to the dominion of GOD.

Reafon cannot give extenfive ideas of GOD, in all his natural and moral perfections; nor is it able to difcover all the moral relations of GOD to our fouls, fo that we may be fure that no idea of GOD is wanting, which is needful to our real duty and final happinefs.

Reafon is unable to give pleafant and lovely ideas of GOD, fuch as fhall fuit a rational tafte, and excite a tender affection to him as an amiable being, full of perfect love, good and beautiful in himfelf; fit to do us the higheft good, worthy to receive all poffible good from us; an object in whom we may expand our nobleft powers with delight; a being that rejoices to do us good, and fill us with happinefs.

Reafon can never furnifh fuch fweet difcoveries of GOD, as fhall fet our hearts at reft, fo as to have no occafion to feek any farther happinefs to eternity.

Reafon cannot give fuch powerful and durable ideas of GOD as fhall abide with great force upon the foul, working from moment to moment, and renewing the impreffion every inftant on the underftanding and confcience; and yet fuch an impreffion is abfolutely neceffary for man's duty and happinefs. Here reafon difcovers its utter weaknefs and infufficiency.

In order that a man fhould know GOD, he muft have fuch an inceffant impreffion of GOD upon his foul, as fhall forcibly influence him to a compliance with every duty, in every inftance, in every ftate of life, from youth to manhood, from manhood to old age, and to the very moment of death.

Reafon cannot difcover the true happinefs of man.

Reafon cannot difcern that good which removes mifery, prevents pain, prepares for happinefs, and makes a man happy in GOD.

Reafon

Reafon cannot difcern wherein true happinefs confifts: it knows not that good which is fuited to our
higheft powers, and is agreeable to every fituation
we can be in all round the globe, and to every character we can fuftain.

Reafon cannot difcern that good which may be
enjoyed without fhame, poffeffed without fufpicion of
wrong conduct, or dread of future bad confequences.

Reafon cannot difcern that good which will fupport us under the troubles of life, refine and fatisfy
our affections, ftand the fevere teft of fober reflection,
improve upon longer experience, afford the higheft
pleafure, upon the moft frequent repetition, and be as
lafting as our eternal exiftence.

Reafon cannot difcover a complete body of morals,
or univerfal virtue, as the means of happinefs.

Reafon never has given us a complete body of morality, without defect or darknefs. A perfect fcheme
of morality muft be eafy and clear, in order to be inftructive and ufeful to man. A confufed rule of duty
is of no ufe; a found plan of morals muft be univerfal, to oppofe every fin, and urge to every duty.
There muft be nothing defective, nothing vicious in
the whole fyftem. Sound morality muft have no
pernicious maxim to draw after it any bad confequences. This plan muft be avowed by GOD himfelf as a rule of duty, and enforced by his dominion
and authority.

Reafon leaves poor man to draw the rule of duty
from the fource of his own nature. Man cannot
frame a complete body of morals: he can make no
progrefs in a fyftem of morality of his own, whilft he
is a raw youth, full of impure appetites and bad paffions. If clear rules could be found out, motives
would be wanting: if motives were difcerned, affiftances of light and ftrength would be wanting. Man
will not be honeft to put himfelf in the way of motives: he will not be honeft to enquire into the defign

of motives: he will not be honeſt to fulfil the intention of motives; and we ſhall freeze to ice, amidſt
maxims of wiſdom and motives to virtue.

Hervey clearly ſaw the utter INSUFFICIENCY of
REASON to furniſh the beſt MOTIVES to VIRTUE.

It cannot give us a full view of the immediate preſence of GOD, the Lawgiver and Judge of the world.
It doth not give us a ſweet ſenſation of the preſent pleaſures of virtue, nor the future rewards of virtue: nor
does reaſon give us to know the preſent puniſhments
of vice, nor the future vengeance of GOD againſt all ſin.

Reaſon cannot give us one good and perfect example of virtue in the whole world, in any age or
nation under heaven.

Reaſon is defective in another motive to virtue:
it cannot diſcover the leaſt help and aſſiſtance from
GOD in the practice of virtue in one inſtance through
life.

Reaſon cannot give us a full view of the immediate
preſence of GOD, and the infinite authority of his
laws, as the invariable rule of virtue.

Reaſon is unable to recommend the law, by ſhew-
ing the glorious qualifications of the Lawgiver in his
power and greatneſs: it cannot ſupply us with right
notions of his wiſdom and goodneſs, juſtice and
truth; and yet the diſcoveries of theſe glorious properties muſt be attained, in order to promote univerſal virtue.

Reaſon cannot give ſuch clear evidence of GOD
from moment to moment as ſhall ſtrike the underſtanding with force, touch the paſſions with fire, leave
a lively impreſſion, and have a pungent influence to
quicken us to the practice of virtue.

Reaſon cannot ſhew us that our Governor is always
near; that he is every moment converſant with us;
that we have every day convincing evidences of his
goodneſs, wiſdom, juſtice, and kindneſs, with all
other perfections, fitting him for government.

Theſe

Thefe notices are abfolutely needful to enforce a re-gard to the will of GOD.

Reafon cannot excite to obedience, by fhewing us that the title of the Lawgiver is indifputable, and the ground of his claim to our affection clearly made known. Such is the tranfcendent excellency of the nature of GOD, as to render him the only fit being to govern; but reafon is blind to this excellence.

Reafon doth not clearly difcern that GOD is the Creator of all worlds, and that he has an abfolute propriety in all his creatures.

· The human underftanding is blind with refpect to GOD's preferving us in being every moment; his taking fpecial care of us, and his infpection into the whole of our frame, with the many precious benefits he has beftowed upon us. All this peculiar attention of GOD to us, and his clofe influence upon us, from moment to moment, is moft ungratefully difregarded by every man in the world.

Reafon is unable to give us a clear and fatisfying difcovery of GOD's concernment in his own laws, *i. e.* that the GOD who is thus qualified for, and rightly poffeffed of the government, has made fuch laws, and ftamped his authority upon them.

No truth in the world is more certain, and we can clearly make it appear, even to demonftration, that the frame of the univerfe, and the whole fyftem of the laws of nature, are adapted to the powers of man, in a ftate of rectitude, which is not the cafe of man now. No, verily; this is infinitely far from being his prefent ftate; and therefore, how to reconcile the per-fection of thefe laws to the moft rational ideas of GOD, and the prefent ftate of man, is an incompre-henfible fpeculation of infinite confequence, and of the moft prodigious difficulty; fo that the human un-derftanding never could have got through it; its ut-moft force could never have furmounted it; the whole united world of minds could never have folved
the

the difficulty, if God had not gracioufly given us another guide above reafon, and the light of nature.

Reafon cannot give a certain knowledge that God has a great regard to his laws, and keenly infpects whether or no thefe laws are obeyed. The knowledge of this would be a ftrong inducement to regard his laws; but here reafon always fails.

Reafon is defective in a fecond motive to virtue, it doth not clearly difcern the prefent pleafures of virtue, nor fatisfy us with refpect to the prefent rewards of virtue.

Reafon cannot produce in us fuch a delightful fenfe of God, nor imprefs upon us fuch a feeling conviction of our momentary dependance upon him, and mighty obligations to him, as fhall excite us to love him with a lively gratitude, zealoufly ftrive to promote his glory, and proclaim to the utmoft of our power the excellency of his perfections.

Reafon is unable to difcern the certainty and evidence of a virtuous life: it cannot fteadily difcover the beauty and excellency of a virtuous life.

Mere Reafon cannot infpire the pleafures and joys of a virtuous life: it cannot fupply the pleafures of a virtuous action: it cannot enable us to enjoy the fweet pleafures of reflection, after the performance of a good action: it cannot furnifh the pleafures of exquifite fruition in the prefence and love of God.

Reafon can never furnifh the pleafures of hope, and truft in God for all future times.

Reafon is unable to exhibit the alluring and inftructive nature of a virtuous life. A fhining light inftructs: an ardent light enflames: a beautiful light perfuades the paffions of the heart, and excites imitation; but where is fuch a fhining, ardent, and beautiful light to be found?

Reafon is infufficient to make an high advancement in the power and beauty of virtue. True religion is of a progreffive nature. Vital virtue refembles sembles the advancing light of the rising sun. As the sun rises higher and higher towards the meridian, so Hervey was still advancing in goodness. Internal virtue urged him on by a rational and forcible stimulus to a farther growth in knowledge, perfection, and usefulness; but here the powers of unassisted reason could do nothing. He, as a virtuous man, improved in the knowledge of GOD and himself: he had an ardent zeal to advance in clearer apprehensions of the infinite perfections of his REDEEMER: his conceptions of the dignity of GOD, and of the powers and affections of his own soul became more vivid and distinct: his mind was more free from pride and haughtiness: his reason more free from error: his judgment more purged from prejudice, and more correct in its decisions. But where is the man to be found in the whole world that is capable of these noble advancements on the principles of reason alone?

Reason is unable to produce a fixed adhesion of the will to GOD and virtue: it cannot give us strength and firmness in true religion. An adhesion of the will to GOD, is properly the strength of virtue. If reason were sufficient for the happiness of man, we should find a natural progress in the life of virtue; and this adhesion of the will to the goodness, rectitude, and beauty of GOD, would grow stronger with time, so as to bear a proportion with the growing apprehension of GOD, and the enlarged views of the human understanding. There is a great degree of strength in the union of the will to GOD; and in this union, true virtue consists: but did reason alone ever produce it? A soul that truly feels it, hopes to have the approbation of GOD before the whole assembled world: but reason can neither produce, nor cherish this hope.

Reason cannot excite us to that sublime virtue which will cause a man to shine in the perfection of his example. Hervey was a man of true virtue: he

proceeded

proceeded to higher degrees of beauty and perfection ; he had fewer blemishes than other men, and fewer than he himself once had: he was more purified from the vices of flesh and spirit: he corrected whatever was amiss in his temper and conduct: his example was formerly good, but of late years it was much brighter and better; more lovely and instructive. This man, of high and delicate virtue, laboured about his example and character*, as a skilful painter doth upon a picture, or a statuary on a piece of first-rate sculpture; who, before he finishes his piece, strives to give beauty to the whole, and to spread a grace over his whole production; but we challenge the whole world to produce one man that hath done this on the mere principles of reason.

Reason can never advance a man in the ease and pleasure of virtuous action. Hervey, as a man of true virtue, found, to his unspeakable pleasure, that he advanced in the ease of virtuous action, and that the pleasure of right conduct was still increasing. He felt his faculties more and more adapted to actions of generous goodness, and the pleasures of devotion, and social benevolence : by a divine and God-like instinct, he proceeded naturally into worthy manners and practices; whilst every bad man will make a swift progressive motion into all the pollutions and plagues of vice; but where is the man who, on the principles of mere reason, hath pursued virtue and avoided wickedness?

Reason alone cannot carry any man into such purity of heart as shall, at last, issue in a state of perfection in the full fruition of God. The perfection of virtue, in the order and operations of our noblest powers, would certainly be the result of a rich advance in perfect goodness ; but here reason eternally fails. The human understanding, in its present state,

* See Grove on the Pleasure and Beauty of Religion.

is

is utterly unable to guide us to that perfection of happiness in God, and that rich enjoyment of the soul, in
all its powers of fruition, which our nature appears
to be designed for in its original constitution. Thus
we have seen that reason is defective in the second
motive to virtue; *i. e.* it cannot display, in a convincing manner, the present pleasures of virtue and
obedience to God.

Reason is defective in a third motive to virtue: it
cannot give us a clear and striking view of future
rewards and pleasures, to repay us for all present
disadvantages and hardships we suffer for the sake of
God and vital virtue.

Reason is defective in a fourth motive to virtue;
i. e. it cannot discover, in a clear and forcible manner, those present pains and horrors which are always
the result of vicious actions; nor, fifthly, can reason
discover those terrible future punishments which God
will certainly execute on all resolute and determined
rebels against his government.

Reason is defective in a sixth motive to virtue: it
cannot shew us one example of spotless virtue in the
whole world. *Præcepta docent, exempla movent.* Precepts teach, examples move to action. Laws and
precepts only instruct us what is to be done; but
reason can neither furnish precepts nor examples to
excite one man to vital virtue.

Reason is defective in a seventh motive and means
to virtue; *i. e.* it cannot discover the least assistance
from God for the great work of devotion or benevolence to mankind.

Reason cannot discover any assistance of the Spirit
of God, to illuminate the understanding, to discern
the divine perfections, and our duty and happiness.

Reason can discover no help of the Holy Spirit, to
give us a savoury taste for all the truths of the Gospel, with a lively sense of all Gospel motives.

Reason

Reafon can never difcover the power of divine grace, to fupprefs all indifference of heart to God, and all inclinations to vice and wickednefs.

Reafon can never difcover the Holy Spirit working in us a willingnefs and readinefs to all manner of duties.

Reafon can never difcover the Holy Spirit as enlivening all graces into pleafing exercifes.

Reafon can never difcover the Holy Spirit as difplaying all the motives to univerfal holinefs.

Reafon can never difcover the Holy Spirit as ftrengthening the foul in its powers and paffions, to comply with every motive that God has propofed.

Thus far we have fhewn the utter infufficiency of reafon to make proper difcoveries of God, and his infinite perfections; to fhew the fupreme good or happinefs of man; to difcover a perfect rule of morality, or plan of found virtue and morals; and to difcern the moft powerful motives to virtue and godlinefs.

We now proceed to fhew that reafon cannot difcover the pardon of fin; the refinement of the foul by fanctification; fupport under the troubles of life, and confolation againft the fears of death.

Reafon is infufficient to difcover the pardon of fin. The clear and determinate idea of pardon, is this: that it is-a voluntary and free act of grace, which remits the punifhment, and releafes the finner from that vengeance he juftly deferved, and which the Lawgiver might juftly have inflicted on him. So that upon the whole, pardon includes four ideas, a total fuppreffion of all defires to punifh—a kind difpofition to do the finner good—a folemn affurance of hearty reconciliation—admiffion into full confidence with God. Pardon of fin is the life of religion, and without this no religion can exift.

Reafon cannot difcern the eftimate which God has made of the firft act of fin; nor can it intimate the

way in which GOD would be propitious to a rebel.
It is unable to difcern GOD inviting men to repentance; nor can it difcover any command of GOD to
repent.   It cannot difcover one finner pardoned from
the beginning of the world to this very moment.   It
is unable to difcern the great defign of GOD's patience towards a wicked world for thoufands of years.
This is an incomprehenfible conduct in GOD, which
no fagacity of man can account for or folve.

Reafon is infufficient to fhew us any happy foul's
burfting into fongs of praife for pardon from GOD as
a merciful being.

Reafon can difcover no holy and fpiritual worfhip
appointed by GOD for any of his rebellious creatures;
nor does it affure us that any worfhip will be acceptable to him: no worfhip is commanded by GOD on
the foot of reafon.   This is an awful thought; i. e.
that GOD commands no man to worfhip; nor by the
light of reafon doth he exhort or command any man
to repent and to turn to GOD.

Reafon can never difcover one purpofe in the heart
of GOD, nor one promife in the mouth of GOD, nor
one action in the conduct of GOD, that gives a fure
and certain indication of the pardon of a fingle fin;
much lefs can it difcover ten thoufand promifes and
actions flowing from the gracious nature of GOD in
ftreams of light and love upon loft rebels.

Reafon cannot difcover one name belonging to
GOD that infpires a folid hope of pardon.   It can
never difcern one perfection in GOD that can pardon:
it cannot poffibly fee the harmony of juftice and
mercy in the pardon of one fin in the whole world.
The united reafon and wifdom of all mankind, can
never difcover how juftice and mercy may be fhewn
at the fame time to a criminal in civil government,
much lefs in the government of GOD. . This thought
deferves to be urged to the utmoft extent.

Reafon

Reafon is not in the leaft able to difcern a fuitable provifion for a divine and infinite Governor, to the end that he may pardon fin with honour to his moral character and laws. It can difcern no ranfom paid to a divine and infinite Conqueror: no facrifice to a divine and injured Monarch: no fatisfaction to a divine and infinite Judge.

Reafon can difcover no able friend to us who could, by the difpofitions of his heart, and by his actions and fufferings, provide for the meridian glory of divine juftice, as making laws; as rewarding obedience to laws; as punifhing the violation of laws in the moft juft and impartial manner; and this friend freely obeying all the righteous commands, and bearing all the righteous curfes of the law which it otherwife required of us, in order to efcape punifhment, and have a right to eternal happinefs in GOD. Concerning all this, reafon is at an utter and eternal lofs.

Reafon cannot difcover one man fent by GOD to proclaim a word of pardon to a guilty world: not any fet of men, nor fo much as one man, can be difcovered by reafon, as fent with a commiffion from GOD, and fealed with a broad feal of heaven, to proclaim a fingle hint of pardon to a guilty world, or to any individual on earth, through thoufands of years. We defy all mankind to deny this, and prove the contrary. The human underftanding is not able to difcover GOD iffuing out any commands to rebels, to forgive the crimes they commit againft each other. No man, by the exercife of reafon alone, can difcern that GOD has ordered him to forgive his fellow creatures their offences: no, not in one fingle inftance through the whole world. Ignorance of the pardoning mercy of GOD, and having no command from GOD to forgive each other, was the blamelefs occafion of producing the oppofite fpirit in the Pagan world. They knew not GOD's mercy; they knew not any command to forgive: the defperate depravity

of

of the human heart took occasion from this to exert the spirit of revenge in every mode of operation, and thus they resemble the most malignant devils.

Reason is utterly insufficient to suppress vicious inclinations, and to root them out of the heart, or to refine and purify the soul by powerful and effectual holiness. How blind was the Heathen world; how dark their wisest philosophers; how childish and silly are all the best means they prescribed. Plato bids you purify your souls by music and mathematics. Can music charm away the lust of the flesh? Can Euclid's Elements subdue your pride? purge out impurity, rash anger, malice, and covetousness?

Reason cannot produce those excellent qualities in the soul which are necessary for a life of virtue and holiness.

Reason cannot discover the true source of holiness, nor the foundation on which it is enjoyed; *i. e.* an union of heart with God, and a new constitution of soul flowing entirely from the grace of Christ. A sufficiency of strength and light from God is absolutely necessary for a life of holiness towards God, and a conformity to his moral perfections. To be like God in wisdom, a man must be made wise: to resemble his goodness, a man must be made good at heart: to bear the likeness of his holiness, a man must be refined in the temper of his soul: to resemble God's justice and truth, a man must be impressed with the sense of the beauty of justice, and be filled with sincerity and integrity of heart. But did mere reason ever produce these charming qualities? Where is the man to be found? In what age or in what country did he live, that performed all this by the power of reason alone? A cordial peace and friendship with God is absolutely necessary to a life of vital virtue and holiness. Nothing less than a powerful sense of peace with God can produce an earnest desire after a resemblance to God: but here reason,

with

with all its united powers, utterly fails. A lively hope of being happy in the prefence of God to eternity, is effentially neceffary to a life of genuine virtue and holinefs in the prefent world.

Without this vigorous hope, no man on earth will ever put himfelf to the expence of practifing univerfal virtue, or a love to God and all mankind. And where is this man to be found, who ever purfued univerfal virtue on the principles of reafon alone? Where was he born? Where was he educated? Where did he live? No anfwer can be given. Our infidels are ftruck dumb for ever. They cannot, if the life of their foul depended upon it, give us a fatisfying anfwer to thefe queftions; confequently the fcheme of their infidelity is ruined for ever, and if they had any moral honefty, or juftice, and truth in their hearts, they would confefs it before the whole world.

For a rational creature in his prefent ftate, and with all the awful imperfections of his internal character, to look for an eternity of happinefs in God, *is to look very high indeed*. It is to form very grand conceptions, and moft exalted hopes; and it is demonftrably certain, that no man in the world will go to the expence of denying all his vile appetites after prefent good, without a ftrong fenfation of vifible and eternal good to reward him for his felf-denial, and the refolute practice of virtue.

Now I afk again, Where is the man to be found, that has preferved in his bofom an high hope of the eternal fruition of God, as the fupreme good, and on this principle alone has denied every bad appetite, every polluted paffion, every impure inclination, every vicious tafte, and has exerted all his powers in love to God and to all mankind? There is no fuch man to be found in the whole world; he is yet to be born.

We

We repeat it again, that reafon cannot produce and cherifh any of thofe noble principles in the foul which are neceffary for a life of virtue and holinefs.

A vigorous bent of the mind, or a powerful and ardent inclination and propenfity of the heart to virtue, is neceffary to the practice of virtue; but here reafon utterly fails.

All mankind have an actual bent of heart to moral evil, or a propenfity to vice and wickednefs: it is neceffary to the end that a man may be virtuous, that his inclinations for good be as lively and forcible for virtue, as the heart of a wicked man is to vice; as an hungry man longs for bread; as a thirfty man eagerly defires to drink; as the hart panteth after the water brooks; as the ambitious man longs for honour; as the covetous man loves gold; as the fenfual profligate purfues pleafure; as a man of fcience and tafte eagerly feeks knowledge: fo it is equally requifite that a man of virtue fhould poffefs an irrefiftible impulfe to every branch of virtue, and an inceffant thirft after univerfal holinefs. This conftitution of foul on the principles of reafon is not to be found in the whole world.

Reafon cannot fupport us under the troubles and bitter afflictions of life. It is utterly infufficient to give us a lively apprehenfion, and a ftrong conception of the weight and worth of eternal good. It cannot infpire the leaft fenfe of the fweetnefs and folidity of invifible things: it knows nothing of the reality and beauty of the perfections of GOD, and his being prefent with us at all times, in all places, and in all conditions.

Reafon can give no relief to the mind in pinching and critical times of diftrefs. It cannot difcover any certain fupplies in want, nor difcern GOD's providence taking fpecial notice of any one of the human race, having a care for fparrows, and numbering the hairs of our head.

Reafon

Reafon knows not that there is any one man in our world whom GOD will vouchfafe to call his friend; nor can it difcern any promife that GOD has made to the human race. Not the utmoft exertion of reafon can tell us that GOD has ever made one promife, or ever will to eternity: it knows not that GOD has any people on earth or in heaven.

Reafon knows not the Son of GOD: it cannot form one thought of him, nor tell us that GOD has a Son. It is totally blind concerning a SAVIOUR.

Reafon knows not the Spirit of GOD, or that GOD's Spirit has any exiftence: all eternity is in horrid darknefs, even the blacknefs of darknefs.

Reafon knows not a word of heaven: an eternal heaven, with all its pleafures and fulnefs of joy, is totally unknown.

Reafon is quite blind concerning GOD's kingdom in our world, or in the world to come: it is totally ignorant of all GOD's falvations of every kind: it has no affurance of intereft in GOD. It has no difcernment of GOD's fpecial favour, or experience of his faithfulnefs in the leaft: it knows of no fweetnefs in GOD our SAVIOUR and REDEEMER.

Reafon cries if the fweetnefs of the world is loft, all is loft to me for ever: it knows not that there is one drop of love in GOD for an immortal foul to eternity.

Reafon is blind concerning the true ufefulnefs of afflictions: it knows not the folid good which fprings up out of the trials, troubles, and diftreffes of life: it cannot difcern their ufe to the fouls of men, nor make all afflictions work for our prefent and eternal good.

Reafon knows not a word or a fyllable of any fear— not from the voice of GOD: it is totally at a lofs as to all the final iffues of our affairs with GOD at death: it is totally ignorant of all notices of GOD's oath,

life,

life, foul, arm, and confolations pledged to one finner in all the world.

Reafon knows nothing of the appearances of God
in our favour; nothing of the laft ftate of the univerfe; nothing of his free interpofitions for our good,
either for time or for eternity; all is dark, dark as
death.

Reafon is infufficient to fupport us in the profpects
and terrors of death. Let us take four diftinct views
of death.

1ft. Confider it as your leaving this world, and
all things in it for ever.

2d. Confider death as the awful time when your
whole internal character fhall be declared by God
himfelf, and your ftate fhall be fealed and fixed for
eternity.

3d. View death as turning the body to corruption
and rottennefs, and reducing it to the duft from
whence it was taken.

4th. View death as an entrance upon a new world,
and a new manner of exifting, thinking, and acting,
in a difembodied ftate.

Reafon is infufficient to give us any ftrong *confolations* againft the *terror* of death.

Reafon in guilty man will awfully declare that
God will forfake us in our moft grievous dying
agonies.

Reafon cannot look upon God as a merciful Father, nor can it truft in his infinite goodnefs to fupport us.

Reafon knows nothing at all of the fufferings and
death of our Lord Jesus Christ: it is totally ignorant of the infinite and eternal merit of his obedience and blood.

Reafon knows nothing at all of our Lord Jesus
Christ as dead in his grave, to make it a fafe refting
place for all his followers.

Reafon

Reason is totally ignorant of the refurrection of CHRIST, and has no idea of the victory of JESUS over death, and fin, and the grave.

Reason is totally ignorant of the afcenfion of JE-SUS into heaven, and his amazing triumph over all his enemies, with the honours that he enjoys at GOD's right hand.

Reason cannot ftart one thought of our vital union with CHRIST by his eternal love; the new and divine nature in the foul; the omnipotence of his arm, and his HOLY SPIRIT, as the firft fruits of our bleffed im-mortality. Here reafon utterly fails. The human underftanding cannot difcern that death will deliver us from all temporal evils which we daily fuffer from a body liable to a thoufand difeafes, from vile ene-mies, falfe friends, loffes of temporal good, pinches and trials in Providence, critical times of diftrefs, and cruel fufpicions of GOD's favour to our fouls.

Reason cannot difcern that death fhall deliver us from all fin, which we fee raging and reigning all over the world in the bodies, and fouls, and lives, of millions of mankind; and likewife from the horrid power and deceit of internal depravity. Here reafon utterly fails.

The human underftanding, without revelation, knows nothing at all of the glory and happinefs of our fouls, the firft moment of their departure out of the body from darknefs to light, from corruption to purity, from conflict to triumph, from weaknefs to ftrength, from bondage to liberty, from enemies to friends, from doubts to full affurance, from forrows to joys, from groans to hallelujahs, in the prefence of GOD. Here reafon appears utterly infufficient.

Reason knows not one fyllable of the glorious and aftonifhing refurrection of the body, and the fweet meeting of body and foul before GOD. All the Greek and Roman philofophers, who lived after the refurrection was publifhed by the apoftles, looked upon the doctrine of the refurrection with fcorn and difdain: and even at Athens, the feat of philofophy and fcience, they treated Paul as a babbling fellow for preaching JESUS and the refurrection of the dead.

Reafon alone is entirely ignorant of the utter deftruction of death, fin and pain, forrow and fadnefs, dark nights and difmal temptations, with the eternal and moft blefied life which true Chriftians fhall enjoy both in foul and body after their refurrection.

Hervey faw as clearly as any man in the world, the utter infufficiency of reafon to difcover the natural and moral attributes of GOD, the fupreme happinefs of man, a fyftem of univerfal virtue, or a plan of perfect morals, without redundancy, error, or defect. He knew the infufficiency of reafon to difcover the moft pungent motives to virtue, arifing from the immediate prefence of GOD; the prefent rewards and pleafures of virtue; the future rewards of virtue; the prefent punifhments of vice; the future punifhments of vice; the beautiful examples of virtue; the rich afiiftances to virtue, or the powerful fuccours of divine grace. He clearly faw the infufficiency of reafon to difcover the pardon of fin, the purification of the heart, and the advancement of the foul in virtue and holinefs. He knew the infufficiency of reafon to fupport us under the troubles of life and the terrors of death.

From a pungent conviction of the truth of all thefe particulars, he clearly faw the neceffity of divine revelation to lead him into the true knowledge of GOD, and final happinefs in the fruition of GOD. This endeared revelation to his inmoft foul; and no man in the whole world had a higher value for the Bible than himfelf. He had thoughts for feveral years before he died, of writing a Series of Letters on the Fulfilment of Prophecies, with refpect to the Four Univerfal Monarchies; the Difperfion of the Jews; the Rife and Progrefs of Popery, and the

the Great MESSIAH. Nothing but the feeblenefs of his conftitution, his other avocations, and his want of a free flow of fpirits, prevented our enjoyment of this rich treafure, which would have been an high entertainment of eloquence and divinity united, to the pious and ingenuous part of the Chriftian world. He entered with ardour into the nature of infpiration: he faw GOD take the fouls of the facred penmen into his own hands, and infufe his own thoughts, ideas, and images, into their underftandings. He faw GOD's Spirit giving them direction in all matters of fact, firing their imaginations, elevating their conceptions, inflaming their paffions, in all the pfalms and devotional exercifes of the Bible. He faw GOD communicating his underftanding to all the prophets, to enable them to foretel ten thoufand future events; to difcover fublime doctrines; to denounce the moft awful threatenings, and to declare the richeft promifes which were hid in GOD from eternal ages. He faw the broad feal of omnipotence in the miraculous operations, confirming the truth of all thefe difcoveries. He faw the holinefs of the penmen; and in the light of eternity, he faw the divine character of the Son of GOD, the great Founder of the Chriftian religion. He faw the omniprefent Spirit of GOD go forth in the name of CHRIST, and enlightening the underftandings, and converting thoufands and millions to the refemblance and fruition of GOD in JESUS CHRIST.

With all thefe facts and objects darting upon his mental eye, he fat down with the utmoft ferioufnefs, with the moft honeft impartiality, and the moft lively gratitude, to fearch into the genuine fenfe and meaning of the Holy Scriptures.

Hervey did not come with a proud underftanding to the Bible, to teach GOD what He ought to fay, or how He ought to fpeak: he had no fcheme of pre-conceived notions to put upon the word of GOD, prior to his approach to the Sacred Scrip-

tures. He was fenfible of the weaknefs of the underftanding to receive truth, to difcern truth, to retain truth: he was fenfible of the weaknefs and wickednefs of the human will, that as it was weak, it could
not choofe Christ; that as it was wicked, it would
moft certainly refufe him. He knew the pollution of
the human imagination, and that every thought of
man's heart was only evil all the day, Heb. Gen. vi.
5. He knew the defperate fury of the human paffions againft God, and their violent oppofition to the
method of juftification by the righteoufnefs of Christ.
He knew the weaknefs of the human memory to recollect truth, and its pronenefs to be a repofitory for trafh
and uncleannefs. He knew the guiltinefs of the human confcience, and how full it was loaded with offences againft God. He knew the depravity of man's
genius and tafte, and what a relifh human nature had
for all the difpofitions of the beaft and the devil.

With thefe convictions full in his eye, and felt to
the very depth of his foul, he came to the Bible to
be taught the whole counfel of God; as dark, to be
enlightened; as ftubborn, to be made willing; as filthy, to be purified; as turbulent, to be humbled in
the duft; as full of trafh, to be cleanfed from all iniquity; as guilty, to be pardoned; as an unclean and
groveling creature, to be elevated and refined.

With thefe fentiments and feelings of foul he came
to the Bible. He was ftedfaftly governed by thefe
immortal principles and rules in his interpretation of
Scripture. He affigned no irrational or abfurd fenfe
to the word of God: he never fixed any meaning to
the Scripture which was contrary to found reafon, or
was an outrage upon common fenfe.

When he attempted to judge of any divine fubject
by reafon, he took care that they were fuch fubjects
as were within the fphere of reafon.

He fubmitted his reafon humbly to divine revelation in all truths and difcoveries of God, which reafon could never attain.

He

He offered no violence or outrage to the language of Scripture, nor gave evasive explanations of it on such subjects as are not branches of natural religion.

He distinguished well between the principles of natural religion, and the principles of revealed religion, although the former are contained in the Bible in their utmost perfection, as well as the latter in their brightest beauty.

He observed the real intention and design of the divine writers; and he took the words and expressions of Scripture in their proper connection and meaning.

He allowed every word of Scripture its obvious and proper sense; that is, the natural sense which Scripture conveys.

He compared the word of God with itself: he collected the several parts of Scripture on the same subjects, and on the same view. By this means he had the most striking evidence of every doctrine, blessing, and precept, set before his eyes in the most attractive light; and his views of the beauty of truth were of unspeakable use and pleasure to his soul.

With these convictions, deep in his conscience, and these modest dispositions of mind, and with these principles and rules in his understanding, he proceeded to consider the Scriptural idea of the character of God; the revealed account of the unity of God; the discovery of a plurality of agents in the undivided being of God, arising from the Hebrew plurals of the Old Testament, and the discoveries of three sacred agents in the works of creation, in the works of providence, in the production of miracles, and in the highest work of all, the work of salvation.

The Scripture Idea of God; or a concise View of the Divine Perfections.

It is certain, by the light of nature, that there is a God; and it is certain that this God can be but one; He is an infinite, eternal, unchangeable, independent,

pendent, and necessarily existent Being, every where
present; the Creator, Preserver, and Governor of all
things; infinite in wisdom, power, holiness, justice,
goodness and truth.

The Scripture wholly agrees with the light of reason, in the notion it gives us of one that is really,
truly, and properly GOD. An account of this, I
shall give in the words of a great writer*, not being
able to express myself better, or more, according to
my own mind. " If we trace (says he) this matter
through the Old Testament, we shall find that the
Scripture notion of a person that is truly GOD, and
should be received as such, includes in it

POWER AND MIGHT IRRESISTIBLE."

O LORD JEHOVAH, what GOD is there in heaven
or in earth, that can do according to thy works, and
according to thy might, Deut. iii. 24.

JEHOVAH, your GOD, is among you, a mighty
GOD and terrible, Deut. vii. 1.

JEHOVAH, your GOD, is a GOD of gods, and a
LORD of lords; a great GOD, a mighty and terrible, Deut. x. 17.

Thine, O JEHOVAH, is the greatness, and the
power, and the glory, and the victory, and the ma-
jesty, 1 Chron. xxix. 11.

He is wise in heart, and mighty in strength; who
hath hardened himself against him and prospered?
Job ix. 4.

With Him is strength and wisdom, Job xii. 13.

I know that thou canst do every thing, Job xlii. 2.

In the LORD is everlasting strength, Isa. xxvi. 5.

GOD, even JEHOVAH, that created the heavens,
and stretched them out; He that spread forth the
earth, and what comes out of it; He that gives
breath to the people upon it, and spirit to them that
walk therein, Isa. xlii. 5.

---

* Dr. Waterland in his Sermons on CHRIST's Divinity.

PERFECT

PERFECT KNOWLEDGE AND CONSUMMATE WISDOM,

He that is perfect in knowledge, is with thee, Job xxxvi. 4.

Doſt thou know the wondrous works of Him that is perfect in knowledge? Job xxxvii. 16.

Bleſſed be the name of GOD, for wiſdom and might are his, Dan. ii. 20.

ETERNITY.

Thy throne is eſtabliſhed of old from everlaſting, Pſa. xciii. 2.

GOD is great; neither can the number of his years be ſearched out, Job xxxvi. 26.

The eternal GOD, Deut. xxxiii. 27.

JEHOVAH, the everlaſting GOD, Gen. xxi. 33.

Holy One, who inhabits eternity, Iſa. lvii. 15.

IMMUTABILITY.

I am JEHOVAH: I change not, Mal. iii. 16.

OMNIPRESENCE.

Whither ſhall I go from thy Spirit; whether ſhall I fly from thy preſence? Pſa. cxxxix. 7.

Am I a GOD at hand, ſaith the LORD, and not a GOD afar off? Can any hide himſelf in ſecret places that I ſhall not ſee him, ſaith the LORD? Do not I fill heaven and earth, ſaith the LORD? Jer. xxiii. 23, 24.

CREATIVE POWERS.

Job xxvi. xxxvii. xxxviii. xxxix. xl. xli. throughout.

O JEHOVAH, thou art GOD alone, 2 Kings xix. 15.

I am JEHOVAH, that makes all things, Iſa. xliv. 24.

I am He who laid the foundation of the earth, Iſa. xlviii. 12, 13.

JEHOVAH! He is the true GOD: He is the living GOD: has made the earth by his power, Jer. x. 10, 12.

SUPREMACY, INDEPENDENCE, AND NECESSARY EXISTENCE.

GOD ſaid, I AM that I AM, Exod. iii. 14.

Theſe are the diſtinguiſhing characters, under
which

which God was pleafed to make himfelf known; and it is upon thefe accounts, that he, in oppofition to all other gods, claims to be received and honoured as God. Thefe are therefore what make up the Scripture idea of a perfon who is truly, really, and properly God. And if the Scripture has informed us what properties, attributes, and perfections muft be fuppofed to meet in one, that is truly and properly God, our own reafon muft tell us, that thefe attributes, properties, and perfections, muft have a fubject, and this fubject we call fubftance; and therefore the Scripture notion of God is, that of an eternal, immutable, omnifcient, omniprefent, almighty fubftance. If it be pretended that thefe are the characters of a Supreme God only, and not of every perfon that is true God, I anfwer, that fupremacy (*negatively confidered, in oppofition to any fuperior nature) is one of the characters belonging to any perfon that is truly God, as much as omnipotence, omnifcience, or any other; and confequently he is not truly God in the Scripture notion of God, who is not Supreme God.

This is the true notion of God, which may be drawn from the writings of the Old Teftament, and the fame runs through thofe of the New.

The Scripture Notion of the Divine Unity †.

As natural reafon affures us, that there can be but one abfolutely infinite being, fo the Scripture eftablifhes the unity of God, in the fulleft and ftrongeft manner. This, Mofes proclaimed in the ears of Ifrael ‡ : " Hear O Ifrael, Jehovah our God is one Jehovah;" and that there can be but one true God, the Moft High Himfelf has affured us, fpeaking thus by the prophet Ifaiah § : " I (Jehovah of Hofts) am the firft and I am the laft, and befides me there is no God: there

---

* I fay, negatively; becaufe pofitive fupremacy over others, could not commence till the creation.

† See Dr. Abraham Taylor on the Trinity.

‡ Deut. vi. 4.   § Ifai xlv. 6, 8.

is

is no GOD befides me; I know not any." CHRIST acknowledged, that the fcribe anfwered difcreetly, when
he faid*, " There is one GOD, and there is none but
He." The apoftle Paul has declared †, " There is
one GOD." And not to multiply quotations in fo plain
a matter, the apoftle James reprefents this truth to
be too clear to be denied by the devils; for he thus
fpeaks to fuch as vainly pretended to faith without
good works‡. " Thou believeft that there is one
GOD; thou doft well: the devils alfo believe and
tremble."

Thefe declarations of the unity of GOD, effectually
guard againft all inferior fubordinate gods, and effectually exclude all creatures from having divine honour
afcribed to them. None that are not gods by nature
can be efteemed truly and properly Gods. The apoftle
Paul tells the Galatian converts, that they were entirely ignorant of the true GOD, while they worfhipped
fuch as by nature were no Gods. " Then when you
knew not GOD, you did fervice to them which by nature are no gods." None can be true God, in a Scripture fenfe, but one infinitely perfect Being, who is GOD
by nature, or neceffarily exiftent.

A VIEW of the PLURALITY of PERSONS in the ETER-
NAL GODHEAD, from the Hebrew Bible.

I. אלהים GODS; Thirty-two times in Genefis i.—
Five hundred times in the Five Books of Mofes.

Why does Mofes ufe the plural five hundred
times, when there is a fingular noun אלוה.

INSTANCES OF A PLURAL NOUN, AND PLURAL
ADJECTIVE.

II. אלהים קרבים GODS nigh, Deut. iv. 7.
III. אלהים חיים Living GODS, Deut. v. 26.

* Mark xii. 32.   † 1 Tim. ii. 5.
‡ James ii. 19.   § Gal. iv. 8.

IV. אלהים חיים Living Gods, 1 Sam. xvii. 26.

V. אלהים חיים Living Gods, verſe 36.

VI. הוא אלהים חיים He is the living Gods, Jer. x. 10

VII. אלהים קדשים הוא The Holy Gods is He, Joſh. xxiv. 19.

VIII. אלהים אדירים Illuſtrious Gods, 1 Sam. iv. 8.

IX. אלהים שפטים בארץ Gods judging in the earth, Pſal. lviii. 11.

X. קדישי עליונין The Holy Supreme Ones, Dan. vii. 18.

INSTANCES OF THE PLURAL NOUN AND PLURAL VERB.

XI. נעשה אדם Let us make man, Gen. i. 26.

XII. נרדה ונבלה Let us go down, and let us confound their language, Gen. ii. 7.

XIII. התעו אתי אלהים Gods cauſed me to wander, Gen. xx. 13.

XIV. ולא נתנו אלהים And Gods ſuffered not, Gen. xxxi. 7.

XV. נגלו אליו אלהים Gods appeared to him, Gen. xxxv. 7.

XVI. אלהים ישפטו Gods judge, Gen. xxxi. 53.

XVII. הלכו אלהים לפדות Gods went to redeem, 2 Sam. vii. 23.

INSTANCES OF THE PLURAL PRONOUN BELONGING TO THE SUPREME GOD.

XVIII. כאחד ממנו The man is become as one of us, Gen. iii. 22.

XIX. ומי ילך לנו And who will go for us, Iſa. vi. 8.

XX. ויגידו לנו Shew us what ſhall happen, Iſa. xli. 22.

INSTAN◆

INSTANCES OF A DIVINE PERSON APPEARING IN THE
CHARACTER OF A MESSENGER.

XXI. מלאך יהוה The Meſſenger of JEHOVAH, Gen.
xvi. 7.

The Meſſenger who appeared to Hagar was JEHO-
VAH, as appears from verſe 13.

שם יהוה הדבר אליה.
The name of JEHOVAH *who ſpake* to her.

XXII. וירא אליו יהוה JEHOVAH in the character of a
Meſſenger converſed with Abraham, Gen. xviii. 1, 2.

It is evident that CHRIST was one of the three men.

XXIII. ויקרא אליו מלאך יהוה--ויאמר בי נשבעתי נאם
יהוה.

JEHOVAH in the character of a Meſſenger, ſwore an
oath to Abraham, Gen. xxii. 11, 12.

XXIV. &c. המלאך הגאל The Meſſenger that redeemed me from all evil, bleſs the lads, Gen. xlviii.
16.

XXV. וירא מלאך יהוה אליו--ויקרא אליו אלהים The
Meſſenger of JEHOVAH appeared unto Moſes—GOD
called to him out of the buſh, Exod. iii. 2, 4.

XXVI. שמי בקרבו The Meſſenger, to whom pay
obedience for my name is in him, Exod. xxiii. 20, 21.

XXVII. העברתי מעליך עונך A Meſſenger ſays to
Joſhua, " I have removed thy iniquity from thee,"
Zech. iii. 4.

MISCELLANEOUS PROOFS OF A PLURALITY IN THE
GODHEAD.

XXVIII. ויהוה המטיר--מאת יהוה JEHOVAH rained
on Sodom from JEHOVAH, Gen. xix. 24.

XXIX. קדשים The HOLY ONES; unto which of
the Holy Ones wilt thou turn, Job v. 1.

XXX. ודעת קדשים And the knowledge of the Holy
Ones, Prov. ix. 10.

XXXI. ודעת קדשים And the knowledge of the
Holy Ones, Prov. xxx. 3.

H h 2   XXXII,

XXXII. קדשים The Holy Ones, Hof. xi. 9.

XXXIII. קדישן The Holy Ones, Dan. iv. 13, 17.

XXXIV. קדוש קדוש קדוש Holy, Holy, Holy, Ifai. vi. 3.

XXXV. גבהים HIGHER ONES, Eccle. v. 7.

XXXVI. וזכר את בוראיך And remember thy CREATORS, Eccle. xii. 1.

XXXVII. איה אלוה עשי Where is GOD my MAKERS, Job xxxv. 10.

XXXVIII. כסאך אלהים Thy throne, O GOD, Pfal. xlv. 7.—Verfe 8. משחך אלהים אלהיך O GOD, thy GOD hath anointed thee.

XXXIX. ישמח ישראל בעשיו Let Ifrael rejoice in his MAKERS, Pfalm cxlix. 2.

XL. ואם אדונים אני איה מוראי If I am LORDS where is my fear, Mal. i. 6.

XLI. בעליך עשיך Thy MAKERS—thy Hufband, Ifai. liv. 5.

XLII. יבעלוך בניך Thy MAKERS fhall marry thee, Ifai. lxii. 5.

XLIII. יהוה צדקנו JEHOVAH our righteoufnefs. JEHOVAH will raife the Branch JEHOVAH, Jer. xxiii. 6.

XLIV. עירין The WATCHERS, Dan. iv. 13. 17.

XLV. אלהא עליא--העדיו The Moft High GOD —THEY took away, Dan. v. 18, 20.

XLVI. והושעתים ביהוה אלהיכם JEHOVAH fays, I will fave them by JEHOVAH their GOD, Hof. i. 7.

SCRIPTURE REPRESENTATION of THREE PERSONS
in the DIVINE NATURE.

PRELIMINARY DEFINITIONS.

A Perfon is fomething intelligent, in oppofition to the brutal creation.

A Perfon is fomething which is the fubject of intelligence, having diftinctive characters of *I, Thou, He,*

He, not divided, nor diftinguifhed into more intelligent agents, capable of the fame character.

The Trinity is not a fingle Perfon, becaufe diftinguifhed into more intelligent agents than one.   See
Dr. Waterland's Second Defence, pages 370, 371.

A BEING is one feparate divided fubftance, divided
from all other beings.

The DIVINE BEING is the one infinite divine nature.

A DIVINE PERSON is one fingle fubfiftent in that
being or fubftance, the Godhead.

Thofe that deny the true and proper Deity of JE-
SUS CHRIST, plainly and flatly deny that two perfons
can be one neceffary being or fubftance.   Dr. Waterland's Second Defence, page 437.

" They fay two perfons cannot be one being, page
438.

" Two perfons cannot be one neceffary exifting
fubftance."

I. CREATION proves a TRINITY.

1. In the beginning GOD created the heavens and
the earth, Gen. i. 1.

2. All things were made by JESUS CHRIST, Eph.
iii. 9.

LORD, Thou art GOD, which haft made heaven and
earth, Acts iv. 24.

All things were made by CHRIST : without Him
no one thing, John i. 3.

For by him were all things created that are in
heaven, and that are in earth, vifible and invifible,
whether they be thrones or dominions, or principali-
ties, or powers, all things were created by him, and
for him, Col. i. 16.

3. The SPIRIT of GOD moved on the face of the
waters, Gen. i. 2.

By his SPIRIT he garnifhed the heavens, and all the
hoft of them ; by the breath or fpirit of his mouth,
Job xxvi. 13.

II. The

II. The Creation of Man.

Let Us make man, Gen. i. 26.

Thy Maker is thy Hufband, Ifa. liv. 5.

Let us kneel before our Maker, Pfal. xcv. 6.

The Spirit of God has made me, and the breath of the Almighty hath given me life, Job xxxiii. 4.

III. The Deliverance of the Israelites out of Egypt, by

1. Jehovah the Father, whofe mercies, &c. Pfal. lxii. 12.

2. The Angel of his Prefence, who faved—redeemed—bare them. Ifa. lxiii. 9.

3. The Spirit led them on—caufed them to reft, ver. 10, 11, 14.

IV. The Covenant of Grace.

The Father made the covenant.

The Son is the Surety, Mediator, and Meffenger.

The Spirit of God ftands by as a witnefs, to fee all the articles agreed upon and performed on each fide.

The Father's part in the covenant was to fill it with all bleffings, Eph. i. 4.

The Son's part was to receive all the bleffings, and keep them. Pfa. lxviii. 18. Thou haft received gifts for men. Col. ii. 3. In whom are hid all the treafures of wifdom and knowledge. Col. i. 19. For it pleafed the sacred Three, that in him fhould all fulnefs dwell*.

The Spirit's part is to apply all the bleffings to elect fouls. He fhall take of mine, and fhall fhew it unto you, John xvi. 15.

For I am with you, faith the Lord of Hofts, with the word by whom I covenanted with you, when ye came out of Egypt; fo my Spirit is ftanding among you, Hag. ii. 4, 5.

* See Dr. Gill's Body of Divinity, Vol. I. page 231.

V. The

V. The Oeconomy of Salvation.

1. The God and Father of Christ elects men, and blesses them; predestinates and adopts them into his family, Eph. i. 5, 6.

2. The Son of God is the Author of Redemption by his blood, Eph. i. 7. Rev. v. 9.

3. The Holy Spirit seals them up for the possession of heaven, Eph. i. 3—11.

VI. Christ sent by the Lord God and his Spirit, Isa. xlviii. 16.

Here we plainly perceive Three Persons.
1. Now the Lord God
2. And his Spirit
3. Have sent Me, Isa. lxi. 1.
Again,
1. The Spirit
2. Of the Lord God
3. Is upon Me.

VII. The Son of God sent into Human Flesh, Gal. iv. 4.

God was manifest in the flesh, 1 Tim. iii. 16.
See a Trinity in Luke i. 32—35.

1. The Highest—Jehovah the Father, ver. 32.
2. The Son of the Highest who took flesh of the virgin.
3. The Holy Ghost who overshadowed the virgin, ver. 35.

VIII. Jesus anointed by God the Father with the Holy Spirit.

Psa. xlv. 7. Thy God hath anointed thee.
Isa. lxi. 1. Jehovah hath anointed me.
Acts x. 38. How God anointed Jesus of Nazareth with the Holy Ghost, and with power.

Note. Here the Holy Spirit is plainly distinguished from a power, or virtue, or an energy, which the Socinians would have us believe. See also

Rom.

Rom. xv. 13. where we read of the power of the
HOLY GHOST; that is, on Socinian principles, the
power of a power! the attribute of an attribute! the
energy of an energy! But this is too contemptible
and abfurd to be admitted by any that are fo modeft
as to take GOD at his word refpecting the perfonality
and divinity of the HOLY SPIRIT.

The UNCTION and SEALING of BELIEVERS.

Now he who eftablifheth us with you in CHRIST,
and hath anointed us, is GOD; who alfo hath fealed
us, and given the earneft of the SPIRIT in our hearts,
2 Cor. i. 21, 22.

IX. The BAPTISM of JESUS.

1. JESUS being baptifed—
2. The HOLY SPIRIT defcending—
3. The FATHER fpeaking from heaven—
This is MY beloved SON—The SPIRIT defcended
upon him, Matt. iii. 16, 17.

Go Arian!—Go Socinian!—Go Unitarian! to
Jordan, and fee a Trinity.

X. JESUS promifes to fend the HOLY SPIRIT from the FATHER.

See a Trinity twice in one verfe, John xv. 26.
1. But when the Comforter is come,
2. Whom I will fend unto you
3. From the FATHER.
   Again, in the fame verfe.
1. Even the SPIRIT of TRUTH,
2. Who proceedeth from the FATHER,
3. He (the HOLY SPIRIT) fhall teftify of ME.
   Again, John xiv. 26.
1. But the Comforter, who is the HOLY GHOST,
2. Whom the FATHER will fend
3. In my Name.
   See alfo John xiv. 16.
1. I will pray.

2. The

2. The FATHER.

3. He fhall give you another Comforter. See chap. xvi. 7.

XI. Our LORD JESUS obtained Eternal REDEMPTION.

1. The price was paid to GOD the FATHER.

Thou haft redeemed us to GOD with thy blood, Rev. v. 9.

2. CHRIST paid the price.

As man, his body and foul were the facrifice, Heb. ix. 12, 14.

As God-Man, he was the Prieft or Sacrificer.

As GOD, he was the Altar on which he facrificed, or offered up his Satisfaction.

3. It was through the eternal SPIRIT.

Grieve not the HOLY SPIRIT of GOD, by whom ye are fealed unto the day of Redemption, Eph. iv. 30.

XII. The RESURRECTION of CHRIST fhews THREE PERSONS.

1. GOD raifed up JESUS, 1 Cor. xv. 15.

2. I have power to take up my life again, John x. 18.

3. The SPIRIT raifed up CHRIST from the dead, Rom. viii. 9.

Again,

1. GOD raifed him, and gave him glory, 1 Pet. i. 21.

2. CHRIST raifed himfelf by his own power—" I will raife it up," John ii. 19.

3. He was declared the SON of GOD with power, according to the SPIRIT, Rom. i. 4.

XIII. In REGENERATION we fee a TRINITY.

1. The FATHER is faid to regenerate —" Blefled be the GOD and FATHER—begotten us again," 1 Pet. i. 3.

2. SON of GOD regenerates—" Quickens whom he will," John v. 21.—" Born of him," 1 John ii. 29.

I i   3. The

3. The Spirit of God regenerates—" Born of water and of the Spirit," John iii. 5.

See the Three Persons in Titus iii. 5.

God the Father is called our Saviour—is said to save by the washing of regeneration, and the renewing of the Holy Ghost, (ἐ ἐξεχεεν) whom he poured out on men, through Jesus Chrit our Saviour.

XIV. Adoption is an Act of Three Persons.

1. The Father's love is admired in bestowing this favour, 1 John iii. 1.

2. Christ gives right and power to become the sons of God, John i. 12. Gal. iv. 5.

A privilege is a right and power to enjoy a peculiar, exclusive blessing, or a blessing from which others are excluded.

3. The Spirit is the Spirit of adoption.

He witnesses to our spirits that we are sons, Rom. viii. 16.

See all three together in one verse.

Because ye are sons, God hath sent forth the Spirit of his Son into your hearts, crying, Abba, Father, Gal. iv. 6.

XV. Fresh Illuminations from God in Three Persons.

That the God of our Lord Jesus Christ, the Father of Glory, may give unto you the Spirit of wisdom and revelation in the knowledge of Him, that is, of Christ, Eph. i. 17. where

1. The Father is prayed to.

2. The Spirit of wisdom is prayed for, that they might have

3. An increase of the knowledge of Christ.

XVI. Fresh

KVI. Fresh Grace and Strength from Three
Persons.

I bow my knee to the Father of our Lord
Jesus Christ, that he would grant you according
to the riches of his glory, to be ſtrengthened with
might by his Spirit in the inner man, Eph. iii. 14,
16. See Zech. x. 12.

XVII. The Holy Ghost given to Believers, by
God the Father, through the Merits of Jesus
Christ.

The Holy Ghost, whom He, that is, God the
Father, poured on us abundantly through Jesus
Christ, Titus iii. 5, 6.

XVIII. Proof from the Object of our Prayers.

The object of prayer is the one God; Father,
Son, and Spirit.

Sometimes the God and Father of Christ is
ſingly addreſſed—" I bow my knee to the Father,"
&c. Eph. iii. 14.

Sometimes Christ himſelf as by Stephen—"Lord
Jesus receive my Spirit," Acts vii. 59.

Sometimes the Holy Spirit—" I beſought the
Lord thrice," 2 Cor. xii. 9.

The Lord direct your hearts into the love of
God, and into the patient waiting for Christ, (or into
the patience of Christ) 2 Theſſ. iii. 5.

Sometimes all three together.

1. Him who is, was, and is to come; (namely, the
Father)

2. The ſeven ſpirits which are before his throne;
(which mean the Holy Spirit in the perfection of
his gifts and graces—See Dr. Gill in Loc.)

3. And from Jesus Christ, Rev. i. 4, 5.

Some think the ſeven ſpirits are angels; but it is
abſurd to imagine that grace and peace ſhould be

prayed for from angels equally as from God. Can angels too be set before the Son of God?

XIX. Inspiration is peculiarly the work of the Holy Spirit, but not to the exclusion of the Father and the Son. All three dictated to David, and doubtless all the writers were inspired in the same manner, and by the same persons.

1. The Spirit of the Lord spake by me, and his word was in my tongue.

2. The God of Israel—(that is, God the Father)

3. The Rock of Israel spake to me, (that is, Jesus Christ) 2 Sam. xxiii. 2, 3.

1. All Scripture is given by inspiration of God, 2 Tim. iii. 16.

2. The Bible is, " the Word of Christ."—Let the Word of Christ dwell in you richly, &c. Col. iii. 16.

3. Holy men of God spake as they were moved by the Holy Ghost, 2 Pet. i. 21.

XX. JEHOVAH in Three Persons.

1. Jehovah bless thee, and keep thee.

2. Jehovah make his face shine upon thee, and be gracious unto thee.

3. Jehovah lift up his countenance upon thee, and give thee peace, Numb. vi. 24, 25, 26.

Jehovah is our Judge.

Jehovah is our Lawgiver.

Jehovah is our King—he will save us, Isai. xxxiii. 22.

O Lord hear.

O Lord forgive.

O Lord hearken and do, Dan. ix. 19.

Christian Preachers adore God in Three Persons.

Holy,

Holy,

Holy, Isa. vi. 3. Rev. iv. 8.

These

These are beautiful inftances of the attention paid to the Three Perfons in the Divine nature; or elfe how comes it to pafs that the repetition is made *only* three times—no more and no lefs.

XXI. The GOVERNMENT of the WORLD by the Sacred THREE.

1. My FATHER worketh hitherto,
2. And I work,
3. Who hath directed the SPIRIT of the LORD, or being his Counfellor, hath taught him, that is, in the affair of the government of the world, as follows: With whom took he counfel? And who inftructed him and taught him in the path of judgment, and taught him knowledge; and fhewed to him the way of underftanding, to manage the important concerns of the world, to do every thing wifely and juftly, and to overrule all for the beft ends and purpofes? See Ifa. xl. 13, 14.—See Dr. Gill's Body of Divinity, Vol. I. page 230.

XXII. Election is afcribed to the FATHER, Sanctification to the SPIRIT, and Atonement to our LORD JESUS CHRIST.

Read 1 Pet. i. 2. Elect, according to the foreknowledge of GOD the FATHER, through fanctification of the SPIRIT unto obedience, and fprinkling of the blood of JESUS.

XXIII. The ACT of JUSTIFICATION is afcribed to each of the Sacred THREE.

1. GOD the FATHER juftifies.
One GOD who fhall juftify, &c. Rom. iii. 30.
Bleffednefs of the man to whom GOD imputeth righteoufnefs without works, Rom. iv. 6.
It is GOD that juftifieth, Rom. viii. 33.
2. It is not only by the righteoufnefs of CHRIST that men are juftified, but he himfelf juftifies by his knowledge, or by faith in him.

By

By his knowledge shall my righteous servant justify many, Isai. liii. 11.

3. It is the SPIRIT of GOD that pronounces the sentence of justification in the conscience of believers: hence they are *justified in the name of the* LORD JESUS, *and by the* SPIRIT *of our* GOD." 1 Cor. vi. 11.—See Dr. Gill's Body of Divinity, Vol. I. page 234.

XXIV. BAPTISM is to be administered,

In the name of the FATHER, and of the SON, and of the HOLY GHOST, Matt. xxviii. 19.

XXV. The General Resurrection proves a TRINITY.

1. GOD the FATHER.

GOD hath both raised up the LORD, and *will also raise up us* by his own power, 1 Cor. vi. 14.

Knowing that he which raised up the LORD JESUS, *shall raise us up also* by JESUS, and shall present us with you, 2 Cor. iv. 14.

2. GOD the SON.

All that are in the graves shall hear his voice, John v. 28.

I am alive for evermore, amen, and have the keys of hell and of death, Rev. i. 18.

The LORD JESUS, who shall change our vile body, that it may be fashioned like unto HIS glorious body, &c. Phil. iii. 21.

3. GOD the HOLY SPIRIT,

Shall also quicken your mortal bodies, by his SPIRIT that dwelleth in you, Rom. viii. 11.

XXVI. We conclude the SCRIPTURE DEMONSTRA-TION of a TRINITY, with the Apostle's benedictory Prayer.

The grace of our LORD JESUS CHRIST,
The love of GOD,
And the communion of the HOLY GHOST, be with you all, amen. 2 Cor. xiii. 14.

1. The form of the fourth was like the Son of God, (בר אלהין) Dan. iii. 25.

2. If thou be the Son of God, (ει υιος ει τȣ θεȣ) Matt. iv. 3.

3. Jefus thou Son of God, Ibid. viii. 29.

4. Thou art the Son of God, Ibid. xiv. 33.

5. Chrift the Son of God, Ibid. xxvi. 63.

6. The Son of God, Ibid. xxvii. 40.

7. I am the Son of God, ver. 43.

8. Truly this was the Son of God, ver. 54.

9. Jefus Chrift the Son of God, Mark i. 1.

10. Thou art the Son of God, Ibid. iii. 11.

11. This Man was the Son of God, (υιος θεȣ) Ibid. xv. 39.

12. That thing born of thee, fhall be called the Son of God, Luke i. 35.

13. Thou art Chrift the Son of God, Ibid. iv. 41.

14. Jefus, thou Son of God Moft High, Ibid. viii. 28.

15. Art thou then the Son of God? Ibid. xxii. 70.

16. This is the Son of God, John i. 34.

17. The only begotten Son of God, Ibid. iii. 18.

18. The voice of the Son of God, Ibid. v. 25.

19. Thou art the Chrift, the Son of the living God, Ibid. vi. 69.

20. Doft thou believe on the Son of God? Ibid. ix. 35.

21. I am the Son of God, (υιος τȣ Θεȣ ειμι) John x. 36.

22. That the Son of God might be glorified, Ibid. xi. 4.

23. Thou art Chrift the Son of God, ver. 27.

24. He ought to die becaufe he made himfelf the Son of God, John xix. 7.

25. Thefe are written that ye might believe that Jefus is the Chrift—the Son of God, Ibid. xx. 31.

26. I believe that Jefus Chrift is the Son of God, Acts viii. 37.

27. He preached Chrift, that he is the Son of God, Ibid. ix. 20.

28. Declared to be the Son of God with power, Rom. i. 4.

29. The Son of God, Jefus Chrift, 2 Cor. i. 19.

30. I live by the faith of the Son of God, Gal. ii. 20.

31. To the faith and knowledge of the Son of God, (υιȣ τȣ θεȣ) Eph. iv. 13.

32. Jefus the Son of God, Heb. iv. 14.

33. Crucify afrefh the Son of God, Ibid. vi. 6.

34. Made like the Son of God, Ibid. vii. 3.

35. Trodden under foot the Son of God, Ibid. x. 29.

36. The Son of God was manifefted to deftroy the works of the devil, 1 John iii. 8.

37. Confefs that Jefus is the Son of God, Ibid. iv. 15.

38. Jefus is the Son of God, Ibid. v. 5.

39. Believeth on the Son of God, ver. 10.

40 Believe on the name of the Son of God, ver. 13.

41. The Son of God is come, ver. 20.

42. Thefe things, faith the Son of God, who hath eyes like fire, Rev. ii. 18.

Thus far we have viewed the Character of Hervey as a divine : we have viewed his faith in the exiftence and perfections of GOD: we have entered, in his own eafy and popular manner, into the cleareft evidences of the divine exiftence; and we have adapted it to the capacity of all the young people of Great Britain. I had not power to give more convincing demonftrations. We then proceeded to confider the natural evidences of the immortality of the foul; and on this fubject our young people will find
fome

some arguments peculiarly suited to their understanding, and some thoughts which are not commonly to be met with in books on this subject. It
will not be easy for the infidels of the present age
to overthrow these arguments: their trash and impertinence on this subject will be found utterly
insufficient for this purpose. We defy every infidel
in Great Britain to prove, that he and his dog
Jouler are upon a level with respect to the nature of their souls; their capacities for virtue and
happiness; their eternity of duration, and final desti-
nation, in the empire of GOD.

We have proceeded to consider the objects and the
actions of imagination, and have shewn that there
are three sources of the pleasures of the imagination
in our survey of outward objects; that is to say, the
great, the new, and the beautiful. We went on to
consider the objects and actions of the passions of the
soul: we viewed a large train of the pleasant passions
of the soul: we proceeded to show the painful passions
of the soul, which agree with our ideas of a GOD, and
show our immortality in a strong point of light. We
went on to consider the objects and actions of the
conscience, which prove the immortality of the soul,
and clearly agree with the idea of a GOD.

We proceeded to consider the objects and actions of
taste: we pursued the nature of taste, as described by
the excellent Rollin: we considered the pleasures and
uses of taste in philosophy and devotion. Here Hervey shone in a most conspicuous point of light.

We have proceeded to consider the insufficiency
of reason to lead man to final happiness. We have
viewed reason as defective in giving us convincing
notions of a GOD; as not being able to show us where
true happiness is to be found, as being exceedingly
defective in giving us a plan of universal virtue,
and equally defective in furnishing us with the very
best motives to virtue. We have proved that reason

K k   cannot

cannot difcover the pardon of fin, the advance-ment of the foul in vital holinefs, fufficient fupport under the trials of life, and ftrong confolations againft the fears of death.

Thefe views of the three facred Perfons in the one divine nature, were perfectly agreeable to his underftanding and his faith. He was quite at home in this great truth of the Trinity. His four Ser-mons on the Divinity of Christ—His Letter upon Christ's eternal Godhead, in Theron and Afpafio, No. 8, and his Letters on the Divinity and Perfon-ality of the Holy Spirit, in anfwer to Martin Tom-kins, of Hackney, No. 24—27, plainly fhew how great a mafter he was on thefe fubjects.

And as he had the moft diftinct and forcible con-ceptions of the facred Perfons in the divine nature, fo he likewife had a clear underftanding of the di-vine decrees. He knew the nature of thefe decrees, as they were determinate purpofes of the divine will, founded on the clear perceptions of the divine underftanding. He confidered the objects and ex-tent of thefe decrees as refpecting every thing in heaven, earth, and hell, from the firft moment of creation to all eternity—the production, preferva-tion, and government of the whole natural world—the great events at the deluge—the difperfion of the nations at Babel—the deftruction of Sodom and Gomorrah—the call of Abraham, and all the great events that took place in his family—the afflictions and the advancement of Jofeph—the terrible plagues on Egypt—the ruin of the mad tyrant at the Red Sea—the wonders that furrounded the Ifraelites for forty years in the wildernefs—their entrance into Canaan, with all the fubfequent train of tranfactions under their judges and kings, quite down to the cap-tivity—the ftrange and terrible punifhment of the ten tribes which took place *feven hundred* years before the birth of Christ, and which has now lafted

twenty-five

twenty-five hundred years without any prefent fign of their ever being recalled—the ruin of Egypt, of Babylon, of Nineveh, of Tyre—the rife of Popery at Rome, with the prefent ftate of all mankind, good and bad, and all the future events that are coming upon the univerfe; *i. e.* the fudden converfion of all the Jews—their call into their own land, and eftablifhment in greater glory than ever—the ruin of Popery and Mahommedifm, and the fpread of the Gofpel all round the globe.

Thefe, with the free actions of all mankind, with the publication and eftablifhment of the Gofpel in different nations, are included in the objects and extent of the divine decrees, and they were the objects of Hervey's fpiritual underftanding. He confidered all the actions of GOD, in time, as forming one grand fyftem, without redundancy, error, or defect, terminating in the happinefs of all GOD's elect, and exhibiting the nobleft affemblage of the divine perfections.

He faw the perfections of the firft man in his original conftitution and powers, who had a clear underftanding to difcern GOD; a rectitude of will conformed to the divine nature; and his affections were like fair water in a cryftal glafs, without any difturbance or fediment; a clear and unclouded imagination; an active and retentive memory, which brought GOD to his recollection every moment. He had a tafte for all that was holy in heaven and earth; and from all thefe qualifications, nothing could flow but perfect happinefs.

Hervey has fhewn his deep fenfe of the DEPRAVITY of HUMAN NATURE, as viewed from experience and Scripture, in Dialogues XI and XIII. A man muft have no reverence for the truth of GOD in Scripture, if he can deny the facts and evidences produced in thofe Dialogues.

He

He had a very clear underſtanding of the doĉtrine
of God's FREE DISTINGUISHING AND SOVEREIGN
LOVE.

He knew that God, before he made the world,
choſe ſome certain perſons of his own free grace to
be made holy and happy; and he conſidered this
whole doĉtrine in the following points of light:

1. There is a manifeſt difference between the children of men in this world. It is evident, from daily
obſervation, that ſome are religious, and others ungodly; ſome are ſpiritual, and others are earthly-
minded; ſome are vicious, and other men are virtuous; ſome are holy, and others are ſinful; ſome have
the temper of angels, other men have the temper of
brutes; ſome are conſecrated to God, others are devoted to the devil; ſome are full of benevolence to
mankind, others are full of hatred and malice; ſome
work for the public happineſs, others work to promote public miſery; ſome are ſtriĉtly temperate,
others are riotous gluttons; ſome are amiably ſober,
others abominable drunkards; ſome have virgin
chaſtity, others are monſters in lewdneſs; ſome revere
the divine name, others are profane ſwearers; ſome
are deeply humble, others are infernals in pride;
ſome have a meek and quiet ſpirit, others are inflamed
with raſh anger; ſome are patient as lambs, others
are fretful as waſps; ſome have a generous public
ſpirit, others are eaten up with the ſcurvy of ſelf-love;
ſome are contented as a weaned child, others are diſ-
contented with every condition; ſome mortify every
ſin, others indulge every luſt of fleſh and ſpirit; ſome
reſiſt the devil, and he flies from them, others yield to
his temptations, and are his tame ſlaves; ſome live
above the ſpirit of the world, others give into all ſinful compliances; ſome are diligent in every good
thought, word, and work, others are lazy ſluggards,
and abſolutely good for nothing; ſome have a boundleſs benevolence to Being, others are envenomed with
                                                    the

the malice of hell; some are ardent lovers of justice, with a deliberate purpose of preserving the rights of men inviolate, others outrage every branch of moral justice, and trample upon the rights of all mankind; some have an ardent love to truth and veracity, others act as if they were possessed with the lying devil; some desire to imitate the faithfulness of GOD, others are unfaithful as the spirits of hell.

2. This difference between men, or this distinction of the righteous from the wicked, is not ascribed in Scripture to the will and power of man, as the cause of it, but to the will and power of GOD, and to GOD the HOLY SPIRIT working in them by his grace. " Who maketh thee to differ ? 1 Cor. iv. 7. You hath he enlivened who were dead in sin, Eph. ii. 1. Who were born, not of the will of man, but of GOD, John i. 13. Ye must be born again, John iii. 5. (Faith is) not of yourselves, it is the gift of GOD," Eph. ii. 8. This work of grace is stiled a creation, or giving existence to new principles: it is stiled regeneration, or a new birth: it is stiled a victory, or a conquest of corrupt nature: it is likewise termed a resurrection from the dead.

3. The distinction that is made by this work of GOD on the heart, is attributed in Scripture not to any merit in man, which GOD foresaw, but to the absolutely free and sovereign grace of CHRIST towards his people, and his special choice of them to be partakers of these blessings. " GOD, who is rich in mercy, Eph. ii. 4. By grace ye are saved, ver. 5. By grace ye are saved, ver. 8. There is a remnant, according to the election of grace; and if by grace, then it is no more of works, Rom. ii. 5, 6. Herein is love; not that we loved GOD, but that he loved us," 1 John iv. 10.

4. This choice of persons to sanctification and salvation by the free grace of GOD, is represented in Scripture as before the foundation of the world, from

from eternity. God has no new defigns. God hath, from the beginning, chofen you to falvation, through fanctification of the Spirit and belief of the truth.

He traced, with great fagacity and delight, the gradual openings of the Gofpel, from *Adam* to *Abraham*; from *Abraham* to *Mofes*; from *Mofes* to *David*; from *David* to *Ifaiah*; from *Ifaiah* to the birth of CHRIST. And in thefe dawnings and gradations of Gofpel knowledge, he was greatly affifted by the *fourth* book of *Witfius's* Economy of the Covenants, which is the fitteft and moft judicious work on the fubject.

His mind was exceedingly inftructed and entertained in viewing the wonderful wifdom and goodnefs of God in the whole Mofaic difpenfation of the Gofpel; the typical inftitutions of perfons and things; the High Prieft; the daily facrifice; the annual atonement; the ark of the covenant; the mercy feat; the golden cherubim, all pointed out to Hervey's faith, the perfon, righteoufnefs, fatisfaction, and grace of the LORD JESUS CHRIST.

The prophetic declarations were another fource of entertainment to the mind of this good man. He was exceedingly fond of the prophecies, and nothing but a want of health and fpirits prevented his writing a volume of letters upon them, as we have obferved above.

The fpecial providences and miraculous operations were another fource of wonders appearing in the Mofaic difpenfation. Every voluntary interpofition of God the REDEEMER in favour of good men, and every miraculous operation wrought by his omnipotence, were the broad feals of heaven fixed to the adminiftration and miffion of Mofes, and all the fubfequent prophets. And let it be obferved once for all, that every man who is not well acquainted with the Mofaic difpenfation, will never have a judicious knowledge of the New Teftament.

He

He clearly faw, with wonder and gratitude, the fuperior advantages which we enjoy under the Chriftian
difpenfation. Here we have a brighter view of the
thoughts that were hid in GOD from eternal ages.
Here we have the meridian terrors of divine juftice
united, with all the fplendors of infinite mercy, at the
fame moment, in the crofs of CHRIST—we have a
larger effufion of the HOLY SPIRIT of GOD—more
aftonifhing acts of pardoning mercy difplayed to the
worft of rebels—the moft endearing invitations of
GOD's tender love—his kindeft expoftulations with
vile finners—the richeft promifes of all forts of grace
and mercy—the brighteft examples of univerfal holinefs—the moft feafonable fuccours of divine grace in
all cafes, and the worft of all imaginable conditions.
All thefe, fealed with the blood of GOD, and confirmed
by his oath; and this oath is an appeal to his life and
perfections for the truth of all his declarations.

Hervey did not, in a proud and arrogant manner,
attempt to explain the modus of our LORD's incarna-
tion, or deny it, becaufe he could not comprehend it;
he left that for other perfons to do, who had more
pride and lefs underftanding. He believed it as a
revealed fact: he received it as a truth of GOD: he
trufted to it as the ground of his faith and falvation:
he triumphed in it as the life and joy of his foul; and
it will be the boaft and bleffednefs of his heart to
eternity.

He confidered CHRIST as the repofitory of all
truth: as the feat and fubject of all the determinations
and decrees of GOD: they were all depofited *in* him,
to be executed *by* him. There is not an event that
takes place, which fhall appear of the greateft or the
leaft confequence in heaven, earth, or hell, but what
paffes through his head and his hands. All tranfactions, quite down to the burning of the world, fall under his cognizance, and are fubject to his controul.
Hervey fat at CHRIST's feet with inceffant affiduity
and

and prayer. He underftood no truth : he valued no truth: he delighted in no truth, but as it was taught him by the infallible Spirit of CHRIST.

After a moft deliberate and attentive ftudy of the Sacred Scriptures, he was brought to as firm a faith as any one man ever poffeffed in the divine and infinite Redemption—the divine and infinite Sacrifice—the divine and infinite Satisfaction—the divine and infinite Righteoufnefs—the divine and infinite Interceffion, (for thefe were his conftant phrafes from which he never would depart).

Thefe led him to confider GOD the FATHER in three characters, as an almighty Conqueror ; an injured Sovereign ; an inexorable Judge. Thefe views led him to confider man as a miferable captive, a traiterous rebel, a moft provoking criminal. Thefe led him to confider CHRIST as an almighty REDEEMER ; a glorious High Prieft and Sacrifice ; and a moft faithful and able Surety, who endured the whole punifhment from the law and juftice of GOD. Thefe views led him to confider the HOLY SPIRIT as in regeneration, delivering us from bondage ; in fanctification, reconciling us to CHRIST's facrifice ; and as enjoying from the Comforter, peace of confcience through CHRIST's righteoufnefs and blood.

He felt the glorious power of CHRIST's refurrection in his own foul. *Garbutt*, on the Refurrection of CHRIST, abridged by Dr. *Watts*, is a performance above all price—*Ditton*, on the Refurrection of CHRIST—The great Mr. *Roger Cotes* on the Refurrection of CHRIST—The late *Bifhop Sherlock*, and the incomparable *Gilbert Weft*, on the Refurrection of CHRIST, deferve inceffant attention and eternal admiration and love. Our amiable author had their fentiments daily fhining in his mind, and warm at his heart. He felt the power of CHRIST's refurrection, and you might continually obferve him rifing to heaven by faith and love.

He

He viewed CHRIST as having carried his fatis-faction into the heaven of heavens, and as having prefented it before the throne of GOD · his FATHER, where he met with the higheft delight and eternal approbation. That righteoufnefs and atonement fpeak the very beft things in favour of all his peo-ple upon earth, and keep up a good underftanding between GOD and his people.

He viewed CHRIST in his abfolute dominion over all worlds, as the King of nature, the King of na-tions, and the King of faints. All nature is CHRIST's temple; all fpace is his abode. The depths of hell; the heights of heaven; the unmea-furable tracts of unbounded fpace, are all equally near to an omniprefent GOD and REDEEMER. Every thing that exifts, is preferved by his care; every thing that lives, lives by his life; and every thing that moves, moves by his animation. He governs ina-nimate nature by certain laws of gravitation and at-traction. He governs the vegetable world by rules of his own inftitution. He governs mere animate nature by the laws of inftinct and inceffant impulfe. He governs the rational world by principles of rea-fon and confcience; by motives fuited to our nature, addreffed to the original fprings in the human heart; fuch are honour and difhonour; fuch are profit and lofs; fuch are pain and pleafure; the prefent pains of vice, and the prefent pleafures of virtue, with all the future pains and pleafures of the invifible world.

Hervey faw and felt, with infinite rapture, this fupreme independent and abfolute dominion of CHRIST over the whole creation ; and he found it to be the joy and the blifs of his foul.

Hervey had a clear underftanding, and a rich ex-perience of the doctrine and bleffing of regeneration, and vital union with JESUS CHRIST.

He felt a change in his underftanding, his will, and his affections : he had new apprehenfions of the at-

tributes

tributes of GOD: he had new apprehenſions of his dependance upon GOD: he had new apprehenſions of his obligations to GOD, and of his awful violation of thoſe obligations.

He had a clear ſenſe of the guiltineſs of his acti- ons before GOD: he knew he was an offenſive crea- ture, and deſerved eternal puniſhment for thoſe of- fences.   He had new apprehenſions of the LORD JESUS CHRIST, as the GOD and ſalvation of a ſinner. He had new apprehenſions of the SPIRIT of GOD, as JEHOVAH LORD and GOD, the Author of all ſpiritual life: the ſource of all holy mental habits: the ſole Agent of the ſpiritual divine change: the divine Wri- ter of the law of GOD upon the heart: the glorious Sealer of the moral image of GOD upon the ſoul, and the ſovereign Author of the divine and heavenly birth.

He was experimentally acquainted with the rich bleſſing of ſanctification.   His value for Mr. Mar- ſhall's book on the Myſtery of Goſpel Sanctification, exceeded all deſcription.   He never thought he could read or recommend it enough.   He has informed me that he let it lye by in his ſtudy, without the leaſt attention, or ſo much as once reading it, till at laſt the providence and grace of CHRIST rouſed his attention to read that book; and when once he came to underſtand the four firſt directions, a heaven of holineſs opened to his ſoul, and darted upon his mental eye.   He then ran like a ſtrong man: he found himſelf brought into a new world: he found new reſolutions for GOD, and againſt ſin: he taſted new pleaſures in the word of GOD: he felt new joy in the worſhip of GOD; and he felt new pleaſure in converſing with the people of GOD.   He underſtood ſanctification, as it conſiſts in putting off the old man, and putting on the new: he felt a vital union with CHRIST: he was glued (κολλωμενος, 1 Cor. vi. 17.) to the LORD JESUS, and made one ſpirit with him:

he

he had a fameneſs of nature, a purity of principles, and a heavenly taſte, reſembling the Son of God.

The doctrine and bleſſing of union with Christ is moſt richly deſcribed by Polhill, in his *Chriſtus in Corde*; and *Chriſt a Chriſtian's Life*, by Mr. Gammon, lately publiſhed by the Rev. Mr. Wills; and *Chriſt a Chriſtian's Pattern*, by the Rev. Mr. Robert Murray. Theſe are books that give the brighteſt deſcription of all the branches of evangelical holineſs.

It was one of the brighteſt glories of his character, that he underſtood, as well as any man in the whole world, the doctrine of juſtification, by the imputed righteouſneſs of Jesus Christ.

He conſidered pardon in the mind of God as a total ſuppreſſion of all deſires to puniſh; as a kind diſpoſition to do the ſinner good; as a ſolemn aſſurance of hearty reconciliation; as an admiſſion into full confidence of favour with God. He conſidered imputation of righteouſneſs as an act of God, placing to the account and credit of a ſinner, the righteouſneſs and blood of Christ for his juſtification.

He was exceedingly pleaſed with the word IMPUTED, which is mentioned in different forms no leſs than eleven times in the fourth chapter of the Epiſtle to the Romans.

Rom. iv. 3. It was counted to him for righteouſneſs, ελογισθη αυτω εις δικαιοσυνην. Ver. 4. Reckoned of grace, λογιζεται κατα χαριν. Ver. 5. Counted for righteouſneſs, λογιζεται εις δικαιοσυνην. Ver. 6. God imputeth righteouſneſs without works, ο θεος λογιζεται δικαιοσυνην χωρις εργων. Ver. 8. The Lord will not impute ſin, Κυριος ου μη λογισηται αμαρτιαν. Ver. 9. Faith was reckoned to Abraham for righteouſneſs, η πιςις ελογισθη τω Αβρααμ εις δικαιοσυνην. Ver. x. How was it then reckoned? πως ουν ελογισθη. Ver. 11. That righteouſneſs might be imputed to them, εις το λογισθηναι και αυτοις την δικαιοσυνην. Ver. 22.

It

It was imputed to him for righteoufnefs, ελογισθη αυτω εις δικαιοσυνην. Ver. 23. That it was imputed to him, οτι ελογισθη αυτω. Ver. 24. But for us alfo to whom IT fhall be imputed, Αλλα και δι ημας, οις μελλει λογιζεσθαι

Note. The felf-fame IT which was imputed to Abraham, is imputed to us, which is not the habit or act of Abraham's faith, but the object of it, *i. e.* the divine and infinite righteoufnefs of JESUS CHRIST.

He faw, that in this method of juftification, none of the parties concerned had any reafon to complain; but every thing was tranfacted with high fatisfaction and joy, to every party affociated in the grand affair of man's falvation. The FATHER could not complain, becaufe the fcheme originated from him—The Son of GOD could not complain, for he thinks it his higheft honour and glory to ftand at the head of the whole redeemed world—The SPIRIT of GOD cannot complain, becaufe he loves to regenerate immortal fouls, and bring them to the higheft pitch of holinefs and happinefs—The Law of GOD cannot complain, becaufe that is obeyed in a higher and nobler manner than by all the beft men upon earth, and faints in glory—The Juftice of GOD cannot complain, becaufe that is fatisfied infinitely better than by all the torments of devils and damned fpirits prolonged through a vaft eternity.

In clofe connection with juftification ftands adoption into God's family. This is an higher act of fovereign grace than the pardon of fin, the juftification of a guilty criminal, or the fanctification of a finner. A man may be releafed from all obligation to punifhment, and not taken into favour: a man may be taken into favour, and yet not taken into the family as a fon. This is a greater privilege and dignity than to be an angel of GOD. To be an heir of GOD, is a greater honour than to be heir of all worlds. To be joint heir of JESUS CHRIST, is a much a much greater privilege than the angels ever did or ever will enjoy. Here they have no fhare with us: here we are their fuperiors to eternity.

Hervey ufually appeared to me with the dignity of an angel; but in reality his dignity was above them all. From this fenfe of the grace of adoption, flowed the fweeteft peace, the ftrongeft hope, the richeft joy.

There was an ardent inclination between the heart of Hervey, and the heart of God, towards the moft perfect friendfhip. Hervey was a friend to God, and to him God was a tender friend. Hence arofe the ftrongeft hope in God: the foundations of hope were well laid: the objects of hope were clearly revealed: the bleffings of hope were powerfully applied, and the exercifes of hope were mightily encouraged. Hence arofe the fweeteft joy in God. Joy is a large quantity of pleafure, or the fweeteft fenfations of the mind, fpringing from a confcioufnefs that we have it in our power to poffefs the greateft poffible good.

Hervey rejoiced in the divine perfon of Christ: he rejoiced in the fitnefs of Christ to fave: in the fulnefs of Christ to fatisfy: in the power of Christ's arm to deliver, and in the beauty and grace of Christ to endear himfelf to the foul. He rejoiced in the offices of Christ: in his prophetic office to teach him wifdom and truth: in his prieftly office, as his glorious righteoufnefs: in his kingly office, as his almighty Friend. In a word, his joys were as high as heaven; wide as unbounded fpace, and lafting as a vaft eternity.

Hervey knew the honours of true religion. The effence of honour confifts in being made honeft by the Spirit of God, and poffeffing a generous fcorn of doing wrong in the fight of God or man. A noblenefs of mind, and dignity of manners, exciting the
efteem

efteem and veneration of mankind, without a taint
of juft fufpicion, or a mark of juft contempt.

Honour is an intellectual pleafure: it is a beautiful
object, a real good, fitted to our original powers of
tafte: it is an object fuited to give our paffions true
pleafure.

To have the approbation of a wife and good GOD,
and marks of attention and diftinction from the
LORD JESUS CHRIST, the perfect Judge of excellence,
gives a fweet fenfation to a holy and virtuous mind;
and no man can defpife this honour, except he who
defpairs of attaining it.

Honour is an affiftant to holinefs: a powerful
helper to virtue: it is laudable to ufe honour as a
fcaffolding to holinefs and virtue, which muft never
be taken down to eternity. Holinefs and honour
will live together in the prefence of GOD, and JESUS
CHRIST will never ceafe to crown holinefs with the
moft perfect honour and glory.

Honour is a glorious engine of ufefulnefs, or an
inftrument of promoting the happinefs of the church
of CHRIST, and the good of mankind. It is truly
becoming a wife man to feek honour for this end,
that he may do the more good. It is the wifdom of
a great mind to gain honour as an engine of diffufing
happinefs.

Mr. Hervey has obtained great degrees of honour,
wherever his name has been well known, and his
writings well read and underftood; but I do him the
juftice to declare, ·that I believe that few men of
equal powers of genius, learning, and virtue, ever
fought the honour of this world lefs than himfelf.

In the whole compafs of my converfe and correfpondence with him, I never faw a mind fo fuperior to the applaufes of mankind. The felfifh paffions
appeared to be not only fuppreffed, but eradicated;
not only mortified, but ftruck dead: he catched fire
at the leaft glimpfe of the glory of CHRIST, and was

all

all life and zeal for the honour of his Master, whilst a fondness for fame appeared to be crucified, dead, buried, and lost.

With respect to the riches of this world, he took no pains to acquire them; but he was not indifferent as to a competence in life. He knew that the God who spared not his own son, would with him freely give us all things. As to temporal supplies, he left it entirely to his heavenly Saviour to give him food and raiment at the time when, and in the manner how, he pleased. He only desired temporal good for a supply of his real wants; the enjoyment of his studies, and of his friends; the purposes of moral justice; and the glorious exertions of a godlike benevolence.

Health of body; ease of mind; a sweet flow of animal spirits; a high degree of cheerfulness; pleasing prospects of the grandeur and novelty of creation; clear views of the beauties of Scripture; with all the ravishing sweetness of the great and precious promises. These were all desirable objects, as they were subservient to the divine honour, and promotive of his own usefulness.

Hervey had the greatest serenity of mind, and self-possession of soul, under all the troubles and afflictions of human life. He felt the presence of a good that was pure, powerful, and permanent; and this good was superior to all the evils he felt or feared. He knew, as well as any man, that all things in heaven, earth, and hell, must needs work for his good.

I never observed in him, for one moment, the least disturbance of mind, with respect to future events, and the calamities of life. With the most placid soul, he left all his affairs in the hands of his best Friend; and he firmly believed that he should be bettered by every thing, and worsted by nothing; and you see, that in the last day of his life, when the

agonies

agonies of death were faſt approaching, nothing could ſhake the godlike dignity of his mind.

He loved the bleſſing of divine aſſiſtances from GOD the HOLY SPIRIT. He ſteered between the two extremes of a cold procedure in religion, upon the meer principles of reaſon, without any aſſiſtance from GOD; and all enthuſiaſtic impulſes, viſions, and voices, which have no ground in clear reaſon, or ſolid foundation in Scripture. He knew that duty and dependence muſt go hand in hand together: he knew that maxim to be exceeding good, *Bene oraſſe eſt bene ſtuduiſſe*; *i. e.* praying is the beſt ſtudy; and this, *Nemo magnus vir ſine afflatu divino*. No man is good without the divine aſſiſtance.

The whole ſcope and tenor of Scripture, lead us to conſider the human mind as every moment dependent upon GOD for its light, favour, inclinations to holineſs, a taſte for virtue, a genius for devotion, ſtrength over ſin, power to plead the promiſes, ability to diſcern what is matter of duty in the moſt difficult circumſtances of human life, an honeſty of heart to put ourſelves in the way of the very beſt motives, with a cheerful alacrity of ſoul to obey thoſe motives with unfainting perſeverance, to the end of life. All that ſteady determination of ſpirit, which lived and reigned in Hervey's heart for the laſt eighteen years of his life, was entirely the fruit and conſequence of the faithful energy of GOD the ſpirit in his ſoul.

It was this glorious ſpirit which infuſed the divine life and preſerved that life. This ſpirit created the holy mental habit, and continued that habit in its full force and virtue. This HOLY SPIRIT paſſed the divine change upon all his faculties, and preſerved that change. This bleſſed Spirit inſcribed the divine law, and preſerved that inſcription. This bleſſed Spirit impreſſed the ſacred image, and preſerved that impreſſion.

preffion. This bleffed Spirit produced the new birth, and preferved it alive and immortal in the foul.

All thefe godlike inftincts and impreffions produced an unbounded zeal for the divine honour, and an ardent defire to live with God in immortal glory.

He ardently loved the law of God in the form of a covenant of works, becaufe Christ his head had perfectly kept it. He loved the law of God as a rule of action, becaufe Christ his King had kindly commanded it.

A law is a rule of action, commanding all that is right, and forbidding all that is wrong.

The covenant of works is more than a law: it is a law with a penalty annexed to difobedience, and a reward of eternal life annexed to obedience.

The covenant of works is natural religion in its utmoft extent, perfection, and glory; and the condition of this covenant is uncontaminated virtue.

On the footing of natural religion, the whole world is guilty before God: all mankind are utterly unable to fulfil the condition, to make fatisfaction for paft offences, or endure the punifhment due to their crimes. In this view of things believers are eternally delivered from the covenant of works. Believers owe an eternal debt of gratitude to Christ the Redeemer, and an eternal debt of loyalty to Christ their King. If Christ could redeem us from hell, and not from fin, he would be no Redeemer at all, or worfe than none. A king without a law is a cypher; and if Christ had no rule of obedience, he would be no king at all. God loves the law in the form of the covenant of works, and he delighted his eyes with feeing Christ obey it as a covenant. Let all mankind know, what devils and angels already know, that God will never fave one foul at the expence and ruin of the covenant of works.

M m   Hervey

Hervey loved the grace of repentance, and had every branch of it wrought into his heart by the eternal SPIRIT of GOD. He was poffeffed of the confidering part of repentance: the refolving part; the turning part; the melting and mourning part; the confeffing part; the returning and working part of repentance; and thefe he has defcribed in the moft pungent and lively manner I ever faw, or expect to fee. Read his Eight Pofthumous Sermons, fold by Mathews, in the Strand.

Hervey was a moft ardent lover of the worfhip of GOD in all its branches. Worfhip is the moft fervent and lively acknowledgment of all the divine attributes in the perfon of CHRIST the MEDIATOR, under the affiftance of the HOLY SPIRIT, with a high degree of admiration and love, and attended with the utmoft gratitude and delight.

Hervey had an exceeding veneration for all the parts of public worfhip. How often have I feen his foul nothing but tendernefs and fire! It was enough to grieve any ferious perfon's heart to fee fuch a celeftial genius pinned down to the thoughts and words of other men, fo vaftly inferior to his own.

I have already hinted at his manner of family worfhip. His two fervants read the Gofpels, Epiftles, and Pfalms, in regular order, throughout the year. When they made any blunder, he always ftopped them. When the chapter and pfalm were finifhed, he chofe out that paffage which ftruck his imagination and pleafed his tafte. He would begin fo flow, and with fuch fimplicity of thought and language, that you would be tempted to imagine he wanted matter; but he foon convinced you to the contrary: the powers of his underftanding began to ferment; his thoughts multiplied; his paffions took fire; his expreffions glowed; and in clear, concife, and energetic words, for fifteen or twenty minutes, he would

fly

fly with your foul to the third heavens, and leave your heart melting in the prefence of GOD.

After confidering him in his manner of family prayer, I intended to defcribe his clofet devotions; but I find myfelf unequal to the tafk.   In order to relieve myfelf, and entertain the reader, I defigned to have introduced his guardian angel, who attended him night and day for the laft twenty years of his life.   I wifh to draw this angel as reprefenting the ardour of his fecret adorations; the depth and pungency of his confeffions of fin; the fervour of his pleadings with GOD for grace and mercy; the fublime fire of his gratitude to GOD; his high delight in the LORD JESUS, as the life and joy of his foul. But here I likewife fail; I can neither, by my own powers, nor by the help of an angel, paint Hervey's heart equal to the life.   If I fhould be favoured with an happy flow of thought, they fhall be inferted in the Appendix.   At prefent we muft difmifs this moft agreeable fubject.

He had the deepeft veneration for the being and attributes of GOD of any man I ever knew: he appeared to feel GOD in all the powers of his foul every moment.   Moft men are practical atheifts; and even religious men appear to think of GOD, and fpeak of Him with fuch coldnefs and indifference of heart, as favours of ingratitude and contempt.

It was obferved of the great Mr. Boyle and Sir Ifaac Newton, that they never fpoke the word GOD without a folemn paufe before hand; and neither of them excelled our Author in his reverential attention to the Deity: he faw God in every thing: he heard his voice in every thing: he tafted the divine goodnefs in his food, and he regarded the movements of his Providence in every ftep of his life; at all times, and in all places, he adverted to the power, prefence, and grace of GOD his SAVIOUR.

He

He had a wonderful delight in the LORD's day: he considered that day as consecrated to contemplation and devotion; as devoted to the pursuit of truth and fruition of goodness: he never slept away his LORD's day mornings: his soul soared away into the perfections of CHRIST, and beauties of Scripture: he had not one moment for trifling and impertinence through the whole day, and yet he kept clear of all Jewish rigours and severities: he had nothing gloomy or sour in his religion, nor did I ever see one fit of gloom or sourness in his temper for one moment. Public worship was the delight and joy of his soul; and had he been allowed at all times the use of free prayer equally as in free preaching, he had been an object for wise men to imitate, and angels to admire.

He considered the fear of GOD as the beginning of wisdom, and a trust in his perfections as the commencement of happiness. He had a serious and delightful sense of GOD, which always issued in obedience to the disposing will of his Providence; the commanding will of his law, and the sanctifying will of his spirit in the Gospel. He had the greatest expectations and trust in GOD. He was free to declare to GOD, that he found himself guilty, and fled to him for pardon: that he found himself filthy, and fled to him for purity: that he found himself in danger, and fled to him for protection: that he found himself needy, and fled to him for supply: that he found himself weak, and fled to him for strength: that he found himself a captive, and fled to him for liberty: that he found himself timorous, and fled to him for fortitude: that he found himself fainting, and fled to him for perseverance. Oh! that all Christians might imitate him in his fear, faith, trust, and confidence in GOD.

His whole soul appeared to be transformed into love to GOD; his esteem for the nature and character of GOD was unbounded; his desires after the vital

presence

preſence of God were infinite upon infinite; his good
will to the cauſe of God had no other limits than
the divine nature and attributes; and his delight in
God reſembled the divine love, which has neither a
bottom, nor a ſhore. There are three admirable
diſcourſes upon love to God; the firſt by Dr. An-
neſly in the Morning Exerciſes; the ſecond by Dr.
Watts, in his Uſe of the Paſſions in Religion; the
third by Dr. Guyſe, in the Berry-ſtreet Lectures;
and to theſe I add a fourth, Mrs. Rowe's Devout
Exerciſes of the Heart. Theſe were all exemplified
in a moſt lively manner by our amiable and excellent
friend; but the principle and grace which peculiarly
diſtinguiſhed him from all mankind, was vital faith: he
had a firm perſuaſion of Christ's power and grace to
ſave: his heart was open to receive him in all his
offices, and he ſurrendered his whole ſoul into
Christ's hands, to be ſaved by him in his own
method of ſalvation; Witſius's Chapter of Faith, in
his Economy of the Covenants; but above all, Mr.
Erſkine's Six Sermons upon the Aſſurance of Faith,
pleaſed him more than every thing he had read.
He aſſured me that he had had a million of doubts;
and when God the Spirit began to make him taſte
the joys of aſſurance, he felt himſelf ardently deſirous
to bring every Chriſtian to the ſame ſtature and
ſtrength with himſelf.

We have already taken notice of his faith in
Christ, and I can aſſure the reader; that it was a faith
not without words; his whole ſoul was perpetually
bent upon doing good: all his thoughts and paſſions: all his words and actions, tended towards the
public happineſs: it ſeemed impoſſible for me to
conceive of him as living a ſingle day, without con-
triving how to do good.

His love to Christ we have deſcribed before; I
muſt only add, in this place, that Mr. Hubbard's
two excellent Sermons upon love to Christ, were
exem-

exemplified by this great and good man in the moſt
ſingular manner. His love to CHRIST was attended
with the higheſt zeal for his glory. Zeal is a compound paſſion made up of love and anger; love to
the objeɛt conſidered as good, and anger at every
thing that has a tendency to eclipſe or injure that
good. He knew that GOD the Father had the higheſt
value for his dear SON, and the keeneſt reſentment
againſt every enemy to his glory. He knew that
GOD the SON had the utmoſt regard for his own
honour, and the diſplay of his illuſtrious power and
grace to ſave to the uttermoſt, and he copied the example of his Divine Maſter. He knew that GOD
the HOLY SPIRIT delighted to glorify CHRIST : that
this was his favourite work in the Churches of CHRIST.
Hervey's delight and glory was to imitate the example of the HOLY SPIRIT.

The objeɛts of the inviſible world were always
very near him, and he realized thoſe objeɛts by faith
in a very lively manner. He viewed all the ſaints
and angels in glory as very near him every moment.
He viewed all the devils and damned ſpirits as very
near him: the two worlds of happineſs and miſery
were ſtrongly preſent in his mental eye : his faith
brought diſtant things very near; he conſidered future things as eternal, and eternity juſt at hand.
Theſe ſtrong and pungent repreſentations of inviſible
objeɛts, kept his whole ſoul alive and awake to the
glory of his great GOD and SAVIOUR.

He had a powerful perſuaſion and confidence that
CHRIST had bought a rich abundance of zeal with
his moſt precious blood to put into his heart, and
that he had purchaſed that heart with the ſame blood
to be the receptacle of holy zeal. This was an almighty motive to all manner of good works.

All the bleſſings of heaven and earth : all the
graces and glories of time and eternity, he conſidered
as the fruit of CHRIST's blood and righteouſneſs;

and

and he confidered his underftanding, with all his immortal powers, to be redeemed by the blood of God,
from darknefs, guilt, and corruption, to be the entire
property of his Redeemer, to be· continually employed in the richeft difplay of all the divine perfections.

He regarded the example of the beft of men in all
ages, in order to roufe his own zeal to the moft unbounded fire. He confidered Phinehas, who was
zealous for his God, as a noble pattern for imitation.
He imitated the example of·the glorious Elijah,
who, amidft a nation of infidels and idolaters, was
very jealous for the Lord God of Hofts. He imitated the example of his Divine Mafter, who could
truly fay, the zeal of thine houfe hath eaten me up.
He copied the glorious zeal of the apoftle Paul, who
declares, with a moft magnificent boldnefs, none of
thefe things move me, neither count I my life dear
unto myfelf, fo that I may finifh my courfe with joy.
What mean ye to weep and to break mine heart: I
am willing not only to fuffer, but to die for the name
of the Lord Jesus.

Hervey confidered that the zeal of a great and
generous foul could be no otherwife employed or ex-
pended, but in glorifying Christ.

His zeal could boldly look God in the face, and
God could look his zeal in the face with a fmiling
approbation, becaufe it was the production of his
own bleffed Spirit in his heart. His zeal was
equally purged from lukewarmnefs on the one hand,
and the mad fire of perfecuting bitternefs on the
other. I never obferved the leaft fpeck of perfecution in his temper, language, and letters. It is almoft impoffible to conceive, of a human foul, in
an imperfect ftate, and dwelling· in frail flefh and
blood, more entirely transformed into love to God
and all mankind; he found, by happy experience,
that as true zeal is a refemblance of God, fo it
always

always lives neareſt to that God, whoſe rectitude and honour is infinite and eternal. As zeal loves to live near to God, as it is immortal as our ſoul, the providence and grace of Christ will never forſake a man of true zeal in the preſent life.

The example and righteouſneſs; the honour and dignity of the great Founder of our religion, is an infinitely touching conſideration, to rouſe us to zeal immortal as our exiſtence. God has in all ages encouraged men of the moſt refined zeal and ardour in the cauſe of Christ.

Self-love and ſelf-intereſt; that is, deep ſelf-concern awakened Hervey to jealouſy or reſentment for the deareſt object, and ſpirited up his paſſions to act with zeal for that object.

Gratitude ſtimulated Hervey's ſoul to a generous zeal for the divine honour: gratitude is a compoſition of the fineſt feelings of the ſoul: gratitude has ſeven ingredients in the compoſition of it, i. e. a lively ſenſe of benefits received; a tender regard to the great Benefactor; an ardent deſire to make all poſſible returns; a ſteady determination to be more grateful when we have better abilities; a reſolution never to lay gratitude aſide; diſapprobation, and ſelf-contempt, when we feel an ungrateful heart, and a high delight in our own exiſtence, when we feel a grateful temper equal to our wiſhes.

He conſidered zeal as an intellectual pleaſure, as a moſt agreeable exerciſe to all the faculties of the ſoul, highly pleaſing to God, who is the object of it, and exceedingly pleaſing to a good man, who is the ſeat and ſubject of it.

Lukewarmneſs in religion has no pleaſure: it is highly diſpleaſing to God, and it is no pleaſure to a carnal profeſſor.

Indifference of heart to the evidences of God's exiſtence; indifference of heart to the evidences of the ſoul's immortality; indifference of heart to the evidences

dences of the infpiration of Scripture; indifference
of heart to the evidences of CHRIST's divinity; indifference of heart to the evidences of his precious
fatisfaction and righteoufnefs; indifference of heart
to the evidences of the divinity of the HOLY SPIRIT;
indifference of heart to the evidences of all the glorious doctrines of the Gofpel; indifference of heart
to every part of practical godlinefs. This temper
marks the character of the prefent generation of profeffors; but whether GOD approves of this temper;
whether CHRIST delights in this treatment of his
perfon and grace; whether the HOLY SPIRIT of GOD
is pleafed with this treatment, the day of death,
which is very near, and the day of judgment, that is
not far off, will moft awfully declare.

At this laft tremendous day, Hervey's zeal for the
glory of CHRIST will ftand confpicuous, and will
fhine out before the whole affembled world of devils,
men and angels. Millions of guilty hypocrites will
blufh to fee the infinite fuperiority of his character:
millions of devils will tremble to fee him applauded:
millions of angels will triumph to hear him approved;
and millions of his fellow Chriftians will rejoice to
fhare with him in the rewards of grace through an
endlefs eternity.

Hervey loved to imitate the example of CHRIST
in his temper and life. There was the fame mind in
him that was in CHRIST JESUS. " He walked as
CHRIST walked," 1 John ii. 6. CHRIST fought his
Father's glory in all things. Hervey fought CHRIST's
glory in all things. CHRIST obeyed his Father's
will in all cafes whatfoever. Hervey obeyed CHRIST
at all times and in all conditions. CHRIST trufted
his Father's providence in all circumftances.   Hervey trufted CHRIST's providence in all things.
CHRIST worfhipped his Father's perfections with
high veneration and delight. Hervey adored the

N n   · perfections

perfections of CHRIST with eternal admiration and efteem.

Thus we have feen that CHRIST aimed at his Father's glory: he trufted his Father's providence: he obeyed his Father's will, and as man worfhipped his Father's perfections with high fatisfaction and joy. In all thefe inftances our amiable Author imitated the LORD JESUS CHRIST. Our LORD JESUS CHRIST had all the human graces in the higheft perfection and beauty; the ftricteft temperance and more than virgin chaftity; the deepeft humility, the fweeteft meeknefs, the moft unwearied patience, the fevereft felf-denial, the moft perfect contentment with the allotments of Providence, the moft undaunted fortitude, the greateft felf-command: thefe all fhone out in the temper and life of the LORD JESUS CHRIST; and in all thefe Hervey copied the temper and life of his dear Mafter, the LORD JESUS CHRIST. The focial graces fhone out in his temper and life in their utmoft brilliancy and beauty: his love to being was unbounded by every thing but the will and decrees of GOD: his uprightnefs to all mankind: his truth and juftice to the whole world: his fpirit of forgivenefs, and his mercy to fouls in mifery, were beyond all defcription.

And through every part of his temper, there ran the golden threads of zeal and tendernefs; of perfeverance and prudence. Hervey had a vaft admiration and the moft affectionate imitation of his Mafter. With refpect to the glorious ordinance of Chriftian baptifm, Hervey was no four bigot on the one fide, or on the other. I never obferved in him the leaft degree of prejudice againft what is called Believers Baptifm. He was not fo happy to be led into it for himfelf. This was one of the difadvantages of his education, and to the connections he had formed in all the firft parts of his life. I ufed fometimes to reprefent to him the fentiments of the moft rigid

rigid Diffenters concerning him. I told him that they wondered he fhould continue in a church which had fo many marks of imperfection, and fo many ble- mifhes from human invention. He freely replied with his ufual franknefs and candour, which hid nothing from me, nor ever denied or difguifed one fenti- ment of his foul. " My dear friend, I had not the " forming of the conftitution of the Church of Eng- " land: I had not the eftablifhing and inftituting " of the modes of worfhip; Divine Providence " brought me forth in the Church; I am in great " weaknefs of conftitution, and have no health and " fpirits to make any great exertions: if I was to " omit reading the prayers, they would fufpend " me; if they did, I would come amongft you, *for I* " *love you dearly*. With refpect to the errors and ble- " mifhes of the Church of England, as I was not " the author of them, fo I can neither correct or " remove them. In truth, I ftrive never to think of " them, but to fix all my attention on the perfon of " our LORD JESUS CHRIST."

Hervey had a moft endeared love to the LORD's fupper: his ideas of it were very fpiritual and hea- venly: he confidered this ordinance in the light of Scripture; and with the eye of faith, he primarily confidered it as a memorial of the fufferings and fatis- faction of CHRIST: he avoided two extremes in his conceptions of this facred inftitution; on the one hand, that it was a mere memorial of the act of an abfent generous friend, and that we fhould keep up mere rational fentiments of CHRIST's fufferings and death, as a martyr for truth; while on the other hand, he defpifed and abhorred all thofe wild and fuperfti- tious notions with which the Papifts and others have difhonoured this bleffed ordinance. He entered into a fevere examination of his ftate and frame before he came to this inftitution: he approached it with the greateft veneration and love for CHRIST: he faw in

. CHRIST's

CHRIST's death the moſt ſtriking proofs of the infinite evil of ſin; of the awful ſtrictneſs of the juſtice
of GOD; the harmony of all the divine attributes in
his ſalvation; the infinite worth of his own immortal
ſoul; the boundleſs love of GOD in the gift of
CHRIST, and the purchaſe of all the precious bleſſings of the new covenant at the hands of juſtice;
an that the kingdom of heaven was now ſet open to
all believers.

He exerciſed the moſt ſublime and glorious affections in his attendance upon this ordinance, eſpecially
theſe four; admiration, gratitude, Godly ſorrow, and
a joyful delight.   He ſaw in this plan of redemption,
that every thing was marvellous belonging to it: the
plan of ſalvation was marvellous: the perſon of the
REDEEMER was wonderful: his ſufferings and death
were marvellous: his conflicts in the garden and
on the croſs were aſtoniſhing: his victories and
triumphs over all oppoſition, were marvellous: his
triumphs over death, and his aſcenſion to heaven,
were marvellous: his application of this redemption
to the ſouls of men was wonderful: his carrying on
the work of grace in the heart, in ſpite of all poſſible
oppoſition; and his finally crowning grace with
glory: theſe were, in his view, actions more than un-
ſpeakable, more than glorious.

All the ſprings of gratitude in his holy and generous heart were ſet open upon this occaſion; and he
had, as we have already obſerved, the ſtrongeſt ſenſe
of benefits received; the greateſt love to his dear
Benefactor, and an ardent diſpoſition to make all poſſible returns, with a reſolution never to lay gratitude
aſide to eternity.

Godly ſorrow ariſes from a clear ſenſe of the evil
of ſin, and a ſenſe of the malignity and guilt that
there is in ſin, and the miſchief and miſery that flows
from it.   This ſorrow does not ſo much ariſe from a
fear of hell, or a dread of damnation for our crimes,

as

as from a fenfe of the great unkindnefs and bafenefs that we have been guilty of in our temper and conduct towards our beft and deareft Friend. A believer never mourns better, than when he has the higheft hope of heaven, and the ftrongeft affurances of the love of CHRIST.

The affection of delight, which is a mixture of love and joy, was powerfully felt, and generoufly exercifed by our excellent friend at this ordinance. Delight ruled all the powers and affections of his foul: delight reigned and triumphed in his heart: every view that he had of CHRIST afforded him new pleafure, and infpired him with greater degrees of joy.

GOD the HOLY SPIRIT affifted him to take a moft refpectful departure from the LORD's table, and to live as becomes the Gofpel of CHRIST, in all holy converfation and godlinefs.

The HOLY SPIRIT opened all the fountains of ftrong confolations, arifing from the LORD's fupper: he was fupported under the fenfe of paft fins, by a knowledge that they were all pardoned: he was fupported under a fenfe of prefent fins, by a promife that they fhould be all fubdued: he was fupported under a fenfe of indwelling fin, by an affurance that it fhould be all eradicated, and expelled from the foul: he was fupported under a fenfe of daily defects and infirmities of his obedience, by a fight of CHRIST's righteoufnefs: he was fupported under troubles of life, by an affurance that all things fhould work together for his good: he was fupported under the approaches and terrors of death, by an affurance that CHRIST had extracted the fting, conquered the power, and altered the property of death for all believers.

He had a moft endeared love and gratitude for GOD the HOLY SPIRIT: he confidered him as JEHOVAH, GOD, and LORD, equal with GOD the FATHER and the

the Son; he viewed him as poffeffor of all poffible
and infinite perfections; as eternal, immutable, and
omniprefent: as the efficient and eternal life of the
whole creation: he confidered him as omnipotent,
and upholding all things by the word of his power:
he confidered him as all-wife, poffeffed of infinite
goodnefs, grace, and love; holy, juft, true, and
faithful.

He viewed the HOLY SPIRIT as the author of the
whole univerfe; as the parent of angels and men; the
former of all things vifible and invifible, mortal and
immortal.

He viewed the HOLY SPIRIT as the author of the
whole body of Scripture; that he took the penmen
into his own hands, and enabled them to record the
facts, by the direction of infpiration: he affifted them
to compofe the pfalms and fongs of Scripture by the
infpiration of elevation.

He affifted them to make all the difcoveries of the
glorious Gofpel; to write all the predictions in the pro-
ph.etic part of Scripture; to denounce all the threatenings againft fin; to prefcribe all the laws of univerfal obedience; to publifh all the exceeding great
and precious promifes, and to open a charming profpect into the heaven of heavens.

From all thefe profpects arofe a moft refpectful
love and veneration for the HOLY SPIRIT: he obeyed
his dictates without referve: he put himfelf in the
way of every motive fuggefted by the HOLY SPI-
RIT in the Sacred Scriptures. No perfon ran with a
fwifter race; no one moved with a fweeter pleafure
in the ways of CHRIST's commandments, when the
HOLY SPIRIT had enlarged his heart.

GOD the HOLY SPIRIT inhabited his whole foul,
and incorporated himfelf with all his immortal
powers and paffions. Hence arofe a mutual delight in each other: GOD the HOLY SPIRIT took
him into his own hands, and made him a living
temple.

temple.   Hence arofe all thofe perfonal graces
that adorned his character: his ftrict temperance in
the government of his appetites: his virgin chaftity,
or the purity of his defires: his deep humility, or
fenfe of his immediate dependance upon GOD for
every thing: his fweet meeknefs in the government
of his anger: his refolute felf-denial with refpect to
his own fame, and his own righteoufnefs: his patience to wait, to work, and to fuffer: his entire contentment of mind with the appointments of providence.

Hence arofe his mortification of all fin: his refiftance of every temptation of the devil, and his
watching againft all the finful compliances of this
world.   Hence arofe his ftriking at fin and felf in all
its fecret actings in the mind.   Hence arofe his readinefs to conflict with every temptation upon its firft
approach to the foul, and his holy contempt of all
the vain riches, the fleeting honours, and the fordid
pleafures of the prefent life.

From the indwelling of the SPIRIT of GOD, arofe
his eagle-eyed prudence and difcretion in the manage-
ment of himfelf and all his affairs in life.   Hence
arofe his undaunted and invincible fortitude, which
made him fuperior to all poffible oppofition in the
way to heaven, and entitled him to thofe rewards and
honours which are fo glorioufly promifed to the conquerors in the Book of the Revelations. Hence arofe
his amazing activity and diligence in all his ftudies
and purfuits of evangelical knowledge: he hardly
knew what it was to have one lazy hour: his working mind was always bufy to glorify CHRIST, and
promote the happinefs of true believers. Nothing
gave him fo great a joy as to be able to difplay the
illuftrious power and grace of CHRIST; and in connection with this, it gave him the higheft delight to
find that his writings were inftructive and ufeful to
mankind.   It is hardly conceiveable how a human

fpirit

spirit, incarnate in fo feeble a conftitution, could ever ufe more diligence in the ways of GOD.

His love to the whole world of mankind was fincere, generous, powerful, and permanent: he had the leaft of a party fpirit of any man I ever knew: he practifed a kind of forgetting himfelf, in order to be agreeable to others, yet in fo delicate a manner as fcarce to let you perceive that he was fo employed: he gave himfelf no airs of fuperiority, on account of his being a minifter of the eftablifhed Church of England: he was always upon a level with his company: he never confidered himfelf as James Hervey, the celebrated writer, but as a poor guilty finner, equally indebted to divine grace with the loweft godly day-labourer in his parifh: he envied no one the honour and happinefs of doing more good than himfelf: he rejoiced in the amiable talents and graces of all his brethren, and all were his brethren who belonged to CHRIST: he was mightily pleafed at any opportunity of affifting and directing the ftudies of pious young men, who were devoted to the miniftry of the Gofpel. Nothing gave him greater pleafure, than to fee them go on well, ftudy wifely, and preach CHRIST fervently and fuccefsfully.

From the indwelling of GOD the HOLY SPIRIT, in this great man's foul, there arofe as great fincerity of heart as perhaps ever exifted in an human foul: he had a moft fincere defire to pleafe GOD in all things: he longed to know the whole will of GOD, and he applied himfelf to obey the will of GOD as far as he knew it: he was vaftly fuperior to the moft refined heathens: they only obeyed their own reafon: they never obeyed GOD for one moment. Hervey did not obey his own carnal reafon, but he obeyed the voice of GOD in his providence, and in his law: his thoughts, words, and actions, were all of a piece; and he preferved a felf-confiftency of character in his whole conduct through life: his words were the copy

of

of his heart; and his actions were his words, carried into execution: a better pattern of veracity and faithfulness did not exist in the whole British empire: he loved universal justice and truth ;, and if ever any man exhibited the golden rule as a living law, Hervey was the man. Dr. Watts's beautiful Sermon on the Golden Rule was copied out in the life and conversation of our excellent friend.

There is an excellent beauty in divine justice. Moral justice amongst mankind, is a very great beauty: it is a return towards our original rectitude in Paradise: it is a restoration of the image of GOD in regeneration, and makes a man lovely in his temper, words, and actions.

How much more beautiful must be the character of GOD as just, having an ardent regard to all his rights, and a deliberate design; a determinate purpose to preserve those rights sacred and inviolate for ever, being just to the LORD JESUS; just to the HOLY SPIRIT; just to all saints and angels in heaven; just to all good men on earth; just to all bad men and devils on earth or in hell to eternity. This was the invariable temper of our excellent friend.

There is an unutterable dignity in divine justice: there is a most excellent dignity in moral justice amongst men. A man of inflexible justice in heart, words, and actions, is a man of superior dignity to the trash of mankind: he hath a generous scorn of doing wrong, and a determined purpose to do all that his understanding perceives to be right. How much greater dignity must there be in the justice of GOD: he knows his own worth: he is conscious of his transcendent excellence above all men and angels; and he scorns to think an unjust thought; to speak an unjust word, or do an unjust action towards one of his creatures in heaven, earth, and hell.

Moral justice is the great bond of union amongst mankind: without justice, families would be in ruin-

ous

ous diforder; focieties would be diffolved; towns and cities in a ftate of war; kingdoms and empires would be the bedlams of the univerfe; and all nations round the globe would be fields of blood.

God has ftamped a copy of his juftice on the confciences of men: and this preferves the world in order; and this fenfe of juftice eftablifhes an eternal order and union in the heaven of heavens.

Hervey was the brighteft mirror of the effential juftice of God that I ever knew; and it was from this principle of univerfal juftice, in connection with invariable truth, that he acted in his conduct towards all mankind. Hence arofe his ftrict regard to all the perfons whom he efteemed his fuperiors: fuch are magiftrates, parents, minifters, with all the rich and honourable in this world.

Hence arofe his tender compaffion for the fouls of all mankind: his tender pity and unfailing generofity to the poor: his great love to children, and his ardent defire that the rifing generation might receive the very beft education. Hence arofe his great juftice to the fouls of his fervants: no man upon earth could take a more prudent care to lead his fervants into the way of falvation.

He was the beft neighbour in the world; and the reafon was, he loved his neighbour as himfelf. If ever there was a man that acted the part of the good Samaritan, Hervey was the man at all times and in all conditions; he was not only the moft dutiful fon, and the moft loving brother that could exift, but he was one of the fincereft and tendereft friends that ever breathed upon earth. I am fure I found him fo; and I fhall relifh the thoughts of his friendfhip to me in the agonies of death itfelf. I can hardly forbear running out into a large difcourfe on the nature, the ingredients, the properties, and actions of true friendfhip; but I muft ftop my hand to prevent

this

this part of my book being difproportionate to the reft.

Let me juft obferve, that Dr. Owen's Differtations on Divine Juftice, tranflated from the Latin, are begun to be publifhed. The whole will make about feven numbers, at fix-pence each; but the reft will not be printed till the firft number is fold off. It may be had of the bookfellers, whofe names are prefixed to this work.

He had a moft ardent love to the whole Church of God upon earth : he knew that there were a body of men chofen by God the Father from eternity to holinefs and happinefs : he knew that the body of Christ confifted of thefe chofen men, and that it was for thefe alone that he laid down his life, and that the ends of Christ's death never could be fruftrated : he knew that this body of men were wrought upon by God the Holy Spirit in regeneration, converfion, and fanctification : that this body of men were mingled with carnal profeffors in the prefent world, and this mixture of people were called the vifible Church of Christ; but that the invifible church were diftinguifhed from all mankind by an inward vital holinefs, which rendered them dearer to God, than all the nations upon earth : for this body of people he ftudied, laboured, and prayed with a conftancy, equal to his life and breath.

He delighted at all times to think of this body of people : he knew that a large part of them were already in heaven, and that the reft would certainly follow : he confidered himfelf as a member of this illuftrious body, and he gloried in Christ his divine friend, who had put him amongft the children. He rejoiced at the enlargement of this church under any denomination; and you could not pleafe him better than by carrying him any good news of the converfion of immortal fouls to the great head of the church.

Hervey

Hervey was an ardent lover of all the pleaſures of vital religion, and he knew its glorious uſes and advantages to his own ſoul: he conſidered religion as a delightful ſenſe of GOD upon the ſoul, produced and cheriſhed by the influences of GOD the Spirit alone: he knew that the origin of this religion was the life of GOD: it was CHRIST formed in the heart, that this noble principle enabled him to live above himſelf in GOD, and gave him a ſweet boldneſs with GOD in prayer and praiſe: he found that this religion ſanctified all his faculties, and conſecrated all his paſſions to CHRIST: he found that this religion ſanctified the whole creation to him, and turned all nature into a ſchool of inſtruction, and a temple of evangelical devotion.

Hence aroſe his fondneſs for the beauties of nature. Hence aroſe his powers of deſcriptive eloquence: every thing, from an angel to an atom, brought GOD the REDEEMER to his mind: his deſcant upon creation, in which he lifts the ſeveral parts of the viſible univerſe into the ſervice of his REDEEMER, is nothing but a copy of the daily effuſions of his heart.

Whenever you came into his company, unleſs he was diſturbed and interrupted by your own impertinence, he would preſently fall upon ſome of his ſublime contemplations. He wanted no prompting from any man: your grand point of wiſdom and intereſt was to let him go on in his own way; and then, if you had the mind of an angel, he would be ſure to entertain you.

Only conſider what a rich and inexhauſtible mind this man muſt have, to be able for twenty years together to go on in the pleaſing inſtruction of mankind, with no other interruptions than what a feeble conſtitution, and the neceſſary intervals of food and ſleep required of him: all the reſt of his time was devoted in the moſt flaming manner to the diſplay of

the

the divine perfon; the divine and infinite fatisfaction;
the divine and infinite righteoufnefs; the glorious offices and grace of the LORD JESUS CHRIST. He
lived upon him as his principle: he lived like him
as his pattern: he lived to him as his end. Exiftence would have been a plague and torment to him,
if every moment of it had not been devoted to the
glory of his redeeming GOD.

Every morning of his life his grand queftion was,
" What fhall I do for the glory of CHRIST and the
good of his kingdom in the world? How fhall I
beft employ myfelf to-day in difplaying the new
beauties of nature and Scripture?"

Dry verbal criticifm had very little of his attention; but devotional criticifm engroffed his whole
heart: he was exceedingly pleafed to have from you
any beautiful remark on the energy and dignity of
the words in the Hebrew Bible; and he was equally
pleafed to have any juft criticifms upon the New
Teftament.

Hervey loved to contemplate the death of the
body, and the immortality of the foul. He always
found himfelf at home among the tombs, and he
could fpeak with equal truth thofe lines of Dr.
Young, in his Poem on the Laft Day.

> Say then, my mufe, whom difmal fcenes delight,
> Frequent at tombs, and in the realms of night;
> Say melancholy maid, if bold to dare
> The laft extremes of terror and defpair:
> O fay, what change on earth, what heart in man,
> This blackeft moment fince the world began.
>
> Second edition, page 10th.

He confidered death in every view of it, and he
confidered death as a part of his treafure and bank
ftock.

The death of good men, the death of bad men,
the death of his deareft friends, the death of his bit-
tereft enemies, the death of prophets and apoftles,
the

the death of martyrs and primitive Chriftians, his own death; but above all, the death of CHRIST, was a rich part of his treafure.

He confidered death as a ceffation of the motion of the heart, and a ftoppage of the circulation of the blood, and the free flow of the animal fpirits. He confidered death as a difunion of foul and body, or a feparation of the two conftituent parts in man, as a diffolution of our earthly frame, and a departure out of this world to an invifible eternity. He confidered death as a turning the body to duft and afhes. He confidered death as iffuing in a declaration of our moral character before the throne of GOD, and affix-ing our ftate for eternity, in heaven or hell. He confidered death as entering upon a new ftate of our thinking powers, and having larger conceptions of GOD to eternity.

With refpect to the body, he confidered death as a fleep, Daniel xii. 2. and it is fo ftiled becaufe fleep is an image of death.

In fleep the fenfes are locked up, and in death a man is wholly deprived of his fenfes. Sleep is but for a fhort time, and fo is death. After fleep a man rifes, and being refrefhed by it, is more fit for labour. So is death to true Chriftians; it is a reft to them, and they will rife in the morning of the refurrection frefh, lively and active, more fit for divine exercifes. See Dr. Gill's Body of Divinity, page 916, 917.

Hervey had as clear views of the immortality of the foul, as any man upon earth. He confidered the proofs from nature; the proofs from the natural and moral perfections of GOD; the proofs from man; the proofs from the fublime and glorious truths of the Gofpel; the proofs from a clear account in Scripture, of fouls, even now, this moment in heaven and hell.

Hervey had the proofs from nature clearly before his underftanding; the grandeur of fpace, as appa-rently refembling the eternity, immutability, omni-.
prefence

prefence of God. Who can contemplate fpace, and conceive it as exifting only for the fake of a block or a brute?

The Revolution of the natural World.

If we could watch every night in the northern and fouthern hemifpheres, we fhould fee every one of the conftellations in the whole vaft concave of the heavens; and who can imagine that thefe grand profpects were all made for a creature of a moment's duration?

The fucceffion of the four feafons evinces the immortality of the foul.

Spring exhibits a new creation.

Summer fhews frefh fcenes of boundlefs goodnefs.

Autumn difplays the new bounties of Providence.

Winter exhibits new profpects of the wifdom, power, and goodnefs of God.

Has God brought on fuch a fucceffion of the feafons for nearly fix thoufand years, merely for the ufe of dogs and bullocks, or birds and fifhes? The regular and beautiful fucceffion of day and night through fo many thoufands of years, gives us a ftriking evidence of our immortality.

Proofs of the Immortality of the Soul, from the natural and moral Perfections of God.

His eternity is a refemblance of our immortality. His Omniprefence refembles the vaft range of thought by which the foul of Hervey could fly in a moment through heaven, earth, and hell. His omnipotence is a ftriking image of the amazing ftrength and activity of this great man's immortal fpirit. The wifdom and knowledge of God refembles the worlds of fcience refiding in the vaft underftanding of this man.

The goodnefs of God was a lively image of the unbounded benevolence which reigned and lived in this good man's heart.

The

The divine holineſs was the pattern and ſource of his holineſs. The juſtice of God was a lively reſemblance and image in the ſoul of this juſt man, and his truth and faithfulneſs was the origin, the pattern, and the end of all truth, veracity, and faithfulneſs, in his immortal ſoul, to eternity.

PROOFS FROM MAN, OF THE IMMORTALITY OF THE SOUL.

His diſcontent with his preſent condition in life. There is not a man in the world in his unregenerate ſtate, but what wiſhes for ſome change in his condition. The gradual growth of reaſon proves immortality; the nature of hope aſpires to immortality, the nature of virtue, which is progreſſive, to eternity. A ſoul is capable of increaſing knowledge, through ten thouſand ages. The grandeur of the paſſions proclaim the ſoul immortal. Unbounded ambition, or the love of honour, fame, and glory, ſhew that we are immortal. The inſatiable appetite for pleaſure evinces our eternal duration; the ſordid paſſion for wealth, or the mean appetite ſtiled avarice, or love of gold, is a proof of our immortality. Our preſent ſtate is quite puzzling and unintelligible, on a ſuppoſition that we die like a bullock or a dog. The abſurdities that follow from the brutal ſtate of the human ſoul, are infinite upon infinite: they confound the human underſtanding, and outrage all the common ſenſe in the world. The ſuppoſition of our dying like brutes makes a wiſe man mad: it drives him to the moſt deſperate circumſtances.

> For non-exiſtence no man ever wiſhed,
> But firſt he wiſhed the DEITY deſtroy'd.
>
> Night VII. line 892.

In a word, the daily war between devils and angels proves our ſouls to be immortal, and therefore we may ſay with Dr. Young,

> Kind is the devil, O infidel! when compared with thee.
>
> Line 874.

PROOFS

The sacred three, who from all eternity entered into a council of peace concerning man's salvation. This council includes three ideas, *i. e.* the deepest wisdom, the utmost sincerity and seriousness concerning man, as being a most important creature in the eye of God.

It likewise includes the utmost union of heart, or the sweetest association of the divine Persons, to effect the eternal salvation of men. See a View of the Plurality of Persons, in the eternal Godhead, from the Hebrew Bible, in forty-six Particulars, page 241 —244 of this book. See a Scripture Representation of three Persons in the Divine Nature, associated in the Salvation of Man, in twenty-six Particulars of this Book, page 245—254.

The glorious doctrine of election to everlasting life, proves our immortality.

The doctrine of particular, absolute, and certain redemption, demonstrates the immortality of the soul.

The glorious blessing of adoption, pardon of sin, and justification by CHRIST's imputed righteousness, demonstrates the immortality of the soul.

The great blessing of regeneration, conversion, sanctification, and vital union with CHRIST, prove the immortality of the soul.

The final perseverance in mental habits of holiness, or the continuation of divine and spiritual principles, demonstrate the immortality of the soul.

We have a clear account in Scripture, of souls now this moment in heaven and hell. This is a bright proof of immortality. We have promises of eternal life to good men, and we have threatenings of eternal death to bad men; all to be fulfilled at our moment of departure from the body.

These are all striking proofs of our immortality.

Let

Let us clofe the evidence with the declarations of GOD himfelf. Men may kill the body, but cannot kill the foul, Matt. i. 28. The fpirit fhall return to GOD who gave it, Ecc. xii. 7. Two men appeared, Mofes and Elias, Luke ix. 31. Beggar died, and was carried by angels, Luke xvi. 22. In hell he lift up his eyes, Luke xvi. 23. To-day fhalt thou be with me in Paradife, Luke xxiii. 43. Stephen faid, LORD JESUS receive my fpirit, Acts vii. 59. Abfent from the body, prefent with the LORD, 2 Cor. v. 8. Whether in the body or out of the body, I cannot tell, GOD knoweth, 2 Cor. xii. 2. Spirits of juft men made perfect, Heb. xii. 23. To live is CHRIST, to die is gain, Phil. i. 21. Life and immortality are illuminated by the Gofpel, 2 Tim. i. 10. I faw the fouls of them that were flain for the word of GOD, Rev. vi. 9.

Hervey had very exalted conceptions of the terror and glory of the refurrection, and the laft conflagration of the univerfe. I cannot fpeak fo well for him, as he can for himfelf: hear him then in his own words.

"Wonder, O man! Be loft in admiration at thofe prodigious events which are coming on the univerfe: events, the greatnefs of which, nothing finite can meafure, fuch as will caufe whatever is confiderable or momentous in the annals of all generations, to fink into littlenefs and nothing: events, (JESUS prepare us for their approach; defend us when they take place!) big with the everlafting fates of all the living and all the dead. I muft fee the graves cleaving, the fea teeming, and fwarms unfufpected, crowds unnumbered, yea, multitudes of thronging nations rifing from both. I muft fee the world in flames: muft ftand at the diffolution of all terreftrial things: and be an attendant on the burial of nature. I muft fee the vaft expanfe of the fky wrapt up like a fcroll; and the incarnate GOD iffuing forth from light inac-
ceffible,

cessible, with ten thousand times ten thousand angels, to judge both men and devils. I must see all eternity disclosed to view ; and enter upon a state of being that will never, never have an end.—Tombs, page 131."

Hervey considered the resurrection of the dead as that grand and astonishing action of the omnipotence of God the Son, by which the bodies of all that are dead in earth and sea shall spring up from the dust, and stand on their feet in a moment, in the twinkling of an eye, never to die any more, but to have their eternal existence determined to the horrors of hell or the joys of heaven, as long as God endures.

Hervey had grand conceptions of the last judgment: in the twenty-first year of his age, as may be seen in a letter to his sister, concerning Dr. Young's poem on the last day, dated Lincoln College, Oxford, May 2, 1734. Collection, Letter III.

He grew in his relish for this poem for twenty-four years, and never lost sight of it.

He considered the last judgment as that great action of God the Son, in which he will accurately search the souls of all men, and attentively examine the internal character of every person, and declare the quality of every temper, and action, and determine the state of damnation and misery, or salvation and happiness, for every immortal soul, to all eternity, in heaven or hell.

If you wish to read the most striking description of the day of judgment I ever read, or expect to read, see Letter V, of Aspasio to Theron, page 413—421, and the conclusion of that letter, page 462—464.— large octavo Edition.

Hervey had a clear sense of hell, or the final misery of the wicked. He considered hell as consisting in the tortures of a guilty conscience, in a keen remorse for all bad tempers, words, and actions. He considered hell as consisting in eternal self-accusation, and self-upbraiding for past crimes.

He

He confidered hell as confifting in a fenfe of
God's will to feparate us from him, and to fill us
with defpair of his love, as loft for ever and ever.

He confidered hell as confifting in a hatred of
God, fettled into malice, which can never eafe itfelf
by revenge.

He confidered hell as confifting in eternal hardnefs
of heart, never to relent for paft crimes; never to
ftoop to the will of Christ to all eternity.

He confidered hell as confifting in intenfe black
forrow, and wild impatience, at the lofs of all poffible
good, with a full conviction that the lofs of that good
never will be reftored.

He confidered hell as confifting in raging defires
for eafe, which never fhall be fatisfied, and in longing
for a drop of pleafure, which never can be gratified.

He confidered hell as confifting in vexation and
envy at all happy fouls in heaven and earth, and in a
bitter ill will to every happy creature in the univerfe
of God.

He confidered hell as confifting in a dread of new
torments, and horrible fears of new punifhment every
moment, through an eternal duration. Thefe were
the tremendous conceptions that Hervey formed of
hell.

Hervey had clear views of heaven, or the final
happinefs of the righteous. He confidered heaven
as confifting in fweet peace of confcience, or a fenfe
of perfect friendfhip with God. He knew that all
ground of offence between God and man was entirely
taken away by the blood of Christ. He knew that
God had no ill will to punifh; that he had not one
angry thought in his heart; that he received the finner into full confidence of favour, that there was no
reafon for the leaft complaint in God againft his
people.

He confidered heaven as confifting in a fenfe of
God's will to unite himfelf to the fouls of his people.

ple.   He knew that in heaven that God's defires to
unite himfelf to his people run out into a moft unbounded length, and indulged themfelves in all the
ardours that a God can feel.

He confidered heaven as confifting in love to God,
rifing into vaft admiration and efteem, and fettled
into the moft intenfe delight.

He confidered heaven as confifting in eternal
fweetnefs of temper, like the brighteft faints of the
Old and New Teftament, and an eternal foftnefs of
heart, without the leaft reluctance, wearinefs, or
difguft.

He confidered heaven as confifting in the moft unbounded pleafures; the pleafures of the frame of foul,
purity and holinefs: the pleafures of the place a holy,
heavenly world; the pleafures of the companv, God
the Father, Son and Holy Spirit, millions of
glorified faints and angels; the pleafures of looking
back on the goodnefs of Christ through our whole
lives; the pleafures of looking forward through a
boundlefs eternity, and feeing that we have entered
upon a ftate of happinefs, which fhall never never have
an end. This delightful eafe in the powers of the foul,
and thefe oceans of pleafure which roll through all the
affections, will be equal to our vaft capacities, and
lafting as our immortal duration.

He confidered heaven as confifting in a great
quantity of relative happinefs, or a joy to fee all the
millions of fouls in heaven equally happy with ourfelves. There is no undervaluation of fouls in heaven:
there is no contempt for fouls in glory: there is no
averfion to one bleffed fpirit: there is no ill will to a
Chriftian brother; no difguft at a fellow Chriftian; but
we fhall furvey the world of fouls with the fame unbounded delight, as though the happinefs was all our
own through eternity. To all thefe we muft add,
one more conception to complete our ideas of
heaven.

                                    Hervey

Hervey confidered heaven as confifting in hourly expectations of new pleafures, burfting from the heart of Jesus, our God and Saviour.

Remarks on Mr. Hervey's Life and Character.

Remark I. All the knowledge of this great and good man was carried on and attained by books. Truly fpeaking, he had no tutors: before he went to college he had none: while he was at college he had none. His nominal tutor taught him nothing, nor were regular lectures to be found in his college; confequently he was left to make his own way, and for a long time that way was in the dark. At laft Mr. Jenks and Rawlin, on Juftification by Christ's Righteoufnefs, octavo, 1741, were put into his hand by divine Providence. Thefe were the books which, under the direction of the Spirit of God, firft directed his apprehenfions to Christ's righteoufnefs. Marfhall on Sanctification firft led him to the great fpring and means of Gofpel holinefs. The great Mr. Thomas Hall on Final Perfeverance, in the Lime-ftreet lectures, firft led him into the comfort of that doctrine; and when he came to read Witfius's Œconomy of the Covenants, he found a treafure, infinitely rich, divinely excellent and inexhauftible. He ufed to lament it as one of his greateft loffes that he was acquainted with that excellent author no fooner.

Bofton's Fourfold State of Man laid very near his heart. He has defcribed from him the whole procefs of conviction and converfion, in a moft lively and inftructive manner. See Theron and Afpafio, Dialogue IX. page 29, large octavo edition.

Remark II. How exceeding defective and erroneous are our public and private fchemes of education! or rather, we have no wife and good fchemes at all. Every man who fets himfelf up as a tutor of youth,

youth, purfues the dictates of his own wild imagination, and the fcholars fare accordingly. But the method of education at our public colleges are beyond defcription defective and bad. This ,is difplayed in moft lively and affecting colours, in the effays of the Rev. Vicefimus Knox.

If we furvey our two univerfities, the beauty and grandeur of the buildings, the pleafantnefs of the gardens, the fhady walks, the pleafant bowers, the public and private libraries, the inftituted lectures upon all the liberal arts and fciences, the noble profefforfhips, the large endowments and rich incomes of thofe colleges, with a thoufand other advantages, which I cannot fo much as name.

Amidft all this profufion of advantages, Hervey had juft as much help as though he had been born on the Coaft of Guinea, or in the Sandwich Iflands; and we have reafon to think that thoufands of our young men, who refide at the colleges, meet with the fame fate. They go thither ignorant of fcience and divinity, and they come away ignorant as they went.

What a moft affecting confideration is this! that a young man of fo fine a genius and capacity to receive all kinds of inftruction, fhould be fo vilely neglected !

I have as great an efteem and veneration for learned and good men at our public colleges, as moft perfons in the world : they muft know that I do not write from a fpirit of ill will and bitternefs. If the concealing thefe errors and blemifhes in public education would cure them, I would be the firft man in the world to keep them fecret, but the matter is impoffible. The ignorance and infufficiency of our young nobility, and the great defects in the knowledge of divinity in the younger minifters of religion, is vifible in every part of Great Britain, and cannot poffibly be concealed from the common people in every parifh.

RE-

REMARK III.   What unfpeakable encouragement doth this example give to excite young perfons to increafe in knowledge and virtue.

In this cafe you fee every obftruction removed, every obftacle demolifhed, every objection anfwered.

The obftructions in the way to knowledge are chiefly thefe three, *i. e.* indolence, cowardice and felf-conceit.

Now what reafon can there be for indolence, when they fee the pattern of a man of indefatigable diligence ?   What ground can they have for cowardice, when they fee a perfon of great tendernefs of conftitution furmount all difficulties, conquer all obftacles, and rife to fuch tranfcendent heights of fcience and virtue ?   What reafon can they have for pride and felf-conceit, when they fee a man of fuch fhining genius and fuch accomplifhments, to be one of the humbleft perfons in the world ?

Only ftand ftill, my reader, and confider for a few moments; here is a poor raw boy, kept at the grammar fchool for ten years, without any perfon to teach him one fcrap of fcience, or fo much as to lead him into the beauties of the claffics, not fuffered to hear Dr. Doddridge preach the Gofpel, though he lived in the fame town for feveral years.

When he was fent to Lincoln College, in Oxford, he had no tutor ; or one that was worfe than none, a proud and haughty man, who had no true tafte ; no genius for teaching ; no humanity and fatherly compaffion ; no faithfulnefs and honefty of foul.   Under this man he was taught nothing ; and after ftaying near five years at college, making his way by his own induftry and the bleffing of CHRIST.

Can you imagine a man labouring under greater difadvantages ? every thing to difcourage him, nothing on earth to prompt him to excel.

I publifh this work not fo much to proclaim the fame of Mr. Hervey, as to promote the glory of GOD and the good of my country.   That country whofe
happinefs

happinefs I have more or lefs fought for above fifty
years. I have now a greater regard than ever to
national honour, to national wealth, to national fcience and virtue; but above all to national religion
and happinefs. I defire to offer up a prayer, with
the warmeft emotions that an immortal foul can feel
for the falvation of our KING and QUEEN, for the
heir of the throne, for our nobles, our judges, and
our clergy of all denominations; for our merchants,
our hufbandmen, and the common people of the
land. I pray the eternal Being, that this book
which I now publifh, may be an inftrument in the
hands of divine Providence, to promote national honour and happinefs, by cherifhing true religion, and
advancing public fpirit, or the love of our country.
I truft I fhall have fome of the wifeft and beft young
people amongft my readers.

There are doubtlefs feveral defects in my book,
and I am not fo blind as to be ignorant of many of
them; but this I can affure the reader, that there is
not one wilful mifreprefentation of facts; and I defy
the malice of hell and earth to prove that I have written one falfhood. It was impoffible to defcribe fuch
a character as this without an appearance of flattery:
fuch fuperior virtues and graces will always appear
extravagant to the people of cold hearts and very
inferior virtue.

My pretended friends, who endeavoured to pour
cold water on my ardent defcription of this great and
good man muft excufe me that I did not choofe to
ftoop to the load of their phlegm: cold dead phlegm
in fpeaking or writing I always defpife, and I affure
them that the authors of it fhall always have it all to
themfelves.

This book will outlive Pagan darknefs, the Ma-
hommedan Alcoran, Jewifh prejudices, Popifh errors
and Proteftant infidelity: it will be read by millions
then, which are now unborn. The wife and worthy

people

people in that happy time will wish that Hervey had had a better biographer; and I wish so too, but however, this book will convey some information concerning the character of a man whose name is written with the beams of the sun, and inscribed amongst the constellations of heaven. If this book shall convey some instruction and entertainment, how much more shall his own immortal writings be read with a fixed attention and fervent admiration. They will read with wonder and delight the works of a man born in the Sardian state of the church, on Friday, the 26th of February, 1714, at HARDINGSTONE, a country village, one mile from Northampton, and who died December 25th, at four o'clock in the afternoon, at Weston Favell, 1758, in the forty-fifth year of his age.

They will wonder to think of a man who was trained up in a total ignorance of the spiritual nature of the Gospel to the year 1733. They will then see the light of God gradually dawning upon his soul to 1741. In that year his letter to Mr. Whitfield shews that his soul centered in CHRIT's righteousness: from this time his path shone brighter and brighter to the year 1746. In that happy period, his Meditations among the Tombs, and his Reflections on a Flower Garden, burst out all at once on the astonished world. People of the finest sense, of the most elegant taste, and the highest relish for the Gospel, saw a new species of writing, which pleased the mind, instructed the understanding, charmed the imagination, fired the passions, and spread a glow of devotion and delight through the whole soul.

They were at a loss which to admire most, the genius of the w.··er, or the productions of his pen. Sometimes they turned their thoughts to the man, and were ready to ask themselves this question, What a strange creature is here? Is this a seraph or a human being? where was he born, where was he educated?

How

How did he attain this knowledge? Who gave him these powers, to paint to the imagination, to prove to our reason the truths of the Gospel, and move the passions of the heart.

THE PECULIAR GOODNESS OF CHRIST TO JAMES HERVEY.

Consider this man as the object of CHRIST's affectionate disposition to make his soul happy. Whatever good he possessed of any kind; whatever genius or excellence he was conscious of in the frame of his nature; in the aptitude of his understanding; in the bent of his will; in the rich powers of his imagination, and his pre-eminence above millions of other men, all flowed from CHRIST and his HOLY SPIRIT.

That largeness in the capacity of his soul, by which he was entertained with a boundless diversity of objects in universal nature, through earth, and sea, and heaven; with all the starry worlds, and the Scriptures of GOD: all these worlds of objects and ideas flowed from the Person and Spirit of CHRIST.

CHRIST, by his Spirit, gave him those divine, affections, and those devout passions, which yielded him a great variety of fruitions and pleasures.

His moral capacities and improvements were accompanied with a high sense of worth, as a new and regenerate creature of GOD, indued with a divine taste, or holy aptitude of understanding, to conceive great and new thoughts of the perfections of GOD his REDEEMER, and his vital union with his soul.

The rich privileges of his condition, as a Christian; or that ample provision which was made for his easy enjoyment of life and existence, whether by means of his own invention, or by the assistance of his friends, whether by the benevolence of his fellow creatures, or by the immediate agency of CHRIST

alone,

alone, it all comes to the fame thing, CHRIST is the fource and giver of all good.

The daily happinefs which he received from CHRIST, and the continual fenfe he had of the fupreme good; the hourly union he had with effential truth; his reft in the love of CHRIST; his delight in the fupreme beauty, and in the ufe and enjoyment of CHRIST's infinite love; all thefe flowed from the fame fource.

All thefe good things, with every other good thing that can be mentioned or thought of, are originally owing to the bounty of CHRIST; and however they were conveyed by the kindnefs of friends, or the intervention of Providence, CHRIST was to be feen in all every moment; and the whole world of good in its vaft variety, is all nothing but cyphers and vanity without CHRIST.

The DECREES *of* GOD, *praƐtically improved by the great* Mr. JOHN HUBBARD, *with* ADDITIONS.

With what calm ferenity and fublime fortitude may a truly good man commit himfelf to GOD in well doing.

What a mighty fpring is the decree of GOD to generous, great, and noble undertakings, in the caufe of GOD, and for the glory of the SON of GOD, in his perfon, perfeƐtions, and offices.

What has a wife and worthy man to fear, that fhould deter or divert, allure or terrify, his foul from the moft difficult aƐtions, the moft laborious and dangerous fervices he is warranted or called by GOD to engage in; for he knows that nothing is left to chance; nothing in all the world left to run at random; nothing left to the will and power of creatures; but all occurrences and operations are regulated and ordered by the decree of heaven: all matters are governed by the purpofe of the all-wife mind of GOD; and the inward thoughts, or mighty decree of GOD,

often

often brings forth what could never be expected from the outward face of things. Which absolute decrees, or inward thoughts and purposes of GOD, are clearly and fully interpreted by GOD's whole word: his voluntary declarations and rich promises in particular, respecting the temporal blessings and spiritual graces of his people: that let the decree of GOD fall how it will, let the mighty thoughts of GOD the SON open to the world in actions and great operations how they may, the wise and good man shall be improved by every thing; he shall be bettered by every thing: he shall be worsted by nothing through the whole of his life, and in the moment of his death.

The heart of GOD, expressed in his promises, interprets all his thoughts concerning his people; and there is no one condition of pain or pleasure, of poverty or riches, of loss or gain, of disgrace or honour, of temptation or victory, of persecution or protection, of oppression or liberty, of sunshine or midnight, of sickness or health, of solitude or company, of social friendship or friendlessness, of the world's favours or its frowns, and of the approach of the king of terrors, in which the wise and good man shall not be bettered by every thing, and worsted by nothing. He shall rise superior to the world, the devil, and the flesh, and triumph in GOD's love for ever and ever.

GOD's decree brings forth what could never be expected from the OUTWARD FACE of THINGS.

This remark is most delightfully illustrated and confirmed by the instances of Charles Rollin and James Hervey.

Here are two poor boys, raised from nothing, to be the first writers in the whole world. Rollin was the son of a cutler at Paris, whose father died when he was but five years of age: his mother was not able to give him a good education. A curate in the neighbourhood

neighbourhood procured him a place in a charity fchool. Here he made fuch a rapid progrefs, as to aftonifh his friends, and gain him an higher fituation in a better feminary. All the world knows the confequences! he became the firft man in France, and his writings will live till the burning of the univerfe and the end of all things.

James Hervey is another inftance of the fingular and fupreme goodnefs of God. He was but one degree above a charity boy: and who could ever have thought that this youth fhould rife to the moft exalted degrees of fcience, eloquence, and devotion; fo as to become the wonder and ornament of the Britifh empire!

The defign of this conclufion of my work is to rouze the ambition of the Britifh youth, to excell in every part of learning and virtue; and efpecially to you in the lower ranks of life. There is no occafion for you to be the fon of a nobleman, in order to be a good fcholar, and an amiable Chriftian. Wealth and honour acquired already to your hands, are rather an obftacle, and a curfe to ftudy and fcience.

Our public fchools produce few or none of the beft men in England: you have therefore every motive to ftimulate you to action, to diligence, to dignity, and folid glory.

Arife! arife then, my dear young friends, and ftrive to make new Rollins and Herveys in the prefent age.

There was a beautiful refemblance in the temper and character of thefe two excellent men.

Their natural genius and tafte.

Their fine perceptions of beauty.

Their love of claffical elegance.

Their delight in the beauties of creation.

Their delicate difcernment of the beauties of hiftory, and the characters of men.

Their

Their natural powers for eloquence, and all kinds of good writing.

Their ardent love to GOD, and delight in his perfections.

Their aftonifhing reverence for, and ftudy of the Holy Scriptures.

Their peculiar love to the perfon of CHRIST, and faith in his precious righteoufnefs and blood for their whole falvation.

Their amazing tendernefs and zeal, for the honour of GOD the HOLY SPIRIT.

Their boundlefs philanthropy, or univerfal love to the whole world of mankind.

Their high fenfe of honour and moral juftice, in all its branches and views.

Their invincible fpirit of benevolence and beneficence all through life.

Their indefatigable love to all the fciences, and their infatiable purfuit of every part of beautiful literature.

Thefe are fome of the features in which Rollin and Hervey refembled each other: and thefe virtues powerfully invite and ftimulate us to a moft diligent imitation.

Great GOD! make it appear that we are dear to thee, and eminent for holinefs, and ufefulnefs all the days of our lives. Let a generous ambition to excel animate our breafts, and under the conduct of GOD the SPIRIT rife higher and higher in the empire of GOD to eternity.

F I N I S.

A

SERIES of LETTERS

FROM THE LATE

Rev. JAMES HERVEY, M. A.

TO THE

Rᴇᴠ. JOHN RYLAND, M.A.

CONTAINING,

SIX YEAR's CORRESPONDENCE BEFORE HIS DEATH,

WHICH HAPPENED

DECEMBER 25, 1758.

Never before printed.

LETTER I.

Rev. and Dear Sir,

I AM afhamed to acknowledge, but acknowledge I
muft, that I received your firft favour by the newfman.   I was then very bufy (at thofe intervals of time
when I was capable of application) in preparing for
the prefs " An Anfwer to Lord Bolingbroke's Animadverfions on the Hiftory of the Old Teftament."
In behalf of which attempt, I intreat an intereft in
your prayers to God, that it may be accompanied
with his blefling, and may advance the honour of his
word.

Since that, I have been feized by a fwelled face
and a fever, which has confined me to my chamber,
and delivered me over to the phyfician.   Being always
fo extremely weak, and often quite ill, I am difcouraged from undertaking either correfpondence or bufinefs.   How can fuch an invalid hope for fpirits to
anfwer the one, or for ftrength to difpatch the other?
This is my cafe; or elfe I fhould, with real delight,
embrace your propofal.   Nothing could be more
agreeable, than a free epiftolary intercourfe, on the
glories, the merits, and the love of our Lord Jesus
Christ.   But I am really become *like a broken veſſel*;
and cannot engage to furnifh out my quota.   Your

friend's

friend's mind was always a penurious, and now is an exhausted soil—can give birth to nothing that is worthy of the subject, or worthy of your perusal.

I desire to bless the God of all power, and the God of free grace, if he has been pleased to make my feeble ministry in any degree edifying to any of your friends. May the person you hint at, increase with the increase of God; be sealed unto the day of redemption; and though I know not the name, have a sweet assurance, that his or her name is written in the Lamb's Book of Life!—My cordial salutation and good wishes wait on Mr. Medley. May He that walketh amidst the golden candlesticks, and has the seven spirits of God, prosper your united labours; that you may train up many, many youths, for a life of distinguished holiness, and extensive usefulness, in the world below, and for a life of consummate happiness and everlasting glory in the mansions above!

I wish you would favour me with your thoughts concerning the righteousness of Christ's life: its excellency and perfection: that righteousness, I mean, which was antecedent to his atoning death, and consisted in his obedience to the whole moral law; I will then send you the result of my meditations on the same subject: to be partly confirmed; partly improved, by your's. Though I have forbore writing, I have taken every opportunity to inquire after you. I have always professed a most affectionate esteem for you; and have often made mention of you at our heavenly Father's throne; which not only has been, but will continue to be, the pleasing practice of,

Dear Sir,

Your sincere Friend,

and Brother in Christ,

JAMES HERVEY.

LETTER II.

Wefton-Favel, Jan. 6, 1753.

Rev. and Dear Sir,

I AM truly obliged, and fincerely thankful, for your laft letter. The fpeed and the weight of your anfwer render it a double favour. I fee it is dated Dec. the 13th; but I received it not till laft Sunday evening, when it refrefhed my fpirits, after they had been exhaufted, delightfully exhaufted, by preaching JESUS CHRIST. From which circumftance, you will perceive, it was impoffible for me to acknowledge your kindnefs fooner.

Herewith I fend you, according to my promife, a few thoughts on the noble fubject which you have confidered, with an energy which, I hope, will ftrike me, on every repeated perufal; and with a propriety, in which I can find nothing to be altered, unlefs it be its brevity. Do not grudge your paper, my dear friend, when you pour out your fentiments on fuch a topic.

My manufcript is part of a pretty large work, which, amidft great infirmities of body and mind, I have been meditating. Let me befeech you to read it; not with the partiality of a friend, but the feverity of a critic; and let me hope; let me promife myfelf, to receive it again, improved and enriched by your free corrections.

The whole work, if the FATHER of Lights fhould vouchfafe ability to finifh it, will confift partly of Dialogues, and partly of Letters: to treat of thofe grand doctrines of Chriftianity, which are of univerfal concernment, and of the laft importance; fuch as the fall of man in Adam; the depravity of our nature; the atonement of CHRIST's death; the imputation of his righteoufnefs; (this is to be confidered very diftinctly and copioufly) the fanctification of our nature &c. To be interfperfed with fome eafy but improving

ftrictures

ftrictures of natural philofophy, and to be decorated
with fome agreeable, but edifying pictures, of rural
nature.

I intreat you to obferve, on a feparate paper, what
is redundant, and ought to be retrenched—what is
deficient, and wants to be fupplied—what is obfcure,
and needs to be cleared up—what is weak, and fhould
be ftrengthened—low, and fhould be elevated. I rejoice to find, that my fentiments fo exactly coincide
with your's. I fhall often befeech Him, in whom are
hid all the treafures of wifdom, to give you all knowledge and utterance. And I humbly requeft the
fame exercife of benevolence in behalf of,

Dear Sir,

Your truly affectionate Brother,

in JESUS CHRIST,

JAMES HERVEY.

P. S. I am obliged for your candid approbation of
Remarks on Lord Bolingbroke. Accompany them,
dear Sir, with your prayers: then, perhaps, though
they touch the argument but fuperficially, they may
be made to penetrate fome hearts.

LETTER III.

Wefton-Favel, Feb. 3, 1753.

Rev. and Dear Sir,

I Received your obliging letter, and very valuable
prefent of Witfius, which I fhall thankfully keep
as a monument of your friendfhip, and attentively
ftudy as a magazine of evangelical wifdom. May the
LORD JESUS CHRIST transfufe the precious truths
from the writer's pen, to the reader's heart!—I had
feen this treatife before; but it was at a time when my
fpirits were funk to a very low ebb, and I had but
little relifh even for the moft excellent things.

I rejoice, and fhall be encouraged to proceed in my
work, if you really approve thofe little fketches; but

hope, and I earneftly beg, that you will beftow upon them your free correĉtions. My piece is at yet only in embryo. Will you, dear Sir, contribute your affift-ance to ripen the defign, and bring it to the birth? With this view, I fend you my four firft Dialogues: they are very incorreĉt, and fhamefully blotted: the firft fault, your pen will mend; the fecond, your can-dor will excufe. But inftead of making any more apo-logies, or making any other requefts, give me leave to lay before you a plan of the whole fcheme.

After the four firft conferences, Theron and Afpafio enter upon the fubjeĉt of our LORD's aĉtive righteouf-nefs. Objeĉtions from reafon, from Scripture, are confidered—The abfolute perfeĉtion of the divine law, and confummate holinefs of the DIVINE MA-JESTY—Sincere obedience, infufficient for our jufti-fication—The end of the law, to convince of fin, and bring to CHRIST—Some other objeĉtions urged and anfwered.—The corruption of our nature; firft proved from Scripture, then difplayed from experience. Be-tween which, to relieve the reader, is introduced a Dialogue on the wonderful Struĉture of the Human Body. The whole fummed up—Our friends part, but agree to correfpond—Theron more attentively obferving his heart and life, comparing both with the divine law, is convinced of his great guilt and total deficiency—Begins to acknowledge the neceffity of a better righteoufnefs than his own—Defires to fee what can be alledged for the fupport of this doĉtrine, which occafions fome letters from Afpafio; wherein the point is proved from our Articles and Homilies; from the Scriptures of the Old and New Teftament; from the writings of our moft eminent divines—The excellency of CHRIST's righteoufnefs difplayed, both from its matchlefs perfeĉtion, and from the dignity of his perfon—A letter or two from Theron, by way of carrying on the intercourfe relating to the wonders of creation, and the goodnefs of the CREATOR; not without fome views to the main fubjeĉt—The influ-

ence

ence of righteoufnefs, on moral virtue and evangelical holinefs—Our friends brought together again
—Theron, under difcouraging impreffions, thinks fo
glorious a righteoufnefs can never be intended for
fo grievous a finner—The freenefs of grace, and of
the gift of righteoufnefs—A difcourfe on faith, by
which we are interefted in our LORD's obedience—
The precious and delightful ufe to be made of this
righteoufnefs—Theron relapfes into fins of infirmity—
his faith is fhaken—fupports proper for fuch a ftate—
A difcourfe or two on fanctification; its nature; its
principles; its progrefs—Afpafio, feized with a fudden illnefs—the manner of his death—the laft enemy
conquered, and the believer departing, with hopes
full of immortality.

This is the platform.—If you approve the defign,
I hope you will recommend it in prayer to the Father
of Mercies, and Fountain of Wifdom.   If any thing
occurs which may be proper to fill up thefe outlines,
and complete the work, I promife myfelf you will be
fo kind as to communicate.

Have you feen a treatife, intitled " The Gofpel
Myftery of Sanctification?" If you have met with it,
pleafe to favour me with your opinion of it.   What
muft I defire you to accept by way of return for your
prefent? I have nothing but my Meditations: thofe
are old and ftale; but fuch as they are, let them ftand
in your ftudy as a memorial of that diftinguifhed place
which you have in the heart of,

Dear Sir,
Your truly affectionate,
and obliged Friend and Brother,
JAMES HERVEY.

P. S. I am afhamed to fend fuch patch-work manufcripts; but methinks I would not tranfcribe them
till they are enriched by your and your affiftant's remarks.

L E T-

LETTER IV.

My dear Friend,

I ALSO received your obliging letter, after I had been preaching; preaching upon thofe important words of our LORD JESUS CHRIST, John xvi. 8—11. O that I had fpoke lefs unworthily of the facred fub-ject, and not fullied the glory, nor enervated the power, of the everlafting Gofpel! But the Mafter whom we ferve, can make his ftrength perfect in weaknefs: can make the voice of ftammering lips become the power of GOD unto falvation. May his good Spirit be with us, and his good hand be upon us, when we ftudy his word, and publifh his grace!

I thank you for taking the trouble of perufing my very imperfect manufcripts; and I defire Mr. Medley to accept my very grateful acknowledgments for the improving remarks he has made. I beg of him to proceed; to ufe the fame kind feverity with the other fketches; and render them, if poffible, fit for public view—*meet for the Mafter's ufe.* I am fenfible the pointing is inaccurate, and fhall be much obliged for every correction in this particular. It will be no lefs beneficial to my piece, if he pleafes to make free ufe of the pruning knife. Prolixity upon fuch a fubject will infallibly create difguft, efpecially with the polite; for whofe perufal, and whofe fervice, I would wifh my attempt was properly calculated.

I do not pretend, nor indeed do I wifh, to write one new truth. The utmoft of my aim is, to reprefent old doctrines in a pleafing light, and drefs them in a fafhionable, or genteel manner.

If it is not too late, I would defire to be in the number of the fubfcribers to the work which Mr. Medley has corrected for the prefs. Did I enquire whether you have feen a piece intitled, "The Gofpel Myftery of Sanctification?" I intended to afk this

B   queftion,

queſtion, but as I find nothing in any of your letters relating to it, I am inclined to think I forgot to execute my deſign.   My beſt thanks for your kind offer of Dr. Gill's curious and valuable ſermon ; but as I have it already, you will not be diſpleaſed, if I take the liberty to return it, when a convenient opportunity preſents itſelf. I have the pleaſure of knowing the author, and I hope the benefit of being intereſted in his prayers.   When I was at London, he was ſo friendly as to viſit me at my brother's, (who lives not far from the Doctor's) and always left me wiſer ; and I am ſure it was not owing to his incapacity or negligence, if I was not better.   If you know, or happen to meet with any books, particularly excellent and uſeful, I ſhould own myſelf obliged by your recommendation of them.   And I promiſe myſelf you will not ceaſe to commend, to the tender mercies of God, your very weak, but

Truly affectionate
Brother in Chriſt,
JAMES HERVEY.

P. S. My moſt cordial ſalutation waits upon Mr. Medley.

L E T T E R V.

Weſton, April 21, 1753.

My dear Friend,

IN how many reſpects am I obliged to you; obliged to you for your affectionate letter ; for your edifying meditation, and for Mr. Fowler's truly valuable book : for all which, accept the poor, but ſincere return of my thanks.

I hope Mr. Medley will not diſcontinue his labour of criticiſm and of love ; but proceed to poliſh thoſe rude ſketches ; for which ſervice I ſhall be bound to

wiſh

wish that he himself may be a polished shaft in our divine REDEEMER's quiver.

I shall be glad to receive the Catalogue of Select Authors, which you mention; for I assure you, I am not so well acquainted with excellent writers as your candor may imagine. Be pleased to mark those which you think more particularly worthy of recommenda-- tion; and if a description of their character and dif- tinguishing excellencies should flow readily into your pen, a few strictures of this kind would be highly welcome. Your sentiments, with relation to Marshal, have excited this wish; from which you will learn, without my particularizing it, how well I like them.

If I read Dr. Owen's Works, I should prefer your books, for that very reason which you mention as a difparagement. The manufcript marginal notes will be entertaining, instructive; and will, in a pleasing manner, quicken and keep up my attention; for I must confefs to you, that in perusing a long com- pofition, my spirits are always languid, flag, sink, are exhaufted.

I admire Mr. Fowler, among other excellencies, for reducing his Treatife to so moderate a compafs. I wish fome judicious hand would give us the quin- teffence of Dr. Owen's works, each in a fize so portable, both for the pocket and the memory: I really think it would be one of the most fubftantial acts of fervice which a fcholar and a divine could per- form for the prefent age. Do you approve this fcheme? If fo, fuppofe you think of executing it.

I cannot fay that I am much verfed in Dr. Owen's writings. I once fet about reading his Expofition of the Epiftle to the Hebrews; but his Differtations and Annotations were fo excefsively prolix, that I could by no means retain them in my mind.—The glorious and delightful fubject of union with our exalted head, CHRIST JESUS, will be confidered in the procefs of thefe effays. O! for an unction from the Holy One,

to

to teach us all things, that are moſt expedient for us to write, and for others to know!

When your ſweet meditation upon Gal. vi. 14. came to my hand, I was conſidering about a proper text for a ſermon to be preached before the Clergy at our approaching viſitation; and I can recollect none that pleaſes me ſo much as, "God forbid," &c. You will excuſe me, if I take the liberty to enrich my diſcourſe with ſome of your hints; and pray for me, dear Sir, I beſeech you, that I may open my mouth boldly, and declare the truth as it is in Jesus. Your heart is made for friendſhip. Though mine is much leſs warm and tender, it has, I aſſure you, a very warm and tender regard for Mr. Ryland: to hear from him, will always be eſteemed a favour: to hear of his hap-pineſs, will always be enjoyed as a pleaſure by,

Dear Sir,

Your truly affectionate Brother

in our Lord Jesus Christ,

JAMES HERVEY.

P. S. My cordial compliments wait on Mr. Medley.

———————

LETTER VI.

Weſton, May 4, 1754.

My dear Friend,

WITH gratitude I received, and with delight I peruſed, Mr. Brine's judicious letter. As God has given him a clear head, and a warm heart, I hope he will give a ſingular bleſſing to the produce of both. May he alſo enable me ſo to connect and interweave theſe ſublime ſentiments, with my own ſuperficial notions, that they may appear, not like pieces of velvet tacked on fuſtian, but like beautiful bloſſoms growing out of the tree.

Pray let me have your thoughts upon the ſubject. Your's are moſt ſuitable to my taſte, (and if I do not

greatly

greatly miftake) will be moft acceptable to the public. Light is good, and heat is good; but the two in conjunction are better than either feparate.

You afk for Letter I. and Letter VI. I fancy you mean Letter V. becaufe that is one of the moft important, and Letter VI. is rather a digreffion of the entertaining and ornamental kind, than an effential part of the fubject; however, that I may not difappoint, I have tranfmitted both. Be critical, be fevere, be caftegatory, in perufing them; and, if divine Providence enables me to publifh, and vouchfafe me fuccefs, I will furnifh, out of my profits, the poor of your congregation, with bibles.

My good friend and pious brother, Hartley, has juft publifhed a volume of Sermons. He is a friend to the righteoufnefs of CHRIST; but fo far as it is formed in our hearts, he does not like the doctrine of imputed righteoufnefs; and faid, at Lady Huntingdon's, from the fincerity and impartiality of his zeal, that it would be better to have my intended work fuppreffed, than publifhed. This I was told under the rofe; and this I fpeak only *inter nos.*—He has given us a very long preface concerning religion, enthufiafm, &c. He fpeaks highly of Mr. Law's works; and among other things fays, " He has refuted that " irreverant, but common notion, of the divine Majefty's being actuated by a fpirit of vindictive wrath, " in his proceedings againft fallen man." If you choofe to fee the Sermons, they fhall compofe, or be a part of my next packet: it is a five fhilling volume. —My bookfeller tells me it will be impoffible to comprize my Effay in lefs than three volumes of the Meditation fize. It is much againft my inclination to exceed the quantity of two volumes; but I believe I muft fubmit, or elfe we fhall cramp the defign, and mutilate the plan.—I heartily wifh my brother Hartley's fermons may be accompanied with an abundant bleffing, and bring much honour to our crucified LORD. And I defire to thank his holy name, for

the

the acceptance which he has been pleafed to give unto my weak attempts. The other day I was agreeably furprifed with a prefent from Amfterdam; a tranfla-tion of my firft volume into Low Dutch; very hand-fomely printed in large octavo, and ornamented with eight lively and expreffive prints. It is now in two languages. O! that a double portion of divine bene-diction may attend it! and more than a double por-tion reft upon my dear brother at Warwick, and all the undertakers, for the honour and intereft of him who was dead, but is alive for evermore. I have given my laft orders with relation to printing the Sche-dule of Promifes; but perhaps fhall not have it in my power to perform my engagement, till I put them into your own hand at Wefton. The expectation of which is pleafing; but let it not fuperfede the plea-fure of hearing from you again.

I am, &c.

JAMES HERVEY.

LETTER VII.

Wefton, July 8, 1754.

My dear Friend,

I Received your printed letter from London, and fhould have been glad to receive the author at Wefton. Though difappointed of this pleafure, I hope, through the new and living way confecrated for us, to meet in a calmer place than the fhades of Wefton, and in a grander place than the ftreets of London.

Did you fhew your Defcant upon the Oath of GOD to Dr. Gill and Mr. Brine? Did it receive the ap-probation of thofe mafter builders in Ifrael? Of each of whom we may fay, in an inferior degree, what was faid in the moft exalted fenfe of their divine LORD,

Ifai.

Ifai. xi. 3. Do not you think our tranflation has happily enough expreffed the fine metaphor contained in the original? Or, can you fuggeft a better rendering, then fhall make him of quick' underftanding in the fear of the LORD?

I prefume this will find you at Warwick; and I truft will find you fafe, living together with your family, under the defence of the Moft High, and abiding under the fhadow of the Almighty. I fend this ticket, principally to beg the favour of you to tranfcribe the fubjects, or heads, of Mr. Hervey's Dialogues and Letters. He himfelf has miflaid and cannot recover them. It will fave him a little trouble, if you will fend him a copy.

I have had my bookfeller's opinion with relation to the number of copies proper to be printed, at which I am fomewhat furprifed, and muft defire your advice. He fays, 5000 in fmall, and 750 in large octavo. To this I have fome objections. In the firft place, the fale of fuch a prodigious quantity, cannot but be hazardous, though I muft confefs I have no reafon to diftruft the goodnefs of that over-ruling Providence, to which I would humbly afcribe the acceptance of a preceding effay. This fcruple, therefore, fhall be fet afide. But what think you of the following confideration? Errors and weakneffes, if fuch a number be printed at once, may never be corrected. Whereas, if we publifh half the propofed number, and a fecond edition is demanded, there may be an opportunity of correcting miftakes, and retouching inaccuracies.

May I not hope to receive a few hints for a Preface, in which I am advifed to declare, that it is my firm refolution to enter no farther into the controverfy? With this view, that in cafe the doctrines are attacked, other and abler champions may fee a clear ftage for their entrance.

I am in poffeffion of Dr. Crifp; the LORD JESUS, who is our wifdom, fanctify my reading; and make it, like the milk collected in the mother's breaft, a little refervoir for the fpiritual nourifhment of his people.

An

An account of the obfervables which you met with
at our metropolis, either in your own preaching and
converfation, or in the works and fentiments of the
learned, will be very acceptable to,
                Dear Sir,
                    Your affectionate Brother,
                        JAMES HERVEY.

LETTER VIII.

Wefton, July 26, 1754.

My dear Friend,

I Congratulate you and Mrs. Ryland, on your fafe
return to Warwick. May the feed which you
have left behind you, grow and profper! and may
the ground before you, be like the harveft of the
fixth year in Ifrael, doubly fruitful!

I am indebted to you for two letters, and as many
parcels.—Mather's Chriftian Philofopher, you are
pleafed to fay, is my own. In fuch a fenfe it is mine,
as the flowers in my garden belong to the bees. My
property is like theirs: may my improvement alfo be
like theirs!—The manufcript letters fent by Mr.
Wallin contain an inftance of true heroifm. I would
fay as I read,

" *Sic mihi Contingal vivere, ficque mori.*"

Mr. Keith has fent me, by your order, the
Dialogue on Preaching, and Blackmore's Effay on
the fame fubject. The former I have in my ftudy
already: it is full of fine words, and pleafes in the
reading. But I don't know how, the benefit vanifhes
with the perufal; the improvement is infenfibly loft.
O that this may not be the cafe with my effays!
Rather let them be " as a nail faftened in a fure place!"
—Would you think it? directions about preaching,
                                            rather

rather difcourage than profit me. They fetch from my breaft, that defponding confeffion,

> *Cupidum, frater, optime, vires defieunt.*

The LORD JESUS ftrengthen my weaknefs! You fhould not have put down my name in the lift of the evangelical league; fome men have Atlantean fhoulders, and can execute any thing; may undertake almoft every thing:—your friend is a dwarf and a cripple. And who would invite fuch a one into fo arduous a fervice? However, I muft not think of engaging in any new work, till Theron and Afpafio's affairs are got off my hands. How my heart trembles, left I fhould fail in this attempt, and betray my divine Mafter's caufe, to the infults of his enemies! LORD, I am intimidated; undertake it for me!—This week came a letter from Dr. S——, that breathed the Chriftian, and fpoke the gentleman: be fo good as to make my grateful acknowledgments to him and Mr. Wallin.—I fhall take your advice, with relation to the number of copies—Will it be proper to introduce the work with a dedication?—Herewith are returned Mr. Hurrion's works; and they are accompanied with one manufcript which you have not feen. Pray examine it; correct its fentiments, and polifh its ftyle; and whenever you publifh, may your works be " as polifhed fhafts," in the victorious Redeemer's quiver!

I am, dear Sir,

Your truly affectionate Brother,

in CHRIST,

JAMES HERVEY.

LETTER IX.

Wefton, Aug. 17, 1754.

My dear Friend,

THIS week I received both your letters, and both your parcels, and as from every fuch favour I

C

. receive

receive pleasure, and hope to reap advantage, it is but just, that I return my thanks.

I wonder how you, who have heard my stammering voice, and seen my withered arm, could think of enlisting such a cripple in your service.—If I was perfectly at leisure, I durst not undertake to furnish out any stated periodical composition for the public. The languor of my constitution is so great, and the failure of my spirits so frequent, that whatever I attempt of this kind, must be attempted—not at such an hour, or such a week ; but whenever a lucid and lively interval returns.

At present, my hands, amidst all their weakness, are so full of employ, that I have not time or ability to pay the indispensable debt of gratitude and friendship due to my correspondents. Letters, both of benevolence and of piety, I am obliged to lay by unanswered; being embarked in an affair that requires all, more than all, my application; and thinking it my duty to be, till it is finished, *totus in illo*.

Give me leave also to hint, that I cannot persuade myself to approve of every thing in your proposals. The execution of them is likely to be premature. Might I offer my opinion, I would humbly advise, that you delay the publication of your Essays for a considerable space, till each member of the society has a stock of materials digested, compleated, and ready to form his quota, otherwise, unexpected avocations may break in upon the time which he intends to allot for his compositions: may oblige him to write when his spirits are dull, and his thoughts stagnate ; by which means, what he writes may fall very short of what is required in your fifth article.

Further. I would strongly remonstrate against article the third. My vote is, not barely that it be altered, but intirely reversed. It should be a standing invariable rule, that nothing be dismissed from the pen ; nothing be committed to the press, but what has undergone the examination, and received the correction

rection of every member; otherwife the principal end, and higheft advantage of an affociation, are loft.

When you quote my letter, you quite miftake my meaning. I fpoke of writing, not with all poffible energy of thought, and all the fire and force of diction; but as Luther fomewhere expreffes himfelf, *Trivialiter, vulgariter,* and, *Ad captum populi.*

I keep your Effay; becaufe I would not only advife, but earneftly intreat you to take time. Beware of being precipitate; your lively imagination wants the curb, almoft as much as my phlegmatic temper the fpur.

See how freely I fpeak my mind. Act the fame part with me: tell me as plainly of my errors: correct the faults of my conduct, and of my writings; for how much better is it to be chaftifed with tendernefs by a friend, than to be wounded and infulted by an enemy! My poor veffel is going to be launched. The LORD JESUS CHRIST give it a profperous gale, and a a fuccefsful voyage. The prefs is at work for the publication. Oh! let your prayers be inftant for a blefling.

I am, dear Sir,
Your affectionate Brother,
JAMES HERVEY.

'LETTER X.

Wefton-Favel, Oct. 19, 1754.

My dear Friend,

LAST night I received your parcel. But I had not the fatisfaction of receiving it from the hands of the bearer: the fine afternoon tempted me abroad; and I was gone out in queft of—what I never find, and what I hope you never want—health.

C 2

I thank

I thank you for your remarks on the little manufcript; and, for that copious variety of phrafes, which
may fupply the fterility of my invention. You judge
right in fuppofing me to have full employ, but am
much out of order, and extremely languid in my
fpirits. You muft expect nothing from me. I am a
bow not barely unftrung, but broken. Have neither
a heart nor a hand for any work. I think with fhame
and difmay of the piece that is publifhing. Had I
formerly been in this mifgiving frame, and very enfeebled ftate, fure I fhould never have adventured to
appear from the prefs. O! that the declaration of
the apoftle might be fulfilled in this weakeft of creatures.

I have read and read again your lively piece; yet
with a cold and dead heart. Two or three very flight
alterations I have ventured to make, but thefe not
without diffidence. The word *attend* appears to me
more proper for your purpofe, and in your connection, than convey, or convoy; becaufe one of the
laft expreffions generally fignifies to guard what is
expofed to danger, or to bear what is unable to tra-
vel, neither of which offices need to be performed to
the triumphant JESUS.

In page 6, 7, the epithet *immortal*, occurs four
times, and the adjective *fublime*, three or four. This,
perhaps, you will alter, when the piece is reprinted,
and bound up with your other works. I could not
fo change them as to improve them, otherwife I
would have done it. The pamphlet fhall be fent with
the manufcript directions to your printer by to-morrow's poft. If you can fuggeft a proper hint for a
preface, I fhall be much obliged: only I muft fay,
(for we are entered upon the third volume, but I
fhall not be able to fend you the fecond till next
week, at which time you may expect, and I, if I live
and am well, will not neglect to fend it,) I will very
readily pay my fhare for a fourth part of your
little tract. Let me know what it comes to. But I
will

will defire you, or your friends, to difpofe of them; for I correfpond with nobody, fee nobody, and am as the Pfalmift fpeaks, *Like unto them that are out of re-membrance, and are cut away from thy hand.* Twenty I fhall order for myfelf, and the remainder fhall wait for your fignal. I am, dear Sir, in great weaknefs, but with great fincerity,

Your Friend and Brother,

in CHRIST JESUS,

JAMES HERVEY.

LETTER XI.

Wefton-Favel, Nov. 2, 1754.

My dear Friend,

LET me thank you for your three extracts: they are very fubftantial vouchers, and give a great fanction to my opinion. I wifh you had touched my cold piece with your torch, and enkindled it here and there with a little of your fire: of that fire which glows in your rapturous teftimony borne to the divine JESUS, and will, I truft, warm the hearts of multitudes.

Pray let me know what I am to pay for my fhare of the copies; and be fo kind as to difpofe of them for my Mafter and me. I am the moft unfit perfon alive to undertake the office of fpreading this, or any fuch work, becaufe, fenfible how often my fpirits fail me, and leave me quite incapable of anfwering the expectations of my correfpondents, I choofe to de-cline almoft all epiftolary intercourfe. Several letters now lie by me, from known and unknown hands, which are not, and I believe never will, be acknow-ledged; any otherwife than by prayers to GOD for the friendly writers. To-day, bleffed be the GOD of my life, I am fomewhat better, than when I wrote laft.

But

But ah ! how long will this gleam of halcyon weather continue ? Well, there is a world in which the voice of joy and health is perpetually heard ; may my infirmities render thofe defirable manfions to me! and may your vivacity fit you for abundant ufefulnefs here !

I now fulfil my promife—fend you Volume II. Laft week my bookfeller difappointed me. Now let me intreat my dear friend to correct it with his pen, and blefs it with his prayers. Any remarks from yourfelf or acquaintance, would be extremely welcome. I had rather have the performance improved than applauded ; by the latter, a vain creature may be made vainer ; by the former, the all-glorious JESUS may vouchfafe to bring fome honour to his name, and fome furtherance to his caufe. My bookfeller thinks there is a probability of a fecond edition, fo that any emendations tranfmitted, may take place.

As foon as the third volume is completed, it will be fure to make one of its firft vifits to you ; who will pity its imperfections, and pray for its author.

Your affectionate Brother,
J. HERVEY.

LETTER XII.

Wefton-Favel, Nov. 23, 1754.

My dear Friend,

I Received your hints, and return my thanks. The Preface is finifhed, and muft be fent to-morrow. I have neglected to compofe it, till it was too late to fhew it to any friend for his revifal and correction. Befeech the unerring wifdom to make it, and the whole performance.

I am obliged for your kind and feafonable reproof. Let the righteous fmite me friendly. I am indeed too unthankful to my heavenly Father ; yet, you do not

know;

know; you cannot conceive; it is impoffible for me to exprefs, what forrow attends fuch inceffant languors of conftitution, and failure of fpirits. Devotion is deadened; joy is extinguifhed; peace is difcompofed, the poor foul is rendered tender and fenfible to every crofs accident, as the inflamed or ulcerated flefh fuffers, even by the flighteft touch. O for faith! as ftrong, long-fuffering, unconquerable faith, to live upon the fulnefs and riches of CHRIST, when there is nothing but penury and defolation in felf!

Mr. F—— has fent me 225 of your pamphlets; pray let me know what I am indebted; what the other gentlemen pay for their quota.—The more I read your piece, the more I like it. O! that I may feel it in my very foul, and carry the impreffions of it; I will not fay to my grave only, but infinitely beyond the grave, even to the heaven of heavens. But if you write for the poor and ordinary clafs of mankind, I really think the ftyle is too enriched, and the fentiments too refined, at leaft in feveral places, for their apprehenfion. Why did you put yourfelf to the expence of printing the Promifes, when I have hundreds and hundreds that want to be diftributed. To let you fee how unfit I am to undertake the monthly difpofal of an edifying pamphlet, I cannot but inform you, that I have hardly put off half a hundred of thefe little fcraps, though I truft, when my larger work is difpatched, to be a little more active, in committing thefe to the exchangers, if fo be they may receive a bleffing from on high, and my LORD, when he cometh, may receive his own with ufury.—I fend you a hundred of your own compofitions, and a hundred of my collections; a hundred fhips of the line, attended with a hundred pinnaces. The LORD JESUS vouchfafe a profperous expedition to them all!

Pray execute your intention. I will fend you a large fet of Theron and Afpafio, if you will return it to me, loaded in the margin, with criticifms, caftigations,

gations, and improvements. Though I cannot fix a time, I know not when the larger fort will be completed. Methinks I would advife thofe who purchafe the larger edition, to have it only half bound in blue covers, and not cut on the edges. The paper feems to be remarkably large. The binder will probably cut away abundance of the margin, which will very much impair the beauty of the volume.— To fee you at Chriftmas, will be a pleafure to my family, and to,

Dear Sir,
Your affectionate Brother,
J. HERVEY.

LETTER XIII.

Wefton, *Jan.* 18, 1755.

My dear Friend,

I Hope this will find you fafely arrived at Warwick, refrefhed in your conftitution by your late journey, and refrefhed in your fpirit by finding your family in profperity.

I fend according to my promife, the third volume of Theron and Afpafio in fheets: any remarks which the truth that dwelleth in you fhall fuggeft; will be gladly received, and gratefully acknowledged. Amidft all my fond partiality, and notwithftanding the dimnefs of my fight, I cannot but difcern many blemifhes; the good LORD of his mercies fake pardon them; and for his own Gofpel's fake enable my friends to correct them.

When you fend me a parcel, be fo kind as to inclofe that print in Stackhoufe's Hiftory of the Bible, which reprefents the interview of King Solomon and Queen of Sheba; together with the number that relates to it, and add your obfervations on this picture, and Hervey's Defcription, Vol. I. p. 231.

I have

J have taken the freedom of writing to Mr. Brine, and have sent him a copy of the work. May the LORD JESUS incline his heart to affist me, and make him of quick underftanding, both to detect and to rectify what is amifs.

What do you take to be the precife meaning and defign of the apoftle James in that remarkable affertion, *Whofoever shall keep the whole law, and offend in one point, he is guilty of all?* The Bifhop of London, in a volume of Sermons, which he has lately publifhed, objects to the fenfe commonly given by expofitors. He fays, it doth not fuit the apoftle's inference, in the latter part of the verfe : it is liable to all the difficulties of the ftoic's paradox, that all offences are equal. It relates, he thinks, to the royal law of love mentioned before ; and is intended to shew, that one injurious action, (even though it be only a partial preference) is as inconfiftent with love, as another; and in this refpect, injurious actions have no difference ; for they are all equally inconfiftent with the great law of charity.

You are often mentioned in our family ; and we truft, you remember us all at the throne of grace. My fervant ftays for the parcel ; fo that I cannot add more than,

Your's, inviolably,
J. HERVEY.

LETTER XIV.

Wefton, Feb. 8, 1755.

My dear Friend,

I Return your picture—obliged for the fight of it; but more obliged for your remarks on it. I think they are perfectly juft : I fubfcribe to them all ; and join with you in pronouncing the performance inde

D

licate

licate, injudicious, contemptible. I wiſh you would examine Theron and Aſpaſio, with the ſame honeſt and friendly rigour, which you have exerciſed on Raphael's pencil.

I hope this will find you thoroughly reſtored to health; freed from every complaint of the conſtitutional kind. O! how deſirable (if ſuch be the LORD's will) is ſome good degree of animal vigour and vivacity! How it expedites the operations of the mind, and tunes the human machine for the nicer and happier agency of grace. In this, as well as the ſublimer ſenſe of the promiſe, may the LORD renew your ſtrength, and make fat your bones! My book is not publiſhed yet: it is ſlow enough in its appearance. O! that it may be equally ſure in its compoſition, its acceptance, and ſucceſs. It is advertiſed for the 18th of this inſtant; but there are ſo many unexpected remoras, that I dare not anſwer for its forth coming, even at the expiration of ten days more. I have ordered my bookſeller to lodge a parcel for you in the hands of Mr. Ward: it will contain ſeven ſets of the ſmall ſize, for the worthy miniſters you mention; and one ſet of the large ſize for yourſelf. When you preſent the piece, you will engage their prayers for a divine bleſſing on the work, and obtain their remarks for the improvement of another edition.

Doctor Criſp ſays, "There is no wrath to believers; CHRIST has bore it all; exhauſted it wholly, and carried it—clean away." This is comfortable doctrine. But how will it conſiſt with ſome Scriptures, that ſeem to ſpeak the contrary ſentiment; with that paſſage in Micah particularly; *I will bear the indignation of the* LORD, *becauſe I have ſinned againſt him.* This is evidently the voice of a believer—of a confirmed believer—of a believer in the very exerciſe of faith: for he calls GOD, My GOD, and the GOD of my ſalvation. He ſays, *The* LORD *will bring me forth to light: I ſhall behold his righteouſneſs.*

May

May our adorable Mafter prepare us both for the
fervice of the fanctuary, and grant that we may come
to our important work, like the Mafter of old, *full of
faith, and of the* HOLY GHOST!

I am, dear Sir, of all your friends, the moft weak,
but not the leaft obliged, nor the leaft affectionate,

J. HERVEY.

LETTER XV.

Wefton, March 8, 1755.

My dear Friend,

I Directed my bookfeller, a confiderable time ago, to
leave a parcel with Mr. Ward, containing feven
fets of Theron and Afpafio, (fmall fize) for your
friends: one fet, (large fize) for yourfelf. I hope he
has executed my orders, and the books are come to
your hand. We have begun another edition, and
ventured to print three thoufand. May the LORD
JESUS CHRIST compaffionate the author, and profper
the work of his hand upon him. O profper thou his
handy work!

Any remarks and improvements will be extremely
welcome; but they muft be communicated foon,
otherwife, perhaps, they cannot take place; for it was
propofed to begin upon each volume at once; and
proceed, by means of feveral hands, and feveral
preffes, with great expedition.

I find, from an advertifement in the Northampton
newfpaper, that the writers of the Review have treated
Mr. Brine with virulence and fcurrility. What may
I expect at their hands? Pray for me, that I may receive their cenfures and invectives with calmnefs, and
neither be exafperated in my temper, nor intimidated
in my fpirit. May this be the language of my heart,
Though they curfe, yet blefs thou.

D 2

I fee

I see there is lately published, a magnificent edition of the Hebrew Bible, with which are connected, the Greek Apocryphal Books. To all which are prefixed, Differtations; and fubjoined, Expofitory Notes, by Monf. Houbigant. Have you ever heard a character of this work?

The Princefs of Wales, and my other noble friends, were pleafed to receive my books in a very candid and obliging manner. May the divine REDEEMER open their hearts; give them admiffion into their fouls; and make them not merely a matter of amufement, but a favour of life unto life!

May he blefs abundantly all your labours, and continue forth his loving kindnefs, his grace, mercy, and peace to,

My dear Sir,
Your affectionate Brother,
J. HERVEY.

L E T T E R XVI.

Wefton, March 15, 1755.

My dear Friend,

I Am glad to hear that the parcel is come fafe, though it was more tardy in its arrival than I propofed, and than you might expect. I am much obliged to you for the two valuable books, which I hope the LORD JESUS will make a bleffing to my own foul, and enable me to recommend them in a proper manner to the perufal of others. I will endeavour to follow your advice, and drop a hint to my reader, of the worth and excellency of Doctor Owen's Treatife.

It may be not only ufeful to the reader, but neceffary for the vindication of the writer. I am already attacked on this head, by a gentleman, in manufcript.

He

He writes thus :—" Theron fays, Vol. III. p. 249,
' When I have been cleanfed, I defile myfelf afrefh.'
" Now St. Paul, in that fo commonly-wrefted chap-
" ter to the Romans, is defcribing the natural man,
" that had not been cleanfed; or there is no good
" Chriftian, but is infinitely better than was Paul."
—To this he fubjoins feveral texts of Scripture,—
*dead to fin—made free from fin—he cannot fin—go
and fin no more.* And proceeds thus : " I believe
" when you confider fo many pofitive texts, as you
" know there are, and that without any fhadow of
" qualification, you will allow there muft be meant a
" comparative perfection; a being in a degree per-
" fect, even as our Father which is in heaven is per-
" fect; or, How are we his fons ?"

" Afpafio replies, ' The efficacy of CHRIST's death
' is new for our application every morning; new
' for this bleffed purpofe every moment.' Let a
" friend, and not an enemy, put thefe fentences to-
" gether; all your angelic pages, I doubt, will not
" refcue you. For my part, I was ftruck with hor-
" ror, as to what comes after: ' My beft hours are
' not free from finful infirmities, nor my beft duties
' from finful imperfections.' It feems to me but a
" part of what I am to underftand by the fpeech,
" that miring and wafhing, and miring again, is too
" like abfolution, and finning the very fin anew."

Thus my correfpondent, and, I believe, my friend.
As to the firft expreffion, I intend to expunge it:
" I defile myfelf," looks too much like voluntary and
allowed tranfgreffion. And I muft own, I have always been inclined to think that the apoftle, in the
latter part of the 7th chapter to the Romans, is not defcribing his adult, but his infantile ftate in Chriftianity, what he experienced in the firft ftage of his
journey to Zion. Does he not give us an account, firft
of his total death in fin, then of his being awakened
by the power of the law, fet home by the convincing
Spirit ? After that, of his conflicts, fore conflicts with
unbelief

unbelief and corruption, before he was eſtabliſhed in grace ? Laſt of all, does he not diſplay his deliverance from this ſtate of bondage and of fear? This I look upon only as a ſkirmiſh, or a prelude to the grand aſſault.

The Author of the London Magazine has taken notice of Theron and Aſpaſio, and really, in a very reſpectful and honourable manner.—My ſentence in the Gentleman's Magazine, is reſpited till next month. I know not whether the Monthly Review has taken me to taſk; but this I know, (O that I could conſtantly believe it) that if GOD be for us, it matters not who is againſt us. If He eſpouſes our cauſe, no weapon formed againſt it ſhall proſper. Do, my dear friend, ſend me what you mention in your laſt, and let me have every day more and more reaſon to profeſs myſelf,

Your obliged, as well as,
affectionate Brother,
J. HERVEY,

L E T T E R XVII.

Weſton, April 5, 1755.

My dear Friend,

I Received your letter by the poſt : I thank you very ſincerely for the contents. As I read them with an eager eye, and eſpecially the Introduction to them, I could not forbear whiſpering to myſelf, " Gallantly " ſaid." I could not forbear wiſhing, that the encouragement and the commiſſion, given by the angel to Gideon, may be given to my friend,—" Go, in this " thy might," with which I truſt the LORD JESUS CHRIST has endowed thee, that thou mayeſt fight his battles, and maintain his truth.

I will, if I live to write another letter, deliver my ſentiments concerning your interpretation of the latter

ter part of Romans vii. and the close spirited queries, suggested on the occasion. My thoughts have been so engaged, and my weak spirits so hurried, about a troublesome vexatious affair of a secular nature, that I have had but little power, and as little leisure, to consider more important points. The tenant, whose mother you saw at my house, continues obstinate and revengeful to the very last, and will leave me no possibility of getting my money for the time past, or my land for the time to come, but only by arresting him, and throwing him into gaol; and this I cannot be prevailed on to do: it would grieve me extremely to reflect, that a man, who has a wife and two small children, lies in a prison, confined by my order.

I have received two long letters, one from Mr. Pike of London, another from Mrs. Dutton of Great Gransden, on the subject of assurance of faith. I will transmit them both for your perusal. If, as you read, any thing should occur, which may strengthen my arguments, or illustrate my tenet—any thing which may temper and qualify the doctrine, and render it less exceptionable, yet equally useful—any point that I should give up, or any concession that I should make, be so kind as to favour me with a hint. Mr. Brine is against me on this subject. He writes thus: —" If by an appropriation of CHRIST, is meant an " application to him for life and salvation, this is es- " sential to faith. But if it designs a conclusion, " springing up in my mind of my own interest in " him, and in his saving benefits, I cannot but ap- " prehend it is a mistake. A poor sinner may dis- " cern his need of CHRIST, and be fully persuaded " of his ability to save him; and upon it apply unto " him for mercy, pardon, and succour, in his dis- " tressed condition, in this language: *If thou wilt thou* " *canst make me clean*; which, I hope, will be found " to be that faith, which is the faith of the operation " of GOD."

Now

Now I would fo conduct my Treatife, that it fhould eftablifh my own opinion, without oppofing the judgment of thefe and other eminent divines: I would recommend and promote the affurance of faith, yet allow that a foul, deftitute of this gift, may be really fafe, though not truly happy. If you could fuggeft fome method of maintaining the Chriftian's privilege, without offending the brother of high or low emdowments, I fhould be glad. What you do of this kind, pray let it be fpeedy, otherwife it cannot take place. I muft beg of you to return thefe letters, with your friendly remarks, next week, without fail; for our new edition goes on at a great rate; they have finifhed very near half of each volume, and my bookfeller, prefuming that I fhould have no objection, took the liberty of making the edition confift of 4000, inftead of 3000, on which we had agreed. I fuppofe he was prompted to do this, by finding a call for the piece.

Now I begin to expect a warm, and no very candid attack, from the authors of the Monthly Review. I fee from their treatment of Mr. Brine, what civility I may promife myfelf. Mr. R——— has let fly upon them, in a manner that is, I think, more zealous than judicious; fuch as fhews him to be gailed by their invectives, though he profeffes the contrary; and fuch as feems to betray refentment, rather than difplay a calm and difpaffionate concern for truth. May the true and great Zapnath-Paaneah fill us with all wifdom and fpiritual underftanding, that we may walk and write, worthy of the LORD, unto all pleafing!

I fend you four franks. I wifh you much of that anointing, which may teach you all things. I beg to hear from you by the firft opportunity; and remain,

Dear Sir,

Moft cordially your's,

J. HERVEY.

LET-

My dear Friend,

YOUR parcel has reached my hand, and your affectionate fympathizing letter has made an impreffion on my heart. I rejoice to hear that GOD has
been with you in your journey, and brought you to
your habitation in peace. May the eternal Spirit
water the feed which you have fown; that on your
next excurfion into thofe parts, you may find the
fields laden with increafe, and white for the harveft!

I am glad you have not fent Mr. Gillies's Hiftorical Collections. I defire you to alter your purpofe,
and to divert your intended favour fome other way.
Do you afk the reafon? It is this; I am already fupplied. The worthy author has made me a prefent of
his work, and may the LORD almighty make his
work as a " torch in the fheaf," to quicken a fupine,
and enflame a lukewarm age!

A confiderable time ago, I gave directions to Mr.
R———, to prepare a fet of the Meditations, in the
manner you defcribed, and to lodge them with Mr.
Ward, to be forwarded with the firft parcel for you.

Do you know one Mr. John Dowley? He lives
at Lutterworth; is, I apprehend, a diffenting teacher;
he has favoured me with a letter, very fenfible, very
obliging, and equally devout. If I live to write to
you again, I will tranfcribe a critical remark, which
he makes, but with a great deal of modefty, upon my
interpretation of Exod. xxxiv. 7.

The plan you mention, pleafes and afflicts me.
Its important nature, joined with a probability of
ufefulnefs, pleafes; but a confcioufnefs of my weaknefs, and a reflection on my incapacity for the fervice,
afflicts. However, may I bow my head and fay, the

E

will

will of the LORD, which is always good, always the
beſt, be done.   When do you publiſh your Deſcription of a Preacher? I hope our divine Maſter will
give it admittance into our univerſities, make it as
the Prophet's ſalt in thoſe ſpring-heads.   Surely, if
beauty of thought, and force of language, are re-
liſhed in thoſe ſeminaries, your little piece will want
no recommendation, but be its own paſſport.

That this, and all your labours of love may find
much acceptance, and under the Redeemer's bleſſing,
diffuſe much good, is the wiſh, the prayer, and will,
when accompliſhed, be the joy of,

Dear Sir,

Your affectionate Brother

in the Goſpel,

J. HERVEY.

LETTER XIX.

Weſton, Auguſt, 1755.

My dear Friend,

I Fully intended to have returned your valuable manuſcript, together with this ticket; but as other
engagements have broke in upon my time, I hope
you will excuſe the delay.

Did I ever mention to you a little book, intitled
Terentius Chriſtianus?   As you proceed upon a new
plan, in the education of youth, and admit none but
edifying books into your ſchool, I am apt to think the
piece I have mentioned, may comport with your deſign.

Pray return Mr. W——'s letter.   I find, by private
intelligence, that he has ſhewn it in London; and has
thought proper to animadvert upon me, by name,
from his pulpit.   I am inclined to take no notice
either of his preaching or his writing.

I have

I have received from Mr. Keith, a fet of Dr. Crifp's Sermons; they are very neatly printed: they entertain the eye, and, I hope, will adminifter much confolation to the heart.

A Gentleman of Edinburgh, a perfect ftranger, fent me, a few days ago, a book, ftiled "The Marrow of Modern Divinity," with Notes by Mr. Bofton. I have not been at leifure to perufe it; but by dipping into it, I feem to like it not a little. Has it fallen into your hands? if fo, favour me with your opinion of it.

My good friend, Mr. Whitefield, is now at my houfe. He purpofes to lift up his voice at North-ampton, and proclaim the acceptable year of the LORD. May the LORD of heaven and earth blefs my vifitant; blefs my correfpondent, and blefs their very unworthy

Servant, Friend, and Brother,

in CHRIST JESUS,

JAMES HERVEY.

LETTER XX.

Wefton, March 9, 1756.

My dear Friend,

LATE on Saturday night, I received the inclofed, together with your ticket; by which circum-ftance, you will perceive, that I could not poffibly return the proof-fheet fooner. Wonder not that I re-mit it to you rather than the printer. *Nefcit vox miffa revertere,* is the confequence of printing; I durft not, therefore, commit it to the prefs, till the alterations which I have ventured to make, have been fubmitted to your own examination. I muft defire; nay, I do infift upon it, that without the leaft complaifance to

E 2 my

my opinion, you reject them, one and all, if they do not fuit your defign, or comport with your ideas.

Alarming reprefentations indeed! May the GOD of Glory accompany them with his fpirit, that they may awaken the fupine, intimidate the hardened, and, like the thunders of Sinai, urge us all to take fhelter in our divine Mediator!

Let me remind my friend, that in eight pages of his Effay, I have made more attempts to improve, than he would make in more than a thoufand pages of Theron and Afpafio. You are unkindly tender; I am feverely kind. Perhaps we are both to blame; but furely mine is the moft excufable fault of the two.

Have you ever feen a little book, intitled "The Eternal Law, and Everlafting Gofpel," by Mr. Beart? It was lately put into my hand, and feems to be a folid, correct, mafterly performance.

You promife me a long letter: let me affure you the longer it is, the more welcome it will be to,

My dear Mr. Ryland,

Your inviolable Friend,

And affectionate Brother,

JAMES HERVEY.

LETTER XXI.

Wefton, Auguft 7, 1756.

My dear Friend,

DO I really defire the continuance of your thoughts? Yes, verily, nor can any thing oblige me more. Pray let me look upon thefe as the firft fruits, and give me leave to expect the harveft.

Herewith I fend you Dr. Owen upon the Hebrews. I defire you will not think of returning the volumes, but look upon them as your own.

I am

I am sorry you ordered Mr. Keith to send me Brooks, because I had procured it before his came: if you will commission him to get Eaton's Honeycomb of Justification, (which Mr. Alt so highly commends) and transmit to me, it will be a favour.

This week I received a parcel and a letter from Mr. B——, of Olney, both which you will find accompanying Mr. Brooks. Mr. B——, I assure you, is a better judge of poetry than I pretend to be: practice makes perfect, and he has practised both in rhyme and blank verse, with considerable success; yet I cannot admire his expunging, *roar and foam,* and substituting in its stead, *sap its base.*

For the letter you mention, I am accountable. But I must desire to keep it a little longer, because it contains the explanation of a charge brought against me by Mr. W——, who is going to unmask his battery, and play his artillery upon me in public. Two persons, formerly his preachers, inform me, that he is now in Ireland, and preparing an Answer to Theron and Aspasio. The LORD JESUS grant, that the truth of his Gospel, not mine, or my opposer's notions, may stand!

Why does not Dr. Gill's Exposition make its appearance? I long to be regaled with his Comment on the elegant, sublime, rapturous Isaiah. I wrote lately to Amsterdam, and desired my correspondent to send Witsius's picture, which I intend as an ornament, not of my parlour, but of your's.

J. H.

My dear Friend,

THIS day fe'nnight I received your packet; and take the first opportunity to thank you for the contents.

Mr. White's Letter, in pursuance of your request, is returned. He is fit for the business he undertakes; has the art of soliciting with force, yet with modesty. I wish him success, whenever he engages in so benevolent a cause. If a guinea per annum will be of any service to the young student, his parents may depend upon such a supply from me, as long as my life continues. The first payment, if acceptable, shall be advanced, when my next packet comes to Warwick.

Is the Honey-comb your present? or must it be returned—No more franks at present; I have enough. If you lend me Bosuet's Universal History, perhaps I may recommend it as a book not improper for young gentlemen or young ladies. I could be glad to furnish Miss Melissa with a little library. Do you recollect any treatises peculiarly proper for this purpose, whose style is perspicuous and polite; whose matter is entertaining, yet edifying?

I have seen the Address to Clergymen, and think it well executed, as it is evidently well designed, affectionate, and spirited; weighty and pointed; yet not overbearing or dogmatical. May the LORD speak to us all, *with a strong hand,* and speak, if it be his will, by this word!

Two of Dr. Gill's numbers are come to hand; but I have not been able to go through them, though they are some of the most flowery walks (the prophecies of Isaiah I mean) in the garden of GOD.

The

The fourth volume of Theron and Aspasio, after which you enquire, is less than an embryo, is a mere nonentity. May He who spoke the universe into being; *who calls the things that are not; as though they were,* endue a poor enervated sinner with Abraham's faith, *who against hope, believed in hope.*

Pray let me have one of your monthly Essays, as they come out. I would willingly take a number, but I really have not proper opportunities of dispersing them. When does your Dialogue in verse make its appearance? Or do you follow Mr. B——'s advice, and persuade the author to execute his work in prose?

Yesterday my old friend, Mr. Hartley, dined with me, and brought a pious clergyman with him; the day before, your brother, (and why should I not add my brother) Mr. Evans, was content with a morsel at my table. O! for that hour, when we shall all sit down at the marriage feast of the LAMB! May we taste it by faith, till our souls are " satiated with its fulness in glory." I shall wait, not with impatience, but with some degree of eagerness, for the packet which you have promised to,

My dear Friend,
Your affectionate,
J. HERVEY.

LETTER XXIII.

Weston, November 29, 1756.

My dear Friend,

MR. S—— is now in my room, sketching out the plan of a house. While he is thus employed, I seize a moment to thank you, for remembering me in my weak estate. Help to so feeble a hand: hints
suggested

suggested to so languid a mind, will be as the " cold of snow in harvest." [By the bye, what is the true meaning, or where is the scriptural, *i. e.* the consummate propriety of this comparison? If I remember right, the original is, as a shield of snow.]

Herewith you have the grand attack from Mr. W. of which I apprized you some time ago. Examine it closely; return it speedily; and if you please, confute it effectually; demolish the battery, and spike up the cannon. I have not answered in any shape; and when I do answer with my pen, I propose nothing more than a general acknowledgment, and an inquiry, whether he proposes to print his animadversions? I shall long for your packet, and pray for a rich unction of the spirit on your invention, your judgment, your elocution.

Ever your's,

J. HERVEY.

LETTER   XXIV.

My dear Friend,

HEREWITH I return Mr. White's letter, which I intended, but forgot to inclose in the last packet. In your advertisement, would not *gradually* be better than *annually?* " Annually, these ten years," seems to be an approach towards tautology. I have some doubt with regard to the exact propriety of your title; all the principal branches of revealed religion, evangelical holiness, and social virtue. By this it should seem, that you look upon evangelical holiness, and social virtue, as branches distinct and different from, not comprehended in, revealed religion. Whereas the possibility of a sinister acceptation would

be

be prevented, if you was to exprefs yourfelf in fome fuch manner,. " On the principal branches of revealed religion, including, Vital Faith — Evangelical Holinefs—Social Virtue."

I query whether the word *fpirited,* being fuppofed to come from your own pen, is fo perfectly free from an air of vanity or oftentation.

See with what freedom I write! in this one particular let me be your pattern; *do fo to me, and more alfo.* In your difcourfe on Full Affurance of Faith, there are fome of the moft grand and important truths that can enter into the heart of man; feveral of them will appear rant and enthufiafm to the carnal mind; fome of them will be like ftrange fayings, even to many ferious perfons. For my part, I fubfcribe to them all, without the leaft hefitation or referve; and though many of my pamphlets I have juft peeped upon, and then laid by, never to be regarded more, this I fhall have at my right hand: this I fhall often ftudy: this I would always remember: and if I may but have its counter-part in my heart, I fhall reach the fummit of my wifhes. An expreffion or two I have marked, as not perfectly pleafing my ear; and one I have inclofed in a parenthefis, as feemingly redundant. Pray let me have half a dozen of your papers as foon as they are printed—no more than this number: I would afk for more if I wanted more, or could difpofe of them properly. As foon as I am come to a determination about Mr. Dry, you fhall be informed. The Father of Compaffions profper you and direct me,

Ever your's,

J. HERVEY.

P. S. Thanks for Boffuet: he is a very delicate writer indeed.

LET-

My dear Friend,

YOU repofe a confidence in my judgment, which gives pain to my mind. Indeed, my difcernment is like my conftitution, utterly enervated; and my tafte for compofition, like my appetite for food, is quite palled and depraved. I can do little elfe, than beg of the LORD, in behalf of my worthy friend, and my other brethren in the miniftry.

The effay which you mention, and which I have expected by every poft, is not yet come to my hand. Since you enjoin me this tafk, I will, as foon as I receive it, perufe it with the clofeft attention, and deal with it juft as if it was to go abroad under my own name. But why, my dear Sir, why do you expofe your writings to fuch hazard? Would you fuffer a fhaking hand to open your vein, or choofe a blind operator to couch your eye? The LORD grant you may not repent your adventrous conduct; and that I may not, inftead of a plane, bring a faw to the work.

As to your plan of education, fill it up by degrees, add a touch to-day, another to-morrow, and thus let it ripen into perfection. GOD only wife, and GOD all-wife, knows that I am abfolutely incapable of executing fuch a fcheme, otherwife I fhould not be averfe, but very defirous to engraft my tree with one of your fcions; and I muft befeech you, when I am releafed from this afflicted ftate, not to make public that little fketch, which I know not how has ftole itfelf into your hand: it will appear, unlefs you re-touch and complete it, very rude and imperfect. Moft fincerely I thank you for your affectionate and fervent prayers. But in this inftance, my faith fails. When I think upon your kind encouragement, I

cannot

cannot forbear calling to mind the humane and pious practice of Nathan, advising David to build the temple. But—*dies aliter visum.*

I wish your son James may be like his namesake under the Old Testament, *a prince·with* GOD, *and mighty in prayer*; or like his no less honourable namesake under the New, *a servant of* GOD, *and of the* LORD JESUS CHRIST. Under the lustre of such characters, I shall be willing to have my meanness eclipsed: I shall be glad to have my unworthiness lost. And can you intend, when you pray for him, to remember me? that is like a true friend; that is like a Christian friend; and like a friend, whose favours will extend, not only through the years of life, but through the ages of eternity. I have great reason, therefore, to profess myself,

Dear Sir,

Inviolably and eternally your's,

J. HERVEY.

LETTER XXVI.

My dear Friend,

ACCEPT my thanks for your valuable letter. It found me just come down from a week's confinement to my bed and my chamber: the LORD was pleased to visit me with a fever, which has left behind it a violent and almost incessant cough. This brings me very low, and if not removed, must soon bring me to the dust. *My flesh and my heart fails; but* GOD *the* SAVIOUR *is the strength of my heart, and my portion for ever.*

As to the apology, &c. my great doubt is, whether it be a ταλαντον committed to me by the LORD. My poor head is now so oppressed, that I have little inclination, and less ability, to think upon the subject. Ex-

F 2

cuse

cufe my brevity, my dear friend; this hand has fcarcely
ftrength to hold the pen. Pray, that I may be ftrong
in faith, and rejoice in the Lord.

Ever your's,
J. HERVEY.

L E T T E R XXVII.

My dear Friend,

THANKS for your kind wifhes, and thanks for
your valuable Treatife on Faith.   May the
former be granted, as far as is confiftent with the divine good pleafure ! May the latter be bleffed, abundantly bleffed, to my edification and comfort !

I have fome thoughts of publifhing two or three
plain Sermons, preached on the late faft days : none
that I have feen on the occafion, fpeak enough of the
one thing needful.   Here I fhall make a facrifice of
all my reputation, (if I ever had any) with the elegant and polite : and let it go, freely let it go, if any
honour may redound to the Lord our righteoufnefs.
What would you advife upon the fubject ?

I am juft going abroad upon an affair that is likely
to be exceeding troublefome to me—law.   I fear law
is unavoidable, unlefs I will tamely give up my rights.
God almighty knows I am for peace; but though I
fpeak unto them thereof, they make ready for battle.

Adieu ! my dear friend.   I need not add, that I
am, though in the midft of much weaknefs, cordially
your's,

Friday morn.

J. HERVEY.

L E T-

LETTER XXVIII.

My dear Friend,

I Hope you received the packet by the newfman; and I muft beg you to return it by the returning newfman. You fee how holy and wife perfons are againft my doctrine: the LORD JESUS guide me continually; guide me efpecially in this important point! The more I think of the matter, the lefs I am inclined to recede from my opinion. I cannot perfuade myfelf that Mr. Brine's account anfwers the ideas of faith, or comes up to the fcriptural defcriptions of it. I fhould be glad not to offend thefe excellent perfons; yet, with a decent firmnefs, would maintain what feems to me the truth of the Gofpel. 'Let me hope for fome affiftance from your pen; you are a much better judge of thefe debates: you have been εντρεφομενος τοις λογοις της αληθειας, whereas I am but της σημερον ο προσηλυτος.

I think you diftinguifh very clearly and juftly concerning the divine indignation; and as to Rom. vii. you fay more to convince me that the Apoftle fpeaks of himfelf, and of his prefent ftate, than I ever heard or read before: it has fuch an effect upon your fcholar, that it has induced me to expunge a paffage in my new edition, which feemed to contradict your opinion. Pray do not neglect to fend the manufcripts. The prefs will want Dialogue XVI. in a very little time. I hope your health is eftablifhed, as well as reftored: mine is rather worfe than better: inceffant and infuperable langours; they unfit me for every bufinefs; render every enjoyment unrelifhing; and what is more deplorable, makes my temper like the fore, inflamed, ulcerated flefh. Any thing that comes unexpected, alarms me: any thing that goes crofs, vexes me: I am fadly inclined to a peevifh humour. Pray for me, dear Sir, that our compaffionate LORD would

give

give me, in his good time, an abundant entrance into a better world, for I am weary of this; yet I would humbly adore and blefs GOD for the everlafting righteoufnefs of my Saviour, and that eternal redemption which he has obtained for finners. Amidft the greateft infirmities of body and foul, this is a rock: here is fafety; from hence flows comfort.

Excufe my fcribble: it partakes of my diforder. I am afhamed of every thing in this fcrap of paper, only of this one profeffion, that

I am,

Your obliged and affectionate,

J. HERVEY.

LETTER XXIX.

Wefton, April 20, 1757.

My dear Friend,

I Know not how to be filent any longer, though I cannot yet anfwer your expectations. The little Collection of Promifes is not yet printed; as foon as they are done, I will fend you two hundred, and as many more as you pleafe. I propofe to have two thoufand worked off: my motto muft be, what Virgil pleads by way of recommendation to his Poem on the Bees,

" *In eft fua gratia parvis.*"

Or rather, what the infpired writer fays, in order to difplay the amiable and wonderful condefcenfion of the LORD JEHOVAH,

He does not defpife the day of fmall things.

Accept the two Sermons that wait upon you: one for yourfelf, and one for a friend. The author is a worthy neighbour, who loves his divine Mafter, and labours in his vineyard. When fhall we have fome of your Difcourfes? I verily think they would be welcome

come to the world, and our LORD would honour them with his blessing. I question whether Mr. B———'s manner of writing will meet with much acceptance: there is something very good and fervent; not correct and noble. However, what GOD blesses, is blessed indeed: when he smiles upon a person, or his performance, both the one and the other shall *have favour with all the people.* May this be with my dear correspondent and brother: be with him in his going out, and coming in, from this time forth, for evermore.

I hope you have a packet of judicious and weighty remarks from Mr. Brine; and will transmit them to me, enriched by an addition of your own. I take this opportunity of sending *Volusenus de Transquillitate*, because I would not have you purchase it, till you have seen whether you like it; and if you like it, then I desire you will seek no farther, but keep that which is in your hand,

Dear Friend,

Ever your's,

J. HERVEY.

LETTER XXX.

Weston, Sept. 3, 1757.

My dear Friend,

ACCORDING to promise, I now desire your acceptance of my feeble Essay: strengthen it with your prayers, that it may go forth in the name of the LORD GOD of hosts, and spread abroad the favour of our DIVINE REDEEMER'S name. I expect a severe attack from the Reviewers; but our GOD and SAVIOUR, whose grace we would magnify; whose interests they would oppose, can turn those wise men backward, and make their knowledge foolish.

For

For any remarks, corrections, and improvements from your pen, I shall be sincerely thankful. Pray transmit whatever of this kind occurs in the perusal; an edition is printing on ordinary paper. Tell me, whether you will have any of these to distribute among the poor.

I have several letters to write, before my servant goes to market. This will be my excuse for adding no more, only, that I am,

Ever your's,

J. HERVEY.

P. S. You will please to deliver Mr. Smith's letter.

L E T T E R   XXXI.

Weston, Sept. 21, 1757.

My dear Friend,

HEREWITH I return your lively and charming manuscript. In giving it this character, I have no design to flatter the author, or elate him with vanity; not to flatter him, because what I say, is the genuine sentiment of my heart: not to elate him, because I ascribe what is beautiful and excellent to the Father of Lights.

Some perhaps may think the beginning of the piece is rather too scholastic. " Is it right to say, the Saviour, (or GOD under the relation of a Saviour) exists by a necessity of nature?" page 1, l. 3. " Is it safe to say, the living GOD, expiring in agonies of dissolution?" Should it not rather be, He who is the living, &c. page 3, line 12. I ask these questions chiefly for my own information. *Ibid.* Would you say " a fountain is cloathed with disgrace?" As it is not customary to cloath fountains, I am in some doubt whether this is proper. Page 5, line 13, " Delicious delight." Is
there

there not too great a fimilarity between the fubftantive and its epithet?   Page *ult.* line 13. " *Brilliant*" is
an elegant word; but as it always leads our ideas to
the luftre of a diamond, it feems not to enlarge, but
diminifh our conceptions of the REDEEMER's glory,
which infinitely tranfcends, not diamonds only, but
ftars and funs.

Thefe, my dear Sir, are the only remarks I have to
offer in a critical view, or in the capacity of a caviller:
I fhall only add my prayers, that your arrow may go
forth as lightning, and be as the whirlwinds of the
fouth; confpicuous as the former, forcible as the
latter!

I fend you, according to promife, the firft volume
of my poor attempt; examine and correct it, that it
may be lefs unworthy the glorious fubjects, in cafe
the good providence of GOD fhould vouchfafe to
honour it with another edition ; and do not fail to implore the blefling of heaven upon it, that it may not
be as duft upon the hedges, but as dew upon the
grafs.   I wifh you much fuccefs in your evangelical
affociation.   As for me, my abilities, which at beft,
and when moft difengaged, are really like a thing of
nought, are now entirely taken up with the work upon
the wheels; no lefs than eight men are conftantly
employed upon it: if therefore you could give me
any affiftance, it would be very fignally ferviceable to
the moft infirm, but not the leaft fincere of your
friends,

J. HERVEY.

                    LET-

My dear Friend,

EXCUSE my delay in returning your truly valuable manufcript. I purpofed to do it feveral
times, but by my frequent indifpofitions, my purpofes were broken off. You muft not expect a punc-
tual correfpondent in me : to will is prefent with me,
but oftentimes how to perform what I wifh, I know
not.

I have read your plan again and again, and each
time with new pleafure. I will now perufe it once
more, with the pen in my hand; and whatever appears to want a retouch, I will freely obferve.

Page 1. " Right noble," is what Mr. Johnfon
would call a cant term, graceful only in the Herald's
office, and in the titles of great perfonages.

Ibid. " Greatnefs of foul, elevation," &c. Is there
not a redundancy of fine expreffions here ?

Ibid. " Evangelical virtue, together with vital
faith." Should not *faith* take the wall of *virtue*, as
being fenior of the two ? I mean, fhould not faith
be mentioned firft ?

Page 2. " Rotting in our graves." The word
rotting is too fordid, unlefs ufed on purpofe to pour
contempt.

Ibid. " Natural education." Is *natural* a proper epithet to this fubftantive ? Is not " defpair-
ing " rather too ftrong a word, unlefs you foften it by
the infertion of *almoft* ?

Thus far I had written laft Saturday, and was un-
expectedly called down to receive a vifitant : he proved
to be a young clergyman, a ftranger, charged with a
meffage from my honourable friend, Lady Francis
Shirley. We had fome ferious converfation, which
he

he feemed to enter upon with readinefs, and purfue
with pleafure.   May the Father of Spirits command
it to leave a favour of CHRIST on our hearts ! I now
refume, not the office of a critic, but the fedulity of
a friend.

Page 4, l. 4, del. *too*; l. 6, r. *and for meer*.   Suppofe you was to enlarge upon the preceding and following articles, add a few finews and a little flefh to
your fkeleton, would it not be more graceful ? Might
it not be more ufeful ?

Page 5. I have inclofed two fentences in Hook's,
which appear not abfolutely needful.

Well, my friend, if you are enabled to form
your youth on the model you propofe, happy are
the children committed to your care.   The LORD
JESUS give you ftrength to execute, as he has
given you wifdom to defign.   I have been guilty
of a fault too common with me, the fault of
miflaying my papers: I cannot find, with all my
fearch, the letter which, at my requeft, you was fo
kind as to return.   It will, I prefume, come to hand,
when I do not look for it.   I will regard it as your
property, and make a confcience of reftoring it,
though it be but as a thread, or a fhoe-latchet!—I wifh
you would fend me one copy of every monthly paper
publifhed by your Evangelical Society : I have none
but thofe written by yourfelf.—The third edition of
Theron and Afpafio has made its appearance : I have
not heard with what acceptance from the public.—I
hope you will pray for the fuccefs of this work.—I
hope the LORD will hear your prayers in behalf of
my projected work; and may all your affectionate
prayers for me, return with an abundant increafe of
bleffings on your own works, your own interefts, and
your own heart. Forgive the delay, and forgive all
the faults of, my dear Friend,

Your unworthy Brother in CHRIST,

J. HERVEY.

LETTER XXXIII.

Saturday Morning, Nov. 1757.

My dear Friend,

ACCEPT my thanks for your precious manuscripts: pray continue thefe epiftolary favours. Excufe the delay of my acknowledgments; I have been very bufy in correcting my three Sermons for the prefs: by to-morrow's poft I return the proof of the laft half fheet, fo that they will foon make their appearance. The LORD, whofe glory they would promote, of whofe grace they teftify, both give them favour, and accompany them with power. This is the title,

The Time of Danger, and The Means of Safety; to which is added, The Way of Holinefs.

I will order my bookfeller to pack up one of the Sermons for you, together with Theron and Afpafio for Mr. Crabtree, to be left with Mr. Ward. If you approve the difcourfes, I will fend you fome of them to give away among your poor neighbours.—Laft night came to hand your Treatife on the Full Affurance of Faith. LORD! let the blefled doctrines defcend into my heart, and ever abiding in my foul, ever operate on my converfation. I will, as the LORD fhall direct, place out your treafure to intereft. My letter is fhort, but my Sermons will be long. I muft now be very fparing of my brown bread, left you foon complain of a glut. Thanks for the perufal of Mr. Witherfpoon's letter; it difcovers tafte and judgment, prudence and piety, in the writer. May thefe, and all other gifts and graces of the Spirit, abound in your correfpondent, yourfelf, and your Brother,

J. HERVEY.

My dear Friend,

MANY thanks for your thoughts on the Covenant. You have indeed set plenty before me: may I be enabled to select what is most proper for my purpose; what may be, under the divine blessing, as a *nail fastened in a sure place.*

You enquire after my intended answer to Mr. Wesley: I am transcribing it for the press, but find it difficult to preserve the decency of the gentleman, and the meekness of the Christian: there is so much unfair dealing running through my opponent's objections, and the most magisterial air all along supplying the place of argument. Pray for me, dear Friend, that I may not betray the blessed cause, by the weakness of my reasoning; nor dishonour it by the badness of my temper.

Whether I shall be enabled to finish this work, is apparently uncertain; my cough seizes me in the night like a lion, and leaves me, before the morning, weaker than a babe. It has so totally destroyed my small remainder of strength, that I am quite unable to preach so much as once on the LORD's day: I am obliged to beg assistance, and am looking out for a curate, to take the whole business on his hand. May the Head of the church vouchsafe to furnish me with a faithful and wise steward, who may supply my lack of service, and give his houshold their portion of spiritual meat in due season.

Pray has Mr. Wood finished his work? Methinks I should be glad to have that volume returned, that in case my life drops, I might have a copy corrected, and so leave it, that my survivors might be at no loss concerning it.

I had,

I had, not long ago, the favour of a visit from your worthy neighbour, Mr. Talbot.   He came, accompanied with Mr. Maddin; and both were like men baptized with the HOLY GHOST and with fire; fervent in spirit, and setting their faces as a flint.

I am, my dear Friend,

Your's, most affectionately,

J. HERVEY.

LETTER XXXV.

Weston, Feb. 18, 1758.

My dear Friend,

I Have sent you a quarter of an hundred of the Fast Sermons; and I thank you for putting me in a way to speak for JESUS CHRIST by my pen, since I am still incapable of pleading for him, or giving honour to him with my tongue. May He, whose countenance is as the sun when it shineth in its strength, vouchsafe to smile upon the distributor, the readers, and the writer!

Do not give yourself much trouble about Neonom Unmasked.   I value it much, but can do without it, or perhaps procure it elsewhere.   There are but few books, whose sentiments I so generally approve, or whose doctrine is so thoroughly evangelical.

The letter from Cirencester you will permit me to keep one week longer, or till another packet; at least till some other dispatch comes to you.   It shall not be mislaid.   I sincerely thank you for your admonition on this subject.   I have of late been guilty of negligence in this particular, almost to a sin.

Let me expect the speedy accomplishment of your promise.   Cannot you get a few moments to run over the alterations in the first volume, when Mr. Wood has transcribed them? together with a cursory glance

of

of your eye, will you not beſtow a few improving touches of your pen?

Excuſe me, if I proceed no farther. I have juſt been writing two letters, one for Wales, another for Scotland; and ſhould write two more before my ſervant goes to market, and that which would be a recreation to your vigorous, is a toil to the enfeebled hand of,

Your very affectionate Friend,
J. HERVEY.

LETTER XXXVI.

Weſton, March, 1758.

My dear Friend,

MR. Carter tells me you have been ill. By this time, I truſt, your ſtrength is renewed. May your ability for the ſervice of our divine Maſter increaſe, as much as mine decreaſes!

I have a curate, a godly man; loves CHRIST; underſtands the Goſpel, and will watch over my flock, with more aſſiduity, I hope with greater ſucceſs, than their original paſtor.

My affectionate reſpects to Mr. Carter: tell him I cannot ſpare Mr. Weſley's book, becauſe I am tranſcribing, though very ſlowly, and with a moſt feeble hand, my remarks for the preſs; in executing which work, I have continual need of having his letter before me. He urges no argument, either to eſtabliſh his own opinion, or to overthrow mine; only denies the validity of my reaſons in ſuch manner as the following:—" How does it appear that CHRIST undertook " this before the foundation of the world, and that " by a poſitive covenant between Him and the Fa- " ther?"—" Neither of theſe texts, nor all of them " prove, what they were brought to prove, that there " ever

" ever was any fuch covenant made between the Fa-
" ther and the Son."

Your thoughts upon the joys of heaven will be
very welcome, and very fuitable to my cafe. Thanks;
everlafting thanks, for the blood of the LAMB, in
which our robes are. wafhed; and all we are, all we
have, yea, all we do, is made whiter than fnow.

Here is an author's mite towards the relief of our
poor brethren in Hampfhire. Let it come to them,
not as from J. H——y, but as from the GOD that
hideth himfelf.

Ever your's,
J. HERVEY.

LETTER XXXVII.

April 15, 1758.

My dear Friend,

I Thank you for your punctuality in returning the
manufcript papers, at the time requefted. I thank
you alfo for your very welcome, and no lefs valuable
obfervations on the fubject. I really am more and
more confirmed in my opinion, notwithftanding
all the objections; or rather, I am more and more
convinced, that Mr. Marfhal's doctrine is the doctrine of the Gofpel. To this my reafon fubfcribes:
this I think is taught in the Scriptures: this I am
fure is approved and ratified by my own daily experience. When I depart from this precious truth,
Affurance by the direct act of Faith, I fall into darknefs and diftrefs; but when, looking for no evidences
in myfelf, I depend on the free promife of GOD in his
word; when regarding myfelf only as a poor finner, I
confidently truft in CHRIST as my righteoufnefs and
falvation; then light beams forth, and comfort fprings
up. I propofe to make fome alterations in Dialogue
XVI. and as it is already too long, to divide it into

two

two conferences. Beseech the Lord Jesus that I may not bewilder my reader, but clear his way, and guide his steps.

By the last post, I received the proof sheet of " A Demonstration, &c." I will return it to Mr. Hayward, by the next mail, according to your desire. I will also venture to make a few slight alterations; but I shall do this with hesitation and timidity. If ever you consign over any of your future compositions to my inspection, I must insist upon it, that you yourself peruse and correct what your friend offers by way of improvement. I will criticise for you, but not pretend to finish for the press. It is impossible I should, like the author, take in the design, comprehend the method, and advert to the language; impossible therefore, that I should be so proper and competent a judge; besides, there are some things that do not please and strike me like others. Upon these I would put a query, Was the determination referred to you? But I dare not alter them, barely upon the report of my own imagination; neither could I alter them entirely to my own satisfaction.

I see you look upon sin as an infinite offence, page 6, line 4. I presume you mean objectively, yet I cannot bring myself to adopt this opinion. I am inclined to think that we should reserve and appropriate the word *infinite* wholly, intirely, and without any exception, to God and his perfections. But I am not positive. In this and every thing, O! that I might have the teachablenefs of a babe! I have the weaknefs, Lord grant me the docility of a weaned child; yea, of a babe and suckling. I shall long to see the Essay mentioned page 12, in the note: this will suit my taste, and, I fancy, be not a little impressive on the generality of your readers. The thoughts in the Dissertation before me, are solemn, grand, and of tremendous import. God from on high accompany them with his blessing, that they may humble us all,

H   and

and bring us to the feet, to the crofs, to the blood of
JESUS.   I fhall defire Mr. Hayward to order a dozen
for me, to be left at Mr. Rivington's. I am, my
dear friend, though very, very weak, yet

Inviolably your's,

J. HERVEY.

LETTER   XXXVIII.

Weſten, May 13, 1758.

My dear Friend,

I Send the fecond volume, and my beſt compliments, to Mr. Wood. If he is not tired of the
work, I would beg of him to be rather expeditious,
than curious. If ever the piece comes again to the
prefs, the compofitors will deface and fpoil the moſt
delicate writing.

When the bearer returns, you will tranfmit the
firſt volume, both the interleaved copy and the other.

Have you feen Mr. Brine's Anfwer to the Letters
on Theron and Afpafio?   I find this piece begins to
be taken into confideration.   Not only Mr. Brine and
Mr. Wefley has animadverted upon it; another
Treatife I fee is advertifed in the public papers, intitled, " A Plain Account of Faith in JESUS CHRIST,
in Remarks on feveral Paffages in the Letters on
Theron and Afpafio."   I hope the attention of mankind will be awakened to this important fubject; and
may the Father of Lights enable his minifters to make
the vifion, the capital doctrine of the Gofpel, plain
upon tables, fo that he who runs may read.

Ever your's,

J. HERVEY.

LET-

LETTER XXXIX.

My dear Friend,

I Will treafure up, and very fafely keep, your fprightly thoughts: may they, through the divine Spirit, be prompters to my dull invention.

Mr. Goldney's letter to his fubfcribers I happened to fee, before he made any overtures for an intercourfe with me; I thought him, if not impaired in his intellects, extremely injudicious; have therefore given no encouragement to his intended vifit. Poor man! he is fo far from having any thing like judgment, that he does not underftand the common rudiments of grammar.

This however I muft fay in his behalf, that he is modeft. When one of my neighbours fignified to him, that on account of my extremely ill ftate of health, I chofe to decline vifits and company, he did not offer to intrude himfelf. He has been at Wefton church feveral times, but I hear no good report of him. This may be owing to that fpirit of defamation which walketh through the earth.

S—— turns out worfe and worfe. I am afraid I fhall have much trouble with him, and much lofs from him. He begins to grow defperate. He told my mother to her face, he would arreft her, and take away the bricks from my ground, though every living creature, from Sir Thomas Drury, the able juftice, to the meaneft mechanic, pronounce them mine. I have been obliged to confult a lawyer upon the occafion. He pays nobody: poor workmen are diftreffed for want of their money; and betwixt you and I, he appears to be —————— fay nothing of thefe things, only, if you can think of any expedient to ferve me, communicate it. He has embroiled him-

felf

felf in fome fcrape, for which the conftable of Wefton is now charged with a warrant to apprehend him.

The inclofed I wrote at Dr. Stonehoufe's particular and repeated defire. Without my knowledge, he committed it to the prefs. Examine it, improve it, and fend it back, lefs unmeet for our divine Mafter's ufe.

I have fome thoughts of anfwering Mr. Wefley's Remarks. I mention this defign, that, unfledged as it is, it may have the benefit of your prayers. Σιωπα is the word on this occafion. Tell it to none, but our unerring Counfellor: to Him the oftner you recommend it, the better.

Our united and cordial compliments attend yourfelf, and your truly amiable fpoufe.

Ever your's,
J. HERVEY.

LETTER XL.

Wefton, Sept 3c, 1758.

My dear Friend,

MR. Wefley, among other objeftions to Theron and Afpafio, finds fault with the doftrine of a Covenant eftablifhed between the Father and the Son —calls upon me to prove it by Scripture, and defies me to prove that it was made from eternity.

I find, from reading Witfius, that Dr. Owen has treated this fubjeft very copioufly, in his fecond volume, Exercife IV. page 49. I wifh you would be fo kind as to perufe this Differtation, and give me an extraft of the thoughts that are moft material, and the arguments that are moft forcible.

By the way, let me defire you to examine your Witfius, and obferve whether it contains this reference to Owen. By this you may know, whether
your's

your's is the beft edition. I have now two impreffions of that excellent book before me; the beft has
the reference, page 142, the other has not.

I expeét, ere long, a parcel from Warwick, which
will be highly welcome to

Your's, moft cordially,
J. HERVEY.

P. S. What is become of S——? Had he finifhed
the work according to contraét, he would now have
feventy pounds to take.

———

LETTER XLI.

Wefton, Oct. 14, 1758.

My dear Friend,

LAST night I received your packet by the poft,
for which you will pleafe to accept my beft
thanks: a continuation of your valuable thoughts
will be very welcome: the LORD render them equally
ufeful! I wifh you was at my right hand, that I
might confult you more particularly about my intended Anfwer. I hope you will not fail to implore
for me, the guidance of the wonderful Counfellor.

My kind refpeéts to good Mr. Carter: I wifh him
much light from the LORD; much comfort in his
heart, and much fuccefs in his work.

I wifh you would fpeak to S—— about paying the
bill of a young man who lately wrote to him. He
rents fome ground of me: his name, J— G——:
he ferved S—— with his team, and now is in great
want of the money. If S—— will write me an
order, I will pay him.

I can now add no more, becaufe the bearer waits,
and is in hafte to be gone, unlefs it be, that I am

Ever your's,
J. HERVEY.
P. S.

P. S. Franks are always welcome to me : however, do not diftrefs yourfelf, for I am in no immediate want.

LETTER XLII.

Saturday, 1758.

My dear Friend,

I Have but a few moments allowed, to anfwer your kind letter—no complaints of the builder. The houfe goes on apace, but I have not been able to go up to the houfe of the LORD, ever fince Chriftmas; no, nor yet am able: bleffed be GOD for the houfe not made with hands! I fhall be very glad to fee your Contemplations on the Perfection and Joy of that happy place.

The franks come at your call, may the LORD's prefence and power profper what you have diftributed, and what you are preparing for the public. Excufe my brevity.   Ever your's,

J. HERVEY.

The following Letters, bearing no Date, cannot be placed in Chro-nological Order.

LETTER XLIII.

My dear Friend,

ON Saturday laft, an accident hindered me from writing by the newfman, and fending as I pro-pofed, your very ingenious Preface. The author feems to be a perfon of fine tafte, folid judgment, very extenfive learning, and no enemy to Chriftianity. I cannot but wifh him fuccefs in his work, and fhould be ftrongly inclined to purchafe it, if I was not pof-feffed

feſſed already, of Chambers's Dictionary. I hope I
ſhall not diſappoint your expectations by the next return of the newſman. In the mean time, be ſo good
as to examine the following attempt to anſwer the
objection made in my laſt.

Theron. Pray do you allow that CHRIST is GOD?

Aſpaſio. We not only allow it, but we inſiſt upon
it, and make our boaſt of it. This is the very foundation of his merit, and the ſupport of our hopes.

Ther. This may aggrandize the merit of CHRIST,
but it will increaſe the difficulty of your taſk; for, according to this opinion, CHRIST muſt make ſatisfaction to himſelf! And is not this a practice quite unprecedented? a notion perfectly abſurd?

Aſp. It is quite unprecedented you ſay. On this
point I ſhall not vehemently contend; only let me
mention one inſtance, *Zaleucus,* you know, the Prince
of the Locrians, made a law, that whoever was con-
victed of adultery, ſhould be puniſhed with the loſs
of both his eyes: his own ſon was apprehended in the
very fact, and brought to a public trial. How could
the father acquit himſelf in ſo tender and delicate a
conjuncture? Should he execute the law in all its
rigour? This would be worſe than death to the unhappy youth. Should he pardon ſo notorious a de-
linquent? This would defeat the deſign of his ſalutary
inſtitution. To avoid both theſe inconveniences, he
ordered one of his own eyes to be pulled out, and
one of his ſons; by which means, the rights of juſtice
were preſerved inviolable; yet the tenderneſs of a
parent was remarkably indulged; and may we not
venture to ſay, that in this caſe, Zaleucus both received and made ſatisfaction? Received it as a legiſ-
lator, even while he made it as a father.

Ther. I cannot ſee how this ſuffering of the father
was, in any degree, ſatisfactory to the law, ſince the
father and the ſon could not be conſidered as one and
the ſame perſon. It may paſs for an extraordinary

and

and romantic inftance of parental indulgence. It may ftrike the fancy of the benevolent and compaf-fionate hearer; but if tried at the bar of equity and reafon, it will hardly be admitted as any legal fatis-faction: it will probably be condemned as a breach of nature's firft and fundamental law, felf-prefervation.

Afp. What you obferve, I muft confefs has weight. It will oblige me, I believe, to give up my illuftra-tion. Neverthelefs, what you urge againft the pro-priety of my exemplification, tends to eftablifh the truth of my doctrine: for CHRIST and his people are actually confidered as one and the fame perfon. They are one myftical body; He the head, they the mem-bers; fo intimately united to him, that they are faid to be bone of his bone, and flefh of his flefh. By virtue of which union, their offences were charged upon him; their fins were punifhed in him; and by his ftripes, they are healed: they obtain impunity and life.

Though there may be nothing in the procedure of men, which bears any refemblance to this miracle of heavenly goodnefs, it receives fufficient confirmation from the language of Scripture.

He who wrote as an amanuenfis to —— ——, in order to receive the finifhing touches of your pen, will probably find promifes more full and ex-plicit on each head; or, perhaps, will think of fome other particulars, that fhould be taken under confide-ration. If you will examine and complete the little collection, they fhall be printed very neatly, fo as to be ornamental to the book, as well as beneficial to the owner.

PROMISES OF PARDON.

Ifai. i. 18, Sin as fcarlet, fhall be white as fnow.—
Ifai. xliii. 25. I am he that blotteth out thy fins.—
Acts xiii. 38, 39. The forgivenefs of fins.—Eph. i. 7.
Redemption—the forgivenefs of fins.—1 Peter ii. 24.

His

His own felf bare our fins.—Rev. i. 5. wafhed us from our fins in his own blood.

OF JUSTIFICATION.

Ifai. xlv. 24, 25. In the LORD I have righteoufnefs, —in the LORD juftified.—Rom. iii. 21. 24. Juftified freely by his grace, through redemption in JESUS.— Rom. viii. 33, 34. It is GOD that juftifieth—it is CHRIST that died.

OF SANCTIFICATION.

Deut. xxx. 6. Thy GOD will circumcife thy heart, to love the LORD thy GOD.—Jer. xxiv. 7. I will give them an heart to know me, the LORD.—1 Cor. vi. 11. Ye are wafhed, ye are fanctified by the Spirit of our GOD.—1 Theff. v. 23. The GOD of Peace fanctify your whole fpirit, foul and body.

IN TEMPTATION.

1 Cor. x. 13. GOD is faithful, who will not fuffer you to be tempted above your ability.—2 Cor. xii. 9. My grace is fufficient for thee ; my ftrength perfect in weaknefs.

IN AFFLICTION.

Job v. 17. Happy the man whom GOD correcteth. Defpife not the chaftening of the almighty.—Pfa. l. 15. Call upon me in thy day of trouble : I will deliver thee.—2 Cor. iv, 17. Our light affliction, but for a moment—worketh for us a weight of glory.

IN DEATH.

Pfal. xxiii. 4. In the valley of the fhadow of death, I will fear no evil, thou art with me.—1 Cor. xv. 55, 57. O death where is thy fting—GOD giveth us the victory.—2 Cor. v. 1. If our earthly houfe is diffolved, we have a building of GOD.—John iii. 16. Whoever believeth fhall not perifh, but have everlafting life.

I   At

At the top I would have this text: God *hath given us exceeding great and precious promises.* At the bottom this: God *being willing to shew unto the heirs of promise, &c.* I have now tasked and tired you, but the latter I shall not often do, in so immoderate a manner. For the former, your work shall be with the Lord, and your reward from your God. Gratitude and love is all you must expect from,

Dear Sir,
Your obliged and affectionate Brother,
in CHRIST JESUS,
J. HERVEY.

L E T T E R   XLIV.

My dear Friend,

I Intended to have made my acknowledgments for your last favour by Saturday's newsman; but an unexpected accident rendered my design impracticable.

I assure you, I esteem such letters to be a favour indeed. Let me beg to have them continued; they breathe the genuine spirit of Christianity. Christianity thus displayed, is supremely noble, and worthy of the blessed God : thus enjoyed, is highly delightful, and constitutes both the dignity and happiness of man.

I believe it will be in a manner impossible to begin my new house this year; we have no other abode, as yet, fit to receive us. Before the commencement of another winter, we hope to be accommodated, and to remove; so that Mr. S—— may proceed as early as he pleases in the following year.

I have not had the pleasure of seeing the Critical Review for December; but I find, from the advertisements in the public papers, that they take Mr.

Jenks

Jenks and his recommender to taſk. I am not diſ-appointed: I expected no quarter from them.

You would ſmile, and be a little ſurpriſed, if you was to ſee what employed my ſpare hours almoſt all laſt week. I never had ſuch an inclination for buf-foonery in all my life: it was occaſioned by the un-worthy and abuſive treatment which the Reviewers beſtow upon all the moſt valuable writers that appear in public; and I verily think if their inſolence can be curbed, it muſt be done in purſuance of Horace's maxim.

> *Ridiculum acri*
>
> *Fortius, &c.*

Or in obedience to that command of unerring wiſdom, *anſwer a fool according to his folly.* I am now there-fore digeſting and tranſcribing a parcel of Remarks, which will amount to a ſhilling pamphlet, and may receive the following title:

N E D   D R Y's   A P O L O G Y

for the CRITICAL REVIEWERS.

With a complimentary Card to thoſe Gentlemen.

This written—That publiſhed.

By JAMES HERVEY, A. M.

" *Ut tu fortunam, ſic nos te celſa teremus.*" HOR.

Whether it be expedient to publiſh ſuch a thing, the LORD JESUS knows; and I truſt the LORD JESUS will direct; they are the enemies of his cauſe, and I ſhould be very well pleaſed to bear my teſtimony againſt them. No mortal knows that I have any ſuch thoughts, you only excepted. Let it remain a pro-found ſecret; beſeech, as I know you will, beſeech HIM who is Head over all things to the church, to vouchſafe his heavenly guidance. Give me your free opinion. If I can get a perſon to tranſcribe, I will ſend you a copy.

Ever your's, in CHRIST JESUS,

J. HERVEY.

I 2

P. S. Will you difpofe of a guinea among your poor people, during this fevère feafon ? I defire you will not let any one know from whom it comes. I inclofe the guinea in the book Mr. Witherfpoon mentions.—A fmart piece truly.

LETTER XLV.

Tuefday Evening.

My dear Friend,

I Thank you for your beautiful exhortation, and fine harangue, which makes me wifh it had been your office, not to encourage, but to execute.

I thank you likewife for your criticifms : *confounded* and *plaguy* are low cant words, not ufed but upon droll fubjects; and though I believe they are proper enough on thofe occafions, yet, as they are feldom heard but from the lips of the licentious, or profane, they would, I am apt to fufpect, offend the ferious ear.

The paragraph, relating to coftivenefs, you and your friends very juftly condemn. It was intended to cenfure the clergyman for his fhameful diligence, in writing notes upon two loofe comedians, and to give a reprefentation of his performance not very inviting : but it may be faid of the attempt, *Peccato corrigendo pecceat.* I have altered it in this manner : Mr. S—n, a reverend clergyman, who has lately been very zealous to edify the pious world, by publifhing and expounding a brace of lufcious comedians, has no lefs obliged and improved the learned world, by letting them into the meaning of the curious word, *coftive:* and I cannot but acknowledge, that the expofitor has been juft as laudably employed as his authors. Such kind of
works

works are the propereſt place in the world for ſuch definitions and explanations. Though, for my own part, I do not much want good Mr. S—n's inſtructions on this ſubjeɛt, becauſe I ſee the thing exemplified whenever the Critical Reviewers point out excellencies, or beſtow praiſe. Whether this is proper, *Te tuorque pines ſit, judicium.*

This Mr. S—n, I am ſorry to ſay it, was a fellow collegian of mine. I well remember him at Lincoln college, but I had not the leaſt intimacy with him. He joined, if I am not miſinformed, with a brother of your late excellent friend, Mr. Seward, to publiſh an edition of Beaumont and Fletcher. I hope God will make Mr. Witherſpoon's pen as ſharp as a razor, to cut the comb of ſuch writers, and their works. I was ſorry to ſee, from a paragraph in a late newſpaper, that, by the command of the Prince, the tragedy of Douglas (to which Mr. Witherſpoon alludes) was re-aɛted at the Theatre Royal. Ah! my brother, this is one ſource, one copious ſource of our miſeries; if princes will encourage ſuch corrupting entertainments, there never will be wanting even miniſters to write for them, and magiſtrates to attend them. O that the Prince of the kings of the earth would give our rulers, and all that are in authority, to *diſcern the things that are excellent.*

Little do you think what I am going to tell you— that my friends, who have ſeen the piece, abſolutely diſapprove of it.

A gentleman in the neighbourhood, a perſon of fine taſte, to whom an acquaintance of mine ſhewed it, ſays, Horace ſhall give my opinion,

———————————*Cave, faxis*
Te quidquam indignum.
—————————*Hæc mea Cura eſt,*
Ne quid tu perdas, natt ſis Jocus.

Dr. Stonehouſe ſays, it is a low, dull, ſpiritleſs thing; that I am no more fit for ſuch kind of writing,

·ing, than a carrier's horfe to run a race. He read it, he tells me, to fome ingenious ladies, who have a regard for my character: they declared they would come over to Wefton, and down upon their knees, (if it were needful) to folicit me not to publifh it. Mention nothing of thefe matters: I have mentioned them to none but yourfelf. Thofe are the only perfons that have feen the manufcript. Amidft fuch a diverfity of opinions, How fhall I determine? Shall Warwick or Northampton turn the fcale? The Lord Jesus Christ overrule the determination. If it may be for his honour, let it appear with courage and confidence; if not, let it be. configned over to filence and oblivion.

I am glad you receive fuch advantage and delight from the great Dr. Owen. Perufe, and tell me what you think of the pamphlet, intitled "A Friendly Attempt," &c. You are not to return it, but only your fentiments of it. Pray have you feen Mr. Goadby's Expofition? The word *farrago*, which you make ufe of, makes me conjecture you have fome knowledge of the work. I faw a fpecimen of it in manufcript, and it feemed to me the very thing which your expreffion denotes. He conftantly fays, in his advertifement, the fale increafes every day, yet I know no mortal in thefe parts that purchafes it.

I have fent, according to your defire, the Appendix; but in cafe the Apology fhould appear, this, I think, had better be fecreted, becaufe it relates pretty much to myfelf; and to fpeak properly in fuch a cafe, is very difficult; to fpeak much, difcovers an inward wound, and tells the world the party is galled, which, though it is not fact, yet, if fuppofed, would give an occafion for triumph. Never was I lefs concerned for any thing of this nature, than for the bad words of the Reviewers. Never did I covet any one's good word lefs than theirs.

Mr.

Mr. S— calls upon me. I hope to return your manuscript by the newsman; and may I never forget Him who says, *Return unto me, for I have redeemed thee.*
Affectionately your's,
J. HERVEY.

P. S. I have sent the guinea for Mr. Underhill to you, having no convenient method of transmitting it to Daventry.

The following are the passages, or some of the passages, which I would have annexed to the Apology.

LETTER XLVI.

THE Character of Mr. Jenks's Meditations, as given by the Critical Reviewers.

Cum notis variorum.

" The Meditations are not in the least adapted to " build up the soul in faith, in holiness, or joy."

This assertion is a full evidence that these men never knew in the least what is the nature of vital faith, holiness, or joy: and as they declared themselves utterly destitute of the spirit of religion, I am confident no one Christian in the world, who reads Mr. Jenks, will believe them.

" They are ridiculous and enthusiastic."

Ridiculous to no man who knows what it is to be serious concerning his GOD, his soul, or his salvation. The Reviewers have not the exalted happiness to possess the least spark of this glorious enthusiasm; an enthusiasm every way consistent with rectified reason; an enthusiasm which Moses and the prophets, CHRIST and the apostles, expressed in its noblest perfection.

" They are like hairs on the greasy coat of a " groom, or like dish-water thrown down the kennel."

These Reviewers are in the eyes of every real Christian upon earth, much better qualified to execute
the

the office of a groom to horfes, than to play the critic's part on books of vital Chriftianity; and if they
were paid only in proportion to their merits, difh water would be their higheft reward for their work.

" They are nonfenfe—one great blot—the author
" can neither write nor read."

An eternal blot in the Reviewer's character. They
can evidently neither write like Chriftians, nor read
like true critics. This every wife man who reads
their monthly productions will immediately fee.

Pray return this paper. I hope you will be enabled to fill up the vacancies, with fome fmart remarks. Sure we may, without offence to piety or
charity, pray with the Pfalmift, *Make their faces afhamed,*
O LORD.

The true Temper and Genius of the Critical Reviewers.

Does there not appear, drawn from their monthly
pamphlets, great felf-efteem for their own fenfe, penetration, learning and diction? A very high idea of
their importance and weight in the literary world.
" We are the men!" A refolute determination to vindicate themfelves with rudenefs and overbearing
fiercenefs and impudence.

A moft rooted and cordial hatred of all the glorious peculiarities of the Gofpel, a fpecial fpite and
venom at the moft fpiritual and evangelical authors;
a fcorn of all reproof, and an expectation that the
public adore them, as the revivers of true tafte.

A hearty contempt of the public appears in their
filthy and foolifh extracts from books of the moft
worthlefs character: they appear almoft deftitute of
true critical tafte, and efpecially of real candour, and
generous benevolence. I can fee nothing lovely in
them as men or as fcholars; and as for religion, they
themfelves tell us that they have not one grain of it.

In a word, the real impiety of infidels— a rooted
fpite at vital godlinefs—a rank venom of heart—a
cruelty

cruelty and hard-heartednefs towards wife and worthy men, infinitely beyond themfelves—a fpirit of contempt towards the public—the real malice of devils and horrid malignity of the damned, feem to me to be the grand conftituent parts of their temper, and the effentials of their compofitions; and if I were to wifh them the finifhed ruin of their immortal fouls, I would wifh they might poffefs eternally the fame contempt and enmity towards GOD, and the fame infernal malevolence towards all good men, as they have abundantly expreffed in their twelve monthly pamphlets!

Liars, in acting oppofite to their plan: I appeal to that public which thefe men have infulted, by fuppofing them to be fo far deftitute of religion, grace, and good manners, as to join thefe Reviewers in prophaning the name of the almighty Majefty: in making a joke of vital devotion, and injuring the blamelefs character of their peaceable fellow fubjects. By ftiling them dirty enthufiafts, they difcover great wantonnefs of cruelty.

Thefe forry wretches have affronted the public, by oppofing the general voice, for the writings and reputation of the author of the Meditations among the Tombs, &c. Do they imagine they can injure his character with any fenfible man, or true Chriftian?

<hr />

LETTER XLVII.

My dear Friend,

THANKS for the inclofed. I have nothing to fend with it, but my cordial wifhes, that the writer and the lender may go on, in their glorious warfare, from conquering to conquer. May I not hope to receive a packet by the return of the bearer? A packet which will lay me under an obligation to

K   Mr.

Mr. Wood and Mr. Ryland? which will always be gratefully acknowledged by,

J. HERVEY.

LETTER XLVIII.

My dear Friend,

JUST before the arrival of your packet, Mr. D——— set out for Warwick, promising himself much pleasure, and equal profit in your conversation. I trust you will meet each other in the fulness of the blessings of the Gospel of CHRIST.

Mintert is at your service, as long as you please. Mr. D——— took with him Douglas, &c. By the bearer, I send two volumes of Voyages and Travels; the other five to follow, whenever you give the signal. No picture, nor any of the works of Witsius from Holland. Mudge upon the Psalms is not at present within reach; it will be soon, then it shall wait upon you. Mr. Davis's letter is again mislaid; that I mean written by his own hand; a much longer, transcribed by Mr. Cruttenden, supplies its place. As to any Dialogues for Vol. IV. there are none in being: I have only some hints, and those chiefly in short hand. I do assure you, though I have a heart to the work, I have neither strength nor spirits to execute it: when I retire to my study, I can but just read, or pray a little, not think or write at all. My design of printing three Sermons, proves an abortion: two Discourses I purpose to correct in a little time; the LORD of all power give them a prosperous voyage, that they may traffic for his honour: mine are merchantmen, your's shall be men of war, and both, I hope, will be the means of spreading abroad the favour of CHRIST's name.

No

No letter from Mr. Witherſpoon; I believe I neglected to anſwer his laſt favour, therefore cannot
expect a renewed inſtance of his friendſhip. I have
not leiſure to peruſe his epiſtle to you, nor your pleaſ-
ingly long letter to me, becauſe the bearer waits to be
diſpatched, and my horſe ſtands ready to receive his
maſter. The former ſhall be returned, and the latter
acknowledged by the firſt opportunity.

I can promiſe nothing to Mr. Wood. Have only
told him, that I ſhall remember his offer, and that a
recommendation from Mr. Ryland will always have
weight with me. Moſt freely I tranſmit another
crown for the poor woman, and another for whomſo-
ever you ſhall judge a proper object. Excuſe my
great haſte and rapid ſcribbling.

Ever your's,
J. HERVEY.

LETTER XLIX.

Weſton, Sunday Evening.

My dear Friend,

I Muſt deſire you to accept my thanks for your eloquent diſplay of the Accompliſhed Preacher; and
may the LORD accept my prayer, when I beſeech him
to grant, that you may be what you deſcribe.

We will expect your company, and I will not deſpair of ſeeing the continuation of your thoughts on
the pleaſure of religion, and the execution of your
promiſe, with regard to your Aphoriſms on Faith.

I have been under the ſurgeons and apothecary's
hands. Have ventured out to day; and GOD be praiſed
was enabled, though with much weakneſs, to teſtify
of the grace of our LORD JESUS CHRIST. O! that
the word may proſper, and the work not recall my
feveriſh diſorder. I ſee you very much commend

K 2

Mr.

Mr. Hubbard, an author with whom I have had no converfe; will you introduce me to his acquaintance? And when opportunity ferves, lend me the difcourfes mentioned page 15, of the Preacher,

"On the Love of CHRIST."

"On the Imitation of CHRIST."

I have fent the firft volume of Theron, &c. with alterations: at your leifure peep upon them, and fee if they are corrections. If Mr. ——— will be fo kind as to tranfcribe into the interleaved volume all the alterations which have your imprimature, or rather transferatur, I fhall be much obliged.

Excufe my fcrawl—I write with my gloves on—am fo warm, I dare not put them off—they call me to my fupper—tea—fo I muft take my leave of my friend, whofe I am in the bonds of the Gofpel, and of fincere affection.

J. HERVEY.

LETTER L.

My dear Friend,

EXCUSE my delay in anfwering your letter, and acknowledging your prefent tranfmitted by Mr. Venner: they both deferve my fpeedier thanks, which you will accept though late. As I expected, by every poft, the packet from London, I purpofely withheld my pen, intending, upon the receipt of your proof-fheet, to fend you any remarks that occurred, by the very firft mail; and refolving, within myfelf, not to fuffer any alterations of mine to take place, till they had been fubmitted to your examination, and received your approbation. In this refolution I ftill perfift, and you muft not defire, I had almoft faid, you fhall not oblige me to depart from it. Criticifing on thefe terms, and with fuch a view, I fhall execute my part
more

more freely, otherwife I fhall hefitate, act with timidity, and fcarcely venture to diminifh a jot, or add a tittle.

I am fomewhat furprifed that you, who take fo many of other people's children under your care, fhould be unwilling to finifh the education of your own, your intellectual children. I mean the offspring of your happy invention. The Treatife you mention, as it is begun, fo let it be finifhed, by yourfelf. You muft look upon me as a *broken veffel*. I have not written a line (fuch languors have oppreffed me) towards the accomplifhment of my intended work, during feveral weeks; and yet I am ftrongly importuned to correct the tranflation of a fmall Latin treatife, *De Eminentiâ Cognitionis Chrifti*, to form it into my own manner, and publifh it under my own name. This method, it is thought, may be a means of making it fpread, and rendering it profitable to the tranflator, who wants gain, almoft as much as others want grace. The piece was written originally in German by Liborius Limmermannus. Have you feen it, or heard any account of it? I fancy you have not: there are fome charming evangelical truths in it, moft comfortable, encouraging, delightful! But it feems to want order, and a proper arrangement. Here it fhould be pruned, and there it fhould be grafted. If I fhould attempt to difpatch this bufinefs, I muft beg, not only your perufal of the piece, but your correction of the tranflation, and efpecially your examination; your exact and rigorous examination of the doctrines.

Another propofal is made to me, and that by a member of your Evangelical Society. Mr. Vivian propofes to print his Vifitation Sermon; one on the like occafion by Mr. Davis of Virginia, and mine. To print them all together in one pamphlet. I told him that mine would rather be as lead upon the heels, than as wings in the body of his intended piece : that fome hundreds of the fecond edition now lie upon the bookfellers

fellers hands. He perfifts in his propofal, notwithftanding this difcouraging circumftance. He would
print, if there be four or five hundred of mine unfold,
an equal number of his own, and of Mr. Davis's,
and ftich them together. What fhall I do in this
cafe? I cannot perfuade myfelf that the fcheme is
likely to fucceed; or rather, I am perfuaded, that the
alliance which their works folicit with mine, will be a
clog, rather than a furtherance.

Pleafe to prefent mine and my families compliments to Mr. Venner, and accept the fame yourfelf,
from, dear Sir,

Your affectionate, and obliged,

J. HERVEY.

LETTER LI.

My dear Friend,

MY laft was fo very long, that I will only trouble
my dear friend with a line at prefent. Did not
you mention, and with applaufe, a method of keeping a diary? which, if I remember right, you told me,
was ufed by Dr. Doddridge. I fhould be obliged,
if, when you have leifure, you would communicate
to me the plan. Thanks for the extremely ingenious
Preface, and Mr. Hurrion's folidly ufeful books.
What entertaining accounts of genius and induftry in
the former! What delightful difcoveries of grace
and love in the latter! We would tafte the firft, but
drink into the laft. Virgil has an expreffion, which,
to a fober and temperate mind, may give a lively idea
of the Apoftle's meaning,

Pleno fe proluit Auro.

Though I fhould be afraid to propofe fuch an illuftration to the world. [This was written to have waited
upon

upon you laſt week, but poſtponed for the reaſon mentioned in my letter.]

Your's,

J. HERVEY.

LETTER LII.

Thurſday Evening.

My dear Friend,

ACCEPT my thanks for your packet. I like the thoughts with which you have filled up the vaca. ſpaces. And would you really have me publiſh Mr. Dry's, &c. ? The good LORD direct me. This will certainly bring upon me the moſt unrelenting perſecution of the Reviewers pen; but what have I to fear? Succeſs they cannot withhold; it is not by might, nor by ſtrength, not by their favour and recommendation, but by HIS SPIRIT. Reputation is not my aim; yet if I had this end in view, it is written, *They that honour me, I will honour.* O! that it might be for the honour of CHRIST! then I would run all hazards, and publiſh it at all adventures; and if He pleaſes to proſper, your ſix bibles for his poor people ſhall be made twelve.

Thanks for Maſon's Catechiſms: ſome ſuch ſmall evangelical treatiſes are greatly wanted. I am ſincerely glad you are going to publiſh ſomething conſiderable; the LORD almighty make it acceptable, and make it powerful. I have been hurried almoſt ever ſince the receiving your packet. If it be poſſible, I will return your manuſcript by the newſman.

Mr. White writes like a man of great politeneſs, as well as eminent piety. The ſecond volume of Jenks waits upon you, together with Marſhal. But you are miſtaken in apprehending, that I have added notes to the new edition, only a kind of preface; in which

which is a fentiment or two, not very paffable even
with the pious world; yet furely they contain the truth
of grace, and the glory of the Gofpel.

If I live, I propofe to fend you in a frank, the Appendix to my intended pamphlet. In what fize fhould
it appear, and what price fhould it bear? You forgot
to give me your opinion about my cenfure of Mr.
Goadby and his Life of Bampfyldë Carew. I would
not do any thing unkind. How would he have acted
in fuch a cafe? who fays, *Be ye followers of me, even as
I am of* CHRIST. Mr. Marfhal, if you pleafe to accept it, is your own; as is, on the fame terms,

J. HERVEY.

LETTER LIII.

Thurfday Evening.

THANKS to my worthy friend for interefting himfelf in behalf of my affairs: I may now fay, *Jacta
eft alea.* I have this moment given my confent to
the terms propofed by Mr. S——, and purely to gratify him, my mother and fifter have departed from my
refolution, with regard to the price. Articles are
drawn up; to thefe I have affented in general; only
have deferred figning them, in order to have them in-
fpected by fome perfons of better judgment than
myfelf, that if there fhould be any little matters neceffary or proper to be added, they may be fuggefted
and inferted. With this provifo I have agreed. I
hope the work will be fo executed, as to give me
little trouble, and get the architect much credit.

Twenty-five Sermons are fent, and accompanied
with my earnest prayers, that they may be among
many people *as a dew from the* LORD, *and as rain upon
the grafs.* You may, if you find them acceptable to
your people, command another cargo.

The

The third and fourth volumes of Voyages are fent.
Mr. Fellows's poem is received, but you muft not expect any thing confiderable from my remarks. My
imagination, as well as my conftitution, fades like
yonder leaves.

I think the Critical Reviewers are fomewhat like
Balaam, who had a ftrong inclination to curfe, but was
overruled to blefs the people. I fend you four franks,
and remain,

Inviolably your's,

J. HERVEY.

LETTER LIV.

Sept. 3, 1758.

My dear Friend,

I Thank you, for taking in good part my free remonftrances, and impartial objections. See what
it is to have to do with a Chriftian! his mind, though
endued with manly wifdom, is meek as the weaned
child. May my foul be more and more caft into this
amiable mould! And as you accede to my opinion,
may I be enabled to imitate your humility.

I thank you alfo for the perufal of your manufcript. I hope the Giver of every good gift will enable you to compofe, to finifh, and to publifh, many
fuch animated pieces. You afk me to correct; but
fhall I venture to alter, or prefume to cenfure Mr.
Ryland's writings? No: I will only tell him, what the
world, when favoured with his works, may poffibly
fay. "We could wifh that our favourite author, in
" fome parts, was not quite fo fcholaftic, and meta-
" phyfical; and that in others, his fentiments, though
" all fhining, and his words, though every one elegant,
" were not quite fo diffufe."

L

My

My own piece is indeed in the prefs, and by this poft I return the fifteenth fheet corrected. I remember my promife; and let me look upon it as my privilege. As fuch, I affure you, I fhall efteem it, if you will freely animadvert upon every inaccuracy, and by your friendly remarks enrich what is empoverifhed, exalt what grovels, and rectify what is erroneous. As foon as ever the firft volume is finifhed, I will fend it to Warwick; and give me leave, till then, to detain your valuable manufcript. I took your advice as to the number of copies to be printed, though fome have thought I have proceeded injudicioufly, becaufe my bookfeller offered to give me two hundred pounds, and fifty copies bound, lettered and gilt, for permiffion to print four thoufand copies of the fmall, and feven hundred and fifty of the large octavo; but I muft own, the hope of correcting and rendering the work lefs unworthy of the incomparable fubject, in cafe Providence fhould command a fecond edition, outweighs with me all pecuniary confiderations. Have you confidered what would be proper to lay before the world in the Preface? You who have lately been at our metropolis, and know the fentiments of mankind, can judge of this particular much better than an invalid and reclufe. I have not got the fecond volume of Vitringa, though I have fent for it four times, and waited, I believe, double the number of weeks. I want it very much, to confult that mafterly author, with relation to fome texts quoted by Afpafio. It is my admired commentator, and what before all others I fhould covet to read, if I live to fee my prefent completed and launched into the world. But to Dr. Gill's requeft, efpecially when feconded by Mr. Ryland, I can deny nothing. As foon as ever I recover the book, I will examine what is written upon thofe particular texts, and then tranfmit them to the Doctor.

What

What do you think of my fentiments and reafonings on the grand fubject of faith? Is the article of
affurance wound up too tight? Can fome of my
brethren bear with me, if I fpeak but flightly of
that celebrated diftinction, the faith of adherence, and
the faith of affurance? A gentleman of eminent
piety and fuperior fenfe told me, that receiving of
CHRIST, is a cafting of the foul upon, and trufting
in him, and him alone, for whole falvation, which is
fucceeded by a ftrong, a lively, heart-cheering affurance.   That this affurance is diftinct from faving
faith, and no part of it, nor infeparably connected
with it; faving faith being exercifed on the perfon
of CHRIST as an all-fufficient and willing SAVIOUR;
whereas the faith of affurance is exercifed upon a
propofition, viz. That CHRIST died for me.   Weigh
thefe thoughts in your balance, and let me know the
refult.

I believe I muft dedicate my book to a lady of
quality, and I would fay fine things, not of my patro-
nefs, but of her religion.   I wifh I could give an amiable picture of the glorious Gofpel. I wifh you would
lend me a few bright tints, fuch as might reprefent it
in a light honourable, amiable, and attractive?

Ever your's,

J. HERVEY.

LETTER LV.

My dear Friend,

I Sent you a Dialogue on Faith, No. XVI. Be fo
kind as to return it with your remarks, alterations,
and improvements.   Laft week I tranfmitted, in loofe
fheets, the firft volume of the work, that has long been
conceived, and is now come to the birth.   Here alfo
your corrections, though too late to enrich this edi-

tion, will be very acceptable. Give me leave to aſk
your opinion with reference to a dedication. This
you know will be a detached piece, of a ſmall ſize,
printed in a large type, and addreſſed to a perſon of
diſtinction. Theſe circumſtances will render it peculiarly conſpicuous, and expoſe it to a more ſevere examination. Anticipate the cenſorious critic, and
freely find fault with the following eſſay:

To the Right Hon. Lady F——— S———,

"*Madam,*

" IF Chriſtianity was inconſiſtent with the trueſt
" politeneſs, or prejudicial to real happineſs, I ſhould
" be extremely injudicious, and inexpreſſibly ungrate-
" ful, in preſenting theſe eſſays to your Ladyſhip,
" But as the religion of CHRIST is the grand orna-
" ment of our nature, and a ſource of the ſublimeſt
" joys, the purport of the following pages cannot be
" unworthy the countenance and protection of the
" moſt accompliſhed perſon; neither can there be a
" wiſh more ſuitable to the obligations, or the dictates
" of a grateful heart, than that you may experience
" what you read, and be what you patronize.

" Did religion conſiſt in a cuſtomary round of ex-
" ternal obſervances, or a forced ſubmiſſion to ſome
" rigorous auſterities, I ſhould not ſcruple to join
" with the infidel in deſpiſing it; and with the ſenſu-
" aliſt in having nothing to do with it. You need not
" be informed, Madam, that it is as much ſuperior to
" all ſuch low or forbidding ſingularities, as the hea-
" vens are higher than the earth: it is deſcribed by
" an author, who learned its theory in the regions of
" Paradiſe, and diſplayed its efficacy in his own exem-
" plary converſation: it is thus deſcribed by that in-
" comparable author, *The kingdom of* GOD *is not meat*
" *and drink, but, &c.*

" To be reconciled to the omnipotent. GOD: to be
" intereſted in the unſearchable riches of CHRIST:
" to

" to be renewed in our hearts, and influenced in our
" lives by the sanctifying operations of the divine
" Spirit; this is evangelical righteousness; this is
" genuine religion. This, Madam, is the kingdom
" of God erected in the soul. How amiable and in-
" viting is such an institution! What a dignity, and
" what a beauty are visible in all its parts! from such
" a state, and such a conduct, what other effects can
" flow, but that peace which passeth all understand-
" ing: that joy which is unspeakable, and full of
" glory!

" Was there any thing in the amusements of the
" gay, the pursuits of the ambitious, or the pomp
" of courts, preferable or comparable to these bles-
" sings of the everlasting Gospel, I should not take
" the liberty of exhorting your Ladyship to perse-
" vere and advance in those paths which you have
" been so wise and happy as to choose, are so consis-
" tent and faithful as to avow; neither would that
" which is now my humble exhortation, have been
" the invariable subject of my prayers, ever since I
" had the honour of professing myself,

" Madam, &c."

Line 17. " Having nothing to do with." I do not
like this expression: How shall I express the same
idea in a more elegant manner? Is there any thing
fulsome in all this? Any thing unbecoming the
preacher of humility, or dangerous to its possessor?
O! that your words—O! that my words, and the
words of all CHRIST's ministers, may be sweet as
the honey, yet penetrating as the sting!—Have
you formed the plan of a Preface? I have thrown
together a few sentiments, but have not time to
transcribe them. The LORD JESUS CHRIST prosper you in all your labours, and enable you to pray
for the weakest of all your brethren. Though weak
even to contempt, one would think the devil seems to
rage against me; he has stirred up some envenomed
tongues

tongues to blacken and asperse my character in all
places; nay, they threaten me by a letter under their
own hand, to expose me in the public papers as a vil-
lain. They spare not to talk of shooting me; and all
this, because hearing no recommending account of
their character, I refused to receive them as my te-
nants, and admit them to occupy my land. Such
treatment I have not deserved from them, but deserve
infinitely greater shame and infamy from the righteous
God; yet, as Christ has bore ignominy in my stead,
surely confusion from God will not cover me; nor
reproach from men hurt me. Say nothing of this,
only pray for me, that I may not be intimidated in
my spirit, nor exasperated in my temper. I fear my
own treacherous and naughty heart, more than their
menaces. 　　　　　　　　　Ever your's,

　　　　　　　　　　　　　　　J. HERVEY.

LETTER LVI.

This for my worthy Friend,

METHINKS I do not like the word *its* when
used as a relative to the Godhead, as it is generally applied to the inanimate or brutal creation.
The idea is low: it would please me better if the sentiment was expressed in some such manner, "On the
eternal Godhead, on all the divine persons, and all the
divine perfections."

I took my pen in hand with a design to have
pointed out other inaccuracies, and to have made
other corrections, but my intention outrun my ability.
I think you ask, what part of the Essay on Faith you
shall leave out? I answer, the less you leave out the
better: is it absolutely impossible to take in the whole?
I am loth to lose a thread, or a shoe-latchet of this
　　　　　　　　　　　　　　　　　　　　very

very important fubject. I befeech you let your paper
be brimful; and I beg of the LORD GOD omnipotent to ftrengthen you with his arm, to accompany
you with his fmile, when you take the field againft
doubts, fears, jealoufies, and evil furmifings of CHRIST,
which are the bane of the Chriftian's comforts, and
the remora to his holinefs.

I forgot to return Mr. Witherfpoon's letter. When
he fends you his Effay againft the Stage, favour me
with a fight of it. The Appendix, be fo good as to
return with improvements; I am quite at a lofs how
to proceed. On one fide, defirous to bear my teftimony againft the enemies of our divine Mafter; on
the other, intimidated by the remonftrances of fome
of my friends. That I have not entirely abandoned
the defign, you may fee from the alteration which I
have made. Inftead of the Appendix, Verax is to
deliver a paper, with a defire that it may be publifhed, in order to prevent all mifreprefentation of his
conduct, and all mifapprehenfion of his defign. The
paper I inclofe, and with it a frank, to bring it back as
foon as you have perufed and corrected it. The fame
vehicle will be roomy enough to contain the Appendix likewife. Sometimes I think fomewhat of this
nature will be proper; fometimes I think it will
fpoil the preceding irony. Judge for me, unable as I
am to determine for myfelf,

J. H.

LETTER LVII.

Nov. 21, 1757.

My dear Friend,

YOU very much oblige my family and myfelf,
by interefting yourfelf in the affair of my new
houfe; I am perhaps timid and cautious to an extreme.

After

After all, I fhall depend more upon your influence
with my architect, than upon the obligation of articles, though executed on ftamped paper.

We are now removed into our new lodgings; and
bleffed be the divine Providence, none of us feem to
have taken cold.   We fhall be very glad of your
company to infpect the building of timber and ftone,
and direct us to the houfe not made with hands, eternal in the heavens.

I have given orders to my bookfeller for an interleaved copy of the Dialogues.   Shall be very thankful to him who has the pen of a ready writer, for
tranfcribing the alterations; and more thankful to
fomebody elfe, who is of quick underftanding in the
fear of the LORD, for revifing and correcting them.

I am glad to find that you have fent the Chriftian
Preacher to the prefs.   May he who walks amidft the
golden candlefticks, fend it through his churches, and
form his minifters upon that excellent model.   I fhall
long to read it in print, as I heard it with much pleafure from your manufcript copy.

Have a care you do not depreciate your works, by
inferting any thing of mine.   My poor character is
going to execution.   The Reviewers have already put
the halter about its neck; if therefore you would obtain diftinction, or are a candidate for fame, ftand
clear and detached from fuch a contemptible fcribbler.

You may put my name among Mr. Turner's fubfcribers.   Send me one copy.   If upon perufal it
appears a proper prefent for any of my few acquaintance, I will very readily take a number.   Upon the
fubject of the church, and its government, I muft
proceed with caution.

· I have, purely in compliance with your requeft,
made a few animadverfions on Philander and Palemon.
Such offices I decline, for this, among other reafons,
that my friends may not be led unawares to rely on a
broken reed, amidft all the languors of enervated nature;

ture; fuch muſt a better judgment and taſte than mine unavoidably be.

It would be a high delight to examine nature, and admire her Maker, in your company, and with the aid of your fine microſcope. Mr. Baker, I really think, deſerves your thanks, as he has given us an excellent comment on theſe words of the Pſalmiſt, *Marvellous are thy works*; and has enabled us to add, *And that my ſoul knoweth right well.*

You may draw upon me for any number of the Faſt Sermons, and your draughts will always receive due honour. May the LORD JESUS, who was himſelf crucified in weakneſs, vouchſafe to work by weakneſs; or in other words, by

Your truly affectionate,
J. HERVEY.

LETTER LVIII.

Weſton, Saturday Evening.

My dear Friend,

YOU have our united thanks for your advice relating to my old houſe; but it is in a manner impoſſible to practice it. As to danger, it is my opinion, that it would ſtand theſe ten years; but I fully purpoſe, GOD willing, to abandon it at the cloſe of the ſummer. I am cutting down ſome timber, that it may be ready for the ſaw-pit this year, and for the building another year.

I have ſent you Mr. Dry's Apology: though it is written, it has been thrown by: I have ſeveral doubts, whether my pen carries any edge, and whether the edge, if there is any, be like the ſaw, or the razor: Is it of the former kind? then it will not anſwer my purpoſe, and will not gall and check the adverſaries of CHRIST and

M

his

his servants, but will give them occasion to triumph more extravagantly. Upon this query judge rigorously, and the good LORD strengthen your judgment. I have some doubt, whether this kind of writing suits my character, as a minister of JESUS CHRIST. Is it not the Ευτραπελια which the apostle condemns and banishes from the conversation of Christians? The principal reason to justify such a manner of address is, that no other method seems to have the least probability of succeeding. All that is solid, these men will evade by a sneer; and all that is serious, they will turn into burlesque: ridicule is the only vein in which they will bleed.

Have you any acquaintance who possess the humourous and satirical talent? Could you get their opinion and their retouches, and without blazing abroad the matter? If it is not fit for publication, I would have it remain a secret. A secret it is in these parts: my own relations know nothing of it: one person only has seen it.

Should I mention the case of Mr. Goadby, page 11? Do you know any thing of him, or his Exposition? He pretends to be a very serious and holy man. He once or twice came to see me, at my brother's house, and talked very devoutly. Is it not strange that such a person should be so eager to spread so vile a book, as the Apology for the King of Beggars? Does not such inconsistency in religious professors, bring a reproach upon Christianity? Does it not, since it is a public offence, deserve a public reprimand? I have reproved this gentleman in a private letter, but to no purpose.

There is one passage in the fourth page capable of bearing a double entendre, where Dr. Busby is introduced, saying, "Then my Lady Birch shall cool your flame." But as it is supposed to be spoken to a boy, sure it must be egregiously wresting of the sense, to apply it loosely. However, sift this and other pas-

fages with as much rigour (if it be poffible for a benevolent heart to exercife fo much) as the Critical Reviewers will certainly ufe, if this piece fhould ever
come abroad.

I have not the Critical Reviews, therefore fome
references want to be filled up. But I can eafily
borrow the former, and I can as eafily execute the
latter. I have fome thought of adding, at the end, a
letter written to me by a very ingenious young clergyman, on feeing the remarks made by the Reviewers on Mr. Jenks's Meditations; and likewife of
extracting the grofs paffages of their calumny, and
printing them (together with the clergyman's letter)
cum notis variorum. I wifh you would read them
again, and put down an ironical obfervation or two.
Do not be unkindly modeft here; your hints will
greatly affift me. All this muft come in under my
own name. Verax, you will foon know, has made
his exit. How fhall I introduce fuch a thing naturally and gracefully?

I have lent the clergyman's letter, otherwife I
would have fent it for your perufal. It is truly judicious, and quite poignant, though not under the
veil of farcafm, but declaring the thing as it is.
The whole of this addition I would comprife in two
or three leaves. If you fhould think, when all points
are weighed, that the piece ought to fee the light, you
muft return it fpeedily. I have expunged my name;
and if you read or fhew the manufcript to any body,
it is of no confequence that the author be known;
but if it is publifhed, I apprehend I fhould put my
name to the title page. This I may venture to imagine would promote its fale; and I fhould not be in
the leaft unwilling to bear my teftimony againft the
enemies of our LORD and his Gofpel: though I
muft expect fuch perfecution of the pen as has not
often been known.

Let

Let me hope for a continuation of your lively thoughts on the subject of CHRIST's religion, and beg of you to remember me, when you beseech the *Father of Lights* to inform the ignorant, and teach them in the way wherein they should go; for I do assure you I am very much at a loss how to proceed. I shall intreat our divine Master to direct your mind, that you may be the messenger of his will to,

A Brother in CHRIST,

J. HERVEY.

LETTER LIX.

December 31.

My dear Friend,

I AM just come up from dinner, and who should be there, but the Rev. Mr. Howen! who was so unseasonably zealous as to attack Mr. S—— on the principles of Antipedo-baptism. I was sorry to observe it, and thought it a breach of delicacy and propriety in conduct, especially to do this to my guest, and at my table; therefore I took up the cudgels, and personated a Baptist. I fear I made my opponent angry, and I am apprehensive I shall be represented as a treacherous or perfidious son of the church.

Thanks, many thanks for your Essay, and for assuring me, that it is an earnest, as well as a gift. I wish you had penned the remarks that occurred on reading the manuscript; whether it is to be printed or not I am ignorant. Mr. Witherspoon's Essay waits upon you, together with a very candid letter which I received by the last post. The latter you will return by the first opportunity. Jenks's Meditations is likewise in the packet. I shall overdo the matter, and make my recommendations thread-bare, by so frequently repeating them. Marshal on Sanctification

is

is ready to come abroad, with a recommendatory letter by Mr. H——y. May our divine Mafter and
Head turn all to his glory! I was really averfe to
this bufinefs: when fhall I be able to withftand im-
portunity? I hope Spence's Remarks on the Poetry of the Odyffey will be of fingular fervice to the
Birmingham Dialogues in verfe. I think it is the
moft inftructing work of the kind: to me it has been
far more ufeful than Longinus, or Dionyfius Hali-
cem. Shall not we fee you this Chriftmas? For my
part I am not defirous of feeing many people; but
your company will be always defirable, becaufe I believe it will always be a bleffing to,

Dear Sir,
Your affectionate Brother,
J. HERVEY,

·LETTER LX.

My dear Friend,

YOUR demand for a number of Sermons, to dif-
tribute among your neighbours, fhall be honoured with due compliance: if the LORD pleafes to
make them acceptable or ufeful, a frefh fupply fhall
be at your fervice, and come at your call. The
meaner fort, through fome ftrange delay of the bookfeller or printer, are not yet publifhed, otherwife they
had been fent in this parcel.

I return your *Synopfis Hiftoria Sacra,* with thanks.
What comes from your pen, is more agreeable to me,
than what is detached from your library. The latter
is reftored, that the former may fucceed in its place.
Remarks upon the Aphorifms, and a Continuation of
the Pleafures of Religion, are the favours defired and
expected,

From

From the Reviewers I expect no quarter; but if the cause be CHRIST's, it is written, *No weapon formed against it, shall prosper.* Mudge upon the Psalms I do not forget; but at present I cannot get at it, nor shall I be able, till I remove my books, and change my habitation. Mr. S —— waits, therefore I detain him and you no longer, than only to add,

Your Friend and Brother,

J. HERVEY.

LETTER LXI.

My dear Friend,

MR. S—— has just informed me, that he is setting out for Warwick. I dismiss all other business to write you a line.

I return, though with reluctance, Neonomianism Unmasked. I thought it had been your own by purchase, and mine by promise. I very much esteem it, because of its excellent evangelical doctrine; and more, because it is improved by several remarks from your pen. If it does not really belong to another person, I must still maintain my claim.

You left two pamphlets, which are restored. If the obliging penman has executed his work in my first volume, let it come back with the bearer, and I will supply him with fresh business, and pay him my best thanks.

I have not been abroad; the weather has been either so damp, or so cold. I hope your health is firm, and your spirits flow. May they both, devoted to the best of masters, be eminently instrumental in displaying his honour, and advancing his interests.

Most cordially your's,

J. HERVEY.

LET-

LETTER LXII.

Weston, Friday Night.

My dear Friend,

I Hope by the newfman of next week, to send you a
quarter of a hundred of the Sermons; they do not
come to me till to-morrow, or elfe they fhould be
tranfmitted to you fooner. Confidering the idle infig-
nificance of our fleets and armies in Europe, and the
formidable advantages gained by the French in America, the voice of alarm feems to be more and more
needful. The GOD and FATHER of our LORD JESUS
CHRIST, grant it may not found in vain, even from
thefe feeble lips!

We begin to be under fome uneafy apprehenfions
about Mr. S———. He has been unaccountably di-
latory in my mother's bufinefs: he talked of getting
her houfe ready to receive us in fpring, and he has
hardly done it by Michaelmas: ill it is true he was,
yet feldom confined to his room; generally able, if
not to work, yet to overfee workmen. He feems to
have but little regard to his word: if I fhould enter
into a bond with him, has he any bottom? Is he a
man of any fubftance? Sad things are conjectured relating to the caufe of his illnefs. I wifh it may
prove a falfe furmife, but circumftances look dark.
Your prudence will incline you to mention nothing of
this kind, only to have a wakeful eye on the occafion:
he appears to be a random conductor of bufinefs.
The bearer, his carpenter, is obliged to come to
Warwick for frefh orders, which journey furely Mr.
S——— fhould have prevented, either by coming this
week, as he promifed, or by giving ampler directions
before he left us.

Pray

Pray advife us how to proceed. In this requeft, as well as in cordial refpects to yourfelf, my mother and fifter join with

Your's, moft fincerely,

J. H.

LETTER LXIII.

My dear Friend,

I Return the fix numbers of the Appendix, together with my thanks to you, for giving me this religious entertainment, not omitting my poor prayers to GOD, that the LORD may be feen over thefe faithful labourers, and the arrow of the Gofpel may go forth from their lips and their pens, as the lightning.

Whether S—— is returned to you, I know not. He is gone from thefe parts, but never called upon me at his departure, nor I believe did he take his leave of any one elfe; for he went off with precipitancy and confufion, a writ being out againft him from the perfon of whom he bought the deals. Many more debts came to light: feveral of the creditors have been with me, defiring I would pay them, or help them to get their money. The time affigned for finifhing the houfe draws near: no chimney pieces, locks, &c. provided; and now nobody will truft that unhappy man, for fo much as a pound of nails. How I am to proceed, I am at a lofs to difcern: may the eye of Omnipotence be my guide!

The continuation of your thoughts on the fubject of female education, will be a welcome favour. When you afk what progrefs I make in this or that work, you fetch a figh from my breaft: my ftrength is indeed become labour and forrow. In about three weeks time, the leaves on the trees will be an exact emblem of my ftate.

As

As to the Anfwer to Mr. Wefley, I am not fully determined; but if life is fpared, I am much inclined to publifh it, hoping it may be a teftimony for the grace of our GOD, and the righteoufnefs of his CHRIST.

I fhall be glad to fee Mr. Johnfon's and Witherfpoon's letters: will return them fpeedily and punctually, as you muft return the inclofed little Poem: it was written by a clergyman of diftinction, brought, I am told, to the knowledge of CHRIST, by Mr. Whitefield's preaching. That he and you may have many fuch feals to your miniftry, is the unfeigned defire of,

Dear Sir,
Your truly affectionate Friend,
J. HERVEY.

LETTER LXIV.

My dear Friend,

ACCEPT my thanks for your advice, relating to S——; the LORD direct me how to proceed! I detain the bricks chiefly for my own fecurity: if he would go on, and finifh the houfe according to agreement, he would find me not very rigorous in this or any other article.

Herewith I fend you three quarters of an hundred of the Thoughts on Sunday Vifits, and a dozen of the Faft Sermons. My ftock of the latter grows low: and Rivington has fold off, a few fcores only excepted, that vaft impreffion of fix thoufand! which is the more extraordinary, as there was an edition printed in Scotland, and one or two in America. If GOD will blefs, who can blaft? O may he blefs the perufal to his own glory, as he has bleffed the fale to my profit.

N   Herewith

Herewith comes likewife my contribution to Mr.
Underhill's education. I have nothing more to add at
prefent—as bufy as it is compatible with my poor frame,
broken and enervated beyond expreffion, let me expect to fee fpeedily the continuation of your thoughts,
and ever to enjoy the continuation of your prayers for,

Dear Sir,

Your Brother in CHRIST,

JAMES HERVEY.

LETTER LXV.

November 12.

My dear Friend,

I Have given my confent to Mr. S——'s propofals.
The articles are not figned: this I deferred, that I
might have opportunity to confult my acquaintance.

They informed me, that a bare note, drawn up and
figned by us both, will be of no force in law. Nothing
is a fecurity in this refpect, but a bond, executed on
ftamp paper: as Mr. S—— has no bottom, is worth
nothing, even this, in cafe of default or neglect, will
be of no fervice.

There are feveral neceffaries, not mentioned in the
eftimate, fuch as hearth ftones, chimney pieces, floors
for hall, kitchen, &c. Thefe, to be fure, ought to be
provided in a manner fuitable to the ftile and genius
of the building. May I depend upon his integrity
as to fuch particulars?

My mother complains that the hair ufed in her
mortar, was bad, and the laths not good; that upon
her objecting to the price, as exorbitant, Mr. S——
offered to have his bill and workmanfhip examined
by any impartial judge, and declared himfelf willing
to abide by his determination; from which offer he
now recedes.

When

When shall I have done with such dry subjects, and receive nothing from you but those words which, in their degree, are spirit and life. The manuscript Poem comes by the first packet, and Mudge's Translation of the Pfalms, which now is disengaged from a load of other books. I am glad to see a couple of new Sermons published by Dr. Gill; when shall I see some published by Mr. Ryland? Are you not dispatching to the press your long-expected work: I wish much, if it be the LORD's will, to peruse it before I die. Will that gentleman, who kindly offered to transcribe any Dialogues in manuscript, take the trouble of writing into an interleaved copy, the alterations and corrections which I have occasionally made in Theron and Afpasio? This would be a piece of service, and a welcome favour; so much the more, as they might be transcribed under your inspection, and receive an improvement from your pen.

I am, my dear Friend,

Inviolably your's,

J. HERVEY.

P. S. Do you correspond with our trusty ingenious friend Densham? Or can you tell me any tidings of him? Pray give us your opinion by the first opportunity.

THE END.

APPENDIX.

To the Rev. Mr. Whitefield.

Dear. Mr. Whitefield,   *Biddeford,* 1741.

YOUR favour ftruck me with an agreeable
furprize: I verily thought my ftubborn filence
had razed me from your remembrance; but fince
you ftill have an affection for an ungrateful friend,
I take this opportunity of returning my thankful acknowledgments.

I rejoice to hear the REDEEMER's caufe revives.
Set up thyfelf, O incarnate GOD! above the heavens,
and diffufe thy glory throughout all the earth. Let
thy enemies perifh, O LORD! Let difappointments
attend the attempts of thy foes and the devices of
hell: but let thy fervants be profperous, and their
meffage crowned with fuccefs.

Dear Sir, I cannot boaft of trophies erected here
by the CAPTAIN of our falvation: I hope the arm of
the LORD will be revealed more and more among
us. I hope the triumphs of FREE GRACE will have
wider fpread and freer courfe, and prevail mightily
over our unbelief. I own with fhame and forrow that I
have been too long a BLIND LEADER of the BLIND: my
tongue and my pen have perverted the good ways of
GOD: they have darkened the glory of redeeming merit
and fovereign grace. I have dared to invade the prerogatives of an all-fufficient SAVIOUR, and to pluck the

A   crown

crown off his head. My writings and difcourfes have derogated from the honours, the everlafting and incommunicable honours of JESUS. They prefumed to give works a fhare in the redemption and recovery of a loft finner: they have placed thofe filthy rags upon the throne of the LAMB, and by that means debafed the SAVIOUR, and exalted the finner.

But I truft the divine truth begins to dawn upon my foul. O may it, like the rifing fun, fhine more and more, till the day break in all its brightnefs, and the fhadows flee away. Now was I poffeft of all the righteous acts that have made faints and martyrs famous in all generations: could they all be transferred to me, and might I call them all my own, I would renounce them all that I might win CHRIST. I would not dare to appear before the bright and BURNING EYE OF GOD with fuch hay, ftraw and ftubble. No, dear Sir, I would long to be clothed in a MEDIATOR'S RIGHTEOUSNESS, and afcribe all my falvation to the moft unmerited and freeft grace.

I have juft been giving an exhortation to my young brethren: I have warned them to remember their CREATOR in the days of their youth. My thoughts were led to the fubject by an alarming PROVIDENCE, which fnatched one of their fellows in the gaiety and bloom of life. May the hand of the ALMIGHTY fet home the word of his minifters: may young perfons come in the vigour of health, to the REDEEMER'S feet, and devote their warm affections to his fervice. And O may the preacher himfelf both lead them in the way, and encourage them to follow. Dear Sir, ceafe not to pray for me: defift not to counfel me, fince I perceive you cannot forbear to love me.

I am,

Your's affectionately,

JAMES HERVEY,

Æt. 27 years.

LET-

A SPECIMEN *of the* AUTHOR's *Correspondence with*
MR. HERVEY.

Rev. and dear Sir.

THE kind favour of your letter dated December 2, came to my hands, but not till the 11th, otherwife I fhould have anfwered it by the laft return of the news carrier. I thank you with all my heart for your goodnefs to me: I read it again and again with great pleafure: I fincerely fympathize with you in your late indifpofition, and am glad you are fomething better. I pray that our dear REDEEMER may long continue you with us, though for yourfelf it would be better to depart and be with HIM. As foon as ever your remarks on Lord Bolingbroke were advertifed, I fent for them, and read them with the greateft relifh and improvement. It has been frequently a pleafing reflection with me, that whenever an infidel of genius and learning has arofe in the polite world, our LORD JESUS CHRIST immediately makes it appear that he has faithful humble fervants in waiting, who, under his influence, with fuperior clearnefs of thought, greater delicacy and beauty of language, and demonftration of truth, plead his righteous caufe, to the confufion of the adverfaries, and the joy of his friends.

I will now proceed to confider the queftion you did me the honour to propofe to me, which I will attempt to anfwer with the greateft freedom and fimplicity of which I am capable; not that I imagine myfelf capable of adding to your treafure one new idea, but in order to fhew you my readinefs to oblige you. The fubject propofed is moft delicious and important; and what is more, I hope for a rich return from my dear and honoured brother, whom I am now addreffing. The queftion you propofe to my confideration, and on which you require my thoughts concerning the righteoufnefs of CHRIST's life, its ex-

A 2   cellency

cellency and perfection; that righteoufnefs which was antecedent to his atoning death, and confifted in his obedience to the whole moral law, I will attempt feebly and imperfectly to anfwer in the following manner:—I believe that the whole human nature of CHRIST, as foon as ever it was formed, and being in the formation of it united to the eternal PERSON of the SON of GOD, who was fully poffeffed of all poffible and infinite perfections, and equal to the FATHER and bleffed SPIRIT. I fay, as foon as' ever the human nature was united to the GODHEAD in the Perfon of the SON, it had a right to glory and bleffednefs above the law; but for the fake of his people, he voluntarily confented to be made under the law, by a fpecial appointment of GOD the FATHER. Being thus made under the law by a peculiar conftitution, the law was wrought into the whole contexture of his heart: his mind had a clear and full perception of its fpirituality and vaft extent: his will and pure paffions had a full propenfity to obey it; and his whole human nature had an entire capacity and power to yield the moft exact and perfect obedience all through life: that he was filled with all the gifts and graces of the eternal SPIRIT in their higheft and richeft perfection; and as the confequence of this, he lived in the continued exercife of the vaft ftedfaft faith in the divine perfections and providence: the moft ardent love to the eternal GOD, the deepeft humility, the moft flaming zeal for the glory of his FATHER: the moft exact government of all his appetites and paffions: the ftrongeft love to all mankind as creatures, and a fpecial good will to all his elect, whom the FATHER had given him. That all thefe graces and this obedience was continually influenced by the infinite wifdom, goodnefs, love, holinefs, juftice and truth of his divine nature, which poffeffed and animated his whole human frame, and infufed into it, and all its operations, an infinite worth and excellency

cellency above all our corruptions and imaginations.
That in all this internal and external obedience of
CHRIST, there was an exact correspondence to all the
moral perfections of GOD : as they resided in the FA-
THER, who stood up for the rights of the whole
Godhead, and demanded the perfect fulfilment of
the covenant of works, in order for man's salvation,
which was gloriously performed by our adorable JE-
SUS, in whom, through his whole life, even to death,
shone the richest constellation of virtues and graces
that ever appeared, or can appear in our world. I
believe that all this was done by him, in the nature,
in the name and stead of his elect ; and that, by virtue
of his divine nature, it was equivalent, yea, superior
to the obedience of all his people, supposing they had
never been guilty of defection from GOD : and I believe that this obedience is accepted of GOD at the
bar of justice, and at the throne of his grace, as the
matter of our full and everlasting justification, in
conjunction with his atoning death, which satisfied the
penalties of the law, and exhausted all its curses. I
believe with the pious and venerable Dr. Owen,
" That the righteousness of CHRIST's life, with his
death, was the highest act of obedience to GOD that ever
was or ever shall be to all eternity." But, alas! what
a mass of darkness and confusion is there in my
heart? How little do I know of this righteousness, and
how broken and clouded are all my ideas? Therefore,
to make my letter worth your acceptance, I will beg
leave to conclude with an immortal paragraph from
the judicious Witsius. " *Hic via ostenditur ad me-*
liorem terrestri Paradisum et ad certiorem stabilioremque
felicitatem, ea qua Adamus excidit. Hic nova spes perdi-
tis mortalibus allucet quæ eo gratior esse debet quo inexspec-
tatior obvenit. Hic conditiones offeruntur quibus æterna
salus annexa est; conditiones non a nobis rursus præstandæ
quod animum despondere faceret : sed ab eo qui vita non
excedet antequam vere dixerit, consummatum est. Hic lu-
cidissima

cidiſſimo ſplendore micant ſtupendæ DEI *noſtri virtutes*
ſapientia, potentia, veritas, juſtitia, ſanctitas, bonitas
φιλανθρωπια *miſericordia et quis omnes fando enumeret ?"*
De Œconomia, 4to. 130.

I am very ſorry I have not room for the whole paſſage ; but doubtleſs your ſelect library is not deſtitute
of ſo excellent a book. I hope you received my laſt
letter on the SATISFACTION OF CHRIST. I am waiting with a mixture of impatience and pleaſure for the
fulfilment of your kind promiſe. Freely cenſure me
if I deſerve it.

I am,

My moſt dear brother in CHRIST,

Your's more than I can expreſs,

Warwick, Dec. 13, 1752. JOHN RYLAND.

PART OF A LETTER TO MR. HERVEY.

Imputation of ADAM's *Sin to all his Children.*

ORIGINAL ſin, imputed preciſely, conſiſts in
GOD's placing to the account of all Adam's children
thoſe unjuſt and unlawful thoughts and actions which
he was the author of in his firſt act of rebellion, when
he ſtood as the public head of all mankind, and GOD's
eſteeming and judging as unjuſt and evil, or guilty,
according to the nature of that firſt grand act of moſt
aggravated ſin, rebellion or diſobedience.

The conſequence and effects of this imputation of
our firſt father's ſin to us.—We are born with an ugly,
deformed, corrupted ſoul and body, and are naturally
and neceſſarily, according to the order of GOD's eſſential juſtice, under wrath, or a ſentence of death, an obligation or bond to ſuffer puniſhment.

Imputation of all the original and actual ſins of the
elect to CHRIST.—It is an act of GOD, of his ſovereign and unchangeable will, whereby, on the conſideration of the ſinful and unclean natures and actions
of his people, he reckons and places to the account of

CHRIST

CHRIST, their HEAD and SURETY, all their perſonal guilt, or their true and proper ſins, and really accounting them as CHRIST's, on the footing of his own act as a ſovereign Judge. He binds CHRIST down as a guilty Perſon in the eye of the law, in all its utmoſt extent and force, without the leaſt mitigation in the proper room and ſtead of his elect, and no other perſons.

The conſequence of this placing of original and actual ſin to the account of CHRIST.—He was from his very birth under an obligation, a moral and unchangeable bond, to pay for all his people the full price of redemption: to offer a pure, ſpotleſs, reconciling ſacrifice: to endure the evil of ſuffering for their evil actions, or undergo the very ſame puniſhment which was due to them, to the end that he might make a full SATISFACTION, or rather ſolution; an eternal and complete ſolution of their debt; and thus, by paying what was in our obligation to pay, and by ſuffering what was in our obligation to ſuffer, we are upon the footing of GOD's ſtrict and inflexible juſtice, releaſed from paying or ſuffering—our obligation is for ever diſſolved.

Imputation of CHRIST's *Righteouſneſs to his People.*—It is an act of GOD, as a FATHER and a juſt JUDGE; an act within GOD, of his meer good will or free love, by which, on the conſideration of the obedience, the all-perfect and glorious * obedience and atoning death of CHRIST, conſidered as a price, or ſacrifice, or puniſhment. He makes an abſolute grant and gift of a true, real, perfect, juſtifying righ-

---

* CHRIST's obedience was perfect with reſpect to the inward ſprings of action, he having an exact rectitude in his moral powers: perfect with regard to the parts of the divine law in its vaſt ſpirituality, extent and obligation; perfect as to the various operations of his mind and body; perfect as to the whole period of his obedience.

teouſneſs

teoufnefs or rectitude in the court of GOD, even that
righteoufnefs of CHRIST himfelf, unto all the elect,
and juftly accounting it as theirs, on his own gracious
and judicial act. He releafes, or frees, from all obligation to fuffer, and juftly grants them a right to all
kinds of bleffings, or all manner of good things, and a
firm and indifputable claim and title to eternal life.

The confequence of this placing of CHRIST'S *holy
nature and actions, fufferings and death to our account.*—All this being reckoned to our perfons, in
GOD's eternal mind, we had before our converfion;
yea, permit me to fay before our being; before the
world; a fecret right in the eye of GOD, to pardon
and life, or a fecret right to all forts of bleffings, confidered in union with, or related to CHRIST: yea, even
a right to the eternal poffeffion and enjoyment of the
adorable GODHEAD, to the utmoft of our immortal
powers and capacities. After regeneration, this fecret
right is laid open to us, and becomes pleadable by us.

My dear brother, I had your laft letter, for which I
am ftill more obliged—your friendfhip more endeared.
My next letter fhall confider the miftakes of Baxter, Williams, Bifhop Stillingfleet and Doctor ——,
with refpect to imputation. Affure yourfelf of the
utmoft exertion of my feeble powers to fubferve your
plan. You have with this No. II. III. and IV. If
the LORD JESUS permit, I will accept of your moft
friendly invitation. I wifh you would expatiate freely
on the feveral names of CHRIST, in the manner you
have already purfued in the Contemplations, efpecially where you run the parallel between CHRIST
and the fun, and the note on Rev. x. time fhall be
no longer. With Solomon's addrefs, will GOD in
very deed dwell with men?—Improve my plan.

I am, dear Sir,
Inviolably your's,

Warwick, Dec. 3, 1753. JOHN RYLAND.